Achilles smiled as Valentina settled herself across the coffee table from him, with a certain inbred grace that whispered of palaces and comportment classes and a lifetime of genteel manners.

Because she thought she was tricking him.

Which meant he could trick her instead. A prospect his body responded to with great enthusiasm as he studied her, this woman who looked like an underling a man in his position would never have touched out of ethical considerations—but wasn't.

She wasn't his employee. He didn't pay her salary. And she wasn't bound to obey him in anything if she didn't feel like it.

But she had no idea that he knew that.

Achilles almost felt sorry for her. Almost.

Scandalous Royal Brides

Married for passion, made for scandal!

When personal assistant Natalie and Princess Valentina meet they can't believe their eyes…they're the very image of one another. They're so similar it's impossible that they're anything but identical twins.

Dissatisfied with their lives, they impulsively agree to swap places for six weeks only…

But will they want to return to their old lives when the alpha heroes closest to them are intent on making these scandalous women their brides?

Read Natalie and Prince Rodolfo's story in

The Prince's Nine-Month Scandal
Available now

And discover Princess Valentina
and Achilles Casilieris's story

The Billionaire's Secret Princess
Available now!

THE BILLIONAIRE'S SECRET PRINCESS

BY

CAITLIN CREWS

MILLS & BOON

First Published in Great Britain 2017
By Mills & Boon, an imprint of HarperCollins*Publishers*
1 London Bridge Street, London, SE1 9GF

© 2017 Caitlin Crews

ISBN: 978-0-263-92529-6

USA TODAY bestselling and RITA® Award–nominated author **Caitlin Crews** loves writing romance. She teaches her favourite romance novels in creative writing classes at places like UCLA Extension's prestigious Writers' Program, where she finally gets to utilise the MA and PhD in English literature she received from the University of York in England. She currently lives in California, with her very own hero and too many pets. Visit her at caitlincrews.com.

Books by Caitlin Crews

Mills & Boon Modern Romance

Castelli's Virgin Widow
At the Count's Bidding

Scandalous Royal Brides

The Prince's Nine-Month Scandal

Wedlocked!

Bride by Royal Decree
Expecting a Royal Scandal

One Night With Consequences

The Guardian's Virgin Ward

The Billionaire's Legacy

The Return of the Di Sione Wife

Secret Heirs of Billionaires

Unwrapping the Castelli Secret

Scandalous Sheikh Brides

Protecting the Desert Heir
Traded to the Desert Sheikh

Vows of Convenience

His for a Price
His for Revenge

Visit the Author Profile page
at millsandboon.co.uk for more titles.

To all the secret princesses
cruelly stuck working in horrible offices:
as long as you know the truth, that's what matters.

CHAPTER ONE

ACHILLES CASILIERIS REQUIRED PERFECTION.

In himself, certainly. He prided himself on it, knowing all too well how easy it was to fall far, far short. And in his employees, absolutely—or they would quickly find themselves on the other side of their noncompete agreements with indelible black marks against their names.

He did not play around. He had built everything he had from nothing, step by painstaking step, and he hadn't succeeded the way he had—building the recession-proof Casilieris Company and making his first million by the age of twenty-five, then expanding both his business and his personal fortune into the billions—by accepting anything less than 100 percent perfection in all things. Always.

Achilles was tough, tyrannical when necessary, and refused to accept what one short-lived personal assistant had foolishly called "human limitations" to his face.

He was a man who knew the monster in himself. He'd seen its face in his own mirror. He did not allow for "human limitations."

Natalie Monette was his current executive assistant and had held the position for a record five years because she had never once asserted that she was human as some kind of excuse. In point of fact, Achilles thought of her as a remarkably efficient robot—the highest praise he could think to bestow on anyone, as it removed the possibility of human error from the equation.

Achilles had no patience for human error.

Which was why his assistant's behavior on this flight today was so alarming.

The day had started out normally enough. When Achilles had risen at his usual early hour, it had been to find Natalie already hard at work in the study of his Belgravia town house. She'd set up a few calls to his associates in France, outlined his schedule for the day and his upcoming meetings in New York. They'd swung by his corporate offices in the City, where Achilles had handled a fire he thought she should have put out before he'd learned of it, but then she'd accompanied him in his car to the private airfield he preferred without appearing the least bit bothered that he'd dressed her down for her failure. And why should she be bothered? She knew he expected perfection and had failed to deliver it. Besides, Natalie was never bothered. She'd acquitted herself with her usual cool competence and attitude-free demeanor, the way she always did or she never would have lasted five minutes with him. Much less five years.

And then she'd gone into the bathroom at the airfield, stayed in there long enough that he'd had to go find her himself, and come out changed.

Achilles couldn't put his finger on *how* she'd changed, only that she had.

She still looked the part of the closest assistant to a man as feared and lauded as Achilles had been for years now. She looked like his public face the way she always did. He appreciated that and always had. It wasn't enough that she was capable of handling the complications of his personal and company business without breaking a sweat, that she never seemed to sleep, that she could protect him from the intrusive paparazzi and hold off his equally demanding board members in the same breath—it was necessary that she also look like the sort of woman who belonged in his exalted orbit for the rare occasions when he needed to escort someone to this or that function and couldn't trouble himself to expend the modicum of charm necessary to squire one of his mistresses. Today she wore one of her usual outfits, a pencil skirt and soft blouse and a feminine sort of sweater that wrapped around her torso and was no different from any other outfit she'd worn a million times before.

Natalie dressed to disappear in plain sight. But for some reason, she caught his eye this odd afternoon. He couldn't quite figure it out. It was as if he had never seen her before. It was as if she'd gone into the bathroom in the airport lounge and come out a completely different person.

Achilles sat back in his remarkably comfortable leather chair on the jet and watched her as she took her seat opposite him. Did he imagine that she hesitated? Was he making up the strange look he'd seen in her eyes before she sat down? Almost as if she was looking for clues instead of taking her seat as she always did?

"What took you so long in that bathroom?" he asked, not bothering to keep his tone particularly polite. "I should not have to chase down my own assistant, surely."

Natalie blinked. He didn't know why the green of her eyes behind the glasses he knew she didn't need for sight seemed…too bright, somehow. Or brighter, anyway, than they'd been before. In fact, now that he thought about it, everything about her was brighter. And he couldn't understand how anyone could walk into a regular lavatory and come out…gleaming.

"I apologize," she said quietly. Simply. And there was something about her voice then. It was almost…musical.

It occurred to Achilles that he had certainly never thought of Natalie's voice as anything approaching *musical* before. It had always been a voice, pure and simple. And she had certainly never *gleamed*.

And that, he thought with impatience, was one of the reasons that he had prized Natalie so much for all these years. Because he had never, ever noticed her as anything but his executive assistant, who was reasonably attractive because it was good business to give his Neanderthal cronies something worth gazing at while they were trying to ignore Achilles's dominance. But there was a difference between noting that a woman was attractive and *being attracted to* that woman. Achilles would not have hired Natalie if he'd been attracted to her. He never had been. Not ever.

But to his utter astonishment that was what seemed to be happening. Right here. Right now. His body was sending him unambiguous signals. He wasn't simply *attracted* to his assistant. What he felt roll in him as she crossed her legs at the ankle and smiled at him was far more than *attraction*.

It was need.

Blinding and impossible and incredibly, astonishingly inconvenient.

Achilles Casilieris did not do inconvenience, and he was violently opposed to *need*. It had been beaten into him as an unwanted child that it was the height of foolishness to want something he couldn't have. That meant he'd dedicated his adult life to never allowing himself to need anything at all when he could buy whatever took his fancy, and he hadn't.

And yet there was no denying that dark thread that wound in him, pulling tight and succeeding in surprising him—something else that happened very, very rarely.

Achilles knew the shadows that lived in him. He had no intention of revisiting them. Ever.

Whatever his assistant was doing, she needed to stop. Now.

"That is all you wish to say?" He sounded edgy. Dangerous. He didn't like that, either.

But Natalie hardly seemed to notice. "If you would like me to expand on my apology, Mr. Casilieris, you need only tell me how."

He thought there was a subtle rebuke in that, no matter how softly she'd said it, and that, too, was new. And unacceptable no matter how prettily she'd voiced it.

Her copper-colored hair gleamed. Her skin glowed as she moved her hands in her lap, which struck him as odd, because Natalie never sat there with her hands folded in her lap like some kind of diffident Catholic schoolgirl. She was always in motion, because she was always working. But tonight, Natalie appeared to be sitting there like some kind of regal Madonna, hands folded in her lap, long, silky legs crossed at the ankles, and an inappropriately serene smile on her face.

If it wasn't impossible, he would have thought that she really was someone else entirely. Because she looked exactly the same save for all that gold that seemed to wrap itself around her and him, too, making him unduly fascinated with the pulse he could see beating at her throat—except he'd never, ever noticed her that way before.

Achilles did not have time for this, whatever it was. There was entirely too much going on with his businesses at the moment, like the hotel deal he'd been trying to put together for the better part of the last year that was by no means assured. He hadn't become one of the most feared and fearsome billionaires in the world because he took time off from running his businesses to pretend to care about the personal lives of his employees.

But Natalie wasn't just any employee. She was the one he'd actually come to rely on. The only person he relied on in the world, to be specific.

"Is there anything you need to tell me?" he asked.

He watched her, perhaps too carefully. It was impossible not to notice the way she flushed slightly at that. That was strange, too. He couldn't remember a single instance Natalie had ever flushed in response to anything he'd done. And the truth was he'd done a lot. He didn't hide his flashes of irritation or spend too much time worrying about anyone else's feelings. Why should he? The Casilieris Company was about profit—and it was about Achilles. Who else's feelings should matter? One of the things he'd long prized about his assistant was that she never, ever reacted to anything that he did or said or shouted. She just did her job.

But today Natalie had spots of red, high on her elegant cheekbones, and she'd been sitting across from him for whole minutes now without doing a single thing that could be construed as her job.

Elegant? demanded an incredulous voice inside him. *Cheekbones?*

Since when had Achilles ever noticed anything of the kind? He didn't pay that much attention to the mistresses he took to his bed—which he deigned to do in the first place only after they passed through all the levels of his application process and signed strict confidentiality agreements. And the women who made it through were in no doubt as to why they were there. It was to please him, not render him disoriented enough to be focusing on their bloody *cheekbones*.

"Like what, for example?" She asked the question and then she smiled at him, that curve of her mouth that was suddenly wired to the hardest part of him, and echoed inside him like heat. Heat he didn't want. "I'll be happy to tell you anything you wish to hear, Mr. Casilieris. That is, after all, my job."

"Is that your job?" He smiled, and he doubted it echoed much of anywhere. Or was anything but edgy and a little but harsh. "I had started to doubt that you remembered you had one."

"Because I kept you waiting? That was unusual, it's true."

"You've never done so before. You've never dared." He tilted his head slightly as he gazed at her, not understanding why everything was different when nothing was. He could see that she was exactly the same as she always was, down to that single freckle centered on her left cheekbone that he wasn't even aware he'd noticed before now. "Again, has some tragedy befallen you? Were you hit over the head?" He did nothing to hide the warning or the menace in his voice. "You do not appear to be yourself."

But if he thought he'd managed to discomfit her, he saw in the next moment that was not to be. The flush faded from her porcelain cheeks, and all she did was smile at him again. With that maddeningly enigmatic curve of her lips.

Lips, he noticed with entirely too much of his body, that were remarkably lush.

This was insupportable.

"I am desolated to disappoint you," she murmured as the plane began to move, bumping gently along the tarmac. "But there was no tragedy." Something glinted in her green gaze, though her smile never dimmed. "Though I must confess in the spirit of full disclosure that I was thinking of quitting."

Achilles only watched her idly, as if she hadn't just said that. Because she couldn't possibly have just said that.

"I beg your pardon," he said after a moment passed and there was still that spike of something dark and furious in his chest. "I must have misheard you. You do not mean that you plan to quit this job. That you wish to leave *me*."

It was not lost on him that he'd phrased that in a way that should have horrified him. Maybe it would at some point. But today what slapped at him was that his assistant spoke of quitting without a single hint of anything like uncertainty on her face.

And he found he couldn't tolerate that.

"I'm considering it," she said. Still smiling. Unaware of her own danger or the dark thing rolling in him, reminding him of how easy it was to wake that monster that slept in him. How disastrously easy.

But Achilles laughed then, understanding finally catching up with him. "If this is an attempt to wrangle more money out of me, Miss Monette, I cannot say that I admire the strategy. You're perfectly well compensated as is. Overcompensated, one might say."

"Might one? Perhaps." She looked unmoved. "Then again, perhaps your rivals have noticed exactly how much you rely on me. Perhaps I've decided that I want more than being at the beck and call of a billionaire. Much less standing in as your favorite bit of target practice."

"It cannot possibly have bothered you that I lost my temper earlier."

Her smile was bland. "If you say it cannot, then I'm sure you must be right."

"I lose my temper all the time. It's never bothered you before. It's part of your job to not be bothered, in point of fact."

"I'm certain that's it." Her enigmatic smile seemed to deepen. "I must be the one who isn't any good at her job."

He had the most insane notion then. It was something about the cool challenge in her gaze, as if they were equals. As if she had every right to call him on whatever she pleased. He had no idea why he wanted to reach across the little space between their chairs and put his hands on her. Test her skin to see if it was as soft as it looked. Taste that lush mouth—

What the hell was happening to him?

Achilles shook his head, as much to clear it as anything else. "If this is your version of a negotiation, you should rethink your approach. You know perfectly well that there's entirely too much going on right now."

"Some might think that this is the perfect time, then, to talk about things like compensation and temper tantrums," Natalie replied, her voice as even and unbothered as ever. There was no reason that should make him grit his teeth. "After all, when one is expected to work twenty-two hours a day and is shouted at for her trouble, one's thoughts automatically turn to what one lacks. It's human nature."

"You lack nothing. You have no time to spend the money I pay you because you're too busy traveling the world—which I also pay for."

"If only I had more than two hours a day to enjoy these piles of money."

"People would kill for the opportunity to spend even five minutes in my presence," he reminded her. "Or have you forgotten who I am?"

"Come now." She shook her head at him, and he had the astonishing sense that she was trying to chastise him. *Him.* "It would not kill you to be more polite, would it?"

Polite.

His own assistant had just lectured him on his manners.

To say that he was reeling hardly began to scratch the surface of Achilles's reaction.

But then she smiled, and that reaction got more complicated. "I got on the plane anyway. I decided not to quit today." Achilles could not possibly have missed her emphasis on that final word. "You're welcome."

And something began to build inside him at that. Something huge, dark, almost overwhelming. He was very much afraid it was rage.

But that, he refused. No matter what. Achilles left his demons behind him a long time ago, and he wasn't going back. He refused.

"If you would like to leave, Miss Monette, I will not stop you," he assured her coldly. "I cannot begin to imagine what has led you to imagine I would try. I do not beg. I could fill your position with a snap of my fingers. I might yet, simply because this conversation is intolerable."

The assistant he'd thought he knew would have swallowed hard at that, then looked away. She would have smoothed her hands over her skirt and apologized as she did it. She had riled him only a few times over the years, and she'd talked her way out of it in exactly that way. He gazed at her expectantly.

But today, Natalie only sat there with distractingly perfect posture and gazed back at him with a certain serene confidence that made him want to…mess her up. Get his hands in that unremarkable ponytail and feel the texture of all that gleaming copper. Or beneath her snowy-white blouse. Or better yet, up beneath that skirt of hers.

He was so furious he wasn't nearly as appalled at himself as he should have been.

"I think we both know perfectly well that while you could snap your fingers and summon crowds of candidates for my position, you'd have a very hard time filling it to your satisfaction," she said with a certainty that…gnawed at him. "Perhaps we could dispense with the threats. You need me."

He would sooner have her leap forward and plunge a knife into his chest.

"I need no one," he rasped out. "And nothing."

His suddenly mysterious assistant only inclined her

head, which he realized was no response at all. As if she was merely patronizing him—a notion that made every muscle in his body clench tight.

"You should worry less about your replacement and more about your job," Achilles gritted out. "I have no idea what makes you think you can speak to me with such disrespect."

"It is not disrespectful to speak frankly, surely," she said. Her expression didn't change, but her green gaze was grave—very much, he thought with dawning incredulity, as if she'd expected better of him.

Achilles could only stare back at her in arrogant astonishment. Was he now to suffer the indignity of being judged by his own assistant? And why was it she seemed wholly uncowed by his amazement?

"Unless you plan to utilize a parachute, it would appear you are stuck right here in your distasteful position for the next few hours," Achilles growled at her when he thought he could speak without shouting. Shouting was too easy. And obscured his actual feelings. "I'd suggest you use the time to rethink your current attitude."

He didn't care for the brilliant smile she aimed at him then, as if she was attempting to encourage him with it. *Him.* He particularly didn't like the way it seemed too bright, as if it was lighting him up from the inside out.

"What a kind offer, Mr. Casilieris," she said in that self-possessed voice of hers that was driving him mad. "I will keep it in mind."

The plane took off then, somersaulting into the London sky. Achilles let gravity press him back against the seat and considered the evidence before him. He had worked with this woman for five years, and she had never spoken to him like that before. Ever. He hardly knew what to make of it.

But then, there was a great deal he didn't know what

to do with, suddenly. The way his heart pounded against his ribs as if he was in a real temper, when he was not the sort of man who lost control. Of his temper or anything else. He expected nothing less than perfection from himself, first and foremost. And temper made him think of those long-ago days of his youth, and his stepfather's hovel of a house, victim to every stray whim and temper and fist until he'd given himself over to all that rage and fury inside him and become little better than an animal himself—

Why was he allowing himself to think of such things? His youth was off-limits, even in his own head. What the hell was *happening*?

Achilles didn't like that Natalie affected him. But what made him suspicious was that she'd never affected him before. He'd approved when she started to wear those glasses and put her hair up, to make herself less of a target for the less scrupulous men he dealt with who thought they could get to him through expressing their interest in her. But he hadn't needed her to downplay her looks because *he* was entranced by her. He hadn't been.

So what had changed today?

What had emboldened her and, worse, allowed her to get under his skin?

He kept circling back to that bathroom in the airport and the fact she'd walked out of it a different person from the one who'd walked in.

Of course, she wasn't a *different person*. Did he imagine the real Natalie had suffered a body snatching? Did he imagine there was some elaborate hoax afoot?

The idea was absurd. But he couldn't seem to get past it. The plane hit its cruising altitude, and he moved from his chair to the leather couch that took pride of place in the center of the cabin that was set up like one of his high-end hotel rooms. He sat back with his laptop and pretended to be looking through his email when he was watching Natalie instead. Looking for clues.

She wasn't moving around the plane with her usual focus and energy. He thought she seemed tentative. Uncertain—and this despite the fact she seemed to walk taller than before. As if she'd changed her very posture in that bathroom. But who did something like that?

A different person would have different posture.

It was crazy. He knew that. And Achilles knew further that he always went a little too intense when he was closing a deal, so it shouldn't have surprised him that he was willing to consider the insane option today. Part of being the sort of unexpected, out-of-the-box thinker he'd always been was allowing his mad little flights of fancy. He never knew where they might lead.

He indulged himself as Natalie sat and started to look through her own bag as if she'd never seen it before. He pulled up the picture of her he kept in his files for security purposes and did an image search on it, because why not.

Achilles was prepared to discover a few photos of random celebrities she resembled, maybe. And then he'd have to face the fact that his favorite assistant might have gone off the deep end. She was right that replacing her would be hard—but it wouldn't be impossible. He hadn't overestimated his appeal—and that of his wildly successful company—to pretty much anyone and everyone. He was swamped with applicants daily, and he didn't even have an open position.

But then none of that mattered because his image search hit gold.

There were pages and pages of pictures. All of his assistant—except it wasn't her. He knew it from the exquisitely bespoke gowns she wore. He knew it from the jewels that flowed around her neck and covered her hands, drawing attention to things like the perfect manicure she had today—when the Natalie he knew almost never had time to care for her nails like that. And every picture he clicked on identified the woman in them not as Natalie Monette, assistant to Achilles Casilieris, but Her Royal Highness, Princess Valentina of Murin.

Achilles didn't have much use for royals, or really anyone with inherited wealth, when he'd had to go to so much trouble to amass his own. He'd never been to the tiny Mediterranean kingdom of Murin, mostly because he didn't have a yacht to dock there during a sparkling summer of endless lounging and, further, didn't need to take advantage of the country's famously friendly approach to taxes. But he recognized King Geoffrey of Murin on sight, and he certainly recognized the Murinese royal family's coat of arms.

It had been splashed all over the private jet he'd seen on the same tarmac as his back in London.

There was madness, Achilles thought then, and then there was a con job that no one would ever suspect—because who could imagine that the person standing in front of them, looking like someone they already knew, was actually someone else?

If he wasn't mistaken—and he knew he wasn't, because there were too many things about his assistant today that didn't make sense, and Achilles was no great believer in coincidence—Princess Valentina of Murin was trying to run a con.

On him.

Which meant a great many things. First, that his actual assistant was very likely pretending to be the princess somewhere, leaving him and her job in the hands of someone she had to know would fail to live up to Achilles's high standards. That suggested that second, she really wasn't all that happy in her position, as this princess had dared to throw in his face in a way he doubted Natalie ever would have. But it also suggested that third, Natalie had effectively given her notice.

Achilles didn't like any of that. At all. But the fourth thing that occurred to him was that clearly, neither this princess nor his missing assistant expected their little switch to be noticed. Natalie, who should have known better, must honestly have believed that he wouldn't notice an imposter in her place. Or she hadn't cared much if he did.

That was enraging, on some level. Insulting.

But Achilles smiled as Valentina settled herself across the coffee table from him, with a certain inbred grace that whispered of palaces and comportment classes and a lifetime of genteel manners.

Because she thought she was tricking him.

Which meant he could trick her instead. A prospect his body responded to with great enthusiasm as he studied her, this woman who looked like an underling whom a man in his position could never have touched out of ethical considerations—but wasn't.

She wasn't his employee. He didn't pay her salary, and she wasn't bound to obey him in anything if she didn't feel like it.

But she had no idea that he knew that.

Achilles almost felt sorry for her. Almost.

"Let's get started," he murmured, as if they'd exchanged no harsh words. He watched confusion move over her face in a blink, then disappear, because she was a royal princess and she was used to concealing her reactions. He planned to have fun with that. The possibilities were endless, and seemed to roll through him like heat. "We have so much work to do, Miss Monette. I hardly know where to begin."

CHAPTER TWO

BY THE TIME they landed in New York, Princess Valentina of Murin was second-guessing her spontaneous, impulsive decision to switch places with the perfect stranger she'd found wearing her face in the airport lounge.

Achilles Casilieris could make anyone second-guess anything, she suspected.

"You do not appear to be paying attention," he said silkily from beside her, as if he knew exactly what she was thinking. And who she was. And every dream she'd ever had since she was a girl—that was how disconcerting this man was, even lounging there beside her in the back of a luxury car doing nothing more alarming than *sitting*.

"I am hanging on your every word," she assured him as calmly as she could, and then she repeated his last three sentences back to him.

But she had no idea what he was talking about. Repeating conversations she wasn't really listening to was a skill she'd learned in the palace a long, long time ago. It came in handy at many a royal gathering. And in many longwinded lectures from her father and his staff.

You have thrown yourself into deep, deep water, she told herself now, as if that wasn't entirely too apparent already. As if it hadn't already occurred to her that she'd better learn how to swim, and fast.

Achilles Casilieris was a problem.

Valentina knew powerful men. Men who ruled countries. Men who came from centuries upon centuries of power and consequence and wielded it with the offhanded superiority of those who had never imagined *not* ruling all they surveyed.

But Achilles was in an entirely different league.

He took over the whole of the backseat of the car that had waited for them on the tarmac in the bright and sunny afternoon, looking roomy and spacious from the outside. He'd insisted she sit next to him on the plush backseat that should have been more than able to fit two people with room to spare. And yet Valentina felt crowded, as if he was pressing up against her when he wasn't. Achilles wasn't touching her, but still, she was entirely too *aware* of him.

He took up all the air. He'd done it on his plane, too.

She had the hectic notion, connected to that knot beneath her breastbone that was preventing her from taking anything like a deep breath, that it wasn't the enclosed space that was the issue. That he would have this same effect anywhere. All that brooding ruthlessness he didn't bother to contain—or maybe he couldn't contain even if he'd wanted to—seemed to hum around him like a kind of force field that both repelled and compelled at once.

If she was honest, the little glimpse she'd had of him in the airport had been the same—she'd just ignored it.

Valentina had been too busy racing into the lounge so she could have a few precious seconds alone. No staff. No guards. No cameras. Just her perched on the top of a closed toilet seat, shut away from the world, breathing. Letting her face do what it liked. Thinking of absolutely nothing. Not her duty. Not her father's expectations.

Certainly not her bloodless engagement to Prince Rodolfo of Tissely, a man she'd tuned out within moments of their first meeting. Or their impending wedding in two months' time, which she could feel bearing down on her like a thick hand around her throat every time she let herself think about it. It wasn't that she didn't *want* to do her duty and marry the Crown Prince of Tissely. She'd been promised in marriage to her father's allies since the day she was born. It was that she'd never given a great deal of thought to what it was she wanted, because *want* had never been an option available to her.

And it had suddenly occurred to her at her latest wedding dress fitting there in London that she was running out of time.

Soon she would be married to a man in what was really more of a corporate merger of two great European brands, the houses of Tissely and Murin. She'd be expected to produce the necessary heirs to continue the line. She would take her place in the great sweep of her family's storied history, unite two ancient kingdoms, and in so doing fulfill her purpose in life. The end.

The end, she'd thought in that bathroom stall, high-end and luxurious but still, a bathroom stall. *My life fulfilled at twenty-seven.*

Valentina was a woman who'd been given everything, including a healthy understanding of how lucky she was. She didn't often indulge herself with thoughts of what was and wasn't fair when there was no doubt she was among the most fortunate people alive.

But the thing was, it still didn't seem fair. No matter how hard she tried not to think about it that way.

She would do what she had to do, of course. She always had and always would, but for that single moment, locked away in a bathroom stall where no one could see her and no one would ever know, she basked in the sheer, dizzying unfairness of it all.

Then she'd pulled herself together, stepped out and had been prepared to march onto her plane and head back to the life that had been plotted out for her since the day she arrived on the planet.

Only to find her twin standing at the sinks.

Her identical twin—though that was, of course, impossible.

"What is this?" the other woman had asked when they'd faced each other, looking something close to scared. Or unnerved, anyway. "How…?"

Valentina had been fascinated. She'd been unable to keep herself from studying this woman who appeared to be wearing her body as well as her face. She was dressed in a sleek pencil skirt and low heels, which showed legs that Valentina recognized all too well, having last seen them in her own mirror. "I'm Valentina."

"Natalie."

She'd repeated that name in her head like it was a magic spell. She didn't know why she felt as if it was.

But then, running into her double in a London bathroom seemed something close enough to magic to count. Right then when she'd been indulging her self-pity about the unchangeable course of her own life, the universe had presented her with a glimpse of what else could be. If she was someone else.

An identical someone else.

They had the same face. The same legs, as she'd already noted. The same coppery hair that her double wore up in a serviceable ponytail and the same nose Valentina could trace directly to her maternal grandmother. What were the chances, she'd wondered then, that they *weren't* related?

And didn't that raise all kinds of interesting questions?

"You're that princess," Natalie had said, a bit haltingly.

But if Valentina was a princess, and if they were related as they surely had to be…

"I suspect you might be, too," she'd said gently.

"We can't possibly be related. I'm a glorified secretary who never really had a home. You're a royal princess. Presumably your lineage dates back to the Roman Conquest."

"Give or take a few centuries." Valentina tried to imagine having a job like that. Or any job. A secretary, glorified or otherwise, who reported to work for someone else and actually *did things* with her time that weren't directly related to being a symbol. She couldn't really wrap her head around it, or being effectively without a home, either, having been a part of Murin since her birth. As much Murin as its beaches and hills, its monuments and its palace. She might as well have been a park. "Depending which branch of the family you mean, of course."

"I was under the impression that people with lineages that could lead to thrones and crown jewels tended to keep better track of their members," Natalie had said, her tone just dry enough to make Valentina decide that given the right circumstances—meaning anywhere that wasn't a toilet—she'd rather like her doppelganger.

And she knew what the other woman had been asking.

"Conspiracy theorists claim my mother was killed and her death hushed up. Senior palace officials have assured me my whole life that no, she merely left to preserve her mental health, and is rumored to be in residence in a hospital devoted to such things somewhere. All I know is that I haven't seen her since shortly after I was born. According to my father, she preferred anonymity to the joys of motherhood."

And she waited for Natalie to give her an explanation in turn. To laugh, perhaps, and then tell her that she'd been raised by two perfectly normal parents in a happily normal somewhere else, filled with golden retrievers and school buses and pumpkin-spiced coffee drinks and whatever else normal people took for granted that Valentina only read about.

But instead, this woman wearing Valentina's face had looked stricken. "I've never met my father," she'd whispered. "My mother's always told me she has no idea who he was. And she bounces from one affair to the next pretty quickly, so I came to terms with the fact it was possible she really, truly didn't know."

And Valentina had laughed, because what else could she do? She'd spent her whole life wishing she'd had more of a family than her chilly father. Oh, she loved him, she did, but he was so excruciatingly proper. So worried about appearances. His version of a hug was a well-meaning critique on her latest public appearance. Love to her father was maintaining and bolstering the family's reputation across the ages. She'd always wanted a sister to share in the bolstering. A brother. A mother. *Someone.*

But she hadn't had anyone. And now she had a stranger who looked just like her.

"My father is many things," she'd told Natalie. It was too soon to say *our father.* And who knew? Maybe they were cousins. Or maybe this was a fluke. No matter that little jolt of recognition inside her, as if she'd been meant to know this woman. As if this was a reunion. "Including His Royal Majesty, King Geoffrey of Murin. What he is not now, nor has ever been, I imagine, is forgettable."

Natalie had shaken her head. "You underestimate my mother's commitment to amnesia. She's made it a life choice instead of a malady. On some level I admire it."

"My mother was the noblewoman Frederica de Burgh, from a very old Murinese family." Valentina watched Natalie closely as she spoke, looking for any hint of...anything, really, in her gaze. "Promised to my father at birth, raised by nuns and kept deliberately sheltered, and then widely held to be unequal to the task of becoming queen. Mentally. But that's the story they would tell, isn't it, to explain why she disappeared? What's your mother's name?"

Natalie sighed and swung her shoulder bag onto the counter. Valentina had the impression that she'd really, truly wanted not to answer. But she had. "She calls herself Erica."

And there it was. Valentina supposed it could be a coincidence that *Erica* was a shortened form of *Frederica*. But how many coincidences were likely when they resulted in two women who'd never met—who never should have met—who happened to be mirror images?

If there was something in her that turned over at the notion that her mother had, in fact, had a maternal impulse after all—just not for Valentina—well, this wasn't the time to think about that. It might never be the time to think about that. She'd spent twenty-seven years trying her best not to think about that.

She changed the subject before she lost her composure completely and started asking questions she knew she shouldn't.

"I saw Achilles Casilieris, out there in the lounge," she'd said instead. The notorious billionaire had been there on her way in, brooding in a corner of the lounge and scowling at the paper he'd been reading. "He looks even more fearsome in person. You can almost *see* all that brash command and dizzying wealth ooze from his pores, can't you?"

"He's my boss," Natalie had said, sounding amused—if rather darkly. "If he was really oozing anything, anywhere, it would be my job to provide first aid until actual medical personnel could come handle it. At which point he would bite my head off for wasting his precious time by not curing him instantly."

Valentina had been flooded with a rash of follow-up questions. Was the biting off of heads normal? Was it fun to work for a man who sounded half-feral? Most important, did Natalie like her life or merely suffer through it?

But then her mobile started buzzing in her clutch. She'd forgotten about ferocious billionaires and thought about things she knew too much about, like the daredevil prince she was bound to marry soon, instead, because their fathers had agreed regardless of whether either one of them liked it. She'd checked the mobile's display to be sure, but wasn't surprised to find she'd guessed correctly. Lucky her, she'd had another meeting with her husband-to-be in Murin that very afternoon. She'd expected it to go the way all their meetings so far had gone. Prince Rodolfo, beloved the world over for his good looks and devil-may-care attitude, would talk. She would listen without really listening. She'd long since concluded that foretold a very happy royal marriage.

"My fiancé," she'd explained, meeting Natalie's gaze again. "Or his chief of staff, to be more precise."

"Congratulations," Natalie murmured.

"Thank you, I'm very lucky." Valentina's mouth curved, though her tone was far more dry than Natalie's had been. "Everyone says so. Prince Rodolfo is objectively attractive. Not all princes can make that claim, but the tabloids have exulted over his abs since he was a teenager. Just as they have salivated over his impressive dating history, which has involved a selection of models and actresses from at least four continents and did not cease in any noticeable way upon our engagement last fall."

"Your Prince Charming sounds…charming," Natalie had said.

Valentina raised one shoulder, then dropped it. "His theory is that he remains free until our marriage, and then will be free once again following the necessary birth of his heir. More discreetly, I can only hope. Meanwhile, I am beside myself with joy that I must take my place at his side in two short months. Of course."

Natalie had laughed, and the sound had made Valentina's stomach flip. Because it sounded like her. It sounded exactly like her.

"It's going to be a terrific couple of months all around, then," her mirror image was saying. "Mr. Casilieris is in rare form. He's putting together a particularly dramatic deal and it's not going his way and he…isn't used to that. So that's me working twenty-two-hour days instead of my usual twenty for the foreseeable future, which is even more fun when he's cranky and snarling."

"It can't possibly be worse than having to smile politely while your future husband lectures you about the absurd expectation of fidelity in what is essentially an arranged marriage for hours on end. The absurdity is that *he* might be expected to curb his impulses for a year or so, in case you wondered. The expectations for *me* apparently involve quietly and chastely finding fulfillment in philanthropic works, like his sainted absentee mother, who everyone knows manufactured a supposed health crisis so she could live out her days in peaceful seclusion. It's easy to be philanthropically fulfilled while living in isolation in Bavaria."

Natalie had smiled. "Try biting your tongue while your famously short-tempered boss rages at you for no reason, for the hundredth time in an hour, because he pays you to stand there and take it without wilting or crying or selling whingeing stories about him to the press."

Valentina had returned that smile. "Or the hours and hours of grim palace-vetted prewedding press interviews in the company of a pack of advisers who will censor everything I say and inevitably make me sound like a bit of animated treacle, as out of touch with reality as the average overly sweet dessert."

"Speaking of treats, I also have to deal with the board of directors Mr. Casilieris treats like irritating schoolchildren, his packs of furious ex-lovers each with her own vendetta, all his terrified employees who need to be coached through meetings with him and treated for PTSD after, and every last member of his staff in every one of his households, who like me to be the one to ask him the questions they know will set him off on one of his scorch-the-earth rages." Natalie had moved closer then, and lowered her voice. "I was thinking of quitting, to be honest. Today."

"I can't quit, I'm afraid," Valentina had said. Regretfully.

But she'd wished she could. She'd wished she could just…walk away and not have to live up to anyone's expectations. And not have to marry a man whom she barely knew. And not have to resign herself to a version of the same life so many of her ancestors had lived. Maybe that was where the idea had come from. Blood was blood, after all. And this woman clearly shared her blood. What if…?

"I have a better idea," she'd said, and then she'd tossed it out there before she could think better of it. "Let's switch places. For a month, say. Six weeks at the most. Just for a little break."

"That's crazy," Natalie said at once, and she was right. Of course she was right.

"Insane," Valentina had agreed. "But you might find royal protocol exciting! And I've always wanted to do the things everyone else in the world does. Like go to a real job."

"People can't *switch places*." Natalie had frowned. "And certainly not with a princess."

"You could think about whether or not you really want to quit," Valentina pointed out, trying to sweeten the deal. "It would be a lovely holiday for you. Where will Achilles Casilieris be in six weeks' time?"

"He's never gone from London for too long," Natalie had said, as if she was considering it.

Valentina had smiled. "Then in six weeks we'll meet in London. We'll text in the meantime with all the necessary details about our lives, and on the appointed day we'll just meet up and switch back and no one will ever be the wiser. Doesn't that sound like *fun*?"

"It would never work," Natalie had replied. Which wasn't exactly a *no*. "No one will ever believe I'm you."

Valentina waved a hand, encompassing the pair of them. "How would anyone know the difference? I can barely tell myself."

"People will take one look at me and know I'm not you. *You* look like a *princess*."

"You, too, can look like a princess," Valentina assured her. Then smiled. "This princess, anyway. You already do."

"You're elegant. Poised. You've had years of training, presumably. How to be a diplomat. How to be polite in every possible situation. Which fork to use at dinner, for God's sake."

"Achilles Casilieris is one of the wealthiest men alive," Valentina had pointed out. "He dines with as many kings as I do. I suspect that as his personal assistant, Natalie, you have, too. And have likely learned how to navigate the cutlery."

"No one will believe it," Natalie had insisted. But she'd sounded a bit as if she was wavering.

Valentina tugged off the ring on her left hand and placed it down on the counter between them. It made an audible *clink* against the marble surface, as well it should, given it was one of the crown jewels of the kingdom of Tissely.

"Try it on. I dare you. It's an heirloom from Prince Rodolfo's extensive treasury of such items, dating back to the dawn of time, more or less." She smiled. "If it doesn't fit we'll never speak of switching places again."

But the ring had fit her double as if it had been made especially for her.

And after that, switching clothes was easy. Valentina found herself in front of the bathroom mirror, dressed like a billionaire's assistant, when Natalie walked out of the stall behind her in her own shift dress and the heels her favorite shoe designer had made just for her. It was like looking in a mirror, but one that walked and looked unsteady on her feet and was wearing her hair differently.

Valentina couldn't tell if she was disconcerted or excited. Both, maybe.

She'd eyed Natalie. "Will your glasses give me a headache, do you suppose?"

But Natalie had pulled them from her face and handed them over. "They're clear glass. I was getting a little too much attention from some of the men Mr. Casilieris works with, and it annoyed him. I didn't want to lose my job, so I started wearing my hair up and these glasses. It worked like a charm."

"I refuse to believe men are so idiotic."

Natalie had grinned as Valentina took the glasses and slid them onto her nose. "The men we're talking about weren't exactly paying me attention because they found me enthralling. It was a diversionary tactic during negotiations, and yes, you'd be surprised how many men fail to see a woman who looks smart."

She'd freed her hair from its utilitarian ponytail and shook it out, then handed the stretchy elastic to Valentina. It took Valentina a moment to re-create the ponytail on her own head, and then it was done.

And it really was like magic.

"This is crazy," Natalie had whispered.

"We have to switch places now," Valentina said softly, hearing the rough patch in her own voice. "I've always wanted to be…someone else. Someone normal. Just for a little while."

And she'd gotten exactly what she'd wanted, hadn't she?

"I am distressed, Miss Monette, that I cannot manage to secure your attention for more than a moment or two," Achilles said then, slamming Valentina back into this car he dominated so easily when all he was doing was sitting there.

Sitting there, filling up the world without even trying.

He was *devastating*. There was no other possible word that could describe him. His black hair was close-cropped to his head, which only served to highlight his strong, intensely masculine features. She'd had hours on the plane to study him as she'd repeatedly failed to do the things he'd expected of her, and she still couldn't really get her head around why it was that he was so…affecting. He shouldn't have been. Dark hair. Dark eyes that tended toward gold when his temper washed over him, which he'd so far made no attempt to hide. A strong nose that reminded her of ancient statues she'd seen in famous museums. That lean, hard body of his that wasn't made of marble or bronze but seemed to suggest both as he used it so effortlessly. A predator packed into a dark suit that seemed molded to him, whispering suggestions of a lethal warrior when all he was doing was taking phone calls with a five-hundred-thousand-dollar watch on one wrist that he didn't flash about, because he was Achilles Casilieris. He didn't need flash.

Achilles was something else.

It was the power that seemed to emanate from him, even when he was doing nothing but sitting quietly. It was the fierce hit of his intelligence, that brooding, unmistakable cleverness that seemed to wrap around him like a cloud. It was something in the way he looked at her, as if he saw too much and too deeply and no matter that Valentina's unreadable game face was the envy of Europe. Besides all that, there was something untamed about him. Fierce.

Something about him left her breathless. Entirely too close to reeling.

"Do you require a gold star every time you make a statement?" she asked, careful not to look at him. It was too hard to look away. She'd discovered that on the plane ride from London—and he was a lot closer now. So close she was sure she could feel the heat of his body from where she sat. "I'll be certain to make a note to celebrate you more often. Sir."

Valentina didn't know what she was doing. In Natalie's job, certainly, but also with this man in general. She'd learned one thing about powerful people—particularly men—and it was that they did not enjoy being challenged. Under any circumstances. What made her think Achilles would go against type and magically handle this well?

But she couldn't seem to stop herself.

And the fact that she had never been one to challenge much of anything before hardly signified. Or maybe that was why she felt so unfettered, she thought. Because this wasn't her life. This wasn't her remote father and his endless expectations for the behavior of his only child. This was a strange little bit of role-playing that allowed her to be someone other than Princess Valentina for a moment. A few weeks, that was all. Why not challenge Achilles while she was at it? *Especially* if no one else ever did?

She could feel his gaze on the side of her face, that brooding dark gold, and she braced herself. Then made sure her expression was nothing but serene as she turned to face him.

It didn't matter. There was no minimizing this man.

She could feel the hit of him—like a fist—deep in her belly. And then lower.

"Are you certain you were not hit in the head?" Achilles asked, his dark voice faintly rough with the hint of his native Greek. "Perhaps in the bathroom at the airport? I fear that such places can often suffer from slippery floors. Deadly traps for the unwary."

"It was only a bathroom," she replied airily. "It wasn't slippery or otherwise notable in any way."

"Are you sure?" And something in his voice and his hard gaze prickled into her then. Making her chest feel tighter.

Valentina did not want to talk about the bathroom, much less anything that had happened there. And there was something in his gaze that worried her—but that was insane. He couldn't have any idea that she'd run into her own twin. How could he? Valentina had been unaware that there was the faintest possibility she might have a twin until today.

Which made her think about her father and his many, many lectures about his only child in a new, unfortunate light. But Valentina thrust that aside. That was something to worry about when she was a princess again. That was a problem she could take up when she was back in Murin Castle.

Here, now, she was a secretary. An executive assistant, no more and no less.

"I beg your pardon, Mr. Casilieris." She let her smile deepen and ignored the little hum of...something deep inside her when his gaze seemed to catch fire. "Are you trying to tell me that you need a bathroom? Should I ask the driver to stop the car right here in the middle of the George Washington Bridge?"

She expected him to get angry again. Surely that was what had been going on before, back in London before the plane had taken off. She'd seen temper all over that fierce, hard face of his and gleaming hot in his gaze. More than that, she'd felt it inside her. As if the things he felt echoed within her, winding her into knots. She felt something a whole lot like a chill inch its way down her spine at that notion.

But Achilles only smiled. And that was far more dangerous than merely devastating.

"Miss Monette," he said and shook his head, as if she amused him, when she could see that the thing that moved over that ruthless face of his was far too intense to be simple *amusement*. "I had no idea that beneath your officious exterior you've been hiding a comedienne all this time. For five years you've worked at my side and never let so much as a hint of this whimsical side of your personality out into the open. Whatever could have changed?"

He knows. The little voice inside her was certain— and terrified.

But it was impossible. Valentina knew it was impossible, so she made herself smile and relax against the leather seat as if she'd never in her life been so at her ease. Very much as if she was not within scant inches of a very large, very powerful, very intense male who was eyeing her the way gigantic lions and tigers and jaguars eyed their food. When they were playing with it.

She'd watched enough documentaries and made enough state visits to African countries to know firsthand.

"Perhaps I've always been this amusing," she suggested, managing to tamp down her hysteria about oversize felines, none of which was particularly helpful at the moment. "Perhaps you've only recently allowed yourself to truly listen to me."

"I greatly enjoy listening to you," Achilles replied. There was a laziness in the way he sat there, sprawled out in the backseat of his car, that dark gold gaze on hers.

A certain laziness, yes—but Valentina didn't believe it for a second. "I particularly enjoy listening to you when you are doing your job perfectly. Because you know how much I admire perfection. I insist on it, in fact. Which is why I cannot understand why you failed to provide it today."

"I don't know what you mean."

But she knew what he meant. She'd been on the plane and she'd been the one to fail repeatedly to do what was clearly her job. She'd hung up on one conference call and failed entirely to connect another. She'd expected him to explode—if she was honest, there was a part of her that wanted him to explode, in the way that anyone might want to poke and poke and poke at some kind of blister to see if it would pop. But he hadn't popped. He hadn't lost his temper at all, despite the fact that it had been very clear to Valentina very quickly that she was a complete and utter disaster at doing whatever it was that Natalie did.

When Achilles had stared at her in amazement, however, she hadn't made any excuses. She'd only gazed right back, serenely, as if she'd meant to do whatever utterly incorrect thing it was. As if it was all some kind of strategy.

She could admit that she hadn't really thought the job part through. She been so busy fantasizing herself into some kind of normal life that it had never occurred to her that, normal or not, a life was still *a whole life*. She had no idea how to live any way but the way she'd been living for almost thirty years. How remarkably condescending, she'd thought up there on Achilles Casilieris's jet, that she'd imagined she could simply step into a job—especially one as demanding as this appeared to be—and do it merely because she'd decided it was her chance at something "normal."

Valentina had found the entire experience humbling, if she was honest, and it had been only a few hours since she'd switched places with Natalie in London. Who knew what else awaited her?

But Achilles was still sprawled there beside her, that unnerving look of his making her skin feel too small for her bones.

"Natalie, Natalie," he murmured, and Valentina told herself it was a good thing he'd used that name. It wasn't her name, and she needed the reminder. This wasn't about her. It wasn't her job to advocate for Natalie when the other woman might not wish for her to do anything like that. She was on a fast track to losing Natalie her job, and then what? Valentina didn't have to worry about her employment prospects, but she had no idea what the market was like for billionaire's assistants.

But maybe there was a part of her that already knew that there was no way Natalie Monette was a stranger to her. Certainly not on the genetic level. And that had implications she wasn't prepared to examine just yet, but she did know that the woman who was in all likelihood her long-lost identical twin did not have to work for Achilles Casilieris unless she wanted to.

How arrogant of you, a voice inside her said quietly. *Her Royal Highness, making unilateral decisions for others' lives without their input.*

The voice sounded a little too much like her father's.

"That is my name," Valentina said to Achilles, in case there had been any doubt. Perhaps with a little too much force.

But she had the strangest notion that he was…*tasting* the name as he said it. As if he'd never said it before. Did he call Natalie by her first name? Valentina rather thought not, given that he'd called her *Miss Monette* when she'd met him—but that was neither here nor there, she told herself. And no matter that she was a woman who happened to know the power of titles. She had many of her own. And her life was marked by those who used the different versions of her titles, not to mention the few who actually called her by her first name.

"I cannot tolerate this behavior," he said, but it wasn't in that same infuriated tone he'd used earlier. If anything, he sounded almost…indulgent. But surely that was impossible. "It borders on open rebellion, and I cannot have that. This is not a democracy, I'm afraid. This is a dictatorship. If I want your opinion, I'll tell you what it is."

There was no reason her heart should have been kicking at her like that, her pulse so loud in her ears she was sure he must be able to hear it himself.

"What an interesting way to foster employee loyalty," she murmured. "Really more of a scorch-the-earth approach. Do you find it gets you the results you want?"

"I do not need to breed employee loyalty," Achilles told her, sounding even lazier than before, those dark eyes of his on hers. "People are loyal to me or they are fired. You seem to have forgotten reality today, Natalie. Allow me to remind you that I pay you so much money that I own your loyalty, just as I own everything else."

"Perhaps," and her voice was a little too rough then. A little too shaky, when what could this possibly have to do with her? She was a visitor. Natalie's loyalty was no concern of hers. "I have no wish to be owned. Does anyone? I think you'll find that they do not."

Achilles shrugged. "Whether you wish it or do not, that is how it is."

"That is why I was considering quitting," she heard herself say. And she was no longer looking at him. That was still far too dangerous, too disconcerting. She found herself staring down at her hands, folded in her lap. She could feel that she was frowning, when she learned a long, long time ago never to show her feelings in public. "It's all very well and good for you, of course. I imagine it's quite pleasant to have minions. But for me, there's more to life than blind loyalty. There's more to life than work." She blinked back a strange heat. "I may not have experienced it myself, but I know there must be."

"And what do you think is out there?" He shifted in the seat beside her, but Valentina still refused to look back at him, no matter how she seemed almost physically compelled to do just that. "What do you think you're missing? Is it worth what you are throwing away here today, with this aggressive attitude and the childish pretense that you don't know your own job?"

"It's only those who are bored of the world, or jaded, who are so certain no one else could possibly wish to see it."

"No one is keeping you from roaming about the planet at will," he told her in a low voice. Too low. So low it danced along her skin and seemed to insinuate itself beneath her flesh. "But you seem to wish to burn down the world you know in order to see the one you don't. That is not what I would call wise. Would you?"

Valentina didn't understand why his words seemed to beat beneath her own skin. But she couldn't seem to catch her breath. And her eyes seemed entirely too full, almost scratchy, with an emotion she couldn't begin to name.

She was aware of too many things. Of the car as it slid through the Manhattan streets. Of Achilles himself, too big and too masculine in the seat beside her, and much too close besides. And most of all, that oddly weighted thing within her, rolling around and around until she couldn't tell the difference between sensation and reaction.

And him right there in the middle of it, confusing her all the more.

CHAPTER THREE

ACHILLES DIDN'T SAY another word, and that was worse. It left Valentina to sit there with her own thoughts in a whirl and nothing to temper them. It left no barrier between that compelling, intent look in his curiously dark eyes and her.

Valentina had no experience with men. Her father had insisted that she grow up as sheltered as possible from public life, so that she could enjoy what little privacy was afforded to a European princess before she turned eighteen. She'd attended carefully selected boarding schools run strictly and deliberately, but that hadn't prevented her classmates from involving themselves in all kinds of dramatic situations. Even then, Valentina had kept herself apart.

Your mother's defection was a stain on the throne, her father always told her. *It is upon us to render it clean and whole again.*

Valentina had been far too terrified of staining Murin any further to risk a scandal. She'd concentrated on her studies and her friends and left the teenage rebellions to others. And once out of school, she'd been thrust unceremoniously into the spotlight. She'd been an ambassador for her kingdom wherever she went, and more than that, she'd always known that she was promised to the Crown

Prince of Tissely. Any scandals she embroiled herself in would haunt two kingdoms.

She'd never seen the point.

And along the way she'd started to take a certain pride in the fact that she was saving herself for her predetermined marriage. It was the one thing that was hers to give on her wedding night that had nothing to do with her father or her kingdom.

Is it pride that's kept you chaste—or is it control? a little voice inside her asked then, and the way it kicked in her, Valentina suspected she wouldn't care for the answer. She ignored it.

But the point was, she had no idea how to handle men. Not on any kind of intimate level. These past few hours, in fact, were the longest she'd ever spent alone in the company of a man. It simply didn't happen when she was herself. There were always attendants and aides swarming around Princess Valentina. Always.

She told herself that was why she was having such trouble catching her breath. It was the novelty—that was all. It certainly wasn't *him*.

Still, it was almost a relief when the car pulled up in front of a quietly elegant building on the Upper West Side of Manhattan, perched there with a commanding view of Central Park, and came to a stop.

The late-afternoon breeze washed over her when she stepped from the car, smelling improbably of flowers in the urban sprawl of New York City. But Valentina decided to take it as a blessing.

Achilles remained silent as he escorted her into the building. He only raised his chin in the barest of responses to the greeting that came his way from the doormen in the shiny, obviously upscale lobby, and then he led her into a private elevator located toward the back and behind another set of security guards. It was a gleaming, shining thing that he operated with a key. And it was blessedly without any mirrors.

Valentina wasn't entirely sure whom she'd see if she looked at her own reflection just then.

There were too many things she didn't understand churning inside her, and she hadn't the slightest idea what she was doing here. What on earth she hoped to gain from this odd little lark across the planet, literally in another woman's shoes.

A break, she reminded herself sternly. A vacation. A little holiday away from all the duties and responsibilities of Princess Valentina, which was more important now than ever. She would give herself over to her single-greatest responsibility in a matter of weeks. She would marry Prince Rodolfo and make both of their fathers and all of their subjects very, very happy.

And a brief escape had sounded like bliss for that split second back there in London—and it still did, when she thought about what waited for her. The terribly appropriate royal marriage. The endlessly public yet circumspect life of a modern queen. The glare of all that attention that she and any children she bore could expect no matter where they went or what they did, yet she could never comment upon lest she seem ungrateful or entitled.

Hers was to wave and smile—that was all. She was marrying a man she hardly knew who would expect the marital version of the same. This was a little breather before the reality of all that. This was a tiny bit of space between her circumscribed life at her father's side and more of the same at her husband's.

She couldn't allow the brooding, unreadable man beside her to ruin it, no matter how unnerving his dark gold gaze was. No matter what fires it kicked up inside her that she hardly dared name.

The elevator doors slid open, delivering them straight

into the sumptuous front hall of an exquisitely decorated penthouse. Valentina followed Achilles as he strode deep inside, not bothering to spare her a glance as he moved. She was glad that he walked ahead of her, which allowed her to look around so she could get her bearings without seeming to do so. Because, of course, Natalie would already know her way around this place.

She took in the high ceilings and abundant windows all around. The sweeping stairs that led up toward at least two more floors. The mix of art deco and a deep coziness that suggested this penthouse was more than just a showcase; Achilles actually *lived* here.

Valentina told herself—sternly—that there was no earthly reason that notion should make her shiver.

She was absurdly grateful when a housekeeper appeared, clucking at Achilles in what it took Valentina longer than it should have to realize was Greek. A language she could converse in, though she would never consider herself anything like fluent. Still, it took her only a very few moments to understand that whatever the danger Achilles exuded and however ruthless the swath he cut through the entire world with a single glance, this woman thought he was wonderful.

She *beamed* at him.

It would not do to let that get to her, Valentina warned herself as something warm seemed to roll its way through her, pooling in the strangest places. She should not draw any conclusions about a man who was renowned for his fierceness in all things and yet let a housekeeper treat him like family.

The woman declared she would feed him no matter if he was hungry or not, lest he get skinny and weak, and bustled back in the direction of what Valentina assumed was the kitchen.

"You're looking around as if you are lost," Achilles

murmured, when Valentina didn't think she'd been looking around at all. "When you have spent more time in this penthouse over the last five years than I have."

Valentina hated the fact that she started a bit when she realized his attention was focused on her again. And that he was speaking in English, which seemed to make him sound that much more knowing.

Or possibly even mocking, unless she was very much mistaken.

"Mr. Casilieris," she said, lacing her voice with gentle reprove, "I work for you. I don't understand why you appear to be quite so interested in what you think is happening inside my head today. Especially when you are so mistaken."

"Am I?"

"Entirely." She raised her brows at him. "If I could suggest that we concentrate more on matters of business than fictional representations of what might or might not be going on inside my mind, I think we might be more productive."

"As productive as we were on the flight over?" His voice was a lazy sort of lash, as amused as it was on target.

Valentina only smiled, hoping she looked enigmatic and strategic rather than at a loss.

"Are *you* lost?" she asked him after a moment, because neither one of them had moved from the great entry that bled into the spacious living room, then soared up two stories, a quiet testament to his wealth and power.

"Careful, Miss Monette," Achilles said with a certain dark precision. "As delightful as I have found today's descent into insubordination, I have a limit. It would be in your best interests not to push me there too quickly."

Valentina had made a study out of humbly accepting all kinds of news she didn't wish to hear over the years. She bent her head, let her lips curve a bit—but not enough to be called a smile, only enough to show she was feeling… something. Then she simply stood there quietly. It was amazing how many unpleasant moments she'd managed to get through that way.

So she had no earthly idea why there was a part of her that wanted nothing more than to look Achilles straight in his dark eyes and ask him, *Or what?*

Somehow, thankfully, she refrained.

Servants came in behind them with luggage—some of which Valentina assumed must be Natalie's and thus hers—but Achilles did not appear to notice them. He kept his attention trained directly on her.

A lesser woman would have been disconcerted, Valentina thought. Someone unused to being the focus of attention, for example. Someone who hadn't spent a part of every day since she turned eighteen having cameras in her face to record every flutter of her eyelashes and rip apart every facet of whatever she happened to be wearing and how she'd done her hair. Every expression that crossed her face was a headline.

What was a cranky billionaire next to that?

"There's no need to repair to our chambers after the flight, I think," he said softly, and Valentina had that odd notion again. That he could see right through her. That he knew things he couldn't possibly know. "We can get right to it."

And there was no reason that that should feel almost… dirty. As if he was suggesting—

But, of course, that was absurd, Valentina told herself staunchly. He was Achilles Casilieris. He was renowned almost as much for his prowess in the sheets as he was for his dominance in the boardroom. In some circles, more.

He tended toward the sort of well-heeled women who

were mainstays on various charity circuits. Not for him the actresses or models whom so many other men of his stature preferred. That, apparently, was not good enough for Achilles Casilieris. Valentina had found herself with some time on the plane to research it herself, after Achilles had finished the final call she'd failed entirely to set up to his liking and had sat a while, a fulminating stare fixed on her. Then he'd taken himself off to one of the jet's finely appointed staterooms, and she'd breathed a bit easier.

A bit.

She'd looked around for a good book to read, preferably a paperback romance because who didn't like hope and happiness with a bit of sex thrown in to make it spicy, but there had been nothing of the sort. Achilles apparently preferred dreary economic magazines that trumpeted out recession and doom from all quarters. Valentina had kicked off her shoes, tucked her legs beneath her on the smooth leather chair she'd claimed for the flight, and indulged herself with a descent into the tabloid and gossip sites she normally avoided. Because she knew how many lies they told about her, so why would she believe anything she read about anyone else?

Still, they were a great way to get a sense of the kind of coverage a man like Achilles suffered, which would surely tell her…something. But the answer was…not much. He was featured in shots from charity events where other celebrities gathered like cows at a trough, but was otherwise not really a tabloid staple. Possibly because he was so sullen and scowling, she thought.

His taste in bedmates, however, was clear even without being splashed across screeching front pages all over the world. Achilles tended toward women who were less celebrated for their faces and more for their actions. Which wasn't to say they weren't all beautiful, of course. That seemed to be a requirement. But they couldn't only be beautiful.

This one was a civil rights attorney of some renown. That one was a journalist who spent most of her time in terrifying war zones. This one had started a charity to benefit a specific cancer that had taken her younger sister. That one was a former Olympic athlete who had dedicated her post-competition life to running a lauded program for at-risk teenagers.

He clearly had a type. Accomplished, beautiful women who did good in the world and who also happened to be wealthy enough all on their own. The uncharitable part of her suspected that last part was because he knew a woman of independent means would not be as interested in his fortune as a woman who had nothing. No gold diggers need apply, clearly.

But the point was, she knew she was mistaken about his potentially suggestive words. Because "assistant to billionaire" was not the kind of profession that would appeal to a man like Achilles. It saved no lives. It bettered nothing.

Valentina found herself glaring at his back as he led her into a lavish office suite on the first level of his expansive penthouse. When she stood in the center of the room, awaiting further instructions, he only crooked a brow. He leaned back against the large desk that stretched across one wall and regarded her with that hot sort of focus that made everything inside her seem to shift hard to the left.

She froze. And then she could have stood there for hours, for all she knew, as surely as if he'd caught her and held her fast in his fists.

"When you are ready, Miss Monette, feel free to take your seat." His voice was razor sharp, cut through with that same rough darkness that she found crept through her limbs. Lighting her up and making her feel something like sluggish. She didn't understand it. "Though I do love being kept waiting."

More chastened than she wanted to admit, Valentina moved to one of the seats set around a table to the right of the desk, at the foot of towering bookshelves stuffed full of serious-looking books, and settled herself in it. When he continued to stare at her as if she was deliberately keeping him waiting, she reached into the bag—Natalie's bag, which she'd liberated from the bathroom when she'd left the airport with Achilles—until she found a tablet.

A few texts with her double had given her the passwords she needed and some advice.

Just write down everything he says. He likes to forget he said certain things, and it's always good to have a record. One of my jobs is to function as his memory.

Valentina had wanted to text back her thoughts on that, but had refrained. Natalie might have wanted to quit this job, but that was up to her, not the woman taking her place for a few weeks.

"Anything else?" Achilles's voice had a dark edge. "Would you like to have a snack? Perhaps a brief nap? Tell me, is there any way that I can make you more comfortable, Miss Monette, such that you might actually take it upon yourself to do a little work today?"

And Valentina didn't know what came over her. Because she wanted to argue. She, who had made a virtue out of remaining quiet and cordial under any circumstances, wanted to fight. She didn't understand it. She knew it was Achilles. That there was something in him that made her want to do or say anything to get some kind of reaction. It didn't matter that it was madness. It was something about that look in his eyes. Something about that hard, amused mouth of his.

It was something about *him*.

But Valentina reminded herself that this was not her life.

This was not her life and this was not her job, and none of this was hers to ruin. She was the steward of Natalie's life for a little while, nothing more. She imagined that Natalie would be doing the same for her. Maybe breathing a little bit of new life into the tired old royal nonsense she'd find waiting for her at Murin Castle, but that was all. Neither one of them was out to wreck what they found.

And she'd never had any trouble whatsoever keeping to the party line. Doing her father's bidding, behaving appropriately, being exactly the princess whom everyone imagined she was. She felt that responsibility—to her people, to her bloodline, to her family's history—deeply. She'd never acted out the way so many of her friends had. She'd never fought against her own responsibilities. It wasn't that she was afraid to do any of those things, but simply that it had never occurred to her to try. Valentina had always known exactly who she was and what her life would hold, from her earliest days.

So she didn't recognize this thing in her that wanted nothing more than to cause a commotion. To stand up and throw the tablet she held at Achilles's remarkably attractive head. To kick over the chair she was sitting in and, while she was at it, that desk of his, too, all brash steel and uncompromising masculinity, just like its owner.

She wanted to do *something*. Anything. She could feel it humming through her veins, bubbling in her blood. As if something about this normal life she'd tried on for size had infected her. Changed her. When it had only been a few hours.

He's a ruthless man, something reckless inside her whispered. *He can take it.*

But this wasn't her life. She had to protect it, not destroy it, no matter what was moving in her, poking at her, tempting her to act out for the first time in her life.

So Valentina smiled up at Achilles, forced herself to remain serene the way she always did, and got to work.

It was late into the New York night when Achilles finally stopped torturing his deceitful princess.

He made her go over byzantine contracts that rendered his attorneys babbling idiots. He questioned her on clauses he only vaguely understood himself, and certainly couldn't expect her to be conversant on. He demanded she prepare memos he had no intention of sending. He questioned her about events he knew she could not possibly know anything about, and the truth was that he enjoyed himself more than he could remember enjoying anything else for quite some time.

When Demetria had bustled in with food, Achilles had waved Valentina's away.

"My assistant does not like to eat while she works," he told his housekeeper, but he'd kept his gaze on Valentina while he'd said it.

"I don't," she'd agreed merrily enough. "I consider it a weakness." She'd smiled at him. "But you go right ahead."

Point to the princess, he'd thought.

The most amazing thing was that Princess Valentina never backed down. Her ability to brazen her way through the things she didn't know, in fact, was nothing short of astounding. Impressive in the extreme. Achilles might have admired it if he hadn't been the one she was trying to fool.

"It is late," he said finally, when he thought her eyes might glaze over at last. Though he would cast himself out his own window to the Manhattan streets below before he'd admit his might, too. "And while there is always more to do, I think it is perhaps wise if we take this as a natural stopping place."

Valentina smiled at him, tucked up in that chair of hers that she had long since claimed as her own in a way he couldn't remember the real Natalie had ever done, her green eyes sparkling.

"I understand if you need a rest," she said sweetly. Too sweetly. "Sir."

Achilles had been standing at the windows, his back to the mad gleam of Manhattan. But at that, he let himself lean back, his body shifting into something…looser. More dangerous.

And much, much hotter than contracts.

"I worry my hearing has failed me. Because it sounded very much as if you were impugning my manhood."

"Only if your manhood is so fragile that you can't imagine it requires a rest," she said, and aimed a sunny smile at him as if that would take away the sting of her words. "But you are Achilles Casilieris. You have made yourself a monument to manhood, clearly. No fragility allowed."

"It is almost as if you think debating me like this is some kind of strategy," he said softly, making no attempt to ratchet back the ruthlessness in his voice. Much less do something about the fire he could feel storming through him everywhere else. "Let me warn you, again, it is only a strategy if your goal is to find yourself without a job and without a recommendation. To say nothing of the black mark I will happily put beside your name."

Valentina waved a hand in the air, airily, dismissing him. And her possible firing, black marks—all of it. Something else he very likely would have found impressive if he'd been watching her do it to someone else.

"So many threats." She shook her head. "I understand that this is how you run your business and you're very successful, but really. It's exhausting. Imagine how many more bees you could get with honey."

He didn't want to think about honey. Not when there were only the two of them here, in this office cushioned by the night outside and the rest of the penthouse. No shared walls on these floors he owned. This late, none of the staff would be up. It was only Achilles and this princess pretending to be his assistant, and the buttery light of the few lamps they'd switched on, making the night feel thick and textured everywhere the light failed to reach.

Like inside him.

"Come here."

Valentina blinked, but her green gaze was unreadable then. She only looked at him for a moment, as if she'd forgotten that she was playing this game. And that in it, she was his subordinate.

"Come here," he said again. "Do not make me repeat myself, I beg you. You will not like my response."

She stood the way she did everything else, with an easy grace. With that offhanded elegance that did things to him he preferred not to examine. And he knew she had no desire to come any closer to him. He could feel it. Her wariness hung between them like some kind of smoke, and it ignited that need inside him. And for a moment he thought she might disobey him. That she might balk— and it was in that moment he thought she'd stay where she was, across the room, that he had understood how very much he wanted her.

In a thousand ways he shouldn't, because Achilles was a man who did not *want*. He took. Wanting was a weakness that led only to darkness—though it didn't feel like a weakness tonight. It felt like the opposite.

But he'd underestimated his princess. Her shoulders straightened almost imperceptibly. And then she glided toward him, head high like some kind of prima ballerina, her face set in the sort of pleasant expression he now knew she could summon and dispatch at will. He admired that, too.

And he'd thrown out that summons because he could. Because he wanted to. And he was experimenting with this new *wanting*, no matter how little he liked it.

Still, there was no denying the way his body responded as he watched her walk toward him. There was no denying the rich, layered tension that seemed to fill the room. And him, making his pulse a living thing as his blood seemed to heat in his veins.

Something gleamed in that green gaze of hers, but she kept coming. She didn't stop until she was directly beside him, so close that if she breathed too heavily he thought her shoulder might brush his. He shifted so that he stood slightly behind her, and jutted his chin toward the city laid out before them.

"What do you see when you look out the window?"

He felt more than saw the glance she darted at him. But then she kept her eyes on the window before them. On the ropes of light stretching out in all hectic directions possible below.

"Is that a trick question? I see Manhattan."

"I grew up in squalor." His voice was harsher than he'd intended, but Achilles did nothing to temper it. "It is common, I realize, for successful men to tell stories of their humble beginnings. Americans in particular find these stories inspiring. It allows them to fantasize that they, too, might better themselves against any odds. But the truth is more of a gray area, is it not? Beginnings are never quite so humble as they sound when rich men claim them. But me?" He felt her gaze on him then, instead of the mess of lights outside. "When I use the word *squalor*, that's an upgrade."

Her swallow was audible. Or perhaps he was paying her too close attention. Either way, he didn't back away.

"I don't know why you're telling me this."

"When you look through this window you see a city. A place filled with people going about their lives, traffic and isolation." He shifted so he could look down at her. "I see hope. I see vindication. I see all the despair and all the pain and all the loss that went into creating the man you see before you tonight. Creating this." And he moved his chin to indicate the penthouse. And the Casilieris Company while he was at it. "And there is nothing that I wouldn't do to protect it."

And he didn't know what had happened to him while he was speaking. He'd been playing a game, and then suddenly it seemed as if the game had started to play him— and it wasn't finished. Something clutched at him, as if he was caught in the grip of some massive fist.

It was almost as if he wanted this princess, this woman who believed she was tricking him—deceiving him—to understand him.

This, too, was unbearable.

But he couldn't seem to stop.

"Do you think people become driven by accident, Miss Monette?" he asked, and he couldn't have said why that thing gripping him seemed to clench harder. Making him sound far more intense than he thought he should have felt. Risking the truth about himself he carried inside and shared with no one. But he still didn't stop. "Ambition, desire, focus and drive—do you think these things grow on trees? But then, perhaps I'm asking the wrong person. Have you not told me a thousand times that you are not personally ambitious?"

It was one of the reasons he'd kept Natalie with him for so long, when other assistants to men like him used positions like hers as springboards into their own glorious careers. But this woman was not Natalie. If he hadn't known it before, he'd have known it now, when it was a full-scale struggle to keep his damned hands to himself.

"Ambition, it seems to me, is for those who have the freedom to pursue it. And for those who do not—" and Valentina's eyes seemed to gleam at that, making Achilles wonder exactly what her ambitions were "—it is nothing more than dissatisfaction. Which is far less worthy and infinitely more destructive, I think we can agree."

He didn't know when he'd turned to face her fully. He didn't know when he'd stopped looking at the city and was looking only at her instead. But he was, and he compounded that error by reaching out his hand and tugging on the very end of her silky, coppery ponytail where it kissed her shoulder every time she moved her head.

Her lips parted, as if on a soundless breath, and Achilles felt that as if she'd caressed him. As if her hands were on his body the way he wished they were, instead of at her sides.

"Are you dissatisfied?" It was amazing how difficult it was not to use her real name then. How challenging it was to stay in this game he suddenly didn't particularly want to play. "Is that what this is?"

Her green eyes, which had been so unreadable, suddenly looked slick. Dark and glassy with some or other emotion. He couldn't tell what it was, and still, he could feel it in him like smoke, stealing through his chest and making it harder than it should have been to breathe.

"There's nothing wrong with dissatisfaction in and of itself," she told him after a moment, then another, that seemed too large for him to contain. Too dark and much too edgy to survive intact, and yet here they both were. "You see it as disloyalty, but it's not."

"How can it be anything else?"

"It is possible to be both loyal and open to the possibility that there is a life outside the one you've committed yourself to." Her green eyes searched his. "Surely there must be."

"I think you will find that there is no such possibility." His voice was harsh. He could feel it inside him, like a stain. Like need. "We must all decide who we are, every moment of every day. You either keep a vow or you do not. There is no between."

She stiffened at that, then tried to force her shoulders back down to an easier, less telling angle. Achilles watched her do it. He watched something like distress cross her lovely face, but she hid that, too. It was only the darkness in her gaze that told him he'd scored a direct hit, and he was a man who took great pride in the strikes he leveled against anyone who tried to move against him. Yet what he felt when he looked at Valentina was not pride. Not pride at all.

"Some vows are not your own," she said fiercely, her gaze locked to his. "Some are inherited. It's easy to say that you'll keep them because that's what's expected of you, but it's a great deal harder to actually *do* it."

He knew the vows she'd made. That pointless prince. Her upcoming royal wedding. He assumed that was the least of the vows she'd inherited from her father. And he still thought it was so much smoke and mirrors to hide the fact that she, like so many of her peers, was a spoiled and pampered creature who didn't like to be told what to do. Wasn't that the reason *poor little rich girl* was a saying in the first place?

He had no sympathy for the travails of a rich, pampered princess. But he couldn't seem to unwind that little silken bit of copper from around his finger, either. Much less step back and put the space between them that he should have left there from the start.

Achilles shook his head. "There is no gray area. Surely

you know this. You are either who you say you are or you are not."

There was something like misery in those eyes of hers then. And this was what he'd wanted. This was why he'd been goading her. And yet now that he seemed to have succeeded, he felt the strangest thing deep in his gut. It was an unpleasant and unfamiliar sensation, and at first Achilles couldn't identify it. It was a low heat, trickling through him, making him restless. Making him as close to uncertain as he'd ever been.

In someone else, he imagined, it might be shame. But shame was not something Achilles allowed in himself. Ever.

This was a night full of things he did not allow, apparently. Because he wanted her. He wanted to punctuate this oddly emotional discussion with his mouth. His hands. The whole of his too-tight, too-interested body pressed deep into hers. He wanted to taste those sweetly lush lips of hers. He wanted to take her elegant face in his hands, tip her head back and sate himself at last. It seemed to him an age or two since he'd boarded his plane and realized his assistant was not who she was supposed to be. An agony of waiting and all that *want*, and he was not a man who agonized. Or waited. Or wanted anything, it seemed, but this princess who thought she could fool him.

What was the matter with him that some part of him wanted to let her?

He did none of the things he longed to do.

Achilles made himself do the hard thing, no matter how complicated it was. Or how complicated it felt, anyway. When really it was so simple. He let her go. He let her silky hair fall from between his fingers, and he stepped back, putting inches between them.

But that did nothing to ease the temptation.

"I think what you need is a good night's sleep," he told

her, like some kind of absurd nurturer. Something he had certainly never tried to be for anyone else in the whole of his life. He would have doubted it was possible—and he refused to analyze that. "Perhaps it will clear your head and remind you of who you are. Jet lag can make that so very confusing, I know."

He thought she might have scuttled from the room at that, filled with her own shame if there was any decency in the world, but he was learning that this princess was not at all who he expected her to be. She swallowed, hard. And he could still see that darkness in her eyes. But she didn't look away from him. And she certainly didn't scuttle anywhere.

"I know exactly who I am, Mr. Casilieris," she said, very directly, and the lenses in her glasses made her eyes seem that much greener. "As I'm certain you do, too. Jet lag makes a person tired. It doesn't make them someone else entirely."

And when she turned to walk from the room then, it was with her head held high, graceful and self-contained, with no apparent second thoughts. Or anything the least bit like shame. All he could read on her as she went was that same distracting elegance that was already too far under his skin.

Achilles couldn't seem to do a thing but watch her go.

And when the sound of her footsteps had faded away, deep into the far reaches of the penthouse, he turned back to the wild gleam of Manhattan on the other side of his windows. Frenetic and frenzied. Light in all directions, as if there was nothing more to the world tonight than this utterly mad tangle of life and traffic and people and energy and it hardly mattered what he felt so high above it. It hardly mattered at all that he'd betrayed himself. That this woman who should have been nothing to him made him act like someone he barely recognized.

And her words stayed with him. *I know exactly who I am.* They echoed around and around in his head until it sounded a whole lot more like an accusation.

As if she was the one playing this game, and winning it, after all.

CHAPTER FOUR

As THE DAYS PASSED, Valentina thought that she was getting the hang of this assistant thing—especially if she endeavored to keep a minimum distance between herself and Achilles when the night got a little too dark and close. And at all other times, for that matter.

She'd chalked up those odd, breathless moments in his office that first night to the strangeness of inhabiting someone else's life. Because it couldn't be anything else. Since then, she hadn't felt the need to say too much. She hadn't defended herself—or her version of Natalie. She'd simply tried to do the job that Natalie, apparently, did so well she was seen by other employees of the Casilieris Company as superhuman.

With every day she became more accustomed to the demands of the job. She felt less as if she really ought to have taken Achilles up on his offer of a parachute and more as if this was something she could handle. Maybe not well or like superhuman Natalie, but she could handle it all the same in her own somewhat rudimentary fashion.

What she didn't understand was why Achilles hadn't fired her already. Because it was perfectly clear to Valentina that her version of handling things in no way lived up to Achilles's standards.

And if she'd been any doubt about that, he was the first to tell her otherwise.

His corporate offices in Manhattan took up several floors at one of Midtown's most esteemed addresses. There was an office suite set aside for him, naturally enough, that sprawled across the top floor and looked out over Manhattan as if to underscore the notion that Achilles Casilieris was in every way on top of the world. Valentina was settled in the immediate outer office, guarded by two separate lines of receptionist and secretarial defense should anyone make it through security. It wasn't to protect Achilles, but to further illuminate his importance. And Natalie's, Valentina realized quickly.

Because Natalie controlled access to Achilles. She controlled his schedule. She answered his phone and his email, and was generally held to have that all-important insight into his moods.

"What kind of day is it?" the senior vice presidents would ask her as they came in for their meetings, and the fact they smiled as they said it didn't make them any less anxious to hear her answer.

Valentina quickly discovered that Natalie controlled a whole lot more than simple access. There was a steady line of people at her desk, coming to her to ask how best to approach Achilles with any number of issues, or plot how to avoid approaching him with the things they knew he'd hate. Over the course of her first week in New York City, Valentina found that almost everyone who worked for Achilles tried to run things past her first, or used her to gauge his reactions. Natalie was less the man's personal assistant, she realized, and more the hub around which his businesses revolved. More than that, she thought he knew it.

"Take that up with Natalie," he would say in the middle of a meeting, without even bothering to look over at her. Usually while cutting someone off, because even he appeared not to want to hear certain things until Natalie had assessed them first.

"Come up with those numbers and run them past Natalie," he would tell his managers, and sometimes he'd even sound irritated while he said such things.

"Why are you acting as if you have never worked a day in my company?" he'd demanded of one of his brand managers once. "I am not the audience for your uncertain first drafts, George. How can you not know this?"

Valentina had smiled at the man in the meeting, and then had been forced to sit through a brainstorming/therapy session with him afterward, all the while hoping that the noncommittal things she'd murmured were, at the very least, not the *opposite* of the sort of things Natalie might have said.

Not that she texted Natalie to find out. Because that might have led to a conversation Valentina didn't really want to have with her double about strange, tense moments in the darkness with her employer.

She didn't know what she was more afraid of. That Natalie had never had any kind of tension with Achilles and Valentina was messing up her entire life...or that she did. That *tension* was just what Achilles did.

Valentina concentrated on her first attempt at a normal life, complete with a normal job, instead. And whether Achilles was aware of it or not, Natalie had her fingers in everything.

Including his romantic life.

The first time Valentina had answered his phone to find an emotional woman on the other end, she'd been appalled.

"There's a crying woman on the phone," she'd told Achilles. It had taken her a day or so to realize that she wasn't only allowed to walk in and out of his office when necessary, but encouraged to do so. That particular afternoon Achilles had been sitting on the sofa in his office, his feet up on his coffee table as he'd scowled down at his laptop. He shifted that scowl to her instead, in a way that made Valentina imagine that whatever he was looking at had something to do with her—

But that was ridiculous. There was no *her* in this scenario. There was only Natalie, and Valentina very much doubted Achilles spent his time looking up his assistant on the internet.

"Why are you telling me this?" he'd asked her shortly. "If I wanted to know who called me, I would answer my phones myself."

"She's crying about you," Valentina had said. "I assume she's calling to share her emotions with you, the person who caused them."

"And I repeat—why are you telling me this." This time it wasn't a question, and his scowl deepened. "You are my assistant. You are responsible for fielding these calls. I'm shocked you're even mentioning another crying female. I thought you stopped bringing them to my attention years ago."

Valentina had blinked at that. "Aren't you at all interested in why this woman is upset?"

"No."

"Not at all. Not the slightest bit interested." She studied his fierce face as if he was an alien. In moments like this, she thought he must have been. "You don't even know which woman I'm referring to, do you?"

"Miss Monette." He bit out that name as if the taste of it irritated him, and Valentina couldn't have said why it put her back up when it wasn't even her name. "I have a number of mistresses, none of whom call that line to manufacture emotional upsets. You are already aware of this." And he'd set his laptop aside, as if he needed to concentrate fully on Valentina before him. It had made her spine prickle, from her neck to her bottom and back up again. "Please let me know exactly what agenda it is we are pursuing today, that you expect to interrupt me in order to have a discussion about nuisance calls. When I assure you, the subject does not interest me at all. Just as it did not interest me five years ago, when you vowed to stop bothering me about them."

There was a warning in that. Valentina had heard it, plain as day. But she hadn't been able to heed it. Much less stop herself.

"To be clear, what you're telling me is that tears do not interest you," she'd said instead of beating a retreat to her desk the way she should have. She'd kept her tone even and easy, but she doubted that had fooled either one of them.

"Tears interest me least of all." She'd been sure that there was a curve in that hard mouth of his then, however small.

And what was the matter with her that she'd clung to that as if it was some kind of lifeline? As if she needed such a thing?

As if what she really wanted was his approval, when she hadn't switched places with Natalie for him. He'd had nothing to do with it. Why couldn't she seem to remember that?

"If this is a common occurrence for you, perhaps you need to have a think about your behavior," she'd pointed out. "And your aversion to tears."

There had definitely been a curve in his mouth then, and yet somehow that hadn't made Valentina any easier.

"This conversation is over," he'd said quietly. Though not gently. "Something I suggest you tell the enterprising actress on the phone."

She'd thought him hideously cold, of course. Heartless, even. But the calls kept coming. And Valentina had quickly realized what she should perhaps have known from the start—that it would be impossible for Achilles to actually be out there causing harm to so many anonymous women when he never left the office. She knew this because she spent almost every hour of every day in his company. The man literally had no time to go out there smashing hearts left and right, the way she'd be tempted to believe he did if she paid attention only to the phone calls she received, laden with accusations.

"Tell him I'm falling apart," yet another woman on the phone said on this latest morning, her voice ragged.

"Sorry, but what's your name again?" Valentina asked, as brightly as possible. "It's only that he's been working rather hard, you see. As he tends to do. Which would, of course, make it extremely difficult for him to be tearing anyone apart in any real sense."

The woman had sputtered. But Valentina had dutifully taken her name into Achilles when he next asked for his messages.

"I somewhat doubted the veracity of her claim," Valentina murmured. "Given that you were working until well after two last night."

Something she knew very well since that had meant she'd been working even longer than that.

Achilles laughed. He was at his desk today, which meant he was framed by the vertical thrust of Manhattan behind him. And still, that look in his dark gold gaze made the city disappear. "As well you should. I have no idea who this woman is. Or any of them." He shrugged. "My attorneys are knee-deep in paternity suits, and I win every one of them."

Valentino was astonished by that. Perhaps that was naive. She'd certainly had her share of admirers in her day, strange men who claimed an acquaintance or who sent rather disturbing letters to the palace—some from distant prisons in foreign countries. But she certainly never had men call up and try to pretend they had relationships with her *to* her.

Then again, would anyone have told her if they had? That sat on her a bit uneasily, though she couldn't have said why. She only knew that his gaze was like a touch, and that, too, seemed to settle on her like a weight.

"It's amazing how many unhinged women seem to think that if they claim they're dating you, you might go along with it," she said before she could think better of it.

That dark gold gaze of his lit with a gleam she couldn't name then. And it sparked something deep inside her, making her fight to draw in a breath. Making her feel unsteady in the serviceable low heels that Natalie favored. Making her wish she'd worn something more substantial than a nice jacket over another pencil skirt. Like a suit of armor. Or her very own brick wall.

"There are always unhinged women hanging about," Achilles said in that quietly devastating way of his. "Trying to convince me that they have relationships with me that they adamantly do not. Why do you imagine that is, Miss Monette?"

She told herself he couldn't possibly know that she was one of those women, no matter how his gaze seemed to pin her where she stood. No matter the edge in his voice, or the sharp emphasis he'd put on *Miss Monette*.

Even if he suspected something was different with his assistant, he couldn't know. Because no one could know. Because Valentina herself hadn't known Natalie existed until she'd walked into that bathroom. And that meant all sorts of things, such as the fact that everything she'd been told about her childhood and her birth was a lie. Not to mention her mother.

But there was no way Achilles could know any of that.

"Perhaps it's you," she murmured in response. She smiled when his brows rose in that expression of sheer arrogance that never failed to make her feel the slightest bit dizzy. "I only mean that you're a public figure and people imagine you a certain way based on the kind of press coverage you allow. Unless you plan to actively get out there and reclaim your public narrative, I don't think there's any likelihood that it will change."

"I am not a public figure. I have never courted the public in any way."

Valentina checked a sigh. "You're a very wealthy man. Whether you like it or not, the public is fascinated by you."

Achilles studied her until she was forced to order herself not to fidget beneath the weight of that heavy, intense stare.

"I'm intrigued that you think the very existence of public fascination must create an obligation in me to cater to it," he said quietly. "It does not. In fact, it has the opposite effect. In me. But how interesting that you imagine you owe something to the faceless masses who admire you."

Valentina's lips felt numb. "No masses, faceless or otherwise, admire me, Mr. Casilieris. They have no idea I exist. I'm an assistant, nothing more."

His hard mouth didn't shift into one of those hard curves, but his dark gold eyes gleamed, and somehow that made the floor beneath her seem to tilt, then roll.

"Of course you are," he said, his voice a quiet menace that echoed in her like a warning. Like something far more dangerous than a simple warning. "My mistake."

Later that night, still feeling as off balance as if the floor really wasn't steady beneath her feet, Valentina found herself alone with Achilles long after everyone else in the office had gone home.

It had been an extraordinarily long couple of days,

something Valentina might have thought was business as usual for the Casilieris Company if so many of the other employees hadn't muttered about how grueling it was. Beneath their breath and when they thought she couldn't hear them, that was. The deal that Achilles was so determined to push through had turned out to have more tangles and turns than anyone had expected—especially, it seemed, Achilles. What that meant was long hour after long hour well into the tiny hours of the night, hunched over tables and conference rooms, arguing with fleets of attorneys and representatives from the other side over take-out food from fine New York restaurants and stale coffee.

Valentina was deep into one of the contracts Achilles had slid her way, demanding a fresh set of eyes on a clause that annoyed him, when she noticed that they were the only ones there. The Casilieris Company had a significant presence all over the planet, so there were usually people coming and going at all conceivable hours to be available to different workdays in distant places. Something Valentina had witnessed herself after spending so much time in these offices since she'd arrived in New York.

But when she looked up from the dense and confusing contract language for a moment to give her ever-impending headache a break, she could see from the long conference room table where she sat straight through the glass walls that allowed her to see all the way across the office floor. And there was no one there. No bustling secretaries, no ambitious VPs putting in ostentatiously late hours where the boss could see their vigilance and commitment. No overzealous interns making busy work for themselves in the cubicles. No late-night cleaning crews, who did their jobs in the dark so as not to bother the workers by day. There wasn't a soul. Anywhere.

Something caught in her chest as she realized that it was only the two of them. Just Valentina and the man across the table from her, whom she was trying very hard not to look at too closely.

It was an extraordinarily unimportant thing to notice, she chastised herself, frowning back down at the contract. They were always alone, really. In his car, on his plane, in his penthouse. Valentina had spent more time with this man, she thought, than with any other save her father.

Her gaze rose from the contract of its own accord. Achilles sat across from her in the quiet of the otherwise empty office, his laptop cracked open before him and a pile of contracts next to the sleek machine. He looked the way he always did at the end of these long days. *Entirely too good*, something in her whispered—though she shoved that aside as best she could. It did no good to concentrate on things like that, she'd decided during her tenure with him. The man's appearance was a fact, and it was something she needed to come to terms with, but she certainly didn't have to ogle him.

But she couldn't seem to look away. She remembered that moment in his penthouse a little too clearly, the first night they'd been in New York. She remembered how close they'd stood in that window, and the things he'd told her, that dark gold gaze of his boring into her. As if he had every intention of looking directly to her soul. More than that, she remembered him reaching out and taking hold of the end of the ponytail she'd worn, that he'd looked at as if he had no idea how it had come to be attached to her.

But she'd dreamed about it almost every time she'd slept, either way.

Tonight Achilles was lounging in a pushed-back chair, his hands on top of his head as if, had he had longer hair, he'd be raking his hands through it. His jaw was dotted with stubble after a long day in the office, and it lent him the look of some kind of pirate.

Valentina told herself—sternly—that there was no

need for such fanciful language when he already made her pulse heat inside her simply by being in the same room. She tried to sink down a bit farther behind the piles and piles of documents surrounding her, which she was viewing as the armor she wished she was wearing. The remains of the dinner she'd ordered them many hours before were scattered across the center of the table, and she took perhaps too much pride in the fact she'd completed so simple a task. Normal people, she was certain, ordered from take-out menus all the time, but Valentina never had before she'd taken over Natalie's life. Valentina was a princess. She'd discussed many a menu and sent requests to any number of kitchens, but she'd never ordered her own meal in her life, much less from stereotypical New Yorkers with accents and attitudes.

She felt as if she was in a movie.

Valentina decided she would take her victories where she found them. Even if they were as small and ultimately pointless as sending out for a takeaway meal.

"It's late," Achilles said, reminding her that they were all alone here. And there was something in his voice then. Or the way his gaze slammed into hers when she looked up again.

Or maybe it was in her—that catch. That little kick of something a little too much like excitement that wound around and around inside her. Making her feel…restless. Undone. Desperate for something she couldn't even name.

"And here I thought you planned to carry straight through until dawn," she said, as brightly as possible, hoping against hope he couldn't see anything on her face. Or hear it in her voice.

Achilles lowered his hand to the arms of his chair. But he didn't shift that gaze of his from hers. And she kept catching him looking at her like this. Exactly like this. Simmering. Dark and dangerous, and spun through with gold. In the cars they took together. Every morning when he walked out of his bedchamber and found her sitting in the office suite, already starting on the day's work as best she could. Across boardroom tables just like this one, no matter if they were filled with other people.

It was worse now. Here in the quiet of his empty office. So late at night it felt to Valentina as if the darkness was a part of her.

And Valentina didn't have any experience with men, but oh, the books she'd read. Love stories and romances and happy-ever-afters, and almost all of them started just like this. With a taut feeling in the belly and fire everywhere else.

Do not be absurd, she snapped at herself.

Because she was Princess Valentina of Murin. She was promised to another and had been since her birth. There wasn't space in her life for anything but that. Not even here, in this faraway place that had nothing at all to do with her real life. Not even with this man, whom she never should have met, and never would have had she not seized that moment in the London bathroom.

You can take a holiday from your life, apparently, she reminded herself. *But you still take you along with you wherever you go.*

She might have been playing Natalie Monette, but she was still *herself*. She was still the same person she'd always been. Dutiful. Mindful of what her seemingly inconsequential behavior might mean to her father, to the kingdom, to her future husband's kingdom, too. Whatever else she was—and she wasn't sure she knew anymore, not here in the presence of a man who made her head spin without seeming to try very hard—Valentina was a person who had always, always kept her vows.

Even when it was her father who had made them, not her.

"If you keep staring at me like that," Achilles said softly, a kind of ferociousness beneath his rough words that made her stomach knot, then seemed to kindle a different, deeper fire lower down, "I am not certain I'll be able to contain myself."

Valentina's mouth was dry. "I don't know what you mean."

"I think you do."

Achilles didn't move, she could see that he wasn't moving, and yet everything changed at that. He filled every room he entered—she was used to that by now—but this was something different. It was as if lightning flashed. It was if he was some kind of rolling thunder all his own. It was as if he'd called in a storm, then let it loose to fill all of the room. The office.

And Valentina, too.

"No," she whispered, her voice scratchy against all that light and rumble.

But she could feel the tumult inside her. It was fire and it was light and it threatened to burst free of the paltry cage of her skin. Surely she would burst. Surely no person could survive this. She felt it shake all through her, as if underlining her fear.

"I don't know what you mean, and I don't like what you're implying. I think perhaps we've been in this office too long. You seem to have mistaken me for one of your mistresses. Or worse, one of those desperate women who call in, hoping to convince you they ought to be one of them."

"On the contrary, Miss Monette."

And there was a starkness to Achilles's expression then. No curve on his stern mouth. No gleaming thing in the seductive gold of his dark eyes. But somehow, that only made it worse.

"You're the one who manages my mistresses. And

those who pretend to that title. How could I possibly confuse you for them?" He cocked his head slightly to one side, and something yawned open inside her, as if in response. "Or perhaps you're auditioning for the role?"

"No." Her voice was no less scratchy this time, but there was more power in it. *Or more fear*, something inside her whispered. "I am most certainly not auditioning for anything like that. Or anything at all. I already have a job."

"But you told me you meant to quit." She had the strangest notion then that he was enjoying himself. "Perhaps you meant you were looking to make a lateral move. From my boardroom to my bed?"

Valentina tried to summon her outrage. She tried to tell herself that she was deeply offended on Natalie's behalf, because of course this was about her, not Valentina herself… She tried to tell herself a whole lot of things.

But she couldn't quite get there. Instead, she was awash with unhelpful little visions, red hot and wild. Images of what a "lateral move" might look like. Of what his bed might feel like. Of him.

She imagined that lean, solidly muscled form stretched over hers, the way she'd read in so many books so many times. Something almost too hot to bear melted through her then, pulling deep in her belly, and making her breath go shallow before it shivered everywhere else.

As if it was already happening.

"I know that this might come as a tremendous shock," Valentina said, trying to make herself sound something like fierce—or unmoved, anyway. Anything other than thrown and yearning. "But I have no interest in your bed. Less than no interest."

"You are correct." And something gleamed bright and hot and unholy gold in that dark gaze of his. "I am in shock."

"The next time an aspiring mistress calls the office," Valentina continued coolly, and no matter that it cost her, "I'll be certain to put her through to you for a change. You can discuss lateral moves all day long."

"What if a random caller does not appeal to me?" he asked lazily, as if this was all a game to him. She told herself it was. She told herself the fact that it was a game made it safe, but she didn't believe it. Not when all the things that moved around inside her made it hard to breathe, and made her feel anything at all but *safe*. "What if it is I who wish to alter our working relationship after all these years?"

Valentina told herself that this was clearly a test. If, as this conversation seemed to suggest, Natalie's relationship with her boss had always been strictly professional, why would he want to change that now? She'd seen how distant he kept his romantic entanglements from his work. His work was his life. His women were afterthoughts. There was no way the driven, focused man she'd come to know a bit after the close proximity of these last days would want to muddy the water in his office, with the assistant who not only knew where all the bodies were buried, but oversaw the funeral rites herself.

This had to be a test.

"I don't wish to alter a thing," she told him, very distinctly, as if there was nothing in her head but thorny contract language. And certainly nothing involving that remarkably ridged torso of his. "If you do, I think we should revisit the compensation package on offer for my resignation."

Achilles smiled as if she delighted him. But in an entirely too wicked and too hot sort of way.

"There is no package, Miss Monette," he murmured. "And there will be no resignation. When will you understand? You are here to do as I wish. Nothing more and nothing less than that. And perhaps my wishes concerning your role here have changed."

He wants you to fall apart, Valentina snapped at herself. *He wants to see if this will break you. He's poking at* Natalie *about her change in performance, not at you. He doesn't know* you *exist.*

Because there could be no other explanation. And it didn't matter that the look in his eyes made her shudder, down deep inside.

"Your wishes concerning my role now involve me on my back?" It cost her to keep her voice that flat. She could feel it.

"You say that as if the very idea disgusts you." And that crook in the corner of his lethal mouth deepened, even as that look in his eyes went lethal. "Surely not."

Valentina forced herself to smile. Blandly. As if her heart wasn't trying to claw its way out of her chest.

"I'm very flattered by your offer, of course," she said.

A little too sweetly to be mistaken for sincerity.

Achilles laughed then. It was an unsettling sound, too rough and too bold. It told her too much. That he knew—everything. That he knew all the things that were moving inside her, white hot and molten and too much for her to handle or tamp down or control. There was a growing, impossible fire raging in places she hardly understood, rendering her a stranger to herself.

As if he was the one in control of her body, even sitting across the table, lounging in his seat as if none of this was a matter of any concern at all.

While she felt as if she was both losing pieces of herself—and seeing her true colors for the very first time.

"Are you letting me down easy?" Achilles asked.

There was still laughter in his voice, his gaze and, somehow, dancing in the air between them despite all that fire still licking at her. She felt it roll through her, as if those big hands of his were on her skin.

And then she was suddenly incapable of thinking about anything at all but that. His hands all over her body. Touching places only she had ever seen. She had to swallow hard. Then again. And still there was that ringing in her ears.

"Do think it will work?" he asked, laughter still making his words sound a little too much like the rough, male version of honey.

"I imagine it will work beautifully, yes." She held on to that smile of hers as if her life depended on it. She rather thought it did. It was that or tip over into all that fire, and she had no idea what would become of her if she let that happen. She had no idea what would be left. "Or, of course, I could involve Human Resources in this discussion."

Achilles laughed again, and this time it was rougher. Darker and somehow hotter at the same time. Valentina felt it slide all over her, making her breasts feel heavy and her hips restless. While deep between her legs, a slick ache bloomed.

"I admire the feigned naïveté," Achilles said, and he looked like a pirate again, all dark jaw and that gleam in his gaze. It lit her up. Everywhere. "I have obviously failed to appreciate your acting talent sufficiently. I think we both know what Human Resources will tell you. To suck it up or find another position."

"That does not sound at all like something Human Resources would say," Valentina replied crisply, rather than spending even a split second thinking about *sucking*. "It sounds as if you're laboring under the delusion that this is a cult of personality, not a business."

If she expected him to look at all abashed, his grin disabused her of it. "Do you doubt it?"

"I'm not sure that is something I would brag about, Mr. Casilieris."

His gaze was hot, and she didn't think he was talking about her job or his company any longer. Had he ever been?

"Is it bragging if it's true?" he asked.

Valentina stood then, because it was the last thing she wanted to do. She could have sat there all night. She could have rung in a new dawn, fencing words with this man and dancing closer and closer to that precipice she could feel looming between them, even if she couldn't quite see it.

She could have pretended she didn't feel every moment of this deep inside her, in places she shouldn't. And then pretend further she didn't know what it meant just because she'd never experienced any of it before outside the pages of a book.

But she did know. And this wasn't her life to ruin. And so she stood, smoothing her hands down her skirt and wishing she hadn't been quite so impetuous in that London bathroom.

If you hadn't been, you wouldn't be here, something in her replied. *Is that what you want?*

And she knew that she didn't. Valentina had a whole life left to live with a man she would call husband who would never know her, not really. She had duty to look forward to, and a lifetime of charity and good works, all of which would be vetted by committees and commented on by the press. She had public adulation and a marriage that would involve the mechanical creation of babies before petering off into a nice friendship, if she was lucky.

Maybe the making of the babies would be fun with her prince. What did she know? All she knew so far was that he didn't do...this. He didn't affect her the way Achilles did, lounging there like hard-packed danger across a conference table, his gaze too dark and the gold in it making her pulse kick at her.

She'd never felt anything like this before. She doubted she'd ever feel it again.

Valentina couldn't quite bring herself to regret it.

But she couldn't stay here tonight and blow up the rest of Natalie's life, either. That would be treating this little gift that she'd been given with nothing but contempt.

"Have I given you leave to go?" Achilles asked, with what she knew was entirely feigned astonishment. "I am clearly confused in some way. I keep thinking you work for me."

She didn't know how he could do that. How he could seem to loom over her when she was the one standing up and looking down at him.

"And because I'd like to continue working for you," Valentina forced herself to say in as measured a tone as she could manage, "I'm going to leave now. We can pick this up in the morning." She tapped the table with one finger. "Pick *this* up, I mean. These contracts and the deal. Not this descent into madness, which I think we can chalk up to exhaustion."

Achilles only watched her for a moment. Those hands that she could picture too easily against her own flesh curled over the armrests of his chair, and her curse was that she imagined she *was* that chair. His legs were thrust out before him, long and lean. His usual suit was slightly rumpled, his tie having been tugged off and tossed aside hours earlier, so she could see the olive skin at his neck and a hint of crisp, black hair. He looked simultaneously sleepy and breathlessly, impossibly lethal—with an intensity that made that hot ache between her legs seem to swallow her whole.

And the look in his eyes made everything inside her draw tight, then pulse harder.

"Do you have a problem with that?" she asked, and she meant to sound impatient. Challenging. But she thought both of them were entirely too aware that what came out instead was rather more plaintive than planned.

As if she was really asking him if he was okay with everything that had happened here tonight. She was clearly too dazed to function.

She needed to get away from him while she still had access to what little of her brain remained in all this smoke and flame.

"Do you require my permission?" Achilles lifted his chin, and his dark eyes glittered. Valentina held her breath. "So far tonight it seems you are laboring under the impression that you give the permission, not me. You make the rules, not me. It is as if I am here for no other purpose than to serve you."

And there was no reason at all that his words, spoken in that soft, if dangerous way, should make her skin prickle. But they did. As if a man like Achilles did not have to issue threats, he was the threat. Why pile a threat on top of the threat? When the look on his face would do.

"I will see you in the morning," Valentina said, resolutely. "When I'll be happy to accept your apology."

Achilles lounged farther down in his chair, and she had the strangest notion that he was holding himself back. Keeping himself in place. Goose bumps shivered to life over her shoulders and down her arms.

His gaze never left hers.

"Go," he said, and there was no pretending it wasn't an order. "But I would not lie awake tonight anticipating the contours of my apology. It will never come."

She wanted to reply to that, but her mouth was too dry and she couldn't seem to move. Not so much as a muscle.

And as if he knew it, Achilles kept going in that same intensely quiet way.

"Tonight when you can't sleep, when you toss and turn and stare up at yet another ceiling I own, I want you to think of all the other reasons you could be wide awake in the small hours of the night. All the things that I could do to you. Or have you do to me. All the thousands of ways I will be imagining us together, just like that, under the same roof."

"That is completely inappropriate, Mr. Casilieris, and I think you know it."

But she knew full well she didn't sound nearly as outraged as she should. And only partially because her voice was a mere whisper.

"Have you never wondered how we would fit? Have you not tortured herself with images of my possession?" Achilles's hard mouth curved then, a wicked crook in one corner that she knew, somehow, would haunt her. She could feel it deep inside her like its own bright fire. "Tonight, I think, you will."

And Valentina stopped pretending there was any way out of this conversation besides the precise images he'd just mentioned, acted out all over this office. She walked stiffly around the table and gave him a wide, wide berth as she passed.

When she made it to the door of the conference room, she didn't look behind her to see if he was watching. She knew he was. She could feel it.

Fire and lightning, thunder and need.

She ran.

And heard his laughter follow behind her like the leading edge of a storm she had no hope of outwitting, no matter how fast she moved.

CHAPTER FIVE

ACHILLES ORDINARILY ENJOYED his victory parties. Reveled in them, in fact. Not for him any nod toward false humility or any pretense that he didn't deeply enjoy these games of high finance with international stakes. But tonight he couldn't seem to get his head into it, and no matter that he'd been fighting to buy out this particular iconic Manhattan hotel—which he planned to make over in his own image, the blend of European elegance and Greek timelessness that was his calling card in the few hotels scattered across the globe that he'd deemed worthy of the Casilieris name—for nearly eighteen months.

He should have been jubilant. It irritated him—deeply—that he couldn't quite get there.

His group had taken over a New York steak house renowned for its high-end clientele and specialty drinks to match to celebrate the deal he'd finally put through today after all this irritating wrangling. Ordinarily he would allow himself a few drinks to blur out his edges for a change. He would even smile and pretend he was a normal man, like all the rest, made of flesh and blood instead of dollar signs and naked ambition—an improvement by far over the monster he kept locked up tight beneath. Nights like this were his opportunity to pretend to be like anyone else, and Achilles usually indulged that impulse.

He might not have been a normal man—he'd never been a normal man—but it amused him to pretend otherwise every now and again. He was renowned for his surliness as much as his high expectations, but if that was all there was to it—to him—he never would have gotten anywhere in business. It took a little charm to truly manipulate his enemies and his opponents and even his acolytes the way he liked to do. It required that he be as easy telling a joke as he was taking over a company or using his fiercest attorneys to hammer out a deal that served him, and only him, best.

But tonight he was charmless all the way through.

He stood at the bar, nursing a drink he would have much preferred to toss back and follow with a few more of the same, his attention entirely consumed by his princess as she worked the room. As ordered.

"Make yourself useful, please," he'd told her when they'd arrived. "Try to charm these men. If you can."

He'd been deliberately insulting. He'd wanted her to imagine he had some doubt that she could pull such a thing off. He'd wanted her to feel the way he did—grouchy and irritable and outside his own skin.

She made him feel like an adolescent.

But Valentina had not seemed the least bit cowed. Much less insulted—which had only made him feel that much more raw.

"As you wish," she'd murmured in that overly obsequious voice she used when, he thought, she most wanted to get her claws into him. She'd even flashed that bland smile of hers at him, which had its usual effect—making his blood seem too hot for his own veins. "Your slightest desire is my command, of course."

And the truth was, Achilles should have known better. The kind of men he liked to manipulate best, especially when it came to high-stakes deals like the one he'd closed tonight, were not the sort of men he wanted anywhere near his princess. If the real Natalie had been here, she would have disappeared. She would have dispensed her usual round of cool greetings and even cooler congratulations, none of which encouraged anyone to cozy up to her. Then she would have sat in this corner or that, her expression blank and her attention focused entirely on one of her devices. She would have done that remarkable thing she did, that he had never thought to admire as much as perhaps he should have, which was her ability to be both in the room and invisible at the same time.

Princess Valentina, by contrast, couldn't have stayed invisible if her life depended on it. She was the furthest thing from *invisible* that Achilles had ever seen. It was as if the world was cast into darkness and she was its only light, that bright and that impossibly silvery and smooth, like her own brand of moonlight.

She moved from one group to the next, all gracious smiles. And not that bland sort of smile she used entirely too pointedly and too well, which invariably worked his last nerve, but one he'd seen in too many photographs he'd looked at much too late at night. Hunched over his laptop like some kind of obsessed troll while she slept beneath the same roof, unaware, which only made him that much more infuriated.

With her, certainly. But with himself even more.

Tonight she was the consummate hostess, as if this was her victory celebration instead of his. He could hear her airy laugh from across the room, far more potent than another woman's touch. And worse, he could see her. Slender and graceful, inhabiting a pencil skirt and well-cut jacket as if they'd been crafted specifically for her. When he knew perfectly well that those were his assistant's clothes, and they certainly weren't bespoke.

But that was Valentina's power. She made everything in her orbit seem to be only hers. Crafted specifically and especially for her.

Including him, Achilles thought—and he hated it. He was not a man a woman could put on a leash. He'd never given a woman any kind of power over him in his life, and he didn't understand how this creature who was engaged in a full-scale deception—who was running a con on him *even now*—somehow seemed to have the upper hand in a battle he was terribly afraid only he knew they were fighting.

It was unconscionable. It made him want to tear down this building—hell, the whole city—with his bare hands.

Or better yet, put them on her.

All the men around her lapped it up, of course. They stood too close. They put their hands on her elbow, or her shoulder, to emphasize a point that Achilles did not have to hear to know did not require emphasis. And certainly did not require touch.

She was moonlight over this grim, focused life of his, and he had no idea how he was going to make it through a world cast in darkness without her.

If he was appalled by that sentiment—and he was, deeply and wholly—it didn't seem to matter. He couldn't seem to turn it off.

It was far easier to critique her behavior instead.

So Achilles watched. And seethed. He catalogued every single touch, every single laugh, every single time she tilted back her pretty face and let her sleek copper hair fall behind her, catching all the light in the room. He brooded over the men who surrounded her, knowing full well that each and every one of them was imagining her naked. Hell, so was he.

But he was the only person in this room who knew what he was looking at. They thought she was Natalie

Monette, his dependable assistant. He was the only one who knew who she really was.

By the time Valentina finished a full circuit of the room, Achilles was in a high, foul temper.

"Are you finished?" he asked when she came to stand by his side again, his tone a dark slap he did nothing at all to temper. "Or will you actually whore yourself out in lieu of dessert?"

He meant that to hurt. He didn't care if he was an ass. He wanted to knock her back a few steps.

But of course Valentina only shot him an arch, amused look, as if she was biting back laughter.

"That isn't very nice," she said simply.

That was all.

And yet Achilles felt that bloom of unfortunate heat inside him all over again, and this time he knew exactly what it was. He didn't like it any better than he had before, and yet there it sat, eating at him from the inside out.

It didn't matter if he told himself he didn't wish to feel shame. All Valentina had to do was look at him as if he was a misbehaving child, tell him he *wasn't being nice* when he'd built an entire life out of being the very opposite of nice and hailing that as the source of his vast power and influence—and there it was. Heavy in him, like a length of hard, cold chain.

How had he given this woman so much power over him? How had he failed to see that was what was happening while he'd imagined he was giving her the rope with which to hang herself?

This could not go on. He could not allow this to go on.

The truth was, Achilles couldn't seem to get a handle on this situation the way he'd planned to when he'd realized who she was on the plane. He'd imagined it would be an amusing sort of game to humble a high and mighty spoiled-rotten princess who had never worked a day in her

life and imagined she could deceive *the* Achilles Casilieris
so boldly. He'd imagined it would be entertaining—and
over swiftly. He supposed he'd imagined he'd be ship-
ping her back to her palace and her princessy life and her
proper royal fiancé by the end of the first day.

But Valentina wasn't at all who he'd thought she'd
be. If she was spoiled—and she had to be spoiled, by
definition, he was certain of it—she hid it. No matter
what he threw at her, no matter what he demanded, she
simply did it. Not always well, but she did it. She didn't
complain. She didn't try to weasel out of any tasks she
didn't like. She didn't even make faces or let out those
long-suffering sighs that so many of his support staff did
when they thought he couldn't hear them.

In fact, Valentina was significantly more cheerful than
any other assistant he'd ever had—including Natalie.

She was nothing like perfect, but that made it worse.
If she was perfect, maybe he could have dismissed her
or ignored her, despite the game she was playing. But he
couldn't seem to get her out of his head.

It was that part he couldn't accept. Achilles lived a
highly compartmentalized life by design, and he liked it
that way. He kept his women in the smallest, most easily
controlled and thus ignored space. It had been many, many
years since he'd allowed sex to control his thoughts, much
less his life. It was only sex, after all. And what was sex
to a man who could buy the world if he so chose? It was
a release, yes. Enjoyable, even.

But Achilles couldn't remember the last time he'd
woken in the night, his heart pounding, the hardest part
of him awake and aware. With nothing in his head but
her. Yet it was a nightly occurrence since Valentina had
walked onto his plane.

It was bordering on obsession.

And Achilles did not get obsessed. He did not *want*.

He did not *need*. He took what interested him and then he forgot about it when the next thing came along.

And he couldn't think of a single good reason why he shouldn't do the same with her.

"Do you have something you wish to say to me?" Valentina asked, her soft, smooth voice snapping him back to this party that bored him. This victory that should have excited him, but that he only found boring now.

"I believe I said it."

"You misunderstand me," she replied, smiling. From a distance it would look as if they were discussing something as light and airy as that curve to her mouth, he thought. Achilles would have been impressed had he not been close enough to see that cool gleam in her green gaze. "I meant your apology. Are you ready to give it?"

He felt his own mouth curve then, in nothing so airy. Or light.

"Do I strike you as a man who apologizes, Miss Monette?" he asked her, making no attempt to ease the steel in his voice. "Have I ever done so in all the time you've known me?"

"A man who cannot apologize is not quite a man, is he, Mr. Casilieris?" This time he thought her smile was meant to take away the sting of her words. To hide the insult a little. Yet it only seemed to make it worse. "I speak philosophically, of course. But surely the only people who can't bring themselves to apologize are those who fear that any admission of guilt or wrongdoing diminishes them. I think we can both agree that's the very opposite of strength."

"You must tell me if I appear diminished, then," he growled at her, and he had the satisfaction of watching that pulse in her neck go wild. "Or weak in some way."

He wasn't surprised when she excused herself and went back to working the crowd. But he was surprised he let her.

Not here, he cautioned that wild thing inside him that he'd never had to contend with before, not over a woman. And never so raw and bold. *Not now.*

Later that night, they sat in his car as it slid through the streets of Manhattan in the midst of a summer thunderstorm, and Achilles cautioned himself not to act rashly.

Again.

But Valentina sat there beside him, staring out the window with a faint smile on her face. She'd settled beside him on the wide, plush seat without a word, as if it hardly mattered to her if he spoke or not. If he berated her, if he ignored her. As if she was all alone in this car or, worse, as if her mind was far away on more interesting topics.

And he couldn't tolerate it.

Achilles could think of nothing but her, she was eating him alive like some kind of impossible acid, yet *her* mind was miles away. She didn't seem to notice or care what she did to him when he was the one who was allowing her grand deception to continue—instead of outing her the way he should have the moment he'd understood who she was.

His hands moved before he knew what he meant to do, as if they had a mind of their own.

He didn't ask. He didn't push or prod at her or fence more words, forcing some sort of temper or explosion that would lead them where he wanted her to go. He didn't stack that deck.

He simply reached across the backseat, wrapped his hand around the back of her neck and hauled her closer to him.

She came easily, as if she really was made of nothing but light. He pulled her until she was sprawled across his lap, one hand braced on his thigh and another at his side. Her body was as lithe and sweetly rounded as he'd imagined it would be, but better. Much, much better.

She smelled like a dream, something soft and something sweet, and all of it warm and female and *her*. Valentina.

But all he cared about was the fact that that maddening mouth of hers was close to his.

Finally.

"What are you doing?" she breathed.

"I should think that was obvious," he growled. "And overdue."

And then, at last, he kissed her.

He wasn't gentle. He wasn't anything like tentative. He was neither soft nor kind, because it was too late for that.

He claimed her. Took her. He reminded her who he was with every slick, intense slide of his tongue. Or maybe he was reminding himself.

And he couldn't stop himself once the taste of her exploded inside him, making him reel. He wanted more. He wanted everything.

But she was still fighting him, that stubbornness of hers that made his whole body tight and needy. Not with her body, which was wrapped around him, supple and sweet, in a way that made him feel drunk. Not with her arms, which she'd sneaked around his shoulders as if she needed to hold on to him to keep herself upright.

It was that mouth of hers that had been driving him wild since the start.

He pulled his lips from hers. Then he slid his hands up to take her elegant cheekbones between his palms. He tilted her face where he wanted it, making the angle that much slicker. That much sweeter.

"Kiss me back," he demanded, pulling back farther to scowl at her, all this unaccustomed need making him impatient. And testy.

She looked stunned. And entirely too beautiful. Her green eyes were wide and dazed behind those clear glasses she wore. Her lips were parted, distractingly soft and faintly swollen already.

Achilles was hard and he was greedy and he wanted nothing more than to bury himself inside her here and now, and finally get rid of this obsession that was eating him alive.

Or indulge in it awhile.

"In case you are confused," he told her, his voice still a growl, "that was an order."

She angled herself back, just slightly. As if she was trying to sit up straighter against him. He didn't allow it. He liked her like this. Off balance and under his control, and he didn't much care if that made him a savage. He'd only ever pretended to be anything else, and only occasionally, at that.

"I *am* kissing you back," she said, and there was a certain haughtiness in her voice that delighted him. It made him grin, imagining all the many ways he could make her pay for that high-born, inbred superiority that he wanted to lap up like cream.

"Not well enough," he told her.

Her cheeks looked crisp and red, but she didn't shrink away from him. She didn't so much as blink.

"Maybe we don't have any chemistry," she theorized in that same voice, making it sound as if that was a foregone conclusion. "Not every woman in the world finds you attractive, Mr. Casilieris. Did you ever think of that?"

Achilles pulled her even more off balance, holding her over his lap and in his arms, right where he wanted her.

"No," he said starkly, and he didn't care if his greed and longing was all over his face, revealing more to her than he had ever shared with anyone. Ever. "I don't think either of those things is a problem."

Then he set his mouth to hers, and proved it.

* * *

Valentina thought she'd died and gone to a heaven she'd never dreamed of before. Wicked and wild and *better*. So very much better than anything she could have come up with in her most brilliant and dark-edged fantasies.

She had never been truly kissed before—if that was even the word to describe something so dominant and so powerful and so deeply, erotically thrilling—but she had no intention of sharing her level of inexperience with Achilles. Not when he seemed so close to some kind of edge and so hell-bent on taking her with him, toppling over the side into all of this sensation and need.

So she simply mimicked him. When he tilted his head, she did the same. She balled up her hands in his exquisitely soft shirt, up there against the hard planes of his chest tucked beneath his dark suit coat. She was aware of his hard hands on her face. She exulted in his arms like steel, holding her and caging her against him. She lost herself in that desperately cruel mouth as it moved over hers, the touch of his rough jaw, the impossible heat.

God help her, the heat.

And she was aware of that hard ridge beneath her, suddenly. She couldn't seem to keep from wriggling against it. Once, daringly. Then again when she heard that deep, wild and somehow savagely beautiful male noise he made in response.

And Valentina forgot about her vows, old and forthcoming. She forgot about faraway kingdoms and palaces and the life she'd lived there. She forgot about the promises she'd made and the ones that had been made in her name, because all of that seemed insubstantial next to the sheer, overwhelming wonder of Achilles Casilieris kissing her like a man possessed in the back of his town car.

This was her holiday. Her little escape. This was nothing but a dream, and he was, too. A fantasy of the life she might have lived had she been anyone else. Had she ever been anything like normal.

She forgot where they were. She forgot the role she was supposed to be playing. There was nothing in all the world but Achilles and the wildness he summoned up with every drag of his mouth against hers.

The car moved beneath them, but all Valentina could focus on was him. That hot possession of his mouth. The fire inside her.

And the lightning that she knew was his, the thunder storming through her, teaching her that she knew less about her body than he did. Much, much less. When he shifted so he could rub his chest against hers, she understood that he knew her nipples had pebbled into hard little points. When he laughed slightly as he rearranged her arms around his shoulders, she understood that he knew all her limbs were weighted down with the force of that greedy longing coursing through her veins.

The more he kissed her, over and over again as if time had no meaning and he could do this forever, she understood that he knew everything.

When he pulled his mouth from hers again, Valentina heard a soft, whimpering sound of protest. It took her one shuddering beat of her heart, then another, to realize she'd made it.

She couldn't process that. It was so abandoned, so thoughtless and wild—how could that be her?

"If we do not get out of this car right now," Achilles told her, his gaze a dark and breathtaking gold that slammed into her and lit her insides on fire, "we will not get out of it for some time. Not until I've had my fill of you. Is that how you want our first time to go, *glikia mou*? In the backseat of a car?"

For a moment Valentina didn't know what he meant. One hastily sucked-in breath later, she realized the car had come to a stop outside Achilles's building. Her cheeks flushed with a bright heat, but worse, she knew that he could see it. He saw everything—hadn't she just realized the truth of that? He watched her as she flushed, and he liked it. That deeply male curve in the corner of his mouth made that plain.

Valentina struggled to free herself from his hold then, to climb off his lap and sit back on the seat herself, and she was all too aware that he let her.

She didn't focus on that. She couldn't. That offhanded show of his innate strength made her feel…slippery, inside and outside and high between her legs. She tossed herself off his lap, her gaze tangling with his in a way that made the whole world seem to spin a little, and then she threw herself out the door. She summoned a smile from somewhere and aimed it at the doormen.

Breathe, she ordered herself. *Just breathe.*

Because she couldn't do this. This wasn't who she was. She hadn't held on to her virginity all this time to toss it aside at the very first temptation…had she?

This couldn't be who she was. It couldn't.

She'd spent her whole life practicing how to appear unruffled and serene under any and all circumstances, though she couldn't recall ever putting it to this kind of test before. She made herself breathe. She made herself smile. She sank into the familiarity of her public persona, wielding it like that armor she'd wanted, because it occurred to her it was the toughest and most resilient armor she had.

Achilles followed her into that bright and shiny elevator in the back of the gleaming lobby, using his key to close the doors behind them. He did not appear to notice or care that she was newly armored, especially while he seemed perfectly content to look so…disreputable.

His suit jacket hung open, and she was sure it had to be

obvious to even the most casual observer that she'd had her hands all over his chest and his shirt. And she found it was difficult to think of that hard mouth of his as cruel now that she knew how it tasted. More, how it felt on hers, demanding and intense and—

Stop, she ordered herself. *Now.*

He leaned back against the wall as the elevator started to move, his dark gold eyes hooded and intent when they met hers. He didn't say a word. Maybe he didn't have to. Her heart was pounding so loud that Valentina was certain it would have drowned him out if he'd shouted.

But Achilles did not shout.

On the contrary, when the elevator doors shut behind them, securing them in his penthouse, he only continued to watch her in that same intense way. She moved into the great living room, aware that he followed her, silent and faintly lazy.

It made her nervous. That was what she told herself that fluttery feeling was, lodged there beneath her ribs. And lower, if she was honest. Much lower.

"I'm going to bed," she said. And then instantly wished she'd phrased that differently when she heard it echo there between them, seeming to fill up the cavernous space, beating as madly within her as her own frenzied heart. "Alone."

Achilles gave the impression of smiling without actually doing so. He thrust his hands into the pockets of his dark suit and regarded her solemnly, save for that glittering thing in his dark gaze.

"If that is what you wish, *glikia mou.*"

And that was the thing. It wasn't what she wished. It wasn't what she wanted, and especially not when he called her that Greek name that she thought meant *my sweet*. It made her want to taste that word on that mouth of his. It made her want to find out exactly how sweet he thought she was.

It made her want to really, truly be someone else so she could do all the things that trampled through her head, making her chest feel tight while the rest of her... yearned.

Her whole life had been an exercise in virtue and duty, and she'd thought that meant something. She'd thought that *said* something about who she was. Valentina had been convinced that she'd held on to her chastity all this time, long after everyone she'd known had rid themselves of theirs, as a gift to her future.

But the night all around her told her something different. It had stripped away all the lies she'd told herself—or Achilles had. All the places she'd run and hid across all these years. Because the truth was that she'd never been tested. Was it truly virtue if she'd never been the least bit tempted to give it away? Or was it only coincidence that she'd never encountered anything that had felt the least bit compelling in that regard? Was it really holding on to something if she'd never felt the least bit like getting rid of it?

Because everything tonight was different. Valentina was different—or, worse, she thought as she stared at Achilles across the little bit of space that separated them, she had never been who she'd imagined she was. She had never understood that it was possible that a body could drown out what the mind knew to be prudent.

Until now.

She had judged passion all her life and told herself it was a story that weak people told themselves and others to make their sins seem more interesting. More complicated and unavoidable. But the truth was, Valentina had never experienced passion in her life.

Not until Achilles.

"I am your assistant," she told him. Or perhaps she was telling herself. "This must never happen again. If it does, I can't work for you."

"I have already told you that I am more than happy to accommodate—"

"There will be no lateral moves," she threw at him, appalled to hear her voice shaking. "You might lie awake at night imagining what that means and what it would look like, but I don't. I won't."

"Liar."

If he had hauled off and hit her, Valentina didn't think she could have been any more surprised. Shocked. No one had ever called her a liar before, not in all her life.

Then again, chimed in a small voice deep inside, *you never used to lie, did you? Not to others and not to yourself.*

"I have no doubt that you enjoy doing as you please," she spat at him, horrified that any of this was happening and, worse, that she'd let it—when Valentina knew who she was and what she'd be going back to in a few short weeks. "No matter the consequences. But not everyone is as reckless as you."

Achilles didn't quite smirk. "And that is why one of us is a billionaire and the other is his assistant."

"And if we were having a discussion about how to make money," Valentina said from between her teeth, no sign of her trademark serenity, "I would take your advice— but this is my life."

Guilt swamped her as she said that. Because, of course, it wasn't her life. It was Natalie's. And she had the sick feeling that she had already complicated it beyond the point of return. It didn't matter that Natalie had texted her to say that she'd kissed Prince Rodolfo, far away in Murin and neck-deep in Valentina's real life, however little Valentina had thought about it since she'd left it behind.

Valentina was going to marry Rodolfo. That her double had kissed him, the way Valentina probably should have, wasn't completely out of line.

But this… This thing she was doing… It was unacceptable on every level. She knew that.

Maybe Natalie has this same kind of chemistry with Rodolfo, something in her suggested. *Maybe he was engaged to the wrong twin.*

Which meant, she knew—because she was that self-serving—that maybe the wrong twin had been working for Achilles all this time and all of this was inevitable.

She wasn't sure she believed that. But she couldn't seem to stop herself. Or worse, convince herself that she should.

Achilles was still watching her too closely. Once again, she had the strangest notion that he knew too much. That he could see too far inside her.

Don't be silly, she snapped at herself then. *Of course he can't. You're just looking for more ways to feel guilty.*

Because whatever else happened, there was no way Achilles Casilieris would allow the sort of deception Valentina was neck-deep in to take place under his nose if he knew about it. She was certain of that, if nothing else.

"This is what I know about life," Achilles said, his voice a silken thread in the quiet of the penthouse, and Valentina had to repress a little shiver that threatened to shake her spine apart. "You must live it. If all you do is wall yourself off, hide yourself away, what do you have at the end but wasted time?"

Her throat was dry and much too tight. "I would take your advice more seriously if I didn't know you had an ulterior motive."

"I don't believe in wasting time or in ulterior motives," he growled back at her. "And not because I want a taste of you, though I do. And I intend to have it, *glikia mou*, make no mistake. But because you have put yourself on hold. Do you think I can't see it?"

She thought she had to be reeling then. Nothing was solid. She couldn't help but put her hand out, steadying herself on the back of the nearest chair—though it didn't seem to help.

And Achilles was watching her much too closely, with far too much of that disconcerting awareness making his dark gaze shine. "Or is it that you don't know yourself?"

When she was Princess Valentina of Murin, known to the world before her birth. Her life plotted out in its every detail. Her name literally etched in stone into the foundations of the castle where her family had ruled for generations. She had never had the opportunity to lose herself. Not in a dramatic adolescence. Not in her early twenties. She had never been beside herself at some crossroads, desperate to figure out the right path—because there had only ever been one path and she had always known exactly how to walk it, every step of the way.

"You don't know me at all," she told him, trying to sound less thrown and more outraged at the very suggestion that she was any kind of mystery to herself. She'd never had that option. "You're my employer, not my confidant. You know what I choose to show you and nothing more."

"But what you choose to show, and how you choose to show it, tells me exactly who you are." Achilles shook his head, and it seemed to Valentina that he moved closer to her when she could see he didn't. That he was exactly where he'd always been—it was just that he seemed to take over the whole world. She wasn't sure he even tried; he just did. "Or did you imagine I achieved all that I've achieved without managing to read people? Surely you cannot be so foolish."

"I was about to do something deeply foolish," she said

tightly. And not exactly smartly. "But I've since come to my senses."

"No one is keeping you here." His hands were thrust deep into his pockets, and he stood where he'd stopped, a few steps into the living room from those elevator doors. His gaze was all over her, but nothing else was touching her. He wasn't even blocking her escape route back to the guest room on this floor.

And she understood then. He was giving her choice. He was putting it on her. He wasn't simply sweeping her off into all that wild sensation—when he must have known he could have. He easily could have. If he hadn't stopped in the car, what would they be doing now?

But Valentina already knew the answer to that. She could feel her surrender inside her like heat.

And she thought she hated him for it.

Or should.

"I'm going to sleep," she said. She wanted her voice to be fierce. Some kind of condemnation. But she thought she sounded more determined than resolved. "I will see you in the morning. Sir."

Achilles smiled. "I think we both know you will see me long before that. And in your dreams, *glikia mou*, I doubt I will be so chivalrous."

Valentina pressed her lips tight together and did not allow herself to respond to him. Especially because she wanted to so very, very badly—and she knew, somehow, that it would lead nowhere good. It couldn't.

Instead, she turned and headed for her room. It was an unremarkable guest room appropriate for staff, but the best thing about it was the lock on the door. Not that she thought he would try to get in.

She was far more concerned that she was the one who would try to get out.

"One of these days," he said from behind her, his voice

low and intense, "you will stop running. It is a foregone conclusion, I am afraid. And then what?"

Valentina didn't say a word. But she didn't have to.

When she finally made it to her room and threw the dead bolt behind her, the sound of it echoed through the whole of the penthouse like a gong, answering Achilles eloquently without her having to open her mouth.

Telling him exactly how much of a coward she was, in case he hadn't already guessed.

CHAPTER SIX

IN THE DAYS that followed that strange night and Achilles's world-altering kiss that had left her raw and aching and wondering if she'd ever feel like herself again, Valentina found she couldn't bear the notion that she was twenty-seven years old and somehow a stranger to herself.

Her future was set in stone. She'd always known that. And she'd never fought against all that inevitability because what was the point? She could fight as much as she wanted and she'd still be Princess Valentina of Murin, only with a stain next to her name. That had always seemed to her like the very definition of futility.

But in the days that followed that kiss, it occurred to her that perhaps it wasn't the future she needed to worry about, but her past. She hadn't really allowed herself to think too closely about what it meant that Natalie had been raised by the woman who was very likely Valentina's own mother. Because, of course, there was no other explanation for the fact she and Natalie looked so much alike. Identical twins couldn't just randomly occur, and certainly not when one of them was a royal. There were too many people watching royal births too closely. Valentina had accepted the story that her mother had abandoned her, because it had always been couched in terms of Frederica's mental illness. Valentina had imagined her mother living out her days in some or other institution somewhere, protected from harm.

But the existence of Natalie suggested that Frederica was instead a completely different person from the one Valentina had imagined all this time. The woman who now called herself Erica had clearly not wasted away in a mental institution, all soothing pastels and injections and no ability to contact her own child. On the contrary, this Erica had lived a complicated life after her time in the palace that had nothing to do with any hospital—and though she'd clearly had two daughters, she'd taken only one with her when she'd gone.

Valentina didn't entirely understand how she could be quite so hurt by a betrayal that had happened so long ago and that she hadn't known about until recently. She didn't understand why it mattered so much to her. But the more she tried to tell herself that it was silly to be so bothered, the more bothered she got.

It was only when she had gone round and round and round on that almost too many times to count that Valentina accepted the fact she was going to have to do something about it.

And all these years, she'd never known how to go about looking for her mother even if she'd wanted to. She would have had to ask her father directly, the very idea of which made her shudder—even now, across an ocean or two from his throne and his great reserve and his obvious reluctance to discuss Frederica at all. Barring that, she would have had to speak to one of the high-level palace aides whose role was to serve her father in every possible way and who therefore had access to most of the family secrets. She doubted somehow that they would have told her all the things that she wanted to know—or even a few of them. And they certainly would have run any questions she had past her father first, which would have defeated the purpose of asking them.

Valentina tried to tell herself that was why she'd never asked.

But now she was tucked up in a lethally dangerous billionaire's penthouse in New York City, away from all the palace intrigue and protocol, and far too aware of the things a man like Achilles could do with only a kiss. To say nothing of his businesses. What was an old family secret to a man like Achilles?

And even though in many ways she had fewer resources at her fingertips and fewer people to ask for ancient stories and explanations, in the end, it was very simple. Because Valentina had Natalie's mobile, which had to mean she had direct access to her own story. If she dared look for it.

The Valentina who had seen her own mirror image in a bathroom in London might not have dared. But the Valentina who had lost herself in the raw fire of Achilles's kiss, on the other hand, dared all manner of things.

It was that Valentina who opened up Natalie's list of contacts, sitting there in her locked bedroom in Achilles's penthouse. She scrolled down, looking for an entry that read *Mom*. Or *Mum*. Or any variation of *Mother* she could think of.

But there was nothing.

That stymied her, but she was aware enough to realize that the sensation deep in her belly was not regret. It was relief. As if, in the end, she preferred these mysteries to what was likely to be a vicious little slap of truth.

You are such a coward, she told herself.

Because it wasn't as if her father—or Valentina herself, for that matter—had ever been in hiding. The truth was that her mother could have located her at any point over these last twenty-seven years. That she hadn't done so told Valentina all she needed to know about Frederica's maternal feelings, surely.

Well. What she *needed* to know perhaps, but there was a great deal more she *wanted* to know, and that was the trouble.

She kept scrolling until she found an entry marked *Erica.* She thought that told her a great deal about Natalie's relationship with this woman who was likely mother to them both. It spoke of a kind of distance that Valentina had certainly never contemplated when she'd thought about her own mother from time to time over the past nearly thirty years. In her head, of course, any reunion with the woman she'd imagined had been locked away in a pleasantly secure institution would be filled with love. Regret. Soft, sweet arms wrapped around her, and a thousand apologies for somehow managing to abandon and then never find her way back to a baby who lived at one of the most famous addresses in the world.

She wasn't entirely sure why the simple fact of the woman's first name in a list of contacts made it so clear that all of that was a lie. Not just a harmless fantasy to make a motherless child feel better about her fate, but something infinitely more dangerous, somehow.

Valentina wanted to shut down the mobile phone. She wanted to throw it across the small room and pretend that she'd never started down this road in the first place.

But it occurred to her that possibly, she was trying to talk herself out of doing this thing she was certain she needed to do.

Because Achilles might have imagined that he could see these mysteries in her, but what scared Valentina was that she could, too. That he'd identified a terrible weakness in her, and that meant anyone could.

Perhaps she wasn't who she thought she was. Perhaps

she never had been. Perhaps, all this time, she'd imagined she'd been walking down a set path when she hadn't.

If she was honest, the very idea made her want to cry.

It had been important, she thought then, sitting crosslegged on the bed with the summer light streaming in from the windows—crucially important, even—to carry on the morning after that kiss as if nothing had changed. Because she had to pretend that nothing had. That she didn't know too much now. That she didn't think of that kiss every time she looked at Achilles. She'd gone to work, and she'd done her job, and she'd stayed as much in his presence as she ever did—and she thought that she deserved some kind of award for the acting she'd done. So cool, so composed.

So utterly unbothered by the fact she now knew how he tasted.

And she tried to convince herself that only she knew that she was absolutely full of it.

But one day bled into the next, and she'd found that her act became harder and harder to pull off, instead of easier. She couldn't understand it. It wasn't as if Achilles was doing anything, necessarily. He was Achilles, of course. There was always that look in his eyes, as if he was but waiting for her to give him a sign.

Any sign.

As if, were she to do so, he would drop everything he was doing—no matter where they were and what was happening around them—and sweep them right back into that storm of sensation that she found simmered inside her, waiting. Just waiting.

Just as he was.

It was the notion that she was the one who held the power—who could make all of that happen with a simple word or glance—that she found kept her up at night. It made her shake. It polluted her dreams and made her drift off entirely too many times while she was awake, only to be slapped back down to earth when Achilles's voice turned silken, as if he knew.

Somehow, this all made her determined to seek out the one part of her life that had never made sense, and had never fit in neatly into the tidy narrative she'd believed all her life and knew back and forth.

Today was a rare afternoon when Achilles had announced that he had no need of her assistance while he tended to his fitness in his personal gym because, he'd gritted at her, he needed to clear his head. Valentina had repaired to her bedroom to work out a few snarls in his schedule and return several calls from the usual people wanting advice on how to approach him with various bits of news he was expected to dislike intensely. She'd changed out of Natalie's usual work uniform and had gratefully pulled on a pair of jeans and a T-shirt, feeling wildly rebellious as she did so. And then a little bit embarrassed that her life was clearly so staid and old-fashioned that she found denim a personal revolution.

Many modern princesses dressed casually at times, she was well aware. Just as she was even more aware that none of them were related to her father, with his antiquated notions of propriety. And therefore none of them would have to suffer his disapproval should she find herself photographed looking "common" despite her ancient bloodline.

But she wasn't Princess Valentina here in New York, where no one cared what she wore. And maybe that was why Valentina pulled the trigger. She didn't cold-call the number that she'd found on her sister's phone—and there was something hard and painful in her chest even thinking that word, *sister*. She fed the number into a little piece of software that one of Achilles's companies had been working on, and she let it present her with information that she supposed she should have had some sort of scruple about using. But she didn't.

Valentina imagined that said something about her, too, but she couldn't quite bring herself to care about that the way she thought she ought to have.

In a push of a button, she had a billing address. Though the phone number itself was tied to the area code of a far-off city, the billing address was right here in Manhattan.

It was difficult not see that as some kind of sign.

Valentina slipped out of the penthouse then, without giving herself time to second-guess what she was about to do. She smiled her way through the lobby the way she always did, and then she set out into New York City by herself.

All by herself.

No guards. No security. Not even Achilles's brooding presence at her side. She simply walked. She made her way through the green, bright stretch of Central Park, headed toward the east side and the address Achilles's software had provided. No one spoke to her. No one called her name. No cameras snapped at her, recording her every move.

After a while, Valentina stopped paying attention to the expression on her face. She stopped worrying about her posture and whether or not her hair looked unkempt as the faint breeze teased at it. She simply...walked.

Her shoulders seemed to slip down an extra inch or two from her ears. She found herself breathing deeper, taking in the people she passed without analyzing them—without assuming they wanted something from her or were look-ing to photograph her supposedly "at large" in the world.

About halfway across the park it occurred to her that she'd never felt this way in her life. Alone. Free. Better yet, anonymous. She could have been anybody on the streets. There were locals all over the paths in the park, walking and talking and taking in the summer afternoon as if that was a perfectly normal pastime. To be out on their own, no one the wiser, doing exactly as they pleased.

Valentina realized that whatever happened next, this was the normal she'd spent her life looking for and dreaming about. This exact moment, walking across Central Park while summer made its cheerful noises all around her, completely and entirely on her own.

Freedom, it turned out, made her heart beat a little too fast and too hard inside her chest.

Once she made it to the east side, she headed a little bit uptown, then farther east until she found the address that had been on that billing statement. It looked like all the other buildings on the same block, not exactly dripping in luxury, but certainly no hovel. It was difficult for Valentina to determine the difference between kinds of dwellings in a place like this. Apartment buildings, huge blocks of too many people living on top of each other by choice, seemed strange to her on the face of it. But who was she to determine the difference between prosperous New Yorkers and regular ones? She had lived in a palace all her life. And she suspected that Achilles's sprawling penthouse wasn't a far cry from a palace itself, come to that.

But once she'd located the building she wanted and its dark green awning marked with white scrollwork, she didn't know what to do. Except wait there. As if she was some kind of daring sleuth, just like in the books she'd read as a little girl, when she was just…that same old motherless child, looking for a better story to tell herself.

She chided herself for that instantly. It felt defeating. Despairing. She was anonymous and free and unremarkable, standing on a city street. Nobody in the entire world knew where she was. Nobody would know where to look and nobody was likely to find her if they tried. Valentina couldn't decide if that notion made her feel small and fragile, or vast and powerful. Maybe both at the same time.

She didn't know how long she stood there. She ignored the first few calls that buzzed at her from Natalie's mobile tucked in her pocket, but then realized that standing about speaking on her phone gave her far more of a reason to be out there in the street. Instead of simply standing there doing nothing, looking like she was doing exactly what she was doing, which was looming around as she waited for somebody to turn up.

So she did her job, out there on the street. Or Natalie's job, anyway. She fielded the usual phone calls from the office and, if she was honest, liked the fact that she had somewhere to put all her nervous energy. She was half-afraid that Achilles would call and demand that she return to his side immediately, but she suspected that she was less afraid of that happening than she was hoping that it would, so she didn't have to follow this through.

Because even now, there was a part of her that simply wanted to retreat back into what she already knew. What she'd spent her life believing.

Afternoon was bleeding into evening, and Valentina was beginning to think that she'd completely outstayed her welcome. That Erica was in one of the other places she sometimes stayed, like the one in the Caribbean Natalie had mentioned in a text. That at any moment now it was likely that one of the doormen in the surrounding buildings would call the police to make her move along at last. That they hadn't so far she regarded as some kind of miracle. She finished up the last of the calls she'd been fielding, and told herself that it had been foolish to imagine that she could simply turn up one afternoon, stand around and solve the mysteries of her childhood so easily.

But that was when she saw her.

And Valentina didn't know exactly what it was that had

caught her eye. The hair was wrong, not long and coppery like her daughters' but short. Dark. And it wasn't as if Valentina had any memories of this woman, but still. There was something in the way she moved. The way she came down the block, walking quickly, a plastic bag hanging from one wrist and the other hand holding a phone to her ear.

But Valentina knew her. She knew that walk. She knew the gait and the way the woman cocked her head toward the hand holding her phone. She knew the way this woman carried herself.

She recognized her, in other words, when she shouldn't have. When, she realized, despite the fact she'd spent a whole summer afternoon waiting for this moment—she really didn't want to recognize her.

And she'd been nursing fantasies this whole time, little as she wanted to admit that, even to herself. She'd told herself all the things that she would do if this woman appeared. She'd worked out scenarios in her head.

Do you know who I am? she would ask, or demand, and this woman she had always thought of as Federica, but who went by a completely different name—the better to hide, Valentina assumed—would... Cry? Flail about? Offer excuses? She hadn't been able to decide which version she would prefer no matter how many times she'd played it out in her head.

And as this woman who was almost certainly her mother walked toward her, not looking closely enough to see that there was anyone standing down the block a ways in front of her, much less someone who she should have assumed was the daughter she knew as Natalie, Valentina realized what she should have known already. Or maybe, deep down, she had known it—she just hadn't really wanted to admit it.

There was nothing this woman could do to fix anything

or change anything or even make it better. She couldn't go back in time. She couldn't change the past. She couldn't choose Valentina instead of Natalie, if that had been the choice she'd made. Valentina wasn't even certain that was something she'd want, if she could go back in time herself, but the fact of the matter was that there was nothing to be done about it now.

And her heart beat at her and beat at her, until she thought it might beat its way straight out through her ribs, and even as it did, Valentina couldn't pretend that she didn't know that what she was feeling was grief.

Grief, thick and choking. Dark and muddy and deep.

For the childhood she'd never had, and hadn't known she'd missed until now. For the life she might have known had this woman been different. Had Valentina been different. Had her father, perhaps, not been King Geoffrey of Murin. It was all speculation, of course. It was that tearing thing in her belly and that weight on her chest, and that thick, deep mud she worried she might never find her way out of again.

And when Erica drew close to her building's green awning, coming closer to Valentina than she'd been in twenty-seven years, Valentina…said nothing. She let her hair fall forward to cover her face where she leaned against the brick wall. She pretended she was on a serious phone call while the woman who was definitely her mother—of course she was her mother; how had Valentina been tricking herself into pretending she could be anything but that?—turned into the building that Valentina had been staking out all afternoon, and was swallowed up into her own lobby.

For long moments, Valentina couldn't breathe. She wasn't sure she could think.

It was as if she didn't know who she was.

She found herself walking. She lost herself in the tumult of this sprawling mess of a bright and brash city, the noise of car horns in the street, and the blasts of conversation and laughter from the groups of strangers she passed. She made her way back to the park and wandered there as the summer afternoon took on that glassy blue that meant the hour was growing late.

She didn't cry. She hardly saw in front of her. She simply walked.

And dusk was beginning to steal in at last, making the long blocks cold in the long shadows, when she finally made it back to Achilles's building.

One of the doormen brought her up in the elevator, smiling at her as she stepped off. It made her think that perhaps she had smiled in return, though she couldn't tell. It was as if her body was not her own and her face was no longer under her control. She walked into Achilles's grand living room, and stood there. It was as if she still didn't know where she was. As if she still couldn't see. And the huge windows that let Manhattan in all around her only seemed to make her sense of dislocation worse.

"Where the hell have you been?"

That low growl came from above her. Valentina didn't have to turn and look to know that it was Achilles from on high, standing at the top of the stairs that led to his sprawling master suite.

She looked up anyway. Because somehow, the most dangerous man she'd ever met felt like an anchor.

He looked as if he'd just showered. He wore a T-shirt she could tell was soft from down two flights, stretched over his remarkable chest as if it was as enamored of him as she feared she was. Loose black trousers were slung low on his hips, and she had the giddy sense that if he did something like stretch, or breathe too heavily, she would be able to see a swathe of olive skin between the waistband and the hem of his T-shirt.

And suddenly, she wanted nothing more than to see exactly that. More than she could remember wanting anything else. Ever.

"Careful, *glikia mou*, or I will take you up on that invitation written all over your face," Achilles growled as if he was irritated…but she knew better.

Because he knew. He always knew. He could read her when no one else ever had. The masks she wore like they were second nature and the things she pretended for the whole of the rest of the world fooled everybody, but never him.

Never, ever him.

As if there was a real Valentina buried beneath the exterior she'd thought for years was the totality of who she was, and Achilles was the only one who had ever met her. Ever seen her. Ever suspected she existed and then found her, again and again, no matter how hard Valentina worked to keep her hidden away.

Her throat was dry. Her tongue felt as if it no longer fit in her own mouth.

But she couldn't bring herself to look away from him.

She thought about her mother and she thought about her childhood. She thought about the pride she'd taken in that virtue of hers that she'd clung to so fiercely all these years. Or perhaps not so fiercely, as it had been so untested. Was that virtue at all, she wondered?

Or was this virtue?

She had spent all of this time trying to differentiate herself from a woman she thought she knew, but who it turned out she didn't know at all. And for what? She was already trapped in the same life that her mother had abandoned.

Valentina was the one who hadn't left her father. She was the one who had prided herself on being perfect. She was the one who was decidedly not mentally ill, never too overwrought to do the job required of her by her blood and her father's expectations, nothing but a credit to her father in all ways. And she'd reveled in it.

More than reveled in it. It had become the cornerstone of her own self-definition.

And all of it was built on lies. The ones she told herself, and more than that, the lies that had been told to her for her entire life. By everyone.

All Valentina could think as she gazed up the stairs to the man she was only pretending was her employer was that she was done with lies. She wanted something honest. Even—especially—if it was raw.

And she didn't much care if there were consequences to that.

"You say that is if it is a threat," she said quietly. Distinctly. "Perhaps you should rethink your own version of an invitation before it gets you in trouble." She raised her brows in challenge, and knew it. Reveled in it, too. "Sir."

And when Achilles smiled then, it was with sheer masculine triumph, and everything changed.

He had thought she'd left him.

When Achilles had come out of the hard, brutal workout he'd subjected himself to that had done absolutely nothing to make his vicious need for her settle, Achilles had found her gone.

And he'd assumed that was it. The princess had finally had enough. She'd finished playing this down-market game of hers and gone back to her palaces and her ball gowns and her resplendent little prince who waited for her across the seas.

He'd told himself it was for the best.

He was a man who took things for a living and made an empire out of his conquests, and he had no business whatsoever putting his commoner's hands all over a woman of her pedigree. No business doing it, and worse, he shouldn't want to.

And maybe that was why he found himself on his treadmill again while he was still sucking air from his first workout, running as if every demon he'd vanquished in his time was chasing him all over again, and gaining. Maybe that was why he'd run until he'd thought his lungs might burst, his head might explode or his knees might give out beneath him.

Then he'd run more. And even when he'd exhausted himself all over again, even when he was standing in his own shower with his head bent toward the wall as if she'd bested him personally, it hadn't helped.

The fact of the matter was that he had a taste of Valentina, and nothing else would do.

And what enraged him the most, he'd found—aside from the fact he hadn't had her the way he'd wanted her— was that he'd let her think she'd tricked him all this time. That she would go back behind her fancy gates and her moats and whatever the hell else she had in that palace of hers that he'd looked up online and thought looked exactly like the sort of fairy tale he disdained, and she would believe that she'd played him for a fool.

Achilles thought that might actually eat him alive.

And now here she stood when he thought he'd lost her. At the bottom of his stairs, looking up at him, her eyes dark with some emotion he couldn't begin to define.

But he didn't want to define it. He didn't want to talk about her feelings, and he'd die before he admitted his own, and what did any of that matter anyway? She was here and he was here, and a summer night was creeping in outside.

And the only thing he wanted to think about was sating himself on her at last.

At last and for as long as he could.

Achilles was hardly aware of moving down the stairs even as he did it.

One moment he was at the top, staring down at Valentina's upturned face with her direct challenge ringing in him like a bell, and the next he was upon her. And she was so beautiful. So exquisitely, ruinously beautiful. He couldn't seem to get past that. It was as if it wound around him and through him, changing him, making him new each time he beheld her.

He told himself he hated it, but he didn't look away.

"There is no going back," he told her sternly. "There will be no pretending this didn't happen."

Her smile was entirely too graceful and the look in her green eyes too merry by far. "Do you get that often?"

Achilles felt like a savage. An animal. Too much like that monster he kept down deep inside. And yet he didn't have it in him to mind. He reached out and indulged himself at last while his blood hammered through his veins, running his fingers over that elegant cheekbone of hers, and that single freckle that marred the perfection of her face—and somehow made her all the more beautiful.

"So many jokes," he murmured, not sure how much of the gruffness in his voice was need and how much was that thing like temper that held him fast and fierce. "Everything is so hilarious, suddenly. How much longer do you think you will be laughing, *glikia mou*?"

"I think that is up to you," Valentina replied smoothly, and she was still smiling at him in that same way, graceful and knowing. "Is that why you require so much legal documentation before you take a woman to bed? Do you make them all laugh so much that you fear your reputation as a grumpy icon would take a hit if it got out?"

It was a mark of how far gone he was that he found that amusing. If anyone else had dreamed of saying such a thing to him, he would have lost his sense of humor completely.

He felt his mouth curve. "There is only one way to find out."

And Achilles had no idea what she might do next. He wondered if that was what it was about her, if that was why this thirst for her never seemed to ebb. She was so very different from all the women he'd known before. She was completely unpredictable. He hardly knew, from one moment to the next, what she might do next.

It should have irritated him, he thought. But instead it only made him want her more.

Everything, it seemed, made him want her more. He hadn't realized until now how pale and insubstantial his desires had been before. How little he'd wanted anything.

"There is something I must tell you." She pulled her bottom lip between her teeth after she said that, a little breathlessly, and everything in him stilled.

This was it, he thought. And Achilles didn't know if he was proud of her or sad, somehow, that this great charade was at an end. For surely that was what she planned to tell him. Surely she planned to come clean about who she really was.

And while there was a part of him that wanted to deny that what swirled between them was anything more than sex, simple and elemental, there was a far greater part of him that roared its approval that she should think it was right to identify herself before they went any further.

"You can tell me anything," he told her, perhaps more fiercely than he should. "But I don't know why you imagine I don't already know."

He was fascinated when her cheeks bloomed with that crisp, bright red that he liked a little too much. More each time he saw it, because he liked his princess a little flustered. A little off balance.

But something in him turned over, some foreboding perhaps. Because he couldn't quite imagine why it was that she should be *embarrassed* by the deception she'd practiced on him. He could think of many things he'd like her to feel for attempting to pull something like that over on him, and he had quite a few ideas about how she should pay for that, but embarrassment wasn't quite it.

"I thought you might know," she whispered. "I hope it doesn't matter."

"Everything matters or nothing does, *glikia mou*."

He shifted so he was closer to her. He wanted to care about whatever it was she was about to tell him, but he found the demands of his body were far too loud and too imperative to ignore. He put his hands on her, curling his fingers over her delicate shoulders and then losing himself in their suppleness. And in the delicate line of her arms. And in the sweet feel of her bare skin beneath his palms as he ran them down from her shoulders to her wrists, then back again.

And he found he didn't really care what she planned to confess to him. How could it matter when he was touching her like this?

"I do not require your confession," he told her roughly. "I am not your priest."

If anything, her cheeks flared brighter.

"I'm a virgin," she blurted out, as if she had to force herself to say it.

For a moment, it was as if she'd struck him. As if she'd picked up one of the sculptures his interior designer had littered about his living room and clobbered him with it.

"I beg your pardon?"

But she was steadier then. "You heard me. I'm a virgin. I thought you knew." She swallowed, visibly, but she didn't look away from him. "Especially when I didn't know how to kiss you."

Achilles didn't know what to do with that.

Or rather, he knew exactly what to do with it, but was

afraid that if he tossed his head back and let himself go the way he wanted to—roaring out his primitive take on her completely unexpected confession to the rafters—it might terrify her.

And the last thing in the world he wanted to do was terrify her.

He knew he should care that this wasn't quite the confession he'd expected. That as far as he could tell, Valentina had no intention of telling him who she was. Ever. He knew that it should bother him, and perhaps on some level it did, but the only thing he could seem to focus on was the fact that she was untouched.

Untouched.

He was the only man in all the world who had ever tasted her. Touched her. Made her shiver, and catch her breath, and moan. That archaic word seemed to beat in place of his heart.

Virgin. Virgin. Virgin.

Until it was as if he knew nothing but that. As if her innocence shimmered between them, beckoning and sweet, and she was his for the taking.

And, oh, how Achilles liked to take the things he wanted.

"Are you sure you wish to waste such a precious gift on the likes of me?" he asked, and he heard the stark greed beneath the laziness he forced into his tone. He heard exactly how much he wanted her. He was surprised it didn't seem to scare her the way he thought it should. "After all, there is nothing particularly special about me. I have money, that's all. And as you have reminded me, I am your boss. The ethical considerations are legion."

He didn't know why he said that. Any of that. Was it to encourage her to confess her real identity to him? Was it to remind her of the role she'd chosen to play—although not today, perhaps?

Or was it to remind him?

Either way, she only lifted her chin. "You don't have to take it," she said, as if it was of no import to her one way or the other. "Certainly not if you have some objection."

She lifted one shoulder, then dropped it, and the gesture was so quintessentially royal that it should have set Achilles's teeth on edge. But instead he found it so completely her, so entirely Princess Valentina, that it only made him harder. Hotter. More determined to find his way inside her.

And soon.

"I have no objection," he assured her, and there was no pretending his tone wasn't gritty. Harsh. "Are we finished talking?"

And the nerves he'd been unable to detect before were suddenly all over her face. He doubted she knew it. But she was braver than she ought to have been, his deceitful little princess, and all she did was gaze back at him. Clear and sure, as if he couldn't see the soft, vulnerable cast to her mouth.

Or maybe, he thought, she had no idea how transparent she was.

"Yes," Valentina said softly. "I'm ready to stop talking."

And this time, as he drew her to him, he knew it wouldn't end in a kiss. He knew they weren't going to stop until he'd had her at last.

He knew that she was not only going to be his tonight, but she was going to be only his. That no one had ever touched her before, and if he did it right, no one else ever would.

Because Achilles had every intention of ruining his princess for all other men.

CHAPTER SEVEN

VALENTINA COULDN'T BELIEVE this was happening.

At last.

Achilles took her mouth, and there was a lazy quality to his kiss that made her knees feel weak. He set his mouth to hers, and then he took his time. As if he knew that inside she was a jangle of nerves and longing, anticipation and greed. As if he knew she hardly recognized herself or all the needy things that washed around inside her, making her new.

Making her his.

He kissed her for a long while, it seemed to her. He slid his arms around her, he pulled her against his chest, and then he took her mouth with a thoroughness that made a dangerous languor steal all over her. All through her. Until she wasn't sure that she would be able to stand on her own, were he to let go of her.

But he didn't let go.

Valentina thought she might have fallen off the edge of the world anyway, because everything seemed to whirl and cartwheel around, but then she realized that what he'd done was stoop down to bend a little and then pick her up. As if she was as weightless as she felt. He held her in his arms, high against his chest, and she felt her shoes fall off her feet like some kind of punctuation. And when he gazed down into her face, she thought he looked like some kind of conquering warrior of old, though she chided herself for being so fanciful.

There was nothing fanciful about Achilles.

Quite the opposite. He was fierce and masculine and ruthless beyond measure, and still, Valentina couldn't think of anywhere she would rather be—or anyone she would rather be with like this. It all felt inevitable, as if she'd been waiting her whole life for this thing she hardly understood to sweep her away, just like this.

And it had come into focus only when she'd met Achilles.

Because he was her only temptation. She had never wanted anyone else. She couldn't imagine she ever would.

"I don't know what to do," she whispered, aware on some level that he was moving. That he was carrying her up those penthouse stairs as if she weighed nothing at all. But she couldn't bring herself to look away from his dark gold gaze. And the truth was, she didn't care. He could take her anywhere. "I don't want to disappoint you."

"And how would you do that?" His voice was so deep. So lazy and, unless she was mistaken, amused, even as that gaze of his made her quiver, deep inside.

"Well," she stammered out. "Well, I don't—"

"Exactly," he said, interrupting her with that easy male confidence that she found she liked a little too much. "You don't know, but I do. So perhaps, *glikia mou*, you will allow me to demonstrate the breadth and depth of my knowledge."

And when she shuddered, he only laughed.

Achilles carried her across the top floor, all of which was part of his great master bedroom. It took up the entire top level of his penthouse, bordered on all sides by the wide patio that was also accessible from a separate staircase below. The better to maintain and protect his privacy, she thought now, which she felt personally invested in at the moment. He strode across the hardwood floor with bold-colored rugs tossed here and there, and she took in the exposed brick walls and the bright, modern works of art that hung on them. This floor was all space and silence, and in between there were more of those breathtaking windows that brightened the room with the lights from the city outside.

Achilles didn't turn on any additional light. He simply took Valentina over to the huge bed that was propped up on a sleek modern platform crafted out of a bright, hard steel, and laid her out across it as if she was something precious to him. Which made her heart clutch at her, as if she wanted to be.

And then he stood there beside the bed, his hands on his lean hips, and did nothing but gaze down at her.

Valentina pushed herself up onto her elbows. She could feel her breath moving in and out of her, and it was as if it was wired somehow to all that sensation she could feel lighting her up inside. It made her breasts feel heavier. It made her arms and legs feel somehow restless and sleepy at once.

With every breath, she could feel that bright, hot ache between her legs intensify. And this time, she knew without a shred of doubt that he was aware of every last part of it.

"Do you have anything else to confess?" he asked her, and she wondered if she imagined the dark current in his voice then. But it didn't matter. She had never wanted anyone, but she wanted him. Desperately.

She would confess anything at all if it meant she could have him.

And it wasn't until his eyes blazed, and that remarkable mouth of his kicked up in one corner, that she realized she'd spoken out loud.

"I will keep that in mind," he told her, his voice a rasp into the quiet of the room. Then he inclined his head. "Take off your clothes."

It was as if he'd plugged her into an electrical outlet. She felt zapped. Blistered, perhaps, by the sudden jolt of power. It felt as if there were something bright and hot, wrapped tight around her ribs, pressing down. And down farther.

And she couldn't bring herself to mind.

"But—by myself?" she asked, feeling a little bit light-headed at the very idea. She'd found putting on these jeans a little bit revolutionary. She couldn't imagine stripping them off in front of a man.

And not just any man. Achilles Casilieris.

Who didn't relent at all. "You heard me."

Valentina had to struggle then. She had to somehow shove her way out of all that wild electrical madness that was jangling through her body, at least enough so she could think through it. A little bit, anyway. She had to struggle to sit up all the way, and then to pull the T-shirt off her body. Her hands went to her jeans next, and she wrestled with the buttons, trying to pull the fly open. It was all made harder by the fact that her hands shook and her fingers felt entirely too thick.

And the more she struggled, the louder her breathing sounded. Until she was sure it was filling up the whole room, and more embarrassing by far, there was no possible way that Achilles couldn't hear it. Or see the flush that she could feel all over her, electric and wild. She wrestled the stiff, unyielding denim down over her hips, that bright heat that churned inside her seeming to bleed out everywhere as she did. She was sure it stained her, marking her bright hot and obvious.

She sneaked a look toward Achilles, and she didn't

know what she expected to see. But she froze when her eyes met his.

That dark gold gaze of his was as hot and demanding as ever. That curve in his mouth was even deeper. And there was something in the way that he was looking at her that soothed her. As if his hands were on her already, when they were not. It was as if he was helping her undress when she suspected that it was very deliberate on his part that he was not.

Because of course it was deliberate, she realized in the next breath. He was giving her another choice. He was putting it in her hands, again. And even while part of her found that inordinately frustrating, because she wanted to be swept away by him—or more swept away, anyway—there was still a part of her that relished this. That took pride in the fact that she was choosing to give in to this particular temptation.

That she was choosing to truly offer this particular man the virtue she had always considered such a gift.

It wasn't accidental. She wasn't drunk the way many of her friends had been, nor out of her mind in some other way, or even outside herself in the storm of an explosive temper or wild sensation that had boiled over.

He wanted her to be very clear that she was choosing him.

And Valentina wanted that, too. She wanted to choose Achilles. She wanted this.

She had never wanted anything else, she was sure of it. Not with this fervor that inhabited her body and made her light up from the inside out. Not with this deep certainty.

And so what could it possibly matter that she had never undressed for a man before? She was a princess. She had dressed and undressed in rooms full of attendants her whole life. Achilles was different from her collection of royal aides, clearly. But there was no need for her to be embarrassed, she told herself then. There was no need to go red in the face and start fumbling about, as if she didn't know how to remove a pair of jeans from her own body.

Remember who you are, she chided herself.

She was Princess Valentina of Murin. It didn't matter that seeing her mother might have shaken her. It didn't change a thing. That had nothing to do with who she was, it only meant that she'd become who she was in spite of the choices her mother had made. She could choose to do with that what she liked. And she was choosing to gift her innocence, the virginity she'd clung to as a badge of honor as if that differentiated her from the mother who'd left her, to Achilles Casilieris.

Here. Now.

And there was absolutely nothing to be ashamed about.

Valentina was sure that she saw something like approval in his dark gaze as she finished stripping her jeans from the length of her legs. And then she was sitting there in nothing but her bra and panties. She shifted up and onto her knees. Her hair fell down over her shoulders as she knelt on the bed, swirling across her bared skin and making her entirely too aware of how exposed she was.

But this time it felt sensuous. A sweet, warm sort of reminder of how much she wanted this. Him.

"Go on," he told her, a gruff command.

"That sounded a great deal like an order," Valentina murmured, even as she moved her hands around to her back to work the clasp of her bra. And it wasn't even a struggle to make her voice so airy.

"It was most definitely an order," Achilles agreed, his voice still gruff. "And I would suggest you obey me with significantly more alacrity."

"Or what?" she taunted him gently.

She eased open the silken clasp and then moved her hands around to the bra cups, holding them to her breasts when the bra would have fallen open. "Will you hold it against me in my next performance review? Oh, the horror."

"Are you defying me?"

But Achilles sounded amused, despite his gruffness. And there was something else in his voice then, she thought. A certain tension that she felt move inside her even before she understood what it was. Maybe she didn't have to understand. Her body already knew.

Between her legs, that aching thing grew fiercer. Brighter. And so did she.

"I think you can take it," she whispered.

And then she let the bra fall.

She felt the rush of cooler air over the flesh of her breasts. Her nipples puckered and stung a little as they pulled tight. But what she was concentrating on was that taut, arrested look on Achilles's face. That savage gleam in his dark gold eyes. And the way his fierce, ruthless mouth went flat.

He muttered something in guttural Greek, using words she had never heard before, in her blue-blooded academies and rarefied circles. But she knew, somehow, exactly what he meant.

She could feel it, part of that same ache.

He reached down to grip the hem of his T-shirt, then tugged it up and over his head in a single shrug of one muscled arm. She watched him do it, not certain she was breathing any longer and not able to make herself care about that at all, and then he was moving toward the bed.

Another second and he was upon her.

He swept her up in his arms again, moving her into the center of the bed, and then he bore her down to the mattress beneath them. And Valentina found that they fit together beautifully. That she knew instinctively what to do.

She widened her legs, he fit himself between them, and

she cushioned him there—that long, solid, hard-packed form of his—as if they'd been made to fit together just like this. His bare chest was a wonder. She couldn't seem to keep herself from exploring it, running her palms and her fingers over every ridge and every plane, losing herself in his hot, extraordinary male flesh. She could feel that remarkable ridge of his arousal again, pressed against her right where she ached the most, and it was almost too much.

Or maybe it really was too much, but she wanted it all the same.

She wanted him.

He set his mouth to hers again, and she could taste a kind of desperation on his wickedly clever mouth.

That wild sensation stormed through her, making her limp and wild and desperate for things she'd only ever read about before. He tangled his hands in her hair to hold her mouth to his, then he dropped his chest down against hers, bearing her down into the mattress beneath them. Making her feel glorious and alive and insane with that ache that started between her legs and bloomed out in all directions.

And then he taught her everything.

He tasted her. He moved his mouth from her lips, down the long line of her neck, learning the contours of her clavicle. Then he went lower, sending fire spinning all over her as he made his way down to one of her breasts, only to send lightning flashing all through her when he sucked her nipple deep into his mouth.

He tested the weight of her breasts in his faintly calloused palm, while he played with the nipple of the other, gently torturing her with his teeth, his tongue, his cruel lips. When she thought she couldn't take any more, he switched.

And then he went back and forth, over and over again,

until her head was thrashing against the mattress, and some desperate soul was crying out his name. Over and over again, as if she might break apart at any moment.

Valentina knew, distantly, that she was the one making those sounds. But she was too far gone to care.

Achilles moved his way down her body, taking his sweet time, and Valentina sighed with every inch he explored. She shifted. She rolled. She found herself lifting her hips toward him without his having to ask.

"Good girl," he murmured, and it was astonishing how much pleasure two little words could give her.

He peeled her panties down off her hips, tugged them down the length of her legs and then threw them aside. And when he was finished with that, he slid his hands beneath her bottom as he came back over her, lifted her hips up into the air and didn't so much as glance up at her before he set his mouth to the place where she needed him most.

Maybe she screamed. Maybe she fainted. Maybe both at once.

Everything seemed to flash bright, then smooth out into a long, lethal roll of sensation that turned Valentina red hot.

Everywhere.

He licked his way into her. He teased her and he learned her and he tasted her, making even that most private part of her his. She felt herself go molten and wild, and he made a low, rough sound of pleasure, deeply masculine and deliciously savage, and that was too much.

"Oh, no," she heard herself moan. "No—"

Valentina felt more than heard him laugh against the most tender part of her, and then everything went up in flames.

She exploded. She cried out and she shook, the pleasure so intense she didn't understand how anyone could live through it, but still she shook some more. She shook until she thought she'd been made new. She shook until she didn't care either way.

And when she knew her own name again, Achilles was crawling his way over her. He no longer wore those loose black trousers of his, and there was a look of unmistakably savage male triumph stamped deep on his face.

"Beautiful," he murmured. He was on his elbows over her, pressing himself against her. His wall of a chest. That fascinatingly hard part of him below. He studied her flushed face as if he'd never seen her before. "Am I the only man who has ever tasted you?"

Valentina couldn't speak. She could only nod, mute and still shaking.

She wondered if she might shake like this forever, and she couldn't seem to work herself up into minding if she did.

"Only mine," he said with a certain quiet ferocity that only made that shaking inside her worse. Or better. "You are only and ever mine."

And that was when she felt him. That broad smooth head of his hardest part, nudging against the place where she was nothing but soft, wet heat and longing.

She sucked in a breath, and Achilles took her face in his hands.

"Mine," he said again, in the same intense way.

It sounded a great deal like a vow.

Valentina's head was spinning.

"Yours," she whispered, and he grinned then, too fierce and too elemental.

He shifted his hips and moved a little farther against her, pressing himself against that entrance again, and Valentina found her hands in fists against his chest.

"Will it hurt?" she asked before she knew she meant

to speak. "Or is that just something they say in books, to make it seem more…"

But she couldn't quite finish that sentence. And Achilles's gaze was too dark and too bright at once, so intense she couldn't seem to stop shaking or spinning. And she couldn't bring herself to look away.

"It might hurt." He kept his attention on her, fierce and focused. "It might not. But either way, it will be over in a moment."

"Oh." Valentina blinked, and tried to wrap her head around that. "I suppose quick is good."

Achilles let out a bark of laughter, and she wasn't sure if she was startled or something like delighted to hear it. Both, perhaps.

And it made a knot she hadn't known was hardening inside her chest ease.

"I cannot tell if you are good for me or you will kill me," he told her then. He moved one hand, smoothing her hair back from her temple. "It will only hurt, or feel awkward, for a moment. I promise. As for the rest…"

And the smile he aimed at her then was, Valentina thought, the best thing she'd ever seen. It poured into her and through her, as bright and thick as honey, changing everything. Even the way she shook for him. Even the way she breathed.

"The rest will not be quick," Achilles told her, still braced there above her. "It will not be rushed, it will be thorough. Extremely thorough, as you know I am in all things."

She felt her breath stutter. But he was still going.

"And when I am done, *glikia mou*, we will do it again. And again. Until we get it right. Because I am nothing if not dedicated to my craft. Do you understand me?"

"I understand," Valentina said faintly, because it was

hard to keep her voice even when the world was lost somewhere in his commanding gaze. "I guess that's—"

But that was when he thrust his way inside her. It was a quick, hard thrust, slick and hot and overwhelming, until he was lodged deep inside her.

Inside her.

It was too much. It didn't hurt, necessarily, but it didn't feel good, either. It felt…like everything. Too much of everything.

Too hard. Too long. Too thick and too deep and too—

"Breathe," Achilles ordered her.

But Valentina didn't see how that was possible. How could she breathe when there was a person *inside* her? Even if that person was Achilles.

Especially when that person was Achilles.

Still, she did as he bade her, because he was *inside* her and she was beneath him and splayed open and there was nothing else to do. She breathed in.

She let it out, and then she breathed in again. And then again.

And with each breath, she felt less overwhelmed and more…

Something else.

Achilles didn't seem particularly worried. He held himself over her, one hand tangled in her hair as the other made its way down the front of her body. Lazily. Easily. He played with her breasts. He set his mouth against the crook of her neck where it met her shoulder, teasing her with his tongue and his teeth.

And still she breathed the way he'd told her to do. In. Out.

Over and over, until she couldn't remember that she'd balked at his smooth, intense entry. That she'd ever had a problem at all with *hard* and *thick* and *long* and *deep*.

Until all she could feel was fire.

Experimentally, she moved her hips, trying to get a better feel for how wide he was. How deep. How far inside her own body. Sensation soared through her every time she moved, so she did it again. And again.

She took a little more of him in, then rocked around a little bit, playing. Testing. Seeing how much of him she could take and if it would continue to send licks of fire coursing through her every time she shifted position, no matter how minutely.

It did.

And when she started to shift against him, restlessly, as if she couldn't help herself, Achilles lifted his head and grinned down her, something wild and dark and wholly untamed in his eyes.

It thrilled her.

"Please…" Valentina whispered.

And he knew. He always knew. Exactly what she needed, right when she needed it.

Because that was when he began to move.

He taught her about pace. He taught her depth and rhythm. She'd thought she was playing with fire, but Achilles taught her that she had no idea what real fire was.

And he kept his word.

He was very, very thorough.

When she began to thrash, he dropped down to get closer. He gathered her in his arms, holding her as he thrust inside her, again and again. He made her his with every deep, possessive stroke. He made her want. He made her need.

He made her cry out his name, again and again, until it sounded to Valentina like some kind of song.

This time, when the fire took her, she thought it might have torn her into far too many pieces for her to ever recover. He lost his rhythm then, hammering into her hard and wild, as if he was as wrecked as she was—

And she held him to her as he tumbled off that edge behind her, and straight on into bliss.

Achilles had made a terrible mistake, and he was not a man who made mistakes. He didn't believe in them. He believed in opportunities—it was how he'd built this life of his. Something that had always made him proud.

But this was a mistake. She was a mistake. He couldn't kid himself. He had never wanted somebody the way that he wanted Valentina. It had made him sloppy. He had concentrated entirely too much on her. Her pleasure. Her innocence, as he relieved her of it.

He hadn't thought to guard himself against her.

He never had to guard himself against anyone. Not since he'd been a child. He'd rather fallen out of the habit—and that notion galled him.

Achilles rolled to the side of the bed and sat there, running a hand over the top of his head. He could hear Valentina behind him, breathing. And he knew what he'd see if he looked. She slept hard, his princess. After he'd finished with her the last time, he'd thought she might have fallen asleep before he'd even pulled out of her. He'd held the weight of her, sprawled there on top of him, her breath heavy and her eyes shut tight so he had no choice but to marvel at the length of her eyelashes.

And it had taken him much longer than it should have to shift her off him, lay her beside him and cover her with the sheets. Carefully.

It was that unexpected urge to protect her—from himself, he supposed, or perhaps from the uncertain elements of his ruthlessly climate-controlled bedroom—that had made him go cold. Something a little too close to the sort of panic he did not permit himself to feel, ever, had pressed down on him then. And no amount of controlling his breath or ordering himself to stop the madness seemed to help.

He rubbed a palm over his chest now, because his heart was beating much too fast, the damned traitor.

He had wanted her too much, and this was the price. This treacherous place he found himself in now, that he hardly recognized. It hadn't occurred to him to guard himself against a virgin no matter her pedigree, and this was the result.

He felt things.

He felt things—and Achilles Casilieris did not *feel*. He refused to *feel*. The intensity of sex was physical, nothing more. Never more than that, no matter the woman and no matter the situation and no matter how she might beg or plead—

Not that Valentina had done anything of the sort.

He stood from the bed then, because he didn't want to. He wanted to roll back toward her, pull her close again. He bit off a filthy Greek curse, beneath his breath, then moved restlessly across the floor toward the windows.

Manhattan mocked him. It lay there before him, glittering and sparkling madly, and the reason he had a penthouse in this most brash and American of cities was because he liked to stand high above the sprawl of it as if he was some kind of king. Every time he came here he was reminded how far he'd come from his painful childhood. And every time he stayed in this very room, he looked out over all the wealth and opportunity and untethered American dreams that made this city what it was and knew that he had succeeded.

Beyond even the wildest dreams the younger version of Achilles could have conjured up for himself.

But tonight, all he could think about was a copper-haired innocent who had yet to tell him her real name, who had given him all of herself with that sweet enthusiasm that had nearly killed him, and left him…yearning.

And Achilles did not yearn.

He did not yearn and he did not let himself want things he could not have, and he absolutely, positively did not indulge in pointless nostalgia for things he did not miss. But as he stood at his huge windows overlooking Manhattan, the city that seemed to laugh at his predicament tonight instead of welcoming him the way it usually did, he found himself tossed back to the part of his past he only ever used as a weapon.

Against himself.

He hardly remembered his mother. Or perhaps he had beaten that sentimentality out of himself years ago. Either way, he knew that he had been seven or so when she had died, but it wasn't as if her presence earlier had done anything to save her children from the brute of a man whom she had married. Demetrius had been a thick, coarse sort of man, who had worked with his hands down on the docks and had thought that gave him the right to use those hands however he wished. Achilles didn't think there was anything the man had not beaten. His drinking buddies. His wife. The family dog. Achilles and his three young stepsiblings, over and over again. The fact that Achilles had not been Demetrius's own son, but the son of his mother's previous husband who had gone off to war and never returned, had perhaps made the beatings Demetrius doled out harsher—but it wasn't as if he spared his own flesh and blood from his fists.

After Achilles's mother had died under suspicious circumstances no one had ever bothered to investigate in a part of town where nothing good ever happened anyway, things went from bad to worse. Demetrius's temper worsened. He'd taken it out on the little ones, alternately kicking them around and then leaving them for seven-year-old Achilles to raise.

This had always been destined to end in failure, if not outright despair. Achilles understood that now, as an adult looking back. He understood it analytically and theoretically and, if asked, would have said exactly that. He'd been a child himself, etcetera. But where it counted, deep in those terrible feelings he'd turned off when he had still been a boy, Achilles would never understand. He carried the weight of those lives with him, wherever he went. No matter what he built, no matter what he owned, no matter how many times he won this or that corporate battle— none of that paid the ransom he owed on three lives he could never bring back.

They had been his responsibility, and he had failed. That beat in him like a tattoo. It marked him. It was the truth of him.

When it was all over—after Achilles had failed to notice a gas leak and had woken up only when Demetrius had returned from one of his drinking binges three days later to find the little ones dead and Achilles listless and nearly unresponsive himself—everything had changed. That was the cut-and-dried version of events, and it was accurate enough. What it didn't cover was the guilt, the shame that had eaten Achilles alive. Or what it had been like to watch his siblings' tiny bodies carried out by police, or how it had felt to stand at their graves and know that he could have prevented this if he'd been stronger. Bigger. *Better.*

Achilles had been sent to live with a distant aunt who had never bothered to pretend that she planned to give him anything but a roof over his head, and nothing more. In retrospect, that, too, had been a gift. He hadn't had to bother with any healing. He hadn't had to examine what had happened and try to come to terms with it. No one had cared about him or his grief at all.

And so Achilles had waited. He had plotted. He had taken everything that resembled a feeling, shoved it down as deep inside him as it would go, and made it over into hate. It had taken him ten years to get strong enough. To hunt Demetrius down in a sketchy bar in the same bad neighborhood where he'd brutalized Achilles's mother, beaten his own children and left Achilles responsible for what had happened to them.

And that whole long decade, Achilles had told himself that it was an extermination. That he could walk up to this man who had loomed so large over the whole of his childhood and simply rid the world of his unsavory presence. Demetrius did not deserve to live. There was no doubt about that, no shred of uncertainty anywhere in Achilles's soul. Not while Achilles's mother and his stepsiblings were dead.

He'd staked out his stepfather's favorite dive bar, and this one in the sense that it was repellant, not attractive to rich hipsters from affluent neighborhoods. He'd watched a ramshackle, much grayer and more frail version of the stepfather roaring in his head stumble out into the street. And he'd been ready.

He'd gone up to Demetrius out in the dark, cold night, there in a part of the city where no one would ever dream of interfering in a scuffle on the street lest they find themselves shanked. He'd let the rage wash over him, let the sweet taint of revenge ignite in his veins. He'd expected to feel triumph and satisfaction after all these years and all he'd done to make himself strong enough to take this man down—but what he hadn't reckoned with was that the drunken old man wouldn't recognize him.

Demetrius hadn't known who he was.

And that meant that Achilles had been out there in the

street, ready to beat down a defenseless old drunk who smelled of watered-down whiskey and a wasted life.

He hadn't done it. It wasn't worth it. He might have happily taken down the violent, abusive behemoth who'd terrorized him at seven, but he'd been too big himself at seventeen to find any honor in felling someone so vastly inferior to him in every way.

Especially since Demetrius hadn't the slightest idea who he'd been.

And Achilles had vowed to himself then and there that the night he stood in the street in his old neighborhood, afraid of nothing save the darkness inside him, would be the absolutely last time he let feelings rule him.

Because he had wasted years. Years that could have been spent far more wisely than planning out the extermination of an old, broken man who didn't deserve to have Achilles as an enemy. He'd walked away from Demetrius and his own squalid past and he'd never gone back.

His philosophy had served him well since. It had led him across the years, always cold and forever calculating his next, best move. Achilles was never swayed by emotion any longer, for good or ill. He never allowed it any power over him whatsoever. It had made him great, he'd often thought. It had made him who he was.

And yet Princess Valentina had somehow reached deep inside him, deep into a place that should have been black and cold and nothing but ice, and lit him on fire all over again.

"Are you brooding?" a soft voice asked from behind him, scratchy with sleep. Or with not enough sleep. "I knew I would do something wrong."

But she didn't sound insecure. Not in the least. She sounded warm, well sated. She sounded like his. She sounded like exactly who she was: the only daughter of one of Europe's last remaining powerhouse kings and the only woman Achilles had ever met who could turn him inside out.

And maybe that was what did it. The suddenly unbearable fact that she was still lying to him. He had this burning thing eating him alive from the inside out, he was cracking apart at the foundations, and she was still lying to him.

She was in his bed, teasing him in that way of hers that no one else would ever dare, and yet she lied to him. Every moment was a lie, even and especially this one. Every single moment she didn't tell him the truth about who she was and what she was doing here was more than a lie. More than a simple deception.

He was beginning to feel it as a betrayal.

"I do not brood," he said, and he could hear the gruffness in his own voice.

He heard her shift on the bed, and then he heard the sound of her feet against his floor. And he should have turned before she reached him, he knew that. He should have faced her and kept her away from him, especially when it was so dark outside and there was still so much left of the night—and he had clearly let it get to him.

But he didn't.

And in a moment she was at his back, and then she was sliding her arms around his waist with a familiarity that suggested she'd done it a thousand times before and knew how perfectly she would fit there. Then she pressed her face against the hollow of his spine.

And for a long moment she simply stood there like that, and Achilles felt his heart careen and clatter at his ribs. He was surprised that she couldn't hear it—hell, he was surprised that the whole of Manhattan wasn't alerted.

But all she did was stand there with her mouth pressed against his skin, as if she was holding him up, and through him the whole of the world.

Achilles knew that there was any number of ways to deal with this situation immediately. Effectively. No matter what name she called herself. He could call her out. He could ignore it altogether and simply send her away. He could let the darkness in him edge over into cruelty, so she would be the one to walk away.

But the simple truth was that he didn't want to do any of them.

"I have some land," he told her instead, and he couldn't tell if he was appalled at himself or simply surprised. "Out in the West, where there's nothing to see for acres and acres in all directions except the sky."

"That sounds beautiful," she murmured.

And every syllable was an exquisite pain, because he could feel her shape her words. He could feel her mouth as she spoke, right there against the flesh of his back. And he could have understood if it was a sexual thing. If that was what raged in him then. If it took him over and made him want to do nothing more than throw her down and claim her all over again. Sex, he understood. Sex, he could handle.

But it was much worse than that.

Because it didn't feel like fire, it felt…sweet. The kind of sweetness that wrapped around him, crawling into every nook and cranny inside him he'd long ago thought he'd turned to ice. And then stayed there, blooming into something like heat, as if she could melt him that easily.

He was more than a little worried that she could.

That she already had.

"Sometimes a man wants to be able to walk for miles in any direction and see no one," he heard himself say out loud, as if his mouth was no longer connected to the rest of him. "Not even himself."

"Or perhaps especially not himself," she said softly, her mouth against his skin having the same result as before.

Then he could feel her breathe, there behind him. There was a surprising amount of strength in the arms she still wrapped tight around his midsection. Her scent seemed to fill his head, a hint of lavender and something far softer that he knew was hers alone.

And the truth was that he wasn't done. He had never been a casual man in the modern sense, preferring mistresses who understood his needs and could cater to them over longer periods of time to one-night stands and such flashes in the pan that brought him nothing but momentary satisfaction.

He had never been casual, but this… This was nothing but trouble.

He needed to send her away. He had to fire Natalie, make sure that Valentina left, and leave no possible opening for either one of them to ever come back. This needed to be over before it really started. Before he forgot that he was who he was for a very good reason.

Demetrius had been a drunk. He'd cried and apologized when he was sober, however rarely that occurred. But Achilles was the monster. He'd gone to that bar to kill his stepfather, and he'd planned the whole thing out in every detail, coldly and dispassionately. He still didn't regret what he'd intended to do that night—but he knew perfectly well what that made him. And it was not a good man.

And that was all well and good as long as he kept the monster in him on ice, where it belonged. As long as he locked himself away, set apart.

It had never been an issue before.

He needed to get Valentina away from him, before he forgot himself completely.

"Pack your things," he told her shortly.

He shifted so he could look down at her again, drawing her around to his front and taking in the kick of those wide green eyes and that mouth he had sampled again and again and again.

And he couldn't do it.

He wanted her to know him, and even though that was the most treacherous thing of all, once it was in his head he couldn't seem to let it go. He wanted her to know him, and that meant he needed her to trust him enough to tell who she was. And that would never happen if he sent her away right now the way he should have.

And he was so used to thinking of himself as a monster. Some part of him—a large part of him—took a kind of pride in that, if he was honest. He'd worked so hard on making that monster into an impenetrable wall of wealth and judgment, taste and power.

But it turned out that all it took was a deceitful princess to make him into a man.

"I'm taking you to Montana," he told her gruffly, because he couldn't seem to stop himself.

And doomed them both.

CHAPTER EIGHT

ONE WEEK PASSED, and then another, and the six weeks Valentina had agreed to take stretched out into seven, out on Achilles's Montana ranch where the only thing on the horizon was the hint of the nearest mountain range.

His ranch was like a daydream, Valentina thought. Achilles was a rancher only in a distant sense, having hired qualified people to take care of the daily running of the place and turn its profit. Those things took place far away on some or other of his thousands of acres tucked up at the feet of the Rocky Mountains. They stayed in the sprawling ranch house, a sprawling nod toward log cabins and rustic ski lodges, the better to overlook the unspoiled land in all directions.

It was far away from everything and felt even farther than that. It was an hour drive to the nearest town, stout and quintessentially Western, as matter-of-fact as it was practical. They'd come at the height of Montana's short summer, hot during the day and cool at night, with endless blue skies stretching on up toward forever and nothing to do but soak in the quiet. The stunning silence, broken only by the wind. The sun. The exuberant moon and all those improbable, impossible stars, so many they cluttered up the sky and made it feel as if, were she to take a big enough step, Valentina could toss herself straight off the planet and into eternity.

And Valentina knew she was running out of time. Her wedding was the following week, she wasn't who she was pretending she was, and these stolen days in this faraway place of blue and gold were her last with this man. This stolen life had only ever been hers on loan.

But she would have to face that soon enough.

In Montana, as in New York, her days were filled with Achilles. He was too precise and demanding to abandon his businesses entirely, but there was something about the ranch that rendered him less overbearing. He and Valentina would put out what fires there might be in the mornings, but then, barring catastrophe, he let his employees earn their salaries the rest of the day.

While he and Valentina explored what this dreamy ranch life, so far removed from everything, had to offer. He had a huge library that she imagined would be particularly inviting in winter—not, she was forced to remind herself, that she would ever see it in a different season. A guest could sink into one of the deep leather chairs in front of the huge fireplace and read away a snowy evening or two up here in the mountains. He had an indoor pool that let the sky in through its glass ceiling, perfect for swimming in all kinds of weather. There was the hot tub, propped up on its own terrace with a sweeping view, which cried out for those cool evenings. It was a short drive or a long, pretty walk to the lake a little ways up into the mountains, so crisp and clear and cold it almost hurt.

But it was the kind of hurt that made her want more and more, no matter how it made her gasp and think she might lose herself forever in the cut of it.

Achilles was the same. Only worse.

Valentina had always thought of sex—or her virginity, anyway—as a single, solitary thing. Someday she would have sex, she'd always told herself. Someday she would get rid of her virginity. She had never really imagined that it wasn't a single, finite event.

She'd thought virginity, and therefore sex, was the actual breaching of what she still sometimes thought of as her maidenhead, as if she was an eighteenth-century heroine—and nothing more. She'd never really imagined much beyond that.

Achilles taught her otherwise.

Sex with him was threaded into life, a rich undercurrent that became as much a part of it as walking, breathing, eating. It wasn't a specific act. It was everything.

It was the touch of his hand across the dinner table, when he simply threaded their fingers together, the memory of what they'd already done together and the promise of more braided there between them. It was a sudden hot, dark look in the middle of a conversation about something innocuous or work-related, reminding her that she knew him now in so many different dimensions. It was the way his laughter seemed to rearrange her, pouring through her and making her new, every time she heard it.

It was when she stopped counting each new time he wrenched her to pieces as a separate, astonishing event. When she began to accept that he would always do that. Time passed and days rolled on, and all of these things that swirled between them only deepened. He became only more able to wreck her more easily the better he got to know her. And the better she got to know him.

As if their bodies were like the stars above them, infinite and adaptable, a great mess of joy and wonder that time only intensified.

But she knew it was running out.

And the more Achilles called her Natalie—which she thought he did more here, or perhaps she was far more sensitive to it now that she shared his bed—the more her terrible deception seemed to form into a heavy ball in the pit of her stomach, like some kind of cancerous thing that she very much thought might consume her whole.

Some part of her wished it would.

Meanwhile, the real Natalie kept calling her. Again and again, or leaving texts, but Valentina couldn't bring herself to respond to them. What would she say? How could she possibly explain what she'd done?

Much less the fact that she was still doing it and, worse, that she didn't want it to end no matter how quickly her royal wedding was approaching.

Even if she imagined that Natalie was off in Murin doing exactly the same thing with Rodolfo that Valentina was doing here, with all this wild and impossible hunger, what did that matter? They could still switch back, none the wiser. Nothing would change for Valentina. She would go on to marry the prince as she had always been meant to do, and it was highly likely that even Rodolfo himself wouldn't notice the change.

But Natalie had not been sleeping with Achilles before she'd switched places with Valentina. That meant there was no possible way that she could easily step back into the life that Valentina had gone ahead and ruined.

And was still ruining, day by day.

Still, no matter how self-righteously she railed at herself for that, she knew it wasn't what was really bothering her. It wasn't what would happen to Natalie that ate her up inside.

It was what would happen to her. And what could happen with Achilles. She found that she was markedly less sanguine about Achilles failing to notice the difference between Valentina and Natalie when they switched back again. In fact, the very notion made her feel sick.

But how could she tell him the truth? If she couldn't tell Natalie what she'd done, how could she possibly tell the man whom she'd been lying to directly all this time?

He thought he was having an affair with his assistant. A woman he had vetted and worked closely with for half a decade.

What was she supposed to say, *Oh, by the way, I'm actually a princess?*

The truth was that she was still a coward. Because she didn't know if what was really holding her back was that she couldn't imagine what she would say—or if she could imagine all too well what Achilles would do. And she knew that made her the worst sort of person. Because when she worried about what he would do, she was worried about herself. Not about how she might hurt him. Not about what it would do to him to learn that she had lied to him all this time. But the fact that it was entirely likely that she would tell him, and that would be the last she'd see of him. Ever.

And Valentina couldn't quite bear for this to be over.

This was her vacation. Her holiday. Her escape—and how had it never occurred to her that if that was true, it meant she had to go back? She'd known that in a general sense, of course, but she hadn't really thought it through. She certainly hadn't thought about what it would feel like to leave Achilles and then walk back to the stifling life she'd called her own for all these years.

It was one thing to be trapped. Particularly when it was all she'd ever known. But it was something else again to see exactly how trapped she was, to leave it behind for a while, and then knowingly walk straight back into that trap, closing the cage door behind her.

Forever.

Sometimes when she lay awake at night listening to Achilles breathe in the great bed next to her, his arms thrown over her as if they were slowly becoming one person, she couldn't imagine how she was ever going to make herself do it.

But time didn't care if she felt trapped. Or torn. It marched on whether she wanted it to or not.

"Are you brooding?" a low male voice asked from behind her, jolting her out of her unpleasant thoughts. "I thought that was my job, not yours."

Valentina turned from the rail of the balcony that ambled along the side of the master suite, where she was taking in the view and wondering how she could ever fold herself up tight and slot herself back into the life she'd left behind in Murin.

But the view behind her was even better. Achilles lounged against the open sliding glass door, naked save for a towel wrapped around his hips. He had taken her in a fury earlier, pounding into her from behind until she screamed out his name into the pillows, and he'd roared his own pleasure into the crook of her neck. Then he'd left her there on the bed, limp and still humming with all that passion, while he'd gone out for one of his long, brutal runs he always claimed cleared his head.

It had been weeks now, and he still took her breath. Now that she knew every inch of him, she found herself more in awe of him. All that sculpted perfection of his chest, the dark hair that narrowed at his lean hips, dipping down below the towel where she knew the boldest part of him waited.

She'd tasted him there, too. She'd knelt before the fireplace in that gorgeous library, her hands on his thighs as he'd sat back in one of those great leather chairs. He'd played with her hair, sifting strands of it through his fingers as she'd reached into the battered jeans he wore here on the ranch and had pulled him free.

He'd tasted of salt and man, and he'd let her play with him as she liked. He let her lick him everywhere until she learned his shape. He let her suck him in, then figure out how to make him as wild as he did when he tasted her in this same way. And she'd taken it as a personal triumph when he'd started to grip the chair. And when he'd lost himself inside her mouth, he'd groaned out that name he called her. *Glikia mou.*

Even thinking about it now made that same sweet, hot restlessness move through her all over again.

But time was her enemy. She knew that. And looking at him as he stood there in the doorway and watched her with that dark gold gaze that she could feel in every part of her, still convinced that he could see into parts of her she didn't know how to name, Valentina still didn't know what to do.

If she told him who she was, she would lose what few days with him she had left. This was Achilles Casilieris. He would never forgive her deception. Never. Her other option was never to tell him at all. She would go back to London with him in a few days as planned, slip away the way she'd always intended to do if a week or so later than agreed, and let the real Natalie pick up the pieces.

And that way, she could remember this the way she wanted to do. She could remember loving him, not losing him.

Because that was what she'd done. She understood that in the same way she finally comprehended intimacy. She'd gone and fallen in love with this man who didn't know her real name. This man she could never, ever keep.

Was it so wrong that if she couldn't keep him, she wanted to keep these sun-soaked memories intact?

"You certainly look like you're brooding." There was that lazy note to his voice that never failed to make her blood heat. It was no different now. It was that quick. It was that inevitable. "How can that be? There's nothing here but silence and sunshine. No call to brood about anything. Unless of course, it is your soul that is heavy." And she could have sworn there was something in his gaze then that dared her to come clean. Right then and there. As if, as ever, he knew what she was thinking. "Tell me, Natalie, what is it that haunts you?"

And it was moments like these that haunted her, but she couldn't tell him that. Moments like this, when she was certain that he knew. That he must know. That he was asking her to tell him the truth at last.

That he was calling her the wrong name deliberately, to see if that would goad her into coming clean.

But the mountains were too quiet and there was too much summer in the air. The Montana sky was a blue she'd never seen before, and that was what she felt in her soul. And if there was a heaviness, or a darkness, she had no doubt it would haunt her later.

Valentina wanted to live here. Now. With him. She wanted to *live*.

She had so little time left to truly *live*.

So once again, she didn't tell him. She smiled instead, wide enough to hide the fissures in her heart, and she went to him.

Because there was so little time left that she could do that. So few days left to reach out and touch him the way she did now, sliding her palms against the mouthwatering planes of his chest as if she was memorizing the heat of his skin.

As if she was memorizing everything.

"I don't know what you're talking about," she told him quietly, her attention on his skin beneath her hands. "I never do."

"I am not the mystery here," he replied, and though his voice was still so lazy, so very lazy, she didn't quite believe it. "There are enough mysteries to go around, I think."

"Solve this one, then," she dared him, going up on her toes to press her mouth to his.

Because she might not have truth and she might not have time, but she had this.

For a little while longer, she had this.

Montana was another mistake, because apparently, that was all he did now.

They spent weeks on his ranch, and Achilles made it all worse by the day. Every day he touched her, every day lost himself in her, every day he failed to get her to come clean with him. Every single day was another nail in his coffin.

And then, worse by far to his mind, it was time to leave.

Weeks in Montana, secluded from the rest of the world, and he'd gained nothing but a far deeper and more disastrous appreciation of Valentina's appeal. He hadn't exactly forced her to the light. He hadn't done anything but lose his own footing.

In all those weeks and all that sweet summer sunshine out in the American West, it had never occurred to him that she simply wouldn't tell him. He'd been so sure that he would get to her somehow. That if he had all these feelings churning around inside him, whatever was happening inside her must be far more extreme.

It had never occurred to him that he could lose that bet.

That Princess Valentina had him beat when it came to keeping herself locked up tight, no matter what.

They landed in London in a bleak drizzle that matched his mood precisely.

"You're expected at the bank in an hour," Valentina told him when they reached his Belgravia town house, standing there in his foyer looking as guileless and innocent as she ever had. Even now, when he had tasted every inch of her. Even now, when she was tearing him apart with that serene, untouchable look on her face. "And the board of directors is adamant—"

"I don't care about the bank," he muttered. "Or old men who think they can tell me what to do."

And just like that, he'd had enough.

He couldn't outright demand that Valentina tell him who she really was, because that wouldn't be her telling him of her own volition. It wouldn't be her trusting him.

It's almost as if she knows who you really are, that old familiar voice inside hissed at him. It had been years since he'd heard it, inside him or otherwise. But even though Demetrius had not been able to identify him on the streets when he'd had the chance, Achilles always knew the old man when he spoke. *Maybe she knows exactly what kind of monster you are.*

And a harsh truth slammed into him then, making him feel very nearly unsteady on his feet. He didn't know why it hadn't occurred to him before. Or maybe it had, but he'd shoved it aside out there in all that Montana sky and sunshine. Because he was Achilles Casilieris. He was one of the most sought-after bachelors in all the world. Legions of women chased after him daily, trying anything from trickery to bribery to outright lies about paternity claims to make him notice them. He was at the top of everyone's *most wanted* list.

But to Princess Valentina of Marin, he was nothing but a bit of rough.

She was slumming.

That was why she hadn't bothered to identify herself. She didn't see the point. He might as well have been the pool boy.

And he couldn't take it. He couldn't process it. There was nothing in him but fire and that raw, unquenchable need, and she was so cool. Too cool.

He needed to mess her up. He needed to do something to make all this…wildfire and feeling dissipate before it ate him alive and left nothing behind. Nothing at all.

"What are you doing?" she asked, and he took a little too much satisfaction in that appropriately uncertain note in her voice.

It was only when he saw her move that he realized he was stalking toward her, backing her up out of the gleaming foyer and into one of the town house's elegant sitting rooms. Not that the beauty of a room could do anything but fade next to Valentina.

The world did the same damned thing.

She didn't ask him a silly question like that again. And perhaps she didn't need to. He backed her up to the nearest settee, and took entirely too much pleasure in the pulse that beat out the truth of her need right there in her neck.

"Achilles…" she said hoarsely, but he wanted no more words. No more lies of omission.

No more *slumming.*

"Quiet," he ordered her.

He sank his hands into her gleaming copper hair, then dragged her mouth to his. Then he toppled her down to antique settee and followed her. She was slender and lithe and wild beneath him, rising to meet him with too much need, too much longing.

As if, in the end, this was the only place they were honest with each other.

And Achilles was furious. Furious, or something like it—something close enough that it burned in him as brightly. As lethally. He shoved her skirt up over her hips and she wrapped her legs around his waist, and she was panting already. She was gasping against his mouth. Or maybe he was breathing just as hard.

"Achilles," she said again, and there was something in her gaze then. Something darker than need.

But this was no time for sweetness. Or anything deeper. This was a claiming.

"Later," he told her, and then he took her mouth with

his, tasting the words he was certain, abruptly, he didn't want to hear.

He might be nothing to her but a walk on the wild side she would look back on while she rotted away in some palatial prison, but he would make sure that she remembered him.

He had every intention of leaving his mark.

Achilles tore off his trousers, freeing himself. Then he reached down and found the gusset of her panties, ripping them off and shoving the scraps aside to fit himself to her at last.

And then he stopped thinking about marks and memories, because she was molten hot and wet. She was his. He sank into her, groaning as she encased his length like a hot, tight glove.

It was so good. It was too good.

She always was.

He moved then, and she did, too, that slick, deep slide. And they knew each other so well now. Their bodies were too attuned to each other, too hot and too certain of where this was going, and it was never, ever enough.

He reached between them and pressed his fingers in the place where she needed him most, and felt her explode into a frenzy beneath him. She raised her hips to meet each thrust. She dug her fingers into his shoulders as if she was already shaking apart.

He felt it build in her, and in him, too. Wild and mad, the way it always was.

As if they could tear apart the world this way. As if they already had.

"No one will ever make you feel the way that I do," he told her then, a dark muttering near her ear as she panted and writhed. "No one."

And he didn't know if that was some kind of endearment, or a dire warning.

But it didn't matter, because she was clenching around him then. She gasped out his name, while her body gripped him, then shook.

And he pumped himself into her, wanting nothing more than to roar her damned name. To claim her in every possible way. To show her—

But he did none of that.

And when it was over, when the storm had passed, he pulled himself away from her and climbed to his feet again. And he felt something sharp and heavy move through him as he looked down at her, still lying there half on and half off the antique settee they'd moved a few feet across the floor, because he had done exactly as he set out to do.

He'd messed her up. She looked disheveled and shaky and absolutely, delightfully ravished.

But all he could think was that he still didn't have her. That she was still going to leave him when she was done here. That she'd never had any intention of staying in the first place. It ripped at him. It made him feel something like crazy.

The last time he'd ever felt anything like it, he'd been an angry seventeen-year-old in a foul-smelling street with an old drunk who didn't know who he was. It was a kind of anguish.

It was a grief, and he refused to indulge it. He refused to admit it was ravaging him, even as he pulled his clothes back where they belonged.

And then she made it even worse. She smiled.

She sat up slowly, pushing her skirt back into place and tucking the torn shreds of her panties into one pocket. Then she gazed up at him.

Achilles was caught by that look in her soft green eyes, as surely as if she'd reached out and wrapped her delicate hands around his throat. On some level, he felt as if she had.

"I love you," she said.

They were such small words, he thought through that thing that pounded in him like fear. Like a gong. Such small, silly words that could tear a man down without any warning at all.

And there were too many things he wanted to say then. For example, how could she tell him that she loved him when she wouldn't even tell him her name?

But he shoved that aside.

"That was sex, *glikia mou*," he grated at her. "Love is something different from a whole lot of thrashing around, half-clothed."

He expected her to flinch at that, but he should have known better. This was his princess. If she was cowed at all, she didn't show it.

Instead, she only smiled wider.

"You're the expert on love as in all things, of course," she murmured, because even here, even now, she was the only person alive who had ever dared to tease him. "My mistake."

She was still smiling when she stood up, then walked around him. As if she didn't notice that he was frozen there in some kind of astonishment. Or as if she was happy enough to leave him to it as she headed toward the foyer and, presumably, the work he'd always adored that seemed to loom over him these days, demanding more time than he wanted to give.

He'd never had a life that interested him more than his empire, until Valentina.

And he didn't have Valentina.

She'd left Achilles standing there with her declaration heavy in his ears. She'd left him half fire and a heart that long ago should have turned to ice. He'd been so certain it had when he was seven and had lost everything, including his sense of himself as anything like good.

He should have known then.

But it wasn't until much later that day—after he'd quizzed his security detail and household staff to discover she'd walked out with nothing but her shoulder bag and disappeared into the gray of the London afternoon—that he'd realized that had been the way his deceitful princess said goodbye.

CHAPTER NINE

VALENTINA COULDN'T KEEP her mind on her duties now that she was back in Murin. She couldn't keep her mind focused at all, come to that. Not on her duties, not on the goings-on of the palace, not on any of the many changes that had occurred since she'd come back home.

She should have been jubilant. Or some facsimile thereof, surely. She had walked back into her well-known, well-worn trap, expecting the same old cage, only to find that the trap wasn't at all what she had imagined it was—and the cage door had been tossed wide open.

When she'd left London that day, her body had still been shivering from Achilles's touch. She hadn't wanted to go. Not with her heart too full and a little bit broken at her own temerity in telling him how she felt when she'd known she had to leave. But it was time for her to go home, and there had been no getting around that. Her wedding to Prince Rodolfo was imminent. As in, the glittering heads of Europe's ancient houses were assembling to cheer on one of their own, and she needed to be there.

The phone calls and texts that she'd been ignoring that whole time, leaving Natalie to deal with it all on her own, had grown frantic. And she couldn't blame her sister, because the wedding was a mere day away. *Your twin sister,* she'd thought, those terms still feeling too unwieldy. She'd made her way to Heathrow Airport and bought herself a ticket on a commercial plane—the first time she'd ever done anything of the sort. One more normal thing to tuck away and remember later.

"Later" meaning after tomorrow, when she would be wed to a man she hardly knew.

It had taken Valentina a bit too long to do the right thing. To do the only possible thing and tear herself away from Achilles the way she should have done a long time ago. She should never have gone with him to Montana. She should certainly never have allowed them to stay there all that time, living out a daydream that could end only one way.

She'd known that going in, and she'd done it anyway. What did that make her, exactly?

Now I am awake, she thought as she boarded the plane. *Now I am awake and that will have to be as good as* alive, *because it's all I have left.*

She hadn't known what to expect from a regular flight into the commercial airport on the island of Murin. Some part of her imagined that she would be recognized. Her face was on the cover of the Murin Air magazines in every seat back, after all. She'd had a bit of a start when she'd sat down in the remarkably uncomfortable seat, pressed up against a snoring matron on one side and a very gray-faced businessman on the other.

But no one had noticed her shocking resemblance to the princess in the picture. No one had really looked at her at all. She flashed Natalie's passport, walked on the plane without any issues and walked off again in Murin without anyone looking at her twice—even though she was quite literally the spitting image of the princess so many were flocking to Murin to see marry her Prince Charming at last.

Once at the palace, she didn't bother trying to sneak

in because she knew she'd be discovered instantly—and that would hardly allow Natalie to switch back and escape, would it? So instead she'd walked up to the guard station around the back at the private family entrance, gazed politely at the guard who waited there and waited.

"But the…the princess is within," the guard had stammered. Maybe he was thrown by the fact Valentina was dressed like any other woman her age on the street. Maybe he was taken back because he'd never spoken to her directly before.

Or maybe it was because, if she was standing here in front of him, she wasn't where the royal guard thought she was. Which he'd likely assumed meant she'd sneaked out, undetected.

All things considered, she was happy to let that mystery stand.

Valentina had aimed a conspiratorial smile at the guard. "The princess can't possibly be within, given that I'm standing right here. But it can be our little secret that there was some confusion, if you like."

And then, feeling heavier than she ever had before and scarred somehow by what she'd gone through with Achilles, she'd walked back in the life she'd left so spontaneously and much too quickly in that London airport.

She'd expected to find Natalie as desperate to leave as she supposed, in retrospect, she had been. Or why else would she have suggested this switch in the first place?

But instead, she'd found a woman very much in love. With Crown Prince Rodolfo of Tissely. The man whom Valentina was supposed to marry the following day.

More than that, Natalie was pregnant.

"I don't know how it happened," Natalie had said, after Valentina had slipped into her bedroom and woken her up—by sitting on the end of the bed and pulling at Natalie's foot until she'd opened her eyes and found her double sitting there.

"Don't you?" Valentina had asked. "I was a virgin, but I had the distinct impression that you had not saved yourself for marriage all these years. Because why would you?"

Natalie had flushed a bit, but then her eyes had narrowed. "*Was* a virgin? Is that the past tense?" She'd blinked. "Not Mr. Casilieris."

But it wasn't the time then for sisterly confessions. Mostly because Valentina hadn't the slightest idea what she could say about Achilles that wasn't…too much. Too much and too unformed and unbearable, somehow, now that it was over. Now that none of it mattered, and never could.

"I don't think that you have a job with him anymore," Valentina had said instead, keeping her voice even. "Because I don't think you want a job with him anymore. You said you were late, didn't you? You're having a prince's baby."

And when Natalie had demurred, claiming that she didn't know one way or the other and it was likely just the stress of inhabiting someone else's life, Valentina had sprung into action.

She'd made it her business to find out, one way or another. She'd assured Natalie that it was simply to put her mind at ease. But the truth was a little more complicated, she admitted to herself as she made her way through the palace.

The fact was, she was relieved. That was what had washed through her when Natalie had confessed not only her love for Rodolfo, but her suspicions that she might be carrying his child. She'd pushed it off as she'd convinced one of her most loyal maids to run out into the city and buy her a few pregnancy tests, just to be certain. She'd shoved it to the side as she'd smuggled the tests back into her rooms, and then had handed them over to Natalie so she could find out for certain.

But there was no denying it. When Natalie had emerged from the bathroom with a dazed look on her face and a positive test in one hand, Valentina finally admitted the sheer relief that coursed through her veins. It was like champagne. Fizzy and a little bit sharp, washing through her and making her feel almost silly in response.

Because if Natalie was having Rodolfo's baby, there was no possible way that Valentina could marry him. The choice—though it had always been more of an expected duty than a choice—was taken out of her hands.

"You will marry him," Valentina had said quietly. "It is what must happen."

Natalie had looked pale. "But you… And I'm not… And you don't understand, he…"

"All of that will work out," Valentina had said with a deep certainty she very badly wanted to feel. Because it had to work out. "The important thing is that you will marry him in the morning. You will have his baby and you will be his queen when he ascends the throne. Everything else is spin and scandal, and none of that matters. Not really."

And so it was.

Once King Geoffrey had been brought into the loop and had been faced with the irrefutable evidence that his daughter had been stolen from him all those years ago—that Erica had taken Natalie and, not only that, had told Geoffrey that Valentina's twin had died at birth—he was more than on board with switching the brides at the wedding.

He'd announced to the gathered crowd that a most blessed miracle had occurred some months before. A daughter long thought dead had returned to him to take her rightful place in the kingdom, and they'd all kept it a secret to preserve everyone's privacy as they'd gotten to know each other.

Including Rodolfo, who had always been meant to be part of the family, the king had reminded the assembled crowd and the whole of the world, no matter how. And feelings had developed between Natalie and Rodolfo, where there had only ever been duty and honor between Valentina and her intended.

Valentina had seen this and stepped aside of her own volition, King Geoffrey had told the world. There had been no scandal, no sneaking around, no betrayals. Only one sister looking out for another.

The crowds ate it up. The world followed suit. It was just scandalous enough to be both believable and newsworthy. Valentina was branded as something of a Miss Lonely Hearts, it was true, but that was neither here nor there. The idea that she would sacrifice her fairy-tale wedding—and her very own Prince Charming—for her long-lost sister captured the public's imagination. She was more popular than ever, especially at home in Murin.

And this was a good thing, because now that her father had two heirs, he could marry one of his daughters off to fulfill his promises to the kingdom of Tissely, and he could prepare the other to take over Murin and keep its throne in the family.

And just like that, Valentina went from a lifetime preparing to be a princess who would marry well and support the king of a different country, to a new world in which she was meant to rule as queen in her own right.

If it was another trap, another cage, it was a far more spacious and comfortable one than any she had known before.

She knew that. There was no reason at all she should have been so unhappy.

"Your attention continues to drift, daughter," King Geoffrey said then.

Valentina snapped herself out of those thoughts in her head that did her no good and into the car where she sat with her father, en route to some or other glittering gala down at the water palace on the harbor. She couldn't even remember which charity it was this week. There was always another.

The motorcade wound down from the castle, winding its way along the hills of the beautiful capital city toward the gleaming Mediterranean Sea. Valentina normally enjoyed the view. It was pretty, first and foremost. It was home. It reminded her of so many things, of her honor and her duty and her love of her country. It renewed her commitment to her kingdom, and made her think about all the good she hoped she could do as its sovereign.

And yet these days, she wasn't thinking about Murin. All she could seem to think about was Achilles.

"I am preparing myself for the evening ahead," Valentina replied calmly enough. She aimed a perfectly composed smile at her father. "I live in fear of greeting a diplomat with the wrong name and causing an international incident."

Her father's gaze warmed, something that happened more often lately than it ever had before. Valentina chalked that up to the rediscovery of Natalie and, with it, some sense of family that had been missing before. Or too caught up in the past, perhaps.

"I have never seen you forget a name in all your life," Geoffrey said. "It's one among many reasons I expect you will make a far better queen than I have been a king. And I am aware I gave you no other choice, but I cannot regret that your education and talents will be Murin's gain, not Tissely's."

"I will confess," Valentina said then, "that stepping

aside so that Natalie could marry Rodolfo is not quite the sacrifice some have made it out to be."

Her father's gaze then was so canny that it reminded her that whatever else he was, King Geoffrey of Marin was a force to be reckoned with.

"I suspected not," he said quietly. "But there is no reason not to let them think so. It only makes you more sympathetic."

His attention was caught by something on his phone then. And as he frowned down at it, Valentina looked away. Back out the window to watch the sun drip down over the red-tipped rooftops that sloped all the way to the crystal blue waters below.

She let her hand move, slowly so that her father wouldn't notice, and held it over that faint roundness low in her belly she'd started to notice only a few weeks ago.

If her father thought she was a sympathetic figure now, she thought darkly, he would be delighted when she announced to him and the rest of the world that she was going to be a mother.

A single mother. A princess destined for his throne, with child.

Her thoughts went around and around, keeping her up at night and distracting her by day. And there were never any answers or, rather, there were never any good answers. There were never any answers she liked. Shame and scandal were sure to follow anything she did, or didn't do for that matter. There was no possible way out.

And even if she somehow summoned the courage to tell her father, then tell the kingdom, and then, far more intimidating, tell Achilles—what did she think might happen then? As a princess with no path to the throne, she had been expected to marry the Crown Prince of Tissely. As the queen of Murin, by contrast, she would be expected to marry someone of equally impeccable lineage. There were only so many such men alive, Valentina had met all of them, and none of them were Achilles.

No one was Achilles. And that shouldn't have mattered to her. There were so many other things she needed to worry about, like this baby she was going to be able to hide for only so long.

But he was the only thing she could seem to think about, even so.

The gala was as expected. These things never varied much, which was both their charm and their curse. There was an endless receiving line. There were music and speeches, and extremely well-dressed people milling about complimenting each other on the same old things. A self-congratulatory trill of laughter here, a fake smile there, and so it went. Dignitaries and socialites rubbing shoulders and making money for this or that cause the way they always did.

Valentina danced with her father, as tradition dictated. She was pleased to see Rodolfo and Natalie, freshly back from their honeymoon and exuding exactly the sort of happy charm that made everyone root for them, Valentina included.

Valentina especially, she thought.

She excused herself from the crush as soon as she could, making her way out onto one of the great balconies in this water palace that took its cues from far-off Venice and overlooked the sea. Valentina stood there for a long while, helplessly reliving all the things she'd been so sure she could lock away once she came back home. Over and over—

And she thought that her memory had gotten particularly sharp—and cruel. Because when she heard a foot against the stones behind her and turned, her smile already in place the way it always was, she saw him.

But it couldn't be him, of course. She assumed it was

her hormones mixing with her memory and making her conjure him up out of the night air.

"Princess Valentina," Achilles said, and his voice was low, a banked fury simmering there in every syllable. "I do not believe we have been introduced properly. You are apparently of royal blood you sought to conceal and I am the man you thought you could fool. How pleasant to finally make your acquaintance."

It occurred to her that she wasn't fantasizing at the same moment it really hit her that he was standing before her. Her heart punched at her. Her stomach sank.

And in the place she was molten for him, instantly, she ached. Oh, how she ached.

"Achilles…"

But her throat was so dry. It was in marked contrast to all that emotion that flooded her eyes at the sight of him that she couldn't seem to control.

"Are those tears, Princess?" And he laughed then. It was a dark, angry sort of sound. It was not the kind of laughter that made the world shimmer and change. And still, it was the best sound Valentina had heard in weeks. "Surely those are not tears. I cannot think of a single thing you have to cry about, Valentina. Not one. Whereas I have a number of complaints."

"Complaints?"

All she could seem to do was echo him. That and gaze at him as if she was hungry, and the truth was that she was. She couldn't believe he was here. She didn't care that he was scowling at her—her heart was kicking at her, and she thought she'd never seen anything more beautiful than Achilles Casilieris in a temper, right here in Murin.

"We can start with the fact that you lied to me about who you are," he told her. "There are numerous things to cover after that, culminating in your extremely bad decision to walk out. *Walk out*." He repeated it with three times the fury. "On *me*."

"Achilles." She swallowed, hard. "I don't think—"

"Let me be clear," he bit out, his dark gold gaze blazing as he interrupted her. "I am not here to beg or plead. I am Achilles Casilieris, a fact you seem to have forgotten. I do not beg. I do not plead. But I feel certain, princess, that you will do both."

He had waited weeks.

Weeks.

Having never been walked out on before—ever— Achilles had first assumed that she would return. Were not virgins forever making emotional connections with the men who divested them of their innocence? That was the reason men of great experience generally avoided virgins whenever possible. Or so he thought, at any rate. The truth was that he could hardly remember anything before Valentina.

Still, he waited. When the royal wedding happened the day after she'd left, and King Geoffrey made his announcement about his lost daughter—who, he'd realized, was his actual assistant and also, it turned out, a royal princess—Achilles had been certain it was only a matter of time before Valentina returned to London.

But she never came.

And he did not know when it had dawned on him that this was something he was going to have to do himself. The very idea enraged him, of course. That she had walked out on him at all was unthinkable. But what he couldn't seem to get his head around was the fact that she didn't seem to have seen the error of her ways, no matter how much time he gave her to open her damned eyes.

She was too beautiful and it was worse now, he thought

darkly, here in her kingdom, where she was no longer pretending anything.

Tonight she was dressed like the queen she would become one day, all of that copper hair piled high on the top of her head, jewels flashing here and there. Instead of the pencil skirts he'd grown accustomed to, she wore a deep blue gown that clung to her body in a way that was both decorous and alluring at once. And if he was not mistaken, made her curves seem more voluptuous than he recalled.

She was much too beautiful for Achilles's peace of mind, and worse, she did not break down and begin the begging or the pleading, as he would have preferred. He could see that her eyes were damp, though the tears that had threatened seemed to have receded. She smoothed her hand over her belly, as if the dress had wrinkles when it was very clear that it did not, and when she looked up from that wholly unnecessary task her green eyes were as guarded as her smile was serene.

As if he was a stranger. As if he had never been so deep inside her she'd told him she couldn't breathe.

"What are you doing here?" she asked.

"That is the wrong question."

She didn't so much as blink, and that smile only deepened. "I had no idea that obscure European charities were of such interest to men of your stature, and I am certain it was not on your schedule."

"Are you questioning how I managed to score an invite?" he asked, making no particular move to keep the arrogant astonishment from his voice. "Perhaps I must introduce myself again. There is no guest list that is not improved by my presence, princess. Even yours."

Her gaze became no less guarded. Her expression did not change. But still, Achilles thought something in her steeled. And her shoulders straightened almost imperceptibly.

"I must apologize to you," she said, very distinctly.

And this was what Achilles had wanted. It was why he'd come here. He had imagined it playing out almost exactly this way.

Except there was something in her tone that rubbed him the wrong way, now that it was happening. It was that guarded look in her eyes perhaps. It was the fact that she didn't close the distance between them, but stayed where she was, one hand on the balcony railing and the other at her side. As distant as if she was on some magazine cover somewhere instead of standing there in front of him.

He didn't like this at all.

"You will have to be more specific, I am afraid," he said coolly. "I can think of a great many apologies you owe me."

Her mouth curved, though he would not call it a smile, precisely.

"I walked into a bathroom in an airport in London and saw a woman I had never met before, who could only be my twin. I could not resist switching places with her." Valentina glanced toward the open doors and the gala inside, as if it called to her more than he did, and Achilles hated that, too. Then she looked back at him, and her gaze seemed darker. "Do not mistake me. This is a good life. It is just that it's a very specific, very planned sort of life and it involves a great many spotlights. I wanted a normal one, for a change. Just for a little while. It never occurred to me that that decision could affect anyone but me. I would never have done it if I ever thought that you—"

But Achilles couldn't hear this. Because it sounded entirely too much like a postmortem. When he had traveled across Europe to find her because he couldn't bear the thought that it had already ended, or that he hadn't picked up on the fact that she was leaving him until she'd already gone.

"Do you need me to tell you that I love you, Valentina?" he demanded, his voice low and furious. "Is that what this is? Tell me what you need to hear. Tell me what it will take."

She jolted as if he'd slapped her. And he hated that, so he took the single step that closed the distance between them, and then there was no holding himself back. Not when she was so close again—at last—after all these weeks. He reached over and wrapped his hands around her shoulders, holding her there at arm's length, like some kind of test of his self-control. He thought that showed great restraint, when all he wanted was to haul her toward him and get his mouth on her.

"I don't need anything," she threw at him in a harsh sort of whisper. "And I'm sorry you had to find out who I was after I left. I couldn't figure out how to tell you while I was still with you. I didn't want to ruin—"

She shook her head, as if distressed.

Achilles laughed. "I knew from almost the first moment you stepped on the plane in London. Did you imagine I would truly believe you were Natalie for long? When you could not perform the most basic of tasks she did daily? I knew who you were within moments after the plane reached its cruising altitude."

Her green eyes went wide with shock. Her lips parted. Even her face paled.

"You knew?"

"You have never fooled me," he told her, his voice getting a little too low. A little too hot. "Except perhaps when you claimed you loved me, then left."

Her eyes overflowed then, sending tears spilling down her perfect, elegant cheeks. And he was such a bastard that some part of him rejoiced.

Because if she cried for him, she wasn't indifferent to him. She was certainly not immune to him.

It meant that it was possible he hadn't ruined this, after all, the way he did everything else. It meant it was possible this was salvageable.

He didn't like to think about what it might mean if it wasn't.

"Achilles," she said again, more distinctly this time. "I never saw you coming—it never occurred to me that I could ever be anything but honorable, because I had never been tempted by anything in my life. Only you. The only thing I lied to you about was my name. Everything else was true. Is true." She shook her head. "But it's hopeless."

"Nothing is hopeless," he growled at her. "I have no intention of losing you. I don't lose."

"I'm not talking about a loss," she whispered fiercely, and he could feel a tremor go through her. "This isn't a game. You are a man who is used to doing everything in his own way. You are not made for protocol and diplomacy and the tedious necessities of excruciating propriety. That's not who you are." Her chin tilted up slightly. "But I'm afraid it is exactly who I am."

"I'm not a good man, *glikia mou*," he told her then, not certain what was gripping him. He only knew he couldn't let her go. "But you know this. I have always known who I am. A monster in fine clothes, rubbing shoulders with the elites who would spit on me if they could. If they did not need my money and my power."

Achilles expected a reaction. He expected her to see him at last as she had failed to see him before. The scales would fall from her eyes, perhaps. She would recoil, certainly. He had always known that it would take so very little for people to see the truth about him, lurking right there beneath his skin. Not hidden away at all.

But Valentina did not seem to realize what had happened. She continued to look at him the way she always did. There wasn't the faintest flicker of anything like re-vulsion, or bleak recognition, in her gaze.

If anything, her gaze seemed warmer than before, for all it was wet. And that made him all the more determined to show her what she seemed too blind to see.

"You are not hearing me, Valentina. I'm not speaking in metaphors. Do you have any idea what I have done? The lives that I have ruined?"

She smiled at that, through her tears. "I know exactly who you are," she said, with a bedrock certainty that shook him. "I worked for you. You did not wine me or dine me. You did not take me on a fancy date or try to impress me in any way. You treated me like an assistant, an underling, and believe me, there is nothing more re-vealing. Are you impatient? Are you demanding and often harsh? Of course." She shrugged, as if this was all so ob-vious it was hardly worth talking about. "You are a very powerful man. But you are not a monster."

If she'd reached over and wrenched his mangled little heart from between his ribs with her elegant hands and then held it there in front of him, it could not possibly have floored him more.

"And you will not convince me otherwise," she added, as if she could see that he was about to say something. "There's something I have to tell you. And it's entirely possible that you are not going to like it at all."

Achilles blinked. "How ominous."

She blew out a breath. "You must understand that there are no good solutions. I've had no idea how to tell you this, but our... What happened between us had consequences."

"Do you think that I don't know that?" he belted out at her, and he didn't care who heard him. He didn't care if the whole of her pretty little kingdom poured out of the party behind them to watch and listen. "Do you think that I would be here if I was unaware of the consequences?"

"I'm not talking about feelings—"

"I am," he snapped. "I have not felt anything in years. I have not wanted to feel. And thanks to you all I do now is feel. Too damned much, Valentina." She hadn't actually ripped his heart out, he reminded himself. It only felt as if she had. He forced himself to loosen his grip on her before he hurt her. "And it doesn't go anywhere. Weeks pass, and if anything grows worse."

"Achilles, please," she whispered, and the tears were falling freely again. "I never wanted to hurt you."

"I wish you had hurt me," he told her, something dark and bitter, and yet neither of those things threaded through him. "Hurt things heal. This is far worse."

She sucked in a breath as if he'd punched her. He forged on, throwing all the doom and tumult inside him down between them.

"I have never loved anything in my life, Princess. I have wanted things and I've taken them, but love has always been for other men. Men who are not monsters by any definition. Men who have never ruined anything—not lives, not companies and certainly not perfect, virginal princesses who had no idea what they were signing up for." He shook his head. "But there is nothing either one of us can do about it now. I'm afraid the worst has already happened."

"The worst?" she echoed. "Then you know…?"

"I love you, *glikia mou*," he told her. "There can be no other explanation, and I feel sorry for you, I really do. Because I don't think there's any going back."

"Achilles…" she whispered, and that was not a look of transported joy on her face. It wasn't close. "I'm so sorry. Everything is different now. I'm pregnant."

CHAPTER TEN

ACHILLES WENT SILENT. Stunned, if Valentina had to guess.

If that frozen astonishment in his dark gold gaze was any guide.

"And I am to be queen," she told him, pointedly. His hands were still clenched on her shoulders, and what was wrong with her that she should love that so much? That she should love any touch of his. That it should make her feel so warm and safe and wild with desire. All at once. "My father thought that he would not have an heir of his own blood, because he thought he had only one daughter. But now he has two, and Natalie has married Rodolfo. That leaves me to take the throne."

"I'm not following you," Achilles said, his voice stark. Something like frozen. "I can think of no reason that you have told me in one breath that I am to be a father and in the next you feel you must fill me in on archaic lines of succession."

"There is very strict protocol," she told him, and her voice cracked. She slid her hands over her belly. "My father will never accept—"

"You keep forgetting who I am," Achilles growled, and she didn't know if he'd heard a word she'd said. "If you are having my child, Valentina, this conversation is over. We will be married. That's an end to it."

"It's not that simple."

"On the contrary, there is nothing simpler."

She needed him to understand. This could never be. They could never happen. She was trapped just as surely as she'd ever been. Why couldn't he see that? "I am no longer just a princess. I'm the Crown Princess of Murin—"

"Princess, princess." Achilles shook his head. "Tell me something. Did you mean it when you told me that you loved me? Or did you only dare to tell me in the first place because you knew you were leaving?"

That walloped Valentina. She thought that if he hadn't been holding on to her, she would have staggered and her knees might well have given out from beneath her.

"Don't be ridiculous." But her voice was barely a whisper.

"Here's the difference between you and me, princess. I have no idea what love is. All I know is that you came into my life and you altered something in me." He let go of her shoulder and moved his hand to cover his heart, and broke hers that easily. "Here. It's changed now, and I can't change it back. And I didn't tell you these things and then leave. I accepted these things, and then came to find you."

She felt blinded. Panicked. As if all she could do was cower inside her cage—and worse, as if that was what she wanted.

"You have no idea what you're talking about," she told him instead. "You might be a successful businessman, but you know nothing about the realities of a kingdom like Murin."

"I know you better than you think. I know how desperate you are for a normal life. Isn't that why you switched places with Natalie?" His dark gaze was almost kind.

"But don't you understand? Normal is the one thing you can never be, *glikia mou*."

"You have no idea what you're talking about," she said again, and this time her voice was even softer. Fainter.

"You will never be normal, Valentina," Achilles said quietly. His fingers tightened on her shoulder. "I am not so normal myself. But together, you and I? We will be extraordinary."

"You don't know how much I wish that could happen." She didn't bother to wipe at her tears. She let them fall. "This is a cage, Achilles. I'm trapped in it, but you're not. And you shouldn't be."

He let out a breath that was too much like a sigh, and Valentina felt it shudder through her, too. Like foreboding.

"You can live in fear, or you can live the life you want, Valentina," he told her. "You cannot do both."

His dark gaze bored into her, and then he dropped his other hand, so he was no longer touching her.

And then he made it worse and stepped back.

She felt her hands move, when she hadn't meant to move at all. Reaching out for him, whether she wanted to or not.

"If you don't want to be trapped, don't be trapped," Achilles said, as if it was simple. And with that edge in his voice that made her feel something a little more pointed than simply restless. "I don't know how to love, but I will learn. I have no idea how to be a father, but I will dedicate myself to being a good one. I never thought that I'd be a husband to anyone, but I will be the husband you need. You can sit on your throne. You can rule your kingdom as you wish. I have no need to be a king. But I will be one for you." He held out his hand. "All you have to do is be brave, princess. That's all. Just be a little brave."

"It's a cage, Achilles," she told him again, her voice ragged. "It's a beautiful, beautiful cage, this life. And there's no changing it. It's been the same for untold centuries."

"Love me," he said then, like a bomb to her heart. What was left of it. "I dare you."

And the music poured out from the party within. Inside, her father ruled the way he always did, and her brand-new sister danced with the man Valentina had always imagined she would marry. Natalie had come out of nowhere and taken her rightful place in the kingdom, and the world hadn't ended when brides had been switched at a royal wedding. If anything, life had vastly improved for everyone involved. Why wasn't that the message Valentina was concentrating on?

She realized that all this time, she'd been focused on what she couldn't do. Or what she had to do. She'd been consumed with duty, honor—but none of it her choice. All of it thrust upon her by an accident of birth. If Erica had taken Valentina instead of Natalie, she would have met Achilles some time ago. They wouldn't be standing here, on this graceful balcony, overlooking the soothing Mediterranean and her father's kingdom.

Her whole life seemed to tumble around before her, year after year cracking open before her like so many fragile eggs against the stones beneath her feet. All the things she never questioned. All the certainties she simply accepted, because what was the alternative? She'd prided herself on her serenity in the face of anything that had come her way. On her ability to do what was asked of her, always. What was expected of her, no matter how unfair.

And she'd never really asked herself what she wanted to do with her life. Because it had never been a factor. Her life had been meticulously planned from the start.

But now Achilles stood before her, and she carried their baby inside her. And she knew that as much as she wanted to deny it, what he said was true. She was a coward. She'd used her duty to hide behind. She could have stayed in London, could have called off her wedding. But she hadn't.

And had she really imagined she could walk down that aisle to Rodolfo, having just left Achilles in London? Had she really intended to do that?

It was unimaginable. And yet she knew she'd meant to do exactly that.

She'd been saved from that vast mistake, and yet here she was, standing in front of the man she loved, coming up with new reasons why she couldn't have the one thing in her life she ever truly wanted.

All this time she'd been convinced that her life was the cage. That her royal blood trapped her.

But the truth was, she was the one who did that.

She was her own cage, and she always would be if she didn't do something to stop it right now. If she didn't throw open the door, step through the opening and allow herself to reach out for the man she already knew she loved.

Be brave, he'd told her, as if he knew she could do it. As if he had no doubt at all.

"I love you," she whispered helplessly. Lost somewhere in that gaze of his, and the simple fact that he was here. Right here in front of her, his hand stretched toward her, waiting for her with a patience she would have said Achilles Casilieris did not possess.

"Marry me, *glikia mou*. And you can love me forever." His mouth crept up in one corner, and all the scars Valentina had dug into her own heart when she'd left him seemed to glow a little bit. Then knit themselves into something more like art. "I'm told that's how it goes. But you know me. I always like to push the boundaries a little bit farther."

"Farther than forever?"

And she smiled at him then, not caring if she was still crying. Or laughing. Or whatever was happening inside her that was starting to take her over.

Maybe that was what it was to be brave. Doing whatever it was not because she felt it was right, but because it didn't matter what she felt. It was right, so she had to do it.

"Three forevers," Achilles said, as if he was promising them to her, here and now. "To start."

And he was still holding out his hand.

"Breathe," he murmured, as if he could see all the tumult inside her.

Valentina took a deep breath. She remembered lying in that bed of his with all of New York gleaming around them. He'd told her to breathe then, too.

In. Out.

Until she felt a little less full, or a little more able to handle what was happening. Until she had stopped feeling overwhelmed, and had started feeling desperate with need.

And this was no different.

Valentina breathed in, then out. Then she stepped forward and slid her hand into his, as easily as if they'd been made to fit together just like that, then let him pull her close.

He shifted to take her face in his hands, tilting her head back so he could fit his mouth to hers. Though he didn't. Not yet.

"Forever starts now," Valentina whispered. "The first one, anyway."

"Indeed." Achilles's mouth was so deliriously hard, and directly over hers. "Kiss me, Valentina. It's been too long."

And Valentina did more than kiss him. She poured herself into him, pushing herself up on her toes and winding her arms around his neck, and that was just the start.

Because there was forever after forever stacked up in front of them, just waiting for them to fill it. One after the next.

Together.

CHAPTER ELEVEN

ACHILLES MADE A terrible royal consort.

He didn't know who took more pride in that, he himself or the press corps, who finally had the kind of access to him they'd always wanted, and adored it.

But he didn't much care how bad he was at being the crown princess's billionaire, as long as he had Valentina. She allowed him to be as surly as he pleased, because she somehow found that charming. She'd even supported him when he'd refused to allow her father to give him a title, because he had no wish to become a Murinese citizen.

"I thank you," he had said to Geoffrey. "But I prefer not to swear my fealty to my wife by law, and title. I prefer to do it by choice."

Their wedding had been another pageant, with all the pomp and circumstance anyone could want for Europe's favorite princess. Achilles had long since accepted the fact that the world felt it had a piece of their story. Or of Valentina, certainly.

And he was a jealous bastard, but he tried not to mind as she waved and smiled and gave them what they wanted.

Meanwhile, as she grew bigger with his child she seemed to glow more by the day, and all those dark things in him seemed to grow lighter every time she smiled at him.

So he figured it was a draw.

She told him he wasn't a monster with that same deep certainty, as if she'd been there. As if she knew. And every time she did, he was more and more tempted to believe her.

She gave birth to their son the following spring, right about the time her sister was presenting the kingdom of Tissely with a brand-new princess of their own, because the ways in which the twins were identical became more and more fascinating all the time. The world loved that, too.

But not as much as Valentina and Natalie did.

And as Achilles held the tiny little miracle that he and Valentina had made, he felt another lock fall into place inside him. Maybe they could not be normal, Valentina and him. But that only meant that the love they would lavish on this child would be no less than remarkable.

And no less than he deserved.

This child would never live in the squalor his father had. He would never want for anything. No hand would be raised against him, and no fists would ever make contact with his perfect, sweet face. His parents would not abandon him, no stepfathers would abuse him, and it was entirely possible that he would be so loved that the world might drown in the force of it. Achilles would not be at all surprised.

Achilles met his beautiful wife's gaze over their child's head, lying with her in the bed in their private wing of the hospital. The public was locked outside, waiting to meet this latest member of the royal family. But that would happen later.

Here, now, it was only the three of them. His brand-new family and the world he would build for him. The world that Valentina would give their son.

Just as she'd given it to him.

"You are mine, *glikia mou*," he said softly as her gaze met his. Fiercely. "More now than ever."

And he knew that Valentina remembered. The first vows they'd taken, though neither of them had called it that, in his New York penthouse so long ago.

The smile she gave him then was brighter than the sun, and warmed him all the same. Their son wriggled in his arms, as if he felt it, too. His mother's brightness that had lit up a monster lost in his own darkness, and convinced him he was a man.

Not just a man, but a good one. For her.

Anything for her.

"Yours," she agreed softly.

And Achilles reckoned that three forevers would not be nearly enough with Valentina.

But he was Achilles Casilieris. Perfection was his passion.

If they needed more forever they'd have it, one way or another.

He had absolutely no doubt.

* * * * *

If you enjoyed
THE BILLIONAIRE'S SECRET PRINCESS
don't forget to read the first part of Caitlin Crews's
SCANDALOUS ROYAL BRIDES duet,

THE PRINCE'S NINE-MONTH SCANDAL

Available now!

'We're engaged?' Alejandro sent Catriona a look.

With the bright lights gleaming from the house, this one was easy to interpret. He was *amused*?

'It's your fault,' she declared, instantly defensive. 'I was trying not to be predictable. You dared me.'

'So it's *my* fault?'

'This entire mess is your fault.' She nodded firmly.

He slowly stepped closer. 'You don't feel *any* responsibility, given you're the one who broke in and tried to steal from me?'

'I didn't break in; I used a key. And I wasn't stealing anything that belongs to you.'

'No? I wonder…' He was watching her closely, and then his smile returned, slow and seductive. 'Catriona, you are going to pay for this, you know.'

'Not in the way you're thinking.'

He laughed and stepped nearer so he was right in her personal space. 'Very much in the way I'm thinking. You think these sparks can be ignored?'

Natalie Anderson adores a happy ending. So you can be sure you've got a happy ending in your hands right now—because she promises nothing less. Along with happy endings she loves peppermint-filled dark chocolate, pineapple juice and extremely long showers. Not to mention spending hours teasing her imaginary friends with dating dilemmas. She tends to torment them before eventually relenting and offering—you guessed it—a happy ending. She lives in Christchurch, New Zealand, with her gorgeous husband and four fabulous children.

If, like her, you love a happy ending, be sure to come and say hi on Facebook.com/authornataliea, follow @authornataliea on Twitter, or visit her website/blog: natalie-anderson.com.

Visit the Author Profile page
at millsandboon.co.uk for more titles.

CLAIMING HIS CONVENIENT FIANCÉE

BY
NATALIE ANDERSON

First Published in Great Britain 2017
By Mills & Boon, an imprint of HarperCollins*Publishers*
1 London Bridge Street, London, SE1 9GF

© 2017 Natalie Anderson

ISBN: 978-0-263-92529-6

Printed and bound in Spain
by CPI, Barcelona

CLAIMING HIS
CONVENIENT
FIANCÉE

This one is for the nurses—Olivia, Akansha, Gavin, Glenda, Jo (and Arnie!), Karl, Maria, Naomi, Salma, Shannon and Shannon, and all the others who have helped us…you guys are amazing. Thank you so much for everything—not least teaching us Beanie!

CHAPTER ONE

FRENETIC DRUM AND bass reverberated down the dark street. Irritation pulsed along Kitty Parkes-Wilson's veins, keeping time with the relentless beat. It was too much to hope the neighbours would complain; no doubt they were wishing they could be at the party, all desperate to suck up to the rich new blood on the block.

Alejandro Martinez. Former management consultant turned venture capitalist. Millionaire. Promiscuous playboy. Party animal. And, since signing the documents three days ago, proud owner of the beautiful building in the heart of London that had, until said three days ago, been her family home. The home she'd grown up in, the one that had been in the family for more than five generations until her father had seized the wad of cash Alejandro Martinez had waved under his nose and skipped off to his sunny retirement villa in Corsica with his third picture-book-pretty wife. He'd cleared his debts and abandoned his failed business—and floored children.

All of which Kitty could handle. Just. Anyway, as much as she'd have liked to, the fact was she couldn't have bought Parkes House herself. But she hadn't even been told before it had been sold, and something had inadvertently been left in the Edwardian mansion. Something her father didn't own and had no right to sell. And *that* she couldn't cope with. Kitty Parkes-Wilson was on a retrieval mission and nothing and no one was going to stop her.

It wasn't the necklace's material worth that made it so important. Its loss meant her twin, Teddy, was in trouble, and her own *heart* was in trouble.

'You *can't* do this.'

She grinned at the way her brother could sound both aghast and excited.

'You can't stop me—I'm already here,' she answered in a low voice, pressing her phone closer to her ear as she slowed down her pace just before arriving at her former home. 'And you know I can do it.'

'Damn it, Kitty, you're crazy,' Teddy growled. 'You're only just off the train; why do you have to rush into this? Come here and we can talk about it.'

If she stopped to talk about it too much, she'd lose her nerve. 'The sooner I get it back the better. Now's the perfect chance, what with the party and all.'

'But what if you get caught—?'

'I won't,' she impatiently interrupted. 'He'll be too busy partying with his models to notice me.'

Alejandro Martinez only dated supermodels, trading them in with efficient regularity. According to the theatre gossip Teddy had shared when he'd told her that the house was being sold, the current model was Saskia, the number one swimwear model in the North American sports magazine market. Kitty figured that with those legs to distract him, Mr Martinez would never notice the quick in-and-out of an uninvited party guest. Especially one who knew the secrets of the house and how to stay hidden as she snuck her way to the second-floor library.

'It's in the library post, right?' She ignored her stomach's hungry rumble and double-checked with her twin. 'You're sure about that?'

'Positive.' Her brother's tone changed to out-and-out concerned again. 'But Kitty, please, I'm really not sure—'

'I'll call you as soon as I'm clear, okay? Stop worrying.' She ended the call before he could reply.

Adrenalin amped her muscles. She needed to concentrate and keep her confidence high. With a quick glance each way along the street, she quietly braced then hopped the fence. She ditched her small carry-on bag between a couple of shrubs and got to work.

Alejandro Martinez was not getting his hands on her Great-Aunt Margot's diamond choker. He was not putting it on any of his many girlfriends. Kitty would go to prison before she let that happen. It was not a flashy bauble for a temporary lover.

The back door key was still hidden in the same spot of the communal gated garden where she'd first hidden it a decade before. No one but she and Teddy knew it existed or that it was there and so, despite the sale of the property, it hadn't been handed to the new owner. She recovered it in less than ten seconds.

Phase one: complete.

She turned to look at the house. Brightly lit and in beautiful condition on the outside at least, it appeared to be the gleaming jewel in a row of similar styles. But Kitty knew the truth hidden beneath that freshly painted facade.

She made short work of the fence again then crossed to the corner of the street and found her way to the mews laneway behind the mansions. Her heart hammered as she neared the rear of the house. The lights were on, and she could see a catering worker at the sink.

That was when she threw her shoulders back and lifted her chin.

She unlocked the door, stepped in and smiled blithely at the kitchen hand, who looked up and gazed at her in astonishment. She waved the key at him and held her finger to her perfectly reddened lips. 'Don't tell him I'm here—I want to surprise him,' she said as she confidently strolled past him and out into the corridor.

The dishwashing chap didn't stop her. He didn't say anything. He just turned back to the plate he was rinsing.

She'd learned a few things from sitting in on Teddy's drama classes over the years.

Act confident. Fake it till you make it. Act like you own the place and people will believe you do.

People chose to believe the easiest option—the least trouble for them. And with her walking in all smiles, and with a key, who would doubt her right to be there?

Phase two: complete.

All she had to do now was head up the stairs to the private library, retrieve the necklace and get out again as fast as possible.

But curiosity bit. It had been months since she'd been home and now her heart ached with nostalgia for what she'd lost. In the three days since he'd taken over, what changes had Alejandro Martinez made?

Apparently he'd liked the look of the street and knocked on everyone's doors to find someone willing to sell. Her father hadn't been willing—he'd been *desperate*. Alejandro had been the answer to all his prayers. And Alejandro had got a good deal. House. Contents. Even the cars.

Winding up the company was one thing, but for her father to sell this home without saying a word to them beforehand was unforgivable. He'd sold everything *in* the house as well—only stopping to parcel up the few personal papers left in here. There were things she and Teddy might have liked, family treasures that had sentimental value. She didn't care about the monetary side of things; she'd grown up knowing most of it would never be hers. Her father hadn't thought of her—then again, he never had. But for once he'd not thought about Teddy either. Not that Teddy cared—he was glad not to have any reminders of the expectation he could never live up to. Except there was the last legacy from Great-Aunt Margot—the one Kitty had got her hair colour from, the one who'd given Kitty what confidence and fun she had. Great-Aunt Margot was her inspiration.

Kitty ventured down the corridor towards the bubble

of music and chatter and laughter and glanced through the open doorway into the atrium.

The lighting there was much dimmer than in the kitchen. The guests probably thought it was low to set the 'mood' and make everyone look even more attractive, but they really didn't need the help. No, the soft lighting was all about helping hide the aged, peeling paintwork and how much refurbishment and restoration work the house needed. It seemed Alejandro had had no hesitation in stripping the house of all its 'maximalist' decor—all the antique furniture, vases and fine china displays had vanished, and in their place were three dozen nubile, beautiful women. Every last one had to be a model. Kitty's heart puckered. It was weird to have all these other women here, all relaxed and happy and looking as if they belonged, when she no longer did.

Stopping to look had been a mistake.

She skirted the back of the room to confidently—but not too quickly—walk up the stairs. She kept her head high, her shoulders back and sent a glimmer of a smile to the person she saw along the hallway glancing up after her.

Faking it. Making it.

The volume of the music lowered the higher up the stairs she went. By the time she got to the second floor it had become bearable background noise. There was no one in sight up here—the entire house had yet to be taken over by pumped-up party people. She'd timed her arrival just right—enough people were present for her to disappear into, but it wasn't yet wild enough for them to be everywhere.

Despite the disappointment of seeing the stripped out interior below, she couldn't resist pausing by the master bedroom. The door was open—inviting her—but when she peered carefully around it, she found she couldn't step into the room. It was stuffed with boxes and furniture. So this was where everything from downstairs had been shoved. Her heart ached more and she quickly stepped along the hallway. Unfortunately, the library door was closed. She hovered a moment to listen, but heard nothing coming from within the room. Nervously, she turned the handle. To her relief it was dark inside and apparently unoccupied. She knew that if she left the door open, enough light would spill from the corridor for her to find her way. She smiled in anticipation as she lightly tiptoed to the shelves lining the farthest wall. This house had several secrets that the new owner would never know about—her father wouldn't have thought to tell him any of it. Sure, the pleasure she felt at having knowledge over Alejandro Martinez was childish, but the way he'd waltzed in and snatched away her home made her smart.

On the fifth shelf up, behind the fourth book along from the left, there was a small lever. She depressed it and listened to the scratchy whirring sound as a small cavity opened up. She didn't need to take the other books out; it was only a tiny safe—only large enough for a pile of notes written by bored children, or a coil of diamonds in a platinum setting left there by her forgetful, beloved, fool of a brother.

Kitty scooped them up, relief washing through her. She'd half expected them not to be there—Teddy's recollections weren't always accurate. But they were *hers* again and she could get them back to where they belonged. She'd hated the thought of letting Margot down—even though Margot was only alive in memory now.

Swallowing hard, she straightened the chain and put it around her neck, angling her head as she secured the clasp and then ran her finger along her throat to ensure the choker was sitting smoothly. The cold heaviness was familiar and made her heart ache all over again.

These were the only diamonds Margot had ever worn.

She'd bought them for herself, by herself. She'd declared that she needed no man to buy her jewels and had lived her life in defiant independence, refusing to settle into any kind of expectation—ahead of her time and leaving Kitty in awe.

She wished the choker could be hers for good, but it was Teddy's birthright and he'd given up everything else already. Kitty had nothing to lose.

She released her hair from the high topknot she'd coiled it into while on the train. To leave looking different from how she'd arrived was part of the plan and her hair served another purpose now—it mostly hid the gleaming necklace. She pushed the lever again and the compartment slid shut.

Phase three: complete.

Satisfied, she turned, ready to leave.

That was when she saw it—the man's silhouette looming in the doorway. She froze. With the lack of light she couldn't see his face, but she could see he held a phone in his hand. And she could see how tall he was. How broad. How impossible to slip past.

'Hello?' She wished she didn't sound so scared.

She wished he'd answer.

Her heart took two seconds to start pumping again and when it did her pulse thumped loudly in her ears. She hadn't heard him arrive. The floor in the library was wooden and she'd been certain she'd have heard approaching footsteps. But apparently this guy could enable stealth mode. Was he Security? How long had he been watching her? Had he seen what she'd done?

Apprehension fluttered in her belly.

'She wasn't wearing a necklace when she arrived,' he slowly mused. Softly. Dangerously. 'Yet she wears one now.'

She froze at that accented English, at that tone. She was definitely in trouble.

'If you'd get your boss for me, I can explain,' she bluffed haughtily.

'My name is Alejandro Martinez,' he replied, still in those soft, dangerous tones that made her skin prickle. 'I am the boss.'

It was the devil himself. Of course. Kitty's heart thundered.

He reached out a hand, casually closing the door. There was a split second of total darkness before he unerringly turned on the light.

Kitty rapidly blinked at the brightness. By the time the dancing spots cleared from her vision, he was less than a foot from her, his phone gone and his hands free.

She swallowed.

He was very close and *very* tall. She wasn't short yet she had to tip her chin to look into his face. His hair was dark brown and thick and he was so good-looking, he ought to have been outlawed as hazardous to any woman's attention span. Yes, Alejandro Martinez was fiendishly handsome with that olive skin, those chiselled features and those serious, assessing eyes.

Nervously, she flicked her hair in the hopes it would curl around her throat. She wasn't getting past him in a hurry; there was only one exit out of this library and he'd closed the door.

'No, there's no point trying to hide it now,' he mocked softly, but his eyes glittered like polished onyx. He slowly lifted a lock of her hair back with a lazy, arrogant finger. His penetrating gaze lingered on her neck, then raked down her body—her breasts, her waist, her legs. Every inch of her felt grazed.

'A diamond collar for a lithe little cat burglar,' he said. 'How appropriate.'

To her horror, her body reacted to his unabashed sensual assessment of her and to his low accented tone. Her skin tightened. Heat flooded her cheeks, her lower belly and she fought the instinct to take a squirming step back.

Alejandro Martinez was so *not* her cup of tea. Too obvious. Too forceful. Too…everything.

'A ginger she-cat,' he added thoughtfully, his focus lifting to her face. 'Rather rare.'

She bristled. She'd always hated her hair. She'd gone through a phase when she'd dyed it darker, only that had made her almost see-through skin and squillions of freckles look worse. In the end she'd given up and gone back to natural and faced the fact she was never going to be a 'beauty'.

'You know about the bookcase?' she asked, trying to take control of the situation—of herself—and draw attention away from this *awareness*. But her voice sounded husky and uncertain. She had to get herself and the necklace out of here as fast as possible.

'I do now. What other secrets do you know about this house?' His gaze seemed to penetrate right through her. 'What else are you planning to steal?'

A hot streak of stubbornness shot through her. She wasn't going to tell him anything—not about the house, not about herself, not about the necklace.

So she just stared up at him silently, waiting for him to make his next move.

His expression hardened. 'Give me the necklace,' he said firmly.

She shook her head. 'Possession is nine-tenths of the law,' she muttered.

'Possession?' He suddenly looked even more intent, even more predatory as his jaw sharpened and his eyes gleamed as they locked on hers.

Heat unfurled low in her belly. Shocking, utterly unwanted, destructive heat.

'It is very valuable,' he noted, continuing to watch her way too closely for her comfort. Standing too close too. When had he moved closer?

Kitty struggled to keep her brain working. The necklace

was valuable, but not only in the way *he* meant. It was all heart and memory to her.

'You know it's not yours,' she said, determinedly meeting his gaze and refusing to step back and show his intimidation was working.

'I am also willing to bet it's not yours.' His return gaze was ruthless. His stance was implacable.

But all that did was fire Kitty's desire to defy him. This man had taken ownership of everything she loved. He wasn't having this too. But she couldn't halt the telltale guilty heat building in her cheeks.

The diamonds might not belong to her legally, but they were hers in her heart. Damn Teddy's uselessness. 'It's mine to retrieve.'

And hers by love. No one loved this necklace more than her—more than that, she'd loved the woman who'd once owned it.

Alejandro shook his head slowly. 'This building and everything in it belongs to me now.' A small smile hovered at his mouth. 'Seeing as you are so insistent to stay, I guess that includes you too.'

Oh, she did *not* belong to anyone—and most certainly not him. This display of ownership was outrageous and beyond arrogant. 'Actually, I was just leaving,' she snapped coldly.

'No.' That tantalising smile vanished and he firmly grasped her wrist.

Kitty couldn't hide the tremble that rippled through her as she fisted her hand and tried to pull free from him.

'I think that both the necklace and you will remain in my possession until we find the rightful owner.' His eyes glinted. 'Of both.'

Defiance burned, sharpening her senses. Surely he was just being provocative, except she had the feeling he meant it. He was clearly used to being in control and having all the power. She didn't want to tell him the truth about the diamonds. She wouldn't try to appeal to his sensitive side—it was all too obvious he didn't have one. Arrogant jerk.

The pressure on her wrist grew—inexorably he drew her closer.

'What are you doing?' she gasped when he firmly ran his other hand across her stomach.

Alejandro didn't answer as he swept his palm further around her waist. She was a slim thing and had little in the way of curves, most unlike the women he usually spent time with. And yet there was something undeniably attractive about her. Undeniably different. She was clad entirely in black—slim three-quarter-length trousers and a fitted black sweater that emphasised her tall but slender frame. Her eyes screamed outrage and he suppressed a smile at the stiffness of her body as he continued his search. Maybe that was it—she presented resistance, challenge. And for him that was novel.

'You're assaulting me?' she snarled venomously.

'Checking for a concealed weapon,' he answered smoothly, but a grim defensiveness rose within at her accusation. Alejandro Martinez would *never* assault any woman. He was not like—*no*.

He forced his attention to his pretty prisoner, not his past. Her eyes were the weapons here and now, striking like twin daggers and making him smile, a respite from the memory that had flickered. Pleased, he removed the phone from where she'd tucked it into the waistband of her trousers.

He released her to study his prize. The phone wasn't the latest model and had one of those covers that had a pocket for a couple of cards—a bank card and driver's licence tucked inside. Perfect.

'Catriona Parkes-Wilson.' He read the name aloud, glancing to watch her reaction to the identification.

Soft colour bloomed in her pale cheeks again, and her emerald eyes flashed. She really was striking.

'Kitty,' she corrected him quickly.

Catriona—Kitty—Parkes-Wilson was the daughter of the man who'd sold him this house.

Alejandro would have guessed that the diamonds—undoubtedly real—would be hers, but she'd looked so guilty when he'd stopped her that he now wondered. He had to be certain of their provenance before relinquishing them to her just like that.

But finally he understood her presence here tonight. She was on a retrieval mission.

She was also the ultimate in spoilt heiresses—so headstrong and so used to getting her way that she thought she could strut straight into any room and take what she wanted. Why not do the normal polite thing and *ask*? The sleek Catriona seemed only able to take. And no doubt she was used to causing trouble with every step.

He dampened down the rising attraction and told himself it would be fun to teach her a lesson in politeness, and *then* possession.

'Catriona…' he repeated her full name, deliberately ignoring her preference, and couldn't stop his smile when she looked more annoyed '… I'm delighted to have you back in your former residence. Welcome.'

His security detail had informed him of her unorthodox arrival via text but Alejandro had already spotted her from his hidden vantage point upstairs where he'd been having a moment away from his guests. She'd climbed the stairs as though she thought she was invisible. As if hair the sparkling colours of an autumnal bonfire could ever blend into the background. Even when it had been tied in that pile on her head it had caught his attention. Now that it hung loose in a tumble of crazy curls, he was tempted to tangle his fingers into it and draw her close for a kiss…

But he wasn't about to give in to this unexpected burst of desire.

Alejandro enjoyed sex and had no shortage of it, but it had been a while since he'd felt such an instant surge of lust for a woman. It was mildly irritating—he had better control than this and, to prove that to himself, he wasn't about to explore the sexual electricity arcing between them right now. Not yet. It would be more amusing to put this petulant princess in her place. He'd met too many spoilt people who'd never had to do a real day's work in their lives and who had no idea what hardship really was. Catriona Parkes-Wilson needed to learn some genuine manners.

An idea came instantly, as they generally did, but this one made his muscles tighten in a searing burst of anticipation.

'Remain here this evening as my date,' he said bluntly. 'Or I call the police. The choice is yours.'

'Your *date*?' Her eyes widened in surprise.

He knew she felt the sensual awareness the way he did. It seemed she didn't like it all that much either. Inexplicably, that improved his mood. He'd have her apology. And then, if it was good, maybe he'd have her.

'The police?' she suddenly added quickly, almost hopefully.

That threat was the lesser of the two evils to her? He needed to make that option more alarming. 'Your fingerprints are all over—'

'They would be anyway,' she interrupted scornfully. 'I lived here, remember?'

'And I have security camera footage.' He smiled.

That silenced her.

'I can't ignore my guests for hours while I iron out this interruption of yours,' he said. 'So you will remain with me until I have the time to deal with you.'

Her eyes didn't waver from his as he stipulated his rules.

'I don't intend to leave your side even for a second,' he informed her quietly, failing to suppress the satisfaction that rose at the thought. 'Slinky cats can be clever escape artists. I'm not having you slip out when I look away for a second.' He read the fire in her gaze and his blood heated. 'And I do expect you to behave.'

Kitty glared at him. The thought of staying as his date should appal her. But what really shocked her was the delicious *anticipation* that shivered down her spine at the thought of such relentless attentiveness from him. What was *wrong* with her?

He bent closer, those full lips twisted ever so slightly into that tantalising smile. Dear Lord, he was too handsome.

'Catriona,' he said softly.

Now he loomed over her. She couldn't tear her gaze away from the bottomless depths of his black eyes. Her mouth parted as she struggled to breathe because her heart was thundering. Anticipation spiralled through every cell. Was he going to kiss her? Was she going to let him? Where had her *will* gone?

He was so close now she could feel his breath on her skin and his eyes were mesmerising and she simply couldn't seem to *move*. Then she felt the warmth of his fingers as he brushed the skin at the nape of her neck. She shivered, drawing in a shocked breath, but it was too late. He'd undone the clasp of the necklace before she'd registered his true intention. Now she could only stare as he stepped back and poured the glittering chain into his inside top pocket—right over the spot where his heart should be. Not that he had one of those.

He'd taken the diamond choker from her and she'd just let him.

She'd stood there like a vacant fool and let him reclaim the necklace. She'd let his good looks and his sexual magnetism render her *brainless*. How stupid could she get?

'I can't be your date,' she snapped, furious with herself.

'Why not?'

'You have a girlfriend already.'

'I do?' He sent her a penetrating look.

'Saskia something.' She straightened and snarled, venting her annoyance on him, 'I'm not helping you cheat on another woman.' She knew how much that sucked. 'Not even pretend cheating. So go ahead and call the police.'

She didn't think for a second he would but, to her apprehension, he pulled his mobile from his pocket again.

Had she misread him? Did he want the police here, interrupting his terribly exclusive party? She'd have to explain all and wear yet more mortification, but that was better than letting this man win. Surely the police would let her off with a warning—as a first time offender, distraught by the loss of her family home and all that… She might even be able to keep Teddy's name out of it.

She watched, breathing rapidly and still feeling too hot, as he held the phone up to his ear.

'Saskia, darling. I wanted to be honest with you and let you know before you heard it from anyone else.' He didn't hesitate. 'I've met someone else.'

Kitty's jaw dropped. He'd phoned the latest model girlfriend? She stared at him in frozen fascination as he kept talking.

'I know it seems sudden, but sometimes that's how life works.'

Had he just broken up with the woman?

OMG. The phone call was swift and to the point and the arrogant bastard smiled at *her* the entire way through.

'You just ended your relationship?' she all but gasped as he ended the call. 'Over the phone?'

'Four dates doesn't really constitute a relationship.' He shrugged and pocketed his mobile.

'And you never go much beyond five dates anyway.'

Teddy had told her that. Apparently, Alejandro's appetite for a rapid succession of beauties caused frequent comment—celebration by some, such as Teddy, and derision from others. Kitty was firmly in the second camp.

His eyebrows flickered. 'Don't I? I don't tend to keep count.'

Of dates or women? 'You can't just do that.'

'I just did.'

'You don't care?' Was it all *that* meaningless for him? His callousness was repellent, yet there was still that fickle, stupid part of her that was attracted to him.

'No. I don't.' He laughed at her expression. 'She doesn't either. We both knew what we were in for.'

And what was that—a few meaningless hours in bed together? Kitty whipped up her anger on behalf of the woman. 'You're sure about that?'

'Utterly.' He looked bored as he glanced at his watch. 'Now you needn't have any scruples about being my date for the night.'

'No way.' She shook her head, still shocked at his callous phone call. As if she'd ever date someone so ruthless. 'You're heartless.'

'If that's the case—' he reached for his pocket again '—then I will have to phone the police. Naturally, I will push for charges to be laid.' He sent her a mock-apologetic glance. 'It's unacceptable for people to unlawfully enter houses and take whatever they find lying around.'

She narrowed her eyes. He was playing a game. He'd have called the police already if that was what he'd really meant to do. 'You'll do whatever necessary to get what you want, won't you?'

He smiled as if that wasn't something to be ashamed of. 'Always.'

No doubt he'd blackmail, coerce, fight dirty and think nothing of it.

She gazed at him. He was hideously self-assured. Going through women like normal people went through pints of milk—on an almost daily basis and simply discarding the bottle when done. But that someone so shallow could be so attractive-looking? It was so wrong—the guy needed a warning label stamped on his forehead. Yet there was a whole roomful downstairs waiting to step up and be the next one. His looks and charisma had made things—women—far too easy for him.

He sent her that soft, suave smile, totally in control and at ease. 'What's it going to be, Catriona?' he prompted her gently. 'A night with me at your side, or a night in the cells?'

Her body recognised his beauty; her brain recognised he was a calculating bastard. She'd ensure her brain won this battle. She was certain he was not interested in her; he just wanted to teach her a lesson. That was obvious.

But *he* was the one who needed a lesson. The palm of her hand itched, but she'd never resorted to violence, not even in her worst attention-seeking teen tantrums and she wasn't letting this devil get to her in a way no one else ever had.

Nor was she letting him win. She had no idea what he thought he was going to achieve by forcing her to stay with him during his party, but she wasn't letting him have it. She'd make the night as difficult as possible for him. Then she'd tell the truth and demand Margot's diamonds back.

'Don't call the police,' she finally responded, answering demurely. 'I'll be your date.'

His eyes narrowed just the slightest, but his smile was ready and heart-stopping. He pocketed the phone again and then reached out and laced his fingers through hers. 'I never thought for a second that you wouldn't.'

CHAPTER TWO

'YOU'RE VERY SURE of yourself,' Kitty said, counting her breathing in an attempt to slow her speeding heart.

'I'm sure of people,' he answered. 'They are predictable.'

Well, he definitely wasn't predictable. And she *refused* to be—at least to him. 'What is it you want from me?' She tried to extricate her hand from his, but he wouldn't release her.

'What do you think I want from you?' That smile now lurked in his eyes.

Her chin lifted. 'If I knew, I wouldn't be asking.'

His glance sharpened, but he spoke calmly. 'Your time. Your undivided attention. And when every guest has gone tonight, we'll have a reckoning.'

Something flipped in her belly. Half horrified, half intrigued, she couldn't resist asking more. 'What kind of reckoning?'

The smile he flashed was nothing short of wicked. 'I think you've already guessed.'

He couldn't possibly mean *that*. She flushed. 'Never. Happening.'

He laughed then, releasing his grip on her to throw both his hands in the air, surprisingly animated. 'See? Predictable.' That foreign element underlying his American accent had deepened deliciously.

He was teasing her? She shouldn't feel even a hint of disappointment. Yet she did. Alejandro Martinez was too much the practised flirt and too sure of his own attractiveness.

'I'm not in the least interested in you in that way,' she said, determined to make the point as clear as possible.

'Of course you're not,' he soothed, turning to lead the way to the door.

'I mean it. You try anything—'

He sighed theatrically. 'Well, it will be difficult, but I'll try to control my animal urges.'

Okay, so now she felt a fool because of course he wasn't really interested in her like that. He'd be back on the phone to his Saskia soon enough and sorting out the lovers' tiff or he'd be off with another of the models downstairs…

Laughter danced in his eyes as he turned and caught her glaring at his back.

'You are very beautiful when cross,' he said provocatively. 'Does that fiery hair bring a temper with it?'

She refused to answer him. Her hair didn't bring rage so much as rashness. Fool that she was, she should have listened to Teddy and calmed down before deciding to come on this crazy mission. She should at least have eaten something, then she wouldn't be feeling this light-headed.

He paused and waited until she'd looked up into his face again before teasing her further. 'If you are a good date, you might get a reward.'

'All I want is the necklace,' she replied stiffly. And maybe some dinner at some point. Hopefully, there'd be some decent canapés downstairs and not just the tiny, calorie-free stuff that models lived on.

He took her hand firmly in his again and drew her towards the door. He was really serious about her mingling?

'What are you planning on telling your guests about me?' she asked.

A mystified expression crossed his face. 'Nothing.'

Clearly the opinion of others didn't bother him at all. Kitty tried very hard not to be bothered by what others thought, but there was still that soft part of her that ached to please someone. Anyone. Everyone.

She worked hard to fight it and protect her stupidly

vulnerable heart. For too long her self-esteem had been bound up in the opinion of men. First her father. Then her fiancé.

She hesitated at the top of the stairs. Alejandro was already on the first step, but he turned. His eyes were almost at the same level as hers.

'Come on, my reluctant date,' he dared in that divine accent. 'Come down and act the mute martyr.'

Was *that* what he expected her to do?

She went from famished to galvanised in less than a second. She'd act the ultimate party person—something she hardly ever was. With just that one look from him her appetite vanished. It was her twin, Teddy, who usually held centre stage, while she was the quiet foil—always his most appreciative audience. But now? Now she was energised. Now she had a game to win.

'You're obviously very bored with your life.' She placed her hand on his upper arm, leaning close in a parody of an adoring, clinging lover—half hoping he'd pull away.

He didn't. His smile broadened. 'Because I have to coerce a beautiful woman into standing alongside me for the night?'

'Exactly. You must be very jaded,' she murmured, trying not to dwell on the size and hardness of the muscles she could feel under the fabric of his oh-so-perfectly tailored suit. 'Having to spice it up like this.'

He chuckled. 'I haven't the time to deal with you the way I want right now; I need to spend time with my guests. We'll deal with each other properly later.'

She wasn't sure if that was a promise or a threat. Worse, she wasn't sure what she *wanted* it to be.

'You don't think taking me down there with you is a risk?' She sent him a sideways look. 'Or do you truly think I'm predictable?'

'I'm very good at taking risks,' he said with no trace of

humility. 'And, in my experience, the higher the risk, the greater the reward.'

'So I'm high risk?'

He hesitated, checking his words ever so slightly. 'You're not afraid to put yourself on the line. That makes you interesting.'

She didn't want to be interesting. She didn't want to feel the flush of pleasure that he'd complimented her.

She refused his murmured offer of a drink as they descended the last stairs. As much as she yearned for the Dutch courage, she figured it would be more of a hindrance than a help. She needed all her wits about her to successfully spar with Alejandro Martinez and combat whatever 'reckoning' it was he had in mind.

Maybe she should have confessed all about the diamond necklace when she had the chance upstairs in the library, but he'd been so irritatingly assured, she'd been unable to resist the urge to bait him right back.

She wasn't sure what she'd expected from him once downstairs, but it wasn't the supremely polite courtesy he showed her. He introduced her to everyone as they walked through the atrium to the formal lounge. Many of them were American, like him, and out to enjoy themselves as much as possible. The first few people he introduced her to looked at her with benign disinterest—clearly used to Alejandro appearing every night with a new woman. No wonder he'd looked bemused when she'd asked what he'd say about her to his guests.

'Meet Catriona,' he said to the fourth group of people they stopped beside.

'Kitty,' she sweetly corrected, yet again, and extended her hand to the nearest of the three women. 'I'm his special date for the night.'

Three sets of eyebrows lifted in unison.

'Special?' one rapier-thin woman queried, her gaze equally dagger-like.

'I had to promise her that, or break out the handcuffs,' Alejandro answered smoothly.

The sensuality of his reply rippled through her—and the rest of the group. Eyes widened, then narrowed. But only Kitty knew the truth of his words. Only she knew he didn't mean fur-lined kinky toys, but tight, unbreakable restraints—yet somehow the thought of them wasn't as repellent as it should be. Not when she envisaged Alejandro wielding the cuffs and the key.

As Alejandro turned and led her further into the room, the look he sent *her* was slightly goading as if he knew he was thwarting her prediction of his behaviour. As if he knew the lurching direction of her thoughts. She refused to let the smile slip from her face. She'd 'sparkle' down here even if it killed her.

Except it wasn't that hard at all because he made her laugh too easily. He was extremely charming. In minutes she knew exactly why there were so many women present. He had that charisma, that X-factor, that way of looking at a woman as if she were the only person in the world who mattered to him in that moment. When she was the object of his focus, a woman felt *good*. It was a terrifyingly unfair talent. And he shared it around. He had his fingers laced through hers, but he talked with everyone equally.

Then she noticed people were watching them more attentively. Their gazes rested on the way he remained close to her the entire time. At the way he constantly touched some part of her—a hand on her back, her arm, or clasping her hand. As time passed into the second hour, he placed his arm over her shoulder and drew her closer to his side.

The guests began looking more assessingly at *her*. She heard the ripple of inquiry as they made their way from room to room. She heard the whisper of her name. Surreptitious glances became openly speculative.

If Alejandro noticed he said nothing, but his attentiveness became even more apparent. Until he then led her to a corner and stepped in close to put himself as a wall between her and the rest of his guests.

'You seem to be causing a stir,' he said, his onyx gaze pinning her in place.

'Not me.'

He was the one doing all the touchy-feely stuff that was causing the stares.

'Absolutely you.' He laughed. That amusement danced in his eyes too and she couldn't tear her attention from him.

'You enjoy messing with people's lives?'

'In what way am I messing with your life?' He raised his eyebrows. 'Don't overdramatize having to spend one night alongside me. It's not going to change your world.'

'It's not?' She furrowed her brow in mock-disappointment. 'But I thought any woman who spent a night with the amazing Alejandro had her world *rocked*.'

'Minx.' He laughed again. 'Come on, we'd better keep moving.'

'Must we, darling?' she murmured as she stepped alongside him.

The look he shot her then promised absolute retribution.

Kitty lifted her chin, feeling more game than ever. But, now she could look more freely about the house, she realised there was much gone from the rooms. Her family had had a 'maximalist' rather than a 'minimalist' style of decor but the mantelpieces were bare and shelves barren—the spaces punctuated by used champagne glasses and platters of stupidly tiny delicacies she'd yet to sample. With a pang she wondered what he'd done with all the smaller items of furniture and the trinkets and sculptures that she'd loved all her life—surely they weren't all crammed into those boxes in the bedrooms upstairs.

'Alejandro?' a woman called from almost halfway across the room and walked over with quick, clipping steps. 'I've just had a text from Saskia,' she added, her eyes cold and wide as she locked her gaze on Kitty. 'Bit of a bombshell, actually.'

'Oh?' Alejandro couldn't have sounded less interested but his arm tightened infinitesimally, pressing Kitty closer to his side.

She wished he wouldn't do that; feeling his hard strength was appallingly distracting, but she had the feeling he did it without even realising—so used to having a woman with him.

'She said you've met someone else.'

There was a split-second of awkward silence and Alejandro was utterly still. The woman's confident expression suddenly faltered.

'Oh, that would be me,' Kitty interjected sweetly before Alejandro had a chance to speak. 'When I've had enough of him she's welcome to have him back.'

She heard Alejandro's sharply drawn breath and braced herself. Was he finally going to tell her to go now?

But he drew her closer still. It wasn't an unconscious, almost undetectable gesture now. 'But sweetheart,' he breathed. 'It's my job to ensure you've never had enough.' He turned to the woman. 'If you'll excuse us, I'd like to get Catriona a drink. I think she needs one.'

'How many times do I have to tell you—it's Kitty?' she muttered as he held her hand tightly and drew her through the crowds with him.

He smiled back at her and his hand tightened. 'What will you have?'

She was aware of everyone watching them as he led her through the room. 'Got any cyanide in the champagne?'

'I'll save you some for later, when it's time to face your—how do you say?—fate worse than death.' He looked pleased with himself at that.

'I already told you, that's never happening.'

He stopped in the centre of the room and faced her, apparently uncaring that everyone was staring, and positively *hauled* her right into his arms. 'No? Not even a kiss to say sorry?' Slowly and deliberately he brushed his thumb across her lower lip. 'Methinks the lady doth protest too much.'

'Methinks the asshole doth have an outsize ego.'

He gazed at her, his expression delighted. He couldn't have looked more proprietorial. Or more smitten. But his whispered words were so sarcastic and his awareness of her unbelievably smug. He was enjoying her discomfort hugely. She could tell by the unholy gleam in his eyes, but every touch made her acutely aware of him and his magnetism grew stronger.

She pulled back and made him keep walking.

So. Not. Happening.

It was his reputation that made her so aware of him. All that history, the list of conquests—the world's most beautiful, desired women. But it wasn't only that. There was no denying *his* physical perfection and the supreme assuredness that went with it.

It was impossible to look away from him for long. She'd never met anyone like him and she'd met plenty of wealthy, entitled people in the course of her life. But if you were to strip all those people bare of their designer dresses and jewels and outsize bank balances, many would fade into nothingness. Not Alejandro. Buck-naked in a bull ring he'd still conquer all. And she had the feeling he intended to conquer her. He thought he already had.

He had another think coming.

The awareness of the guests was even more apparent

now. She felt the heat from a zillion hard gazes and fought to keep the polite smile on her face. She wasn't going to lose her confidence. She was going to keep her head high and weather these last couple of hours. But she was quieter as she stood alongside Alejandro, her hand still firmly bound in his, as he talked work with a couple.

That was when she recognised two of the women on the far side of the room. A small British contingent seemed to be standing together. Kitty's heart sank—of course they'd be there. Those two were like pearl hat pins—ultra pretty but with a sharp point they liked to stick into someone given the chance. She hadn't seen Sarah in months, but she didn't imagine she'd had a personality transplant in that time. The woman was a childhood chum of James's—one who'd never approved of his engagement to Kitty and she was with another couple who were also very much 'team James'. And great, they'd spotted her too and were circling closer like a school of sharks honing in for a feeding frenzy.

'Kitty Parkes-Wilson!' the first exclaimed loudly.

'Hi, Sarah.' Kitty smiled, turning to angle herself slightly away from Alejandro. Given he was engrossed in discussing the prospects of another hedge fund, she crossed her fingers he wouldn't hear this conversation—because if anyone here was going to be predictable, it would be this woman.

'Fancy seeing you here this week of all weeks.' Sure enough, Sarah launched her first salvo in a loud chime.

'You mean in my former family home the week we lost possession?' Kitty smiled through her teeth. 'Funny how life works, isn't it?'

'Oh, it is,' Sarah answered as she glanced at Alejandro's hand curling around Kitty's despite the fact he was facing the other couple. 'I never thought you'd be another of Alejandro's notches,' she 'whispered' conspiratorially.

'I'm not!' Kitty flared at the thought and replied swiftly

before thinking better of it. 'I'm only here because he's bullied me into staying.'

Sarah's eyebrows lifted and she laughed a little too loudly. 'Bullied?' Her pointed laugh chimed loudly again. 'Yeah, it really looks like that.'

Was it Kitty's imagination or had Alejandro tensed?

'We haven't seen you in so long,' Sarah added when Kitty didn't elaborate. 'You left London in such a hurry.'

The woman was such a cow to bring that up. Of course she'd left in a hurry. She'd been *hurt*. She'd just found out James hadn't wanted *her* at all. He'd only wanted the wealth he'd assumed came with her. And when he'd found out all the cold hard cash had gone, he hadn't bothered to break up with her before searching the field for her replacement. He'd been trying them all out behind her back. Now, barely six months later, he was engaged to another woman. A beautiful, wealthy one who didn't seem at all bothered about his cheating past.

This time Kitty didn't imagine the sensation. Alejandro's fingers definitely tightened about hers again. But he didn't break his conversation and turn towards her.

'You're finally over James then?' Sarah queried.

She knew it hadn't been her fault, but it still hurt. She'd truly thought he loved her. That he'd got her, and found her attractive. But it was only the money he'd loved. And she'd been so starved for attention, so desperate to believe that a guy finally wanted *her*, she'd not seen through his fickle facade.

She'd been such a fool. And she was a fool now for letting this woman get to her.

Because she was too angry.

She straightened, channelled her inner Great-Aunt Margot and rewrote the rules.

'Oh, yes.' Kitty smiled sunnily at Sarah. 'You know, I didn't want to make things public yet,' she 'whispered'—

every bit as loudly as Sarah had. 'As you've alluded to, it has been a stressful week.'

Sarah's eyes widened and she leaned closer. 'Make what public?' This time her volume really did lower.

'Our relationship,' Kitty answered as if it was obvious.

'Your...' Sarah's jaw slackened in shock, then she almost squeaked. 'You mean with Alejandro? *You're* why he bought this house? He bought it for you?'

It was amazing how the smallest suggestion could snowball into something so out of control so quickly.

'It's a secret, you understand,' Kitty murmured guiltily, not quite correcting Sarah's assumption and hoping Alejandro was still deeply involved with his conversation and not eavesdropping.

'The two of you are that...*serious*?' Sarah's voice rose.

She was so obviously thunderstruck at the notion that Kitty was suddenly irate. Why was it so shocking that an attractive man might want *her*? Just for once she wanted to knock the superior smirk from this woman's face—and every other person who'd looked at her as if she were a loser freak. 'We're—'

Sarah's eyes narrowed on the way Alejandro was holding Kitty's left hand so firmly. 'You're *never* engaged,' she breathed.

'We're...er...' Kitty suddenly realised a metaphorical crevasse had opened at her feet. She was in real trouble.

That was when Alejandro turned.

If only the earth really would open up and swallow her whole.

'Kitty's just told me the news.' Sarah reached out and put a hand on his wrist and shot Kitty a sharp look before Kitty could even draw breath. 'Congratulations.'

Kitty couldn't bring herself to look at him.

And then Sarah did it. She asked so loudly that several heads turned. 'Are you two really engaged, Alejandro?'

CHAPTER THREE

ALEJANDRO'S FINGERS TIGHTENED again on Kitty's—extremely firmly.

But Kitty didn't wince. She held her breath, waiting for the ultimate in public humiliation. It was suddenly so quiet, it was as if the rest of the world was holding its breath with her. This would actually be worse than when she'd finally found out about James's infidelity. At least she'd been alone then and not in the centre of a roomful of people.

'Sarah guessed,' Kitty muttered as she finally braved a glance up at him and recklessly killed the silence that had been a fraction too long already. 'She's always been astute.'

His gaze imprisoned hers and for a second everyone in the room faded. His eyes were like banked furnaces, so very black but so very deep and there was a level of emotion in them that she'd not expected and that she couldn't interpret.

Oh, God, she should just run away now.

His fingers tightened even more—to the point of pain—as if he'd read her mind and was physically preventing her escape. But she wanted to run. She *had* to. How could she ever explain?

Sarah—the one who'd never told her that her fiancé was sleeping with someone else. Sarah—who'd never been nice, who'd never welcomed her into the group, who'd never seemed to want her to succeed.

'You've caught her out, Sarah,' Alejandro said quietly.

Kitty started to die inside.

'Catriona was reluctant to announce it so soon…' He trailed off.

Sarah's jaw dropped. So did Kitty's, but she caught herself in time. She licked her lips, her heart thundering as she gazed at Alejandro. He was smiling? He was looking...*satisfied*?

He turned to face her nemesis intently. 'We can trust you, can't we?'

'Of course,' Sarah said weakly. 'But I...er...might have been a bit loud just then.'

'No matter.' Alejandro smiled. 'We're all friends here.'

Did he underline the word 'friends'? He still held Kitty's hand in a vice but he was smiling.

'Congratulations.' Sarah looked stunned.

Alejandro lifted his free hand to place a finger over his lips and winked at her. 'Shh, remember?' Finally he turned to Kitty again. 'Come along, Catriona. I think you need some fresh air.'

He set off at such a pace Kitty almost stumbled. If it weren't for the grip he had on her hand, she might have. Instead he wrapped his other arm around her waist and—under the guise of attentive affection—practically dragged her out through the back room, past that bland dishwashing guy and out into the small private courtyard at the back.

Only once they were alone outside did he release her. Kitty took a quick few steps to the corner of the tiled courtyard. Then turned to face him.

'We're engaged?' He sent her a look.

With the bright lights gleaming from the house, this one was easy to interpret. He was *amused*?

'It's your fault,' she declared, instantly defensive. 'I was trying not to be predictable. You dared me.'

'So it's *my* fault?'

'This entire mess is your fault.' She nodded firmly.

He slowly stepped closer. 'You don't feel any responsibility, given you're the one who broke in and tried to steal from me?'

'I didn't break in; I used a key. And I wasn't stealing anything that belongs to you.'

'No? I wonder.' He was watching her closely, then his smile returned, slow and seductive. 'Catriona, you are going to pay for this, you know.'

'Not in the way you're thinking.'

He laughed and stepped so he was right in her personal space. 'Very much in the way I'm thinking. You think these sparks can be ignored?'

She really wished his accent didn't make his atrocious words sound so damn attractive. His laugh was low and did things to her insides and the cool air did nothing to settle the fever in her bones.

Now she really wished he'd stop looking at her like that. It made her hot and it was even harder to concentrate. And he knew it. He knew he was like catnip to every woman in the world. He loved it. She didn't want to want him at all. But her stupid body recognised the talent and experience in his.

'Is this the bit where you attempt to exert your sexual dominance over me?' she growled as he stepped closer still.

He let out another burst of laughter, but he caught both her hands in his and forced them behind her back in a move of total sexual dominance. 'No, this is the bit where I stop you from saying more stupid things in public.'

'You have no right to censor me.' She had no idea where the wildness came from. She'd never normally speak to anyone like this. Usually she'd duck her head and mind her own business and let Teddy do the talking.

'Not censoring you,' he chided wickedly. 'Kissing you. To leave you speechless.'

'You're...*what*?' Her jaw dropped. 'You're unbelievable.'

'I know. So good.' He mock preened.

But his proximity was getting to her—she could feel his strength and his size and, appallingly, she wanted to lean up against him! She stiffened instead. 'You don't think you're hyping yourself up too much? I'm going to expect something so amazing you're never going to be able to live up to it.'

'I'm willing to take the risk.'

'You're willing to take a lot of risks.'

'Possibly. But this is my home and you will not cause trouble when I have this many guests present.'

'Then let me leave. With my necklace.' She looked up and sent him a brilliant smile, pleased with her comeback. 'It's a very simple solution.'

'No, that can't happen now,' he answered bluntly, his expression intent. 'Stupid talk earns kissing, remember?'

Kitty didn't get the chance to breathe, let alone reply. Because he'd bent his head and brushed his lips over hers. It was the softest, lightest kiss and not at all what she'd have expected. Silenced, stilled, she waited. There was another light, gentle caress—lips on lips. And then another.

That was when she realised he was the kind of lover who would take his time. Infinite time and care, to arouse her. The thing was, she didn't need that much time. Her toes curled in the ends of her shoes as he kissed her again and she couldn't help her slight gasp, the parting of her suddenly needy mouth. But he didn't press closer, harder—instead, he kept the kiss light, almost sweet, and he was utterly in control. There was just that underlying edge as she absorbed the rigidity of his body…and started to realise that the tightness of his grasp on her wrists was no longer to hold her in place, but to hold himself back.

She looked up at him, bemused by his tender, go softly approach. He threw her a small smile, as if he knew exactly how much she'd anticipated a punishing kiss from him— all frantic passion and a duelling race to the finish line.

And she was *not* disappointed it hadn't become that kind of kiss. Nor was she yearning for another.

'That wasn't enough?' he teased knowingly. 'You want a little more?'

'That was more than enough,' she lied with a little shrug. 'I guess this is where you say we English have no passion.'

'I've yet to meet a woman who doesn't feel passion when she's with me—'

'You mean anger? Rage?'

He chuckled and brushed his thumb across her hypersensitised lips. 'Too easy.'

Awareness rippled down her spine, a warm tide of liquid desire. It was impossible that she be so drawn to this man. He was a philanderer—a total playboy who'd had more lovers than she had freckles. And she had a *lot* of freckles.

He was just toying with her—too aware of his sensual power and utterly assured of his success.

'I won't be another of your numbers.' She promised herself that.

'No?' He laughed and shook her gently. 'You already are. More than that—you're my fiancée.'

She died of mortification all over again. In the heat of that kiss she'd forgotten that nightmare moment. 'Why didn't you deny it?' She swallowed.

'I don't like seeing anyone ganged up on,' he said simply. 'I dislike bullies. It was evident what was going on.'

What would the supremely successful Alejandro Martinez know about bullies? As she frowned at him another emotion flickered across his face. But he suddenly stepped back, looking as suavely in control as ever. He extended his hand to her and waited. That he was so astute surprised her. Now she knew why he hadn't denied that outrageous engagement story to Sarah. He'd felt *sorry* for her. She felt worse than ever.

She hesitated, looking into his eyes, unable to read him at all now.

'Let's go back inside,' he said quietly.

With a small sigh she put her hand in his and walked back into the house. But they didn't return to the packed ground floor reception rooms; instead he led her up the stairs that she had previously used to get to the private library.

'Stay here awhile, make yourself at home,' he teased wolfishly as he showed her into the room.

She should have known that moment of kindness and humanity wouldn't last in him.

'Where are you going?' She eyed him suspiciously.

He had his phone out and a key in his hand—one of the large old-fashioned keys that fitted the internal doors in this house.

'I'm going to get rid of all my guests. I can do that better if you're not with me.'

'And you're going to lock me in here while you do that?' She folded her arms and called him on it. 'What if there's a fire?'

'I'll play the hero and rescue you.' He simply smiled and looked rakish.

'You're no hero—you're all villain.'

He flashed another smile. 'Women always like the bad boy, isn't that so?'

That was *not* so. She felt like flinging the cushions at him, except she wasn't that childish. Guiltily she remembered her lies downstairs. She'd definitely acted like a proud, childish idiot then.

'Don't fret.' He winked at her just before closing—and locking—the door. 'I won't be long.'

He was an inordinately long time. Eventually she heard voices spilling out into the street and resisted the urge to stand at the window and scream for a saviour. She'd made enough of a fool of herself here tonight. What had she been thinking when she'd led Sarah to think Alejandro had bought the house for her? That they were *engaged*?

Tired defeat permeated her. She'd been up since six, ready to get the train from Cornwall back to London. She'd not eaten on the journey and now she felt queasy. She turned off the main light and switched on the reading lamp, pouring herself a finger of whiskey from the decanter still on the table in the study.

She rarely drank spirits but right now she needed *something* and she trusted her father's old single malt more than the concoctions that had been on offer downstairs. And, anyway, this was for medicinal purposes. The liquid hit her stomach and lit a ball of fire in it. She breathed out and closed her eyes, aching to relax properly. She'd spark up again when Alejandro returned. She just needed a bit of a rest now.

The heat drained from her. That kick of adrenalin vanished, leaving her tired and with a headache threatening. She kicked off her shoes and walked to the deep leather sofa that had been in her father's study all her life, trying not to remember the number of times she'd curled up on it and waited late into the night for him to get home.

She'd spent so long trying to get her father's attention. But he'd been preoccupied lecturing Teddy, the son and heir, and he'd been too busy wooing the glamorous women he'd had affairs with. She'd gifted him her best sculptures as a kid. She'd poured her heart into them, only to see them admired for a half second and then relegated to a bottom shelf to gather dust. They were never properly displayed, never shown off with pride, merely indulged for a brief moment before he turned elsewhere. Which was exactly the way he treated *her*.

All she'd wanted was for him to know her, to love her, to let her *be*… She was such a needy fool.

She'd thought James had understood and that he'd be true to her. But he'd been even worse. At least her father had never hidden his affairs from everyone.

'I was just…I couldn't help myself.' Her father had tried to explain it to her the last time she'd seen him, just after she'd broken up with James, and she'd railed at him for being the same kind of *cheat*.

Impulse. Making that snap decision that was so often wrong. She'd inherited that faulty gene from him. Not when it came to lovers, but in every other aspect of her life for sure.

Her father had made bad business choices; he'd needed to sell property to get a cash injection because he'd known his time as a businessman was up. He'd wanted to retire to his flash estate in Corsica while he still could. And so he had. Leaving Teddy and her alone. But they were almost twenty-four and able to look after themselves.

Now she was exhausted from maintaining smiles in front of all those people. From restraining herself from losing her temper with Alejandro in front of them all. From reining in her reaction to the torment of his touches. From hiding the heartbreak at being back here and knowing she no longer belonged. That she'd never really belonged. There was nothing here for her any more.

She curled her legs under her on the sofa and told herself to shrug it off. She was fine. She'd go and stay with Teddy at one of his friends' places tonight after having it out with Alejandro. She'd go back to Cornwall in the morning and get on with her new life. It was all going to be okay.

But in the meantime she slumped lower in the soft leather.

It took longer than Alejandro desired for his guests to get the idea it was time for them to leave. Admittedly his parties usually went on far later, but he needed to be alone with the vexatious redhead who'd tipped his night upside down. So he smiled, firmly shooting down the teasing pleas for the DJ to play on.

Finally he closed the door on the last couple of guests, who were still shocked and avidly curious. Yeah, that 'friend' of Catriona's hadn't kept her mouth shut. But he'd known she wouldn't. They'd all known that.

Rolling his shoulders to ease the tension mounting in them, he lightly jogged up the stairs. His smile was tight. She was going to be furious with him for taking so long. But when he unlocked the door he wasn't greeted with the instant volley of verbal abuse he'd expected. His breath froze in his lungs at the total silence in the room. Had she escaped somehow? He strode into the library then drew up short—the sight before him rendered him speechless. He simply stared.

She was fast asleep on the sofa, her body a sleek, long shadow of woman. Her skin shone pale in the soft light, but her hair was a riot of flames cascading about her face and shoulders. God, she was beautiful. Different. Sexy as hell.

Desire ripped through him—igniting a fierce animal urge to wake her, kiss her, claim her body with his, here and now. The longing to feel her beneath him was sudden and acute. He clenched his fists at the ferocity of the ache and forced himself to take a calming breath.

No. *No.*

He never wanted any woman as intensely as all that. He never felt *anything* as intensely as all that. He refused. He had reason to.

He breathed deeply again and reminded himself of his rational decisions. He hadn't been going to *make* her stay the night—despite the teasing and the incredibly erotic pleasure of her kiss. He'd been planning to get to the bottom of the necklace situation and then say goodbye to her, hadn't he?

But now here she was with her shoes off, fast asleep on the old sofa. He guessed it wasn't the first time she'd slept on it.

He frowned as he quietly stepped closer to study her. He hadn't seen just how pale she was earlier, or noticed those smudges under her eyes. She looked exhausted.

'Catriona?' he softly called to her. 'Kitty?'

She didn't stir. He'd known she wouldn't. She was in too deep a sleep. Something twisted inside Alejandro as he understood how vulnerable she was in this moment and the degree to which he was entrusted with her *care*. An icy droplet snaked down his spine. This was a complication he hadn't foreseen and didn't particularly want. Maintaining the care and wellbeing of another was not his forte. But he fetched a blanket from his room and covered her to make her more comfortable until she woke of her own accord. He hoped she would soon.

He sat in the large armchair opposite the sofa and pulled the necklace from his pocket to inspect it properly in the lamplight. It was definitely worth serious money and she'd risked a lot to get it back. But it wasn't hers.

Over the years, so many of those wealthy people he'd studied alongside had annoyed him when they'd shown a lack of appreciation of how damn lucky they were. He'd never taken his success or his security for granted. How could he when he'd come from worse than nothing? So he'd worked harder than any of them. Ensured his grades were the best. Swinging from one scholarship to the next, climbing higher and higher out of a life of poverty, misery, desperation. And his 'party lifestyle' that claimed all the headlines was but a tiny fraction of his time. The rest was spent working. Still working. Still achieving. Still ensuring success. And now a spoilt young woman had waltzed in to reclaim—what—her inheritance? The wealth she'd never had to earn for herself.

She'd been brazen and bold in her initial dismissal of him, outrageous in the reckless way she'd back-chatted him, and he'd fully planned to teach her a thing or two. Except he'd then heard the tone in which that other woman had spoken to her and there'd been no mistaking it. He hated bullies—whether they were the kind who used vicious words or the violent fists he'd experienced. So he hadn't shamed her publicly. He'd backed her and there'd been no missing the bright relief in her eyes. But then her nerve in the private courtyard when she'd insisted it was all *his* fault? When he'd given in to that urge to kiss her?

He glanced at his Sleeping Beauty again—remembering the softness of her lips, the stirring in her muscles… the *spark*. He couldn't regret that—no matter the complication that now arose.

But now he was stuck with the story that she and he were engaged. He'd smiled his way through the shocked shouts of congratulations from every one of his guests as he'd ushered them out. He'd explained that Catriona had been overwhelmed by the attention and that they'd have another party soon. It was ridiculous but he hadn't been able to find it within himself to reveal the truth. He'd seen that vulnerability when she'd looked at him. He'd seen that hurt. It echoed within him. Didn't he know what it was like to be that isolated? And afraid.

She was a contrary mix of assertiveness and insecurity, a bit broken but bluffing anyway. He liked that spirit. And he wanted her.

Well, if he was going to have her, he was going to have to play it carefully. She obviously wasn't someone who went from affair to affair.

He felt the vibration again and quietly extracted her phone from his pocket. He didn't want to wake her yet, not when she was so obviously wiped out, but it seemed someone was concerned for her welfare. The name 'Teddy' was written across the screen and the photo beneath the lettering was of the two of them. The resemblance was impossible to miss. The man was blond rather than red-haired, but he shared the same smile, the same shaped eyes. He had to be her brother.

Alejandro didn't answer the call; rather he put the phone on the wide arm of the chair he was sitting in and picked up his own phone. A simple Internet search was all it took to remind himself of the family details. Teddy—Edward—and Kitty—Catriona—Parkes-Wilson were the twin children of the man he'd bought this house from. He entered another search and soon enough came up with a photo of an elderly woman—Margot Parkes—wearing the diamond choker Kitty had come here to collect.

And then there were the pictures of Kitty herself. It seemed she was something of an artist—a sculptor. She'd had a few mentions in the society pages; there was the announcement of an engagement to some man named James that hadn't lasted. Another reason to take care with her. But Alejandro was confident; his affairs always ended easily and well and maybe something light and sexual was exactly what the woman needed. Something fun—he did fun really well.

There were more mentions of her brother. And then there was the item about Alejandro's purchase of Parkes House. Apparently it had been in her family for generations. He didn't feel bad about the transaction. He'd paid more than a fair price and if businesses failed, they failed. He'd needed a London base and he'd got one.

When her phone rang for the tenth time he finally relented, feeling only the smallest sympathy for the man who'd allowed his sister to put herself at such risk for his sake.

He touched the screen to take the call. Teddy spoke before Alejandro had the chance to say hello.

'Kitty? For God's sake, are you okay? Did you get the diamonds?'

'I'm sorry, Teddy,' Alejandro replied calmly. 'Both your sister and the diamonds are with me.'

CHAPTER FOUR

KITTY OPENED HER EYES, blinking at the bright light streaming in through the gap in the heavy brocade curtains. She frowned as she took in the familiar surroundings. She was in the second floor library on her father's sofa—

She froze as it all came flooding back. Alejandro Martinez now owned Parkes House. He'd coerced her into being his date. He'd kissed her. He'd said they'd have a reckoning and here she was, waking the next *day*—

'Good morning.'

She sat up quickly, clutching the soft woollen blanket to her, taking a split second to realise she was still fully clothed. Then she looked up, gaping as he took a seat in the armchair opposite. For a moment all she could do was stare. He looked even more striking in the daylight. So gorgeously striking.

Then she snapped herself together.

'What happened?' Warily she brushed her hair back from her face and shifted so she was sitting up properly, her feet on the floor ready to run.

'You fell asleep while I was getting rid of the other guests,' he said easily. 'You've been out for hours; I was starting to get concerned.'

Kitty's skipping pulse didn't settle. He must've showered not that long ago because his hair was still damp and now he wore jeans and a white tee, but he looked no less wolfish than he had the night before. No less to-die-for.

Half her innards melted. She loathed her reaction to him. How superficial could she get? Wowed by chiselled cheekbones, a fit body and a cockier-than-hell attitude.

In that instant he smiled at her as if he knew exactly what she was thinking.

'I have a proposition for you,' he said.

'I already said no thank you,' she said primly. *Determinedly.*

He gestured to a mug of coffee on the low table beside her. Steam curled in the light. 'I'm guessing you like it strong and unsweetened.'

Clearly she *was* that predictable after all. 'Why do you think that?'

'You're a starving artist who needs to make the most of every drop she gets.'

Silently she reached out for the coffee. He'd been doing some research.

'I made your father an offer he couldn't refuse,' he said. 'I'll make you one too.'

'My father didn't much care for this place anyway,' Kitty muttered and drank the coffee. She needed to kick-start her grey matter. 'He thought it was cold.'

'It is cold,' Alejandro said dryly. 'I've ordered a new heating system.'

Because he had the bajillions required to maintain and upgrade a heritage building like this one. She knew it was petty, but she hated him for that. He had no idea of the history of this house.

'But you like this building.' He smiled when she didn't answer. 'I can tell by the way you look around it. Listen to my offer.'

'I'll refuse anything you offer me,' she said fiercely. She wouldn't be bought as easily as her father had been. She'd never say yes to this man.

Now she remembered the humiliation of Sarah being here last night and seeing her. And the story she'd spun— that they were *engaged*? Oh, hell, the sooner she ran back to Cornwall the better.

'Maybe.' He smiled. 'But you might not want to. Why not hear me out first and then decide?'

He stood and walked over to the desk and returned with a large platter. Kitty looked at the freshly sliced fruit and pastries and swallowed to stop herself drooling. She was *starving*.

'Go ahead and eat,' Alejandro commented lazily. 'It'll make you feel better.'

She restrained herself from sending him a stabbing glance. He might be right, but he didn't need to sound so patronising.

'What's your ever so fabulous offer?' she asked, reaching for the fruit.

He watched as she bit into the pineapple before replying and for a moment Kitty wouldn't have heard or understood a word he said anyway. She was famished—and this fruit was so fresh it was all she could do to stop herself devouring it all in two seconds flat.

She heard his low chuckle and he sat back in the chair and pulled the diamond choker from his pocket.

'Tell me about this,' he said.

She gazed sadly at the coil of glittering stones in his hand but shook her head.

'You think you're protecting someone?' His eyebrows lifted. 'I know it belongs to your brother.'

He *had* been doing his research. 'Yes.'

'But you're the one who loves it.'

She bristled at the hint of censure. Did he think she was a materialistic, do-anything-for-diamonds kind of girl? 'I loved the woman it originally belonged to,' she said haughtily. 'I love what the diamonds symbolise, not what they're worth. They have irreplaceable *sentimental* value.'

His frown hadn't lessened. 'So why do they belong to your brother?'

She sighed. 'Because he's the firstborn and the boy.'

Now a baffled look crossed his face. 'Are we still in the Middle Ages?'

'*You're* the one who forced me to be your date last night, so I'd say I'm currently living in the Neanderthal era. Barbaric caveman,' she muttered beneath her breath.

'Poor baby.' His smile flashed and he leaned back in his seat, oozing sensual confidence. 'So what are you willing to do to get your necklace back?'

'Not that.' She picked up a *pain au chocolat* and chomped on it.

'I'm not that crass. We'll sleep together only when you've grown up enough to admit how much you want to.'

He laughed at her expression. His arrogance knew no bounds.

But then he sobered. 'You didn't think that you could have just contacted my lawyer? Or perhaps knocked on the front door and asked me politely? Explained there was a mix-up?'

Was that a glimpse of hurt in his eyes? Surely not.

'Am I such a monster you had to resort to breaking the law to get what belonged to your family?'

Kitty finally managed to swallow the lump of concrete masquerading as pastry in her mouth. 'You're the one who admitted to doing whatever necessary to get what you want. At the time I thought this was necessary.'

'Fair enough, but you know there are consequences to your actions. All your actions.'

'You're calling the police?'

'You should be so lucky.' His smile this time wasn't so nice. 'No, if you want the necklace back, then you make amends.'

'How do you want me to do that?'

'You fulfil the role you claimed last night. You be my fiancée.'

'What?'

Calmly he put the choker back into his pocket and then shot her a look. 'You remain here as my fiancée for a few weeks until we amicably break up and then you leave.'

'Why would you want me to do that?'

'Because it suits me.'

'And it's all about you.'

'Right now, yes, it is.' He shrugged. 'You broke into my house. You spread stories about me to all my friends. I think you owe me.'

She felt guilty enough already; she didn't need him laying it on with a trowel.

'I'm opening up the London office of my company,' he went on. 'It's a big investment and I don't want this sideshow overshadowing or impacting on its success. It doesn't need to be a big deal; interest will fade very quickly once the company set-up is fully underway.'

'I can't just stay here as your fiancée. I have a job.'

'You have a part-time position in a failing art gallery in the south of England where you don't actually get paid; you merely get a roof over your head and use of the small studio out the back.'

Yes, he'd done a *lot* of research. She'd gone to Cornwall on a whim when her engagement to James had ended in that blaze of exposure and humiliation. She'd been there for the last six months. Happy enough, but lonely. She'd been unable to resist Teddy's call for help.

'It's not failing,' she grumbled, just so she could fight with him about something. 'It's a beautiful gallery. The light down there is amazing.'

'I want you to work here and catalogue everything in this mausoleum. There are things in piles of boxes that I haven't the time to open and sift through.'

'So you can auction it off and make money from every little thing?'

'I don't need the money from these trinkets. They'd add less than a drop to my financial ocean.'

Oh, please—bully for him for being so wealthy. 'I could steal from you, you know.'

'I'm willing to take that risk.' He smiled.

'Don't you have ten personal assistants or something?'

'My PA is extremely efficient and I'm sure she'd do a good job, but her talents are better spent on the work she knows best. It's better for this to be done by someone familiar with the content. The place is in a mess and you know it.'

He was right and it wasn't just the boxes; there were years of repairs that had been left undone. Like his business, her father had left the house in a mess.

'It needs an upgrade, and you can make the arrangements, at least for the chattels to begin with. A full restoration programme will take much longer, of course.' Alejandro regarded her steadily. 'So what do you think?'

She thought it was a flimsy excuse to keep her here just because…he simply wanted it. And he always got what he wanted, that was obvious. Yet his plan appealed to the spot where she was most vulnerable. She'd loved this home and she wanted to save some of those things. 'So you're not going to modernise, but restore?'

'The building has many beautiful features that I find attractive and would like to keep.' He nodded. 'Of course I want to see it restored to its glory—not just the shell, but the interior as well.'

She felt her flush of gratitude mounting. It was so stupid, but he'd got her there. And he knew it.

'You have an understanding of the items that are here; you can assess their value and importance. Catalogue them with a sell or keep recommendation and I'll make my decision when I have time.'

She thought about it for a long moment. It was so tempting, but it was also impossible. And insane. She shook her head. 'I can't go from one engagement to another.'

Not even to a fake one.

'It's been about six months, hasn't it?' Alejandro pointed out, lazily selecting one of the grapes she'd left behind on the platter.

'Who have you been talking to?' She was mortified that he knew of her past.

He swallowed the fruit and laughed. 'What does it matter?' He reached forward, his teasing expression back. 'You know a rebound romance is the perfect solution for that bad temper.'

'This will never be a *romance*,' she snarled, shocked at the way she was suddenly burning up.

'No?' He looked amused. 'I was trying to make it sound less…raw.'

'Less tacky, you mean.' He was talking about lust and nothing but.

'You need a system cleanse.' He lifted his hands in that unexpectedly animated way that made her want to smile back at him. 'A little light fun to restore your confidence and independence.'

'And you're offering?' Like the generous, do-good kind of guy he so wasn't. 'A little light fun?'

What, exactly, would that entail? And why was it suddenly so hot in here?

'I'm offering many things. All of them good.' Still leaning forward, he propped his chin in his hand as he watched her. 'You don't have anywhere else to stay in London at the moment. I believe your brother is between apartments as well.'

Oh, hell, he knew it all. And the truth was, the prospect of couch-surfing with Teddy's theatre friends for the next few days was depressing. Her father hadn't thought it necessary to consider whether she'd have a place to stay.

And nor should he. She was twenty-three and perfectly capable of finding her own accommodation. But she hadn't realised how adrift she really was. 'Is there *anything* you don't know?'

'There are many things I don't know about you. Yet.'

The implied intimacy brought more colour to her cheeks.

'It is the organisation of the house that earns you back the diamonds,' he said. 'Our sexual relationship is outside of that bargain.'

'We have no sexual relationship,' she said firmly.

'Yet,' he repeated with a smile. 'It's only a matter of time, Catriona.'

'Not everything is that predictable.'

'This is.'

She drew in a shallow breath. 'And if I refuse to organise the house?'

'No necklace.'

'But it's not yours. It wasn't part of the house sale and you know it.'

'As you said yourself, possession is nine-tenths of the law. I have it, Catriona.' He patted his pocket. 'I'll tell the world about your attempt to break in and steal from me. That initially I covered for you last night to spare your mortification, but that in the end you had to be charged.'

'Wouldn't that bring the "sideshow" you're so keen to avoid?' she asked, delighting in pointing out his own contradiction.

He shrugged. 'I would prefer to avoid that, but I've been through worse. I'm not the villain in this—*you're* the crazy woman.'

She was. She'd be labelled the desperate woman who'd faked a fiancé to save face. Humiliation sucked. This was a way of escaping with some pride intact. And it wasn't all beneficence on his part; she knew what he wanted and frankly she was amazed—and stupidly flattered. She wasn't anything like the beautiful, curvy models he dated.

The sound of a phone ringing startled her. Even more so when she realised it was *her* phone ringing.

Alejandro took her phone from his other pocket and tossed it to her, his gaze alert and speculative. 'You'd better answer this time. He keeps ringing.'

She glanced at the screen. Teddy. He'd be having conniptions.

'Kitty? You're still in his house?' her brother said as soon as she answered.

So Alejandro had spoken to Teddy. No wonder he knew about the diamonds and everything else. Her brother couldn't keep a secret if he tried.

'How did he catch you?' Teddy's astonishment rang down the phone the second she answered. 'You got in and out so many times over the years and *never* got caught.'

Mainly because no one had cared enough to notice if she was missing. 'Well, I did this time.' The guy had to have eyes like a hawk. There'd been so many people present, she never should have been spotted.

'Well, there's the most preposterous story going around. My phone's been ringing flat-out. Everyone thinks you've been seeing him in secret all this time. They're saying you're *engaged.*'

'Oh, hell…' She covered her face with her hand. She'd made the most colossal fool of herself.

She peeked through her fingers and saw Alejandro had sat back more comfortably in his chair and was smiling, as if enjoying her mortification. She realised then that he was waiting for her to decide. That maybe he didn't actually care that much either way.

'So it's not true?'

She heard the disappointment in her brother's voice. And the anxious edge. She didn't want Teddy to worry or try to come charging in here and sorting it out and making it all even more embarrassing. Maybe this situation could be resolved best if the details were kept between her and the devil in front of her. Between *only* them. She'd suffer this mortification in front of Alejandro alone.

'They're saying he stepped in to save Dad's cash flow because he's been in love with you all this time,' Teddy said.

She laughed a little hysterically. 'Oh, Teddy, it's not quite that simple.'

'But you *are* his fiancée?'

She hesitated, glancing up to meet Alejandro's penetrating gaze for a long moment.

'Kitty...' Teddy's voice lowered. 'Are you okay? When I phoned last night he was very short with me.'

'Everything's fine, Teddy.' She tore her gaze from Alejandro's, straightened her shoulders and made herself smile. 'They're more than fine. But things are a little...complicated—'

'I didn't think you even knew him. Last night you were—' He broke off almost as soon as he'd interrupted. 'Shit, is that why you were in such a hurry to get there?'

'Look, I'll come and see you in a couple of days, okay? I'll explain it then. But for now I am staying here.'

'*With* him?' Teddy's excitement barrelled down the phone. 'You're really staying with him?'

'Yes.'

It took almost a full minute after ending the call with Teddy before she could lift her chin and look Alejandro in the face again. She was just waiting for him to gloat with some smart comment. But when she did look at him, she found he was watching her with just the smallest of smiles. It wasn't even a smug one.

'At least here you can have a bed,' he offered blandly.

'My own bed?'

'Of course, until you ask to share mine.'

'Not going to happen.'

He laughed then. 'You're too constricted by your own naivety,' he jeered. 'Believing in some fairy tale version of romance and being in a relationship "happily-ever-after".'

'You don't believe in relationships?' Why wasn't she surprised?

'Not lasting ones.' His smile flashed.

'So not marriage.'

'Definitely not. I will never marry.'

'That's sad,' she said glibly.

'What's sad is the vast number of people who stay in unhappy marriages because they think they have to.' He shrugged carelessly. 'I like indulging—in nice food, pleasant company, good sex. Then a gentle goodbye. What's wrong with that?' He breathed it with utter confidence and arrogance.

'Nothing.' She couldn't fault him for what seemed to be the perfect life. For him. Because she didn't think the goodbye Saskia had got had been all that gentle.

'I work hard. I achieve. I get what I deserve.'

'I hope you do,' she said pointedly.

He didn't look remotely abashed. 'The women I tend to date have worked every bit as hard as I have to achieve their successes.'

'With plastic surgery and liberal use of the casting couch,' she muttered.

'You judge your sisters so harshly?'

She wrinkled her nose, hating that he was right and she'd been bitchy.

'I treat all my lovers with respect and courtesy,' he said meaningfully. 'A little kindness goes a long way.'

'But you have no desire to be faithful?'

His eyes widened. 'I sleep with one woman at a time. I don't date another until I have ensured anyone else I had been seeing is clear that we are no longer an item.'

As he'd done with poor Saskia.

'Is that what you'll do with me if we have an affair? Just flick me a text before jumping into bed with another woman?'

Her cheeks heated. James hadn't done even that. He'd cheated on her.

'We will formally end our engagement. There will be no miscommunication or misunderstanding.'

'And now you think I should just fall into bed with you?'

'I think if you were honest about what you want, that's exactly what you'd do.' He watched her closely. 'There's nothing wrong with lust, Catriona.'

Maybe there wasn't, but she wasn't ready for it. And not for him. 'Okay, here's some honesty for you,' she said, trying to take control of the situation and clarify her intentions. 'You're an attractive man and you know it. But we don't share the same desires. I don't want that kind of empty pleasure. I want something more meaningful and complicated. So I'll do the house. I'll stay until this stupid story blows over. But that's all. And when that's done, then I go.'

He was not winning. He was not getting everything his own way. She'd be his first failure.

'You think you can resist this chemistry?' He grinned, hugely amused. 'Are you one of those women who has to believe she's in love before she'll have sex with a man?'

'Not love necessarily. But something a little warmer than loathing.'

He laughed and stood. 'I will not muddy this affair with false declarations or meaningless promises. When you want me, just let me know.'

'I'll send you a telegram.' She blew him a kiss. 'Now, go to work, darling, so I can steal from you while your back is turned.'

Alejandro knew he could have her far sooner than she pretended. Knew that it would take only a few kisses and she'd be heavy-eyed and restless in his arms, as she'd been for those too brief moments last night. But now he wanted more than that from her. Now he'd seen her defiant rise to his challenge, the determined denial sparking in her eyes. That spirit and courage showed she wasn't so much broken as bruised. He'd help her forget the stupid ex-fiancé.

But he wanted her to hit the ignition on their affair. To be unable to deny this chemistry without his provocation. He didn't know why. Usually he wasn't that bothered— either he took a lover or he didn't. It was straightforward. But Catriona presented a challenge that he couldn't resist engaging with. Maybe some old-fashioned seduction was required, until the electricity was too high a voltage to be ignored and she came to him.

He'd worked like a demon this morning to arrange everything. He'd sent his assistant to stay in a hotel for the week. He'd be at work most of the time, but when he was here he didn't want anyone interrupting him and Catriona. It struck him that things might get fiery at any moment. He was looking forward to that. And, with her unconventional beauty, she fitted in this house. The fact she could help with excavating all the residual stuff that was seemingly cemented inside it was pure bonus.

'I'm happy to have you as my fiancée for the foreseeable future,' he said, pleased with the outcome.

It was the perfect solution. He got someone to sort the house and he'd get to sleep with the most vexingly sexy woman he'd encountered in a while.

'I'm not staying here for long.' She suddenly looked uneasy.

Was she attempting to back out of the deal already? Because she knew she wasn't going to win?

He smothered his smile. 'Why not? The house is big; there's a lot of rubbish to get rid of.'

'It's not rubbish—' Indignation flared in her eyes.

'Well, you'd better do it then—else I'll just dump the lot,' he interrupted dismissively.

She narrowed her gaze at him. 'As if you'd be that reckless with an investment.'

'No, you're the reckless one. I'm on damage control. One month.'

Her mouth opened. Then shut. Then opened again. 'You're not going to get *everything* you want.' She sent him another speaking look. 'No more parties.'

'Pardon?'

'While I'm here as your fiancée there'll be no parties.'

Was she trying to dictate terms to him, to renegotiate when she had zero bargaining power? He stifled another laugh. 'I thought you Bohemian types liked parties.'

'Your definition of a party is very different to mine.'

'How so?' He spread his hands in bewilderment. 'I like parties.'

'You like being surrounded by women who pander to your ego.'

He clamped down another smile. She really didn't want other women around, did she? 'No parties at home,' he conceded, happy to be alone with her for what little time he'd have in the house. 'But we dine out. We dance.'

He liked the ambience of a busy restaurant.

'No dancing.'

'Why not?' He folded his arms, amused by her determined rejection of what he had to offer. 'Don't tell me you can't.'

'Of course I can't,' she declared in total irritation. 'I have no interest in it.'

'I'll teach you,' he said, unbothered. 'Next item?'

'No…' She hesitated. 'No…'

Yes, this was where she really was most vulnerable. 'You don't need to worry.' Hadn't he just told her he only dated one woman at a time?

'I'm not having two fiancés leave me for another woman,' she blurted it out anyway. 'I'm not going through that again. Not even pretend.'

So she had been hurt by the ex-fiancé.

'Fine. You'll break my heart. Unable to get over my rampantly lusty past even though I'll have been nothing but true to you.' He offered the solution softly, watching her closely.

'As if anyone would believe you had.' She rolled her eyes. 'You'll have plenty of women offering to soothe your hurts.'

She was painfully insecure, and breathtakingly insulting, but he didn't blame her. She'd been hurt. 'And you'll have your pride restored.'

A slightly stunned look crossed her face. 'It's not pride.'

'What is it then?'

She shook her head, that expression shutting down. 'You wouldn't understand. You don't seem to have the same kinds of emotions as I do.'

Her words were barbed, and they hit a spot he hadn't realised was exposed. He had emotions all right. It was just that he worked hard to control them. He *had* to. Suddenly raw, he turned and walked towards the door. 'I have to get to work. Be ready for dinner at seven.'

'I don't have any decent clothes with me,' she called after him sulkily.

Drawing in a calming breath, he turned back to face her. 'So buy some more.'

'In case you hadn't noticed, my family has hit the skids. You want to be ashamed by your fiancée when you take her out looking like a bag lady?'

He knew she was deliberately putting obstacles in his way to be as annoying as possible. Too bad, he wasn't going to be bothered. 'You don't look like a bag lady. I like the catsuit thing.' He smiled patronisingly at her. 'But feel free to go out and buy whatever you want for tonight. My treat.'

Her gaze narrowed on his mouth. Awareness arrowed to his groin. He'd known she'd loathe the offer of his money and that her temper would flare. His smile deepened to genuine pleasure in anticipation of her bite.

But she didn't give him a verbal lashing. If anything, she sounded as sultry as a siren. 'What's my budget?'

Only then did she lift her lashes and reveal the fury in her green eyes.

'Will a hundred thousand do to start?' he suggested roughly, unable to resist absorbing her dare and raising the stakes.

She didn't bat an eyelid at that.

He strolled back over to where she still sat on the sofa, enjoying himself immensely. 'We'll have to get you an engagement ring too.' He picked up her hand and studied her long, delicate fingers. 'Just to really set the whole thing off.'

'That's not necessary,' she clipped, tilting her chin so she could keep burning holes in him with her fiery gaze. 'I'm not wearing a ring.'

So she did have a few scruples. Or maybe she was superstitious.

'You've worn one before.' And he felt a twinge of guilt about pointing that out to her so bluntly.

She tried to pull her hand from his but he gripped it harder.

'And it brought me nothing but trouble,' she muttered.

'Poor Catriona.' He couldn't hold back a second longer. He tugged her hand, drawing her into a standing position, and reached out with his other hand to run his fingers down the length of her beautiful hair. 'Go indulge in some retail therapy,' he suggested with a mercilessly condescending tease. 'Spend hard.'

She sent him another foul look. 'You know I could walk out with all this money of yours and skip the country, never to return.'

'You're too polite to do that. And you know that if you did, I would hunt you down.' His gut clenched at the words. It was only a joke; he didn't mean it. Not truly.

'I'm not afraid of you.'

But he was close enough to have felt her shiver and fought his own primal response to pull her closer and keep her. He wasn't going down that possessive route, not when he knew how destructive it could be. How terrifying. He'd rein this in and get it back to nothing more than a seductive, light tease. 'No, but you're afraid of what I can offer.'

'What do you think that you can offer me that I would be afraid of?'

'The kind of passion you think you can't cope with,' he taunted, leaning that last inch into her space.

'Oh, please.' She rolled her eyes, but he'd seen the rise of that pink under her cheeks.

He put his hands on her slender waist. Satisfaction burst within him, desire for more slammed in on its heels. 'I won't deny I want you in my bed, little Cat,' he muttered, his words tumbling, rough and unstoppable now. 'I'm looking forward to hearing you—'

She suddenly stunned him by clamping her hand over his mouth. 'You think I haven't heard those kinds of sleazy lines before? You want to "pet me until I purr"?' She pushed her hand, forcing him to turn his head away for a second. 'If you really want me, you need to try harder.'

Harder? His laugh was harsh as he pulled her flush against him, pressing his lips on hers. For a spilt-second it was pure passion, lip-to-lip, breast-to-chest, hip-to-hip and straining…but then he made himself go gently again.

Slow. Slow right down.

He'd have his control back, thanks. And he'd surprise her into that deliciously unguarded reaction she'd given him last night.

He softened, pressing small kisses on her plump pouting mouth until she opened it with the smallest of sighs. She tasted like fruit and pastry, a little tart, a lot sweet. And hot. So damn hot and vital. She might be slender, but she was strong. He slid his hand up her back, pressing her closer, needing to feel her where he was aching most. Her hands skated up his chest, curling around his shoulders as she arched her back and her neck, pressing her breasts more firmly against him, letting him deepen the kiss even more. And, heaven knew, he did. Slowly and thoroughly, he explored her mouth, caressing her with his tongue because he couldn't get enough of her taste. He widened his stance so he could gather her closer, aching to absorb all her passion. Gentle was all but forgotten. She felt so good pressed up against him.

And, as she kissed him back, his control started to slip again. He wanted more. He wanted it now.

When she breathed so quickly? When she moaned? When her lips were soft and submissive and hungrily seeking, all at the same time? When her hips circled against his in that way that maddened him to the point of *grinding*?

He teetered on the brink of tumbling her to the sofa, tearing clothing and taking her in a frenzy of unfettered, uncontrolled lust—

He pulled back quickly, resisting the urge. It hurt. His breathing sounded loud in his ears.

But so did hers. To his relief—and pleasure—she still felt warm and soft in his arms. Willing. Ready. So close to *his*. Oh, yes, she wanted him too.

Well, she was going to get what they both wanted. When she was ready. When she asked. And when he was in control. He'd keep it light. Always.

Lit up with amusement and arousal and burning-hot satisfaction, he eyed her lazily. 'I don't think I need to try that hard at all.'

CHAPTER FIVE

'SEXUAL ATTRACTION IS easy enough to ignore,' Kitty argued breathlessly, basically hauling herself upright to stop herself leaning on him.

The man packed a serious sexual punch and she'd succumbed again *so* easily. How on earth did she think she could simply ignore the effect he had on her?

'But why would you want to?' He looked mystified.

She pushed out of his arms and walked away from him, needing the space to clear her head. But goodness, her legs felt wobbly. 'You really are bored, aren't you?'

This was just so easy to him—as natural as breathing. But her heart ached for that something *more*. Surely there had to be more?

'And you really are suffering from a lack of self-esteem.'

She shook her head. 'Don't try to flatter me.'

'I'm being honest. Come on.' He flicked his fingers at her. 'Get ready. I've got to go to work and now we have an errand to run first.'

She stiffened. He was used to calling the shots, wasn't he? 'Then fetch my bag from the communal garden, will you?'

'You stashed your bag in the garden?' He sent her an astounded look, ignoring her attempt at a commanding tone to match his. 'You really are a cat burglar.'

'Bet you can't find it.' She smiled at him coyly.

He sent her another look—a lowering one. 'I know what you're doing.' But he left the room anyway.

Amused, Kitty crossed the library, opened the window and leaned out of it to watch him. He glanced back up to the building, somehow knowing she'd do exactly that. She could feel the heat of his glare across the distance, but then he turned his back on her to study the garden for a few minutes and unerringly went to the bush where she'd hidden the bag.

At that point Kitty flounced away from the window.

A few moments later he returned, triumphantly brandishing her bag. 'You don't have much with you.'

'Because I wasn't planning on staying long.' She snatched it from him and stalked from the room.

'You won't need much anyway…' His sensual laughter followed her down the hall.

Kitty locked the bathroom door and showered quickly, briskly soaping herself and ignoring her hyper-sensitised skin and still trembling legs. She was *crazy* to have accepted this arrangement when he could make her want him so easily.

But chemistry *could* be ignored. And a week or so spent here was a chance to say goodbye to her home. A chance to keep her head high the next time she saw those society wenches. And a chance to prove Alejandro wrong— he wasn't going to get everything he wanted. He wasn't going to get her.

As long as she kept her distance from him. No more touching. No more kissing.

She'd been truly hurt by the end of her engagement to James, but she doubted that Alejandro could ever understand the concept. He was total Teflon. Indestructible and impervious to any pain—of feeling any deep emotion, for that matter. As far as she could tell, life was all a party to him. It was all about the next affair while wheeling and dealing the rest of the time. Well, he wasn't having an affair with her, no matter how good he kissed. She refused to be yet another easy conquest.

When she emerged refreshed she found he'd showered again too and changed into a suit. It was navy with a crisp white shirt but he wore no tie with it and his hair was damp; he looked so sharp her eyes hurt. Her resolve wavered. Did she really think she could resist? That unholy smile lurked in his eyes as he watched her walk towards him and she straightened. Of course she could resist. She wasn't an *animal*.

A car was idling for them just outside the house, an enormous, luxurious thing with a suit-and-sunglasses-clad giant sitting behind the steering wheel.

'You might get away with this kind of ostentatiousness in New York, but it's really not the done thing in London, you know,' she offered faux helpfully once they were ensconced in the back seat. 'Better to take a taxi next time.'

'I prefer to rely on my own driver, but thanks for the advice anyway,' he replied blandly.

The car stopped outside a beautiful old building and Alejandro insisted she went inside with him. Only the subtly placed logo near the heavy wooden door clued her in— this wasn't the kind of bank that had tellers behind security grilles and queues of impatient people. This was exclusivity and discretion to the max. The private banker didn't bat an eyelid when Alejandro insisted he issue Kitty a card then and there, preloaded with his wads of cash.

'Show off,' Kitty murmured as they returned to the waiting car less than twenty minutes later.

Alejandro smiled, but she sensed his attention was flicking from her; his expression had become serious and distant—he was entering 'work mode'. A few minutes later the car pulled in again.

'Paolo and the car are at your disposal all day. Get yourself whatever you need,' he said as he looked out of the window at his new office premises. 'Be there when I get home.'

'Or?'

At her tone he turned back to face her and she realised

she'd been wrong about his slipping attention. In this moment, she was the sole object of his searing focus. Her toes curled in her shoes; she was almost melting on the spot.

'Until tonight, sweet fiancée.' He didn't bother replying to her question; he knew he didn't need to.

For a breathless second she wondered if he might take his part too far and kiss her again. But she'd be ready for him this time, right? She'd resist the temptation to slide into his sensuality.

But he didn't lean closer, he didn't kiss her. He just got out of the car.

And that *wasn't* a kernel of disappointment she was feeling. Alejandro waved her off with such a smug, knowing look in his eye that Kitty didn't wave back. The infuriating creature seemed to know everything she was thinking.

'Where would you like to go, Miss Parkes-Wilson?' Paolo asked politely.

Right now? The moon.

'Could you just drive for a bit while I decide?' She pressed a hand to her hot cheeks.

She needed to come up with a decent plan for the next few days—Alejandro was too confident, but she didn't blame him, only herself. She needed something to combat his intensity.

She'd had no intention of spending a penny of his money when she'd made such a drama about her clothes, but now she felt like making him pay in some small way for his intolerable arrogance.

Maybe she should buy the most outrageous couture item she could find? Maybe she should go for something totally off the wall and appalling that she'd never normally be seen dead in. Amused at the thought, she asked Paolo to take her to the flagship store of a high end designer. But, once she was inside, she was almost immediately distracted by a simple black number hanging on a polished rack right near the door. She moved to take a closer look, inwardly grimacing when she saw there was no price tag.

'Would you like to try it on, madam?' A soft-spoken, impossibly groomed man stepped forward to offer assistance.

'Um…maybe?' she mumbled doubtfully, feeling like a fraud.

She was so used to her 'work wardrobe' of black on black—three-quarter-length trousers and long-sleeved sweaters—she was going to feel weird in anything else. She might have long limbs, but there was so much else required to carry off clothing like this.

One summer in her mid-teen years she'd been scouted by a modelling agency. Not to model swimwear, of course, given her pallor and lack of curves, but high-end fashion. At the time she'd been pleased to get the attention and for a few blissful days had actually believed someone thought she was pretty. But then she'd seen the completed booking sheet with her name on it:

Freak chic. Angular, androgynous, tall with red hair, pale skin. Freckles.

She'd filled out a bit since then, but there was no denying she was still the 'freak' and there was no 'chic' about it. After that dose of reality she'd covered up and come up with her own year-in-year-out version of starving artist attire.

'I believe it would suit you, madam.'

He was clearly paid to say that, but she let him lead her to the changing room anyway.

She straightened her shoulders and followed his example of confident posture. She'd never be considered conventionally pretty, but maybe she could wear the damn designer dresses anyway. A dress like this would be like armour, hiding the weaknesses—the imperfections—underneath. Protecting her. She was *so* tempted.

'I need some statement pieces,' she confided to the attendant as he waited at the entrance to the spacious private room. 'Some dresses that scream exclusive.'

'If I may suggest, nothing screams exclusive more than subtlety,' he replied with a quiet courtesy that had her believing him. 'You go ahead and try this on and I'll be back with more in a moment.'

Kitty quickly stripped and then stepped into the dress, blinking as she regarded her reflection in the gleaming mirror. The dress was beautifully cut and sat perfectly on her waist, but it didn't reveal vast quantities of skin. Maybe the man was right about subtlety?

'Madam—?'

She opened the door and saw the saviour of a salesman had returned with an armload of other options for her to try. But now he paused and studied her with a critical eye.

'Yes.' He nodded as she stood in front of the mirror and she felt as if he actually meant it. 'Our dresses never date,' he informed her confidently. 'And they never lose their value.'

Didn't they? She could well believe that, given they were beautifully tailored and had that sleek sort of design that was recognised the world over. And if they didn't lose their value, then perhaps, as soon as these few weeks were over, she could auction any dresses she bought and then give the proceeds to charity?

That would *definitely* work. She'd be making Alejandro pay, but for her own benefit—not ultimately. And if she did that, then she could spend every last penny of his ridiculous 'budget' just to serve him right. She turned to the assistant, inspired and more enthusiastic about shopping than she'd ever been in her life. 'Then let's see what else you have.'

Somehow four hours flew past. After the dress purchases, she succumbed to the temptation of some lacy lingerie. Sure, she couldn't exactly auction those pieces, but the dresses needed the right level of support and discretion—

no visible panty lines or bra straps. It wasn't as if there was any chance of Alejandro seeing her in the lacy smalls...

And then there were shoes—but she chose only a couple of pairs to see her through.

Lastly she ducked into a beauty parlour and spent a little of her own money on a spot of personal grooming. Again, if she was going to look the part, she needed to feel it.

Six and a half hours later she got Paolo to return her to Parkes House, guiltily figuring she'd better get on with her actual 'job'. To be honest, she didn't quite know where to begin. There were so very many boxes, frankly she wouldn't blame Alejandro at all if he decided to just send the lot to the rubbish dump. But she had to start somewhere—and she had to get it *done*.

'You've been busy,' Alejandro called as he stopped by the door of the box-filled room two hours later.

Kitty glared at him from where she stood drowning in boxes, overwhelmed by the enormity of all the stuff she had to process. She'd made the mistake of opening too many too soon.

Alejandro's mouth twitched, as if he was suppressing a laugh at her expense. 'Did you have fun shopping?'

'Oh, yes, I spent all your money,' she lied, turning on a brilliant, totally fake smile.

'Well done.' He nodded approvingly. 'I bet that took some doing.'

She sighed and examined her fingernails in mock boredom. 'Not really—a handful of dresses, a few pairs of shoes...' she shrugged '...and poof, all the money was gone.'

'Wonderful. You can leave the receipts on the desk in the library for me.' He leaned against the doorjamb and frowned at her black trousers. 'Yet you're not ready to go out?'

'We're going out?' She glanced at the mass of boxes

blocking her escape from the room. Her nerves prickled. She was going to have to wear one of those dresses now. She was going to have to live up to the pretence. And she was going to have to look at him across the table... He was too handsome. Too assured. Too damn knowing.

She'd be better off buried in the boxes here.

'Are you not hungry?' Alejandro was feeling extremely hungry and not just for food. She looked beautiful standing there glaring back at him with a raft of emotions flickering across her striking features. 'I believe it's a good restaurant.'

And they needed to get there soon, before he threw all caution to the wind and tried to seduce her here and now.

'Don't you ever just eat at home?' Her glare became less defensive and more curious.

'Why would I?' He didn't enjoy cooking for himself. Usually he went straight to a restaurant from the office. 'I enjoy socialising with lots of people.'

'Oh.' She nodded and seemed to think about it for a moment. 'So you're aware of how boring your own company is.'

He was stunned into silence briefly, but then laughed grudgingly. 'You witch.'

Her smile of acknowledgement lit up her whole face and made him want to step nearer and feel the warmth of it on his skin. But at the same time he felt compelled to get a dig in.

'So you stay home and cook something gourmet for yourself every night?' he challenged her.

Her smile actually deepened. 'I cook instant noodles every night.'

He grimaced and didn't bother commenting.

'I add fresh vegetables,' she added piously.

'As if that makes it any better.'

'I'm a starving artist,' she said loftily. 'What did you expect me to eat?'

'Well, tonight you can eat like a queen. If you'll only hurry up and get ready,' he groaned.

'Okay, darling, I won't be long.'

He watched her navigate the cardboard obstacles with an impressively swift glide, and walk past him and out of the room with a small toss of her head. Shaking his own, he walked down to the library, pulling his phone from his pocket to check on any mail that might have arrived in the thirty minutes since he'd left the office. He might as well do some more work while he waited. But, to his surprise, it was less than fifteen minutes before she cleared her throat.

He looked up to the doorway and promptly forgot his own name, let alone what it was he'd been writing. 'You can spend every last cent of mine if you're going to end up looking like that.'

Her death stare felled him.

'I'm sensing a colour theme.' He noted the black. Again. He'd not seen her in anything else so far. Black clothes that clung, but covered up almost all of her pale, pale skin. *His* skin tightened. He was looking forward to finally getting a proper glimpse of her.

'I'm grieving the loss of my freedom,' she drawled. 'Hence the mourning outfits.'

He laughed appreciatively. 'It's so hard for you, isn't it? Losing the family home.'

'The long goodbye to the family fine china,' she mused. 'It is a burden.'

'Poor baby, the silver spoon's been snatched from you.'

He wasn't going to make it to the damn restaurant if she kept looking at him like that. He was used to dating very beautiful, perfectly proportioned women, but he'd found none as attractive as he found Catriona right now, with her angular defiance and glittering eyes and her chin jutting in the air. He laughed, more to expend some of the energy coiling inside him than from genuine amusement.

In some ways, his reaction to her wasn't funny at all. He'd been so looking forward to seeing what she had in store for him that he'd actually left work a fraction early because he couldn't wait any longer to find out. It was the first time he'd ever done that for a woman. He'd wanted to check she was still there. Catriona Parkes-Wilson wasn't quite as predictable as all that. But, given he'd instructed Paolo to keep his eye on her, he knew she hadn't left the house again since returning from the epic shopping spree. He also knew exactly how much she'd spent and had to admit it had surprised him. But nothing about Catriona was quite as it seemed and he was interested to see how she was going to play this out.

'Shall we go?'

'Where are we going?' she asked.

He named a new restaurant that—according to his PA—had a waiting list of months.

'There'll be celebrities there.' She frowned and glanced down at her dress.

'Are you going to ask for their autographs?'

A giggle burbled out of her.

'You look amazing,' he assured her briefly. 'We need to leave. Now.'

Now or never. Fortunately, Paolo was waiting with the engine running.

'You can't drive yourself anywhere?' she asked pointedly as he held the door for her.

'Why would I when I can hold hands with you in the back seat instead?' he answered, sliding in after her.

He picked up her hand and felt her curl it into a fist. His sensual awareness was stronger now he knew how good she felt pressed against him. Hell, he wanted that again. Now. The energy between them crackled in the air in the confined space. It took all his willpower not to pull her right into his arms and kiss her into saying yes. Instead, he made himself stay a safe distance away. He could stay in control of this. He would always stay in control.

'Sorry we're late,' he said smoothly as he led her to the two vacant seats his colleagues had left in the middle of the large table at the rear of the restaurant. 'I hope you've gone ahead and ordered.'

Catriona's hand tightened on his. 'You promised no parties,' she whispered as she sat in the seat next to him.

'This isn't a party. This is dinner.' He released her to hold her chair out for her.

'It's a dinner party,' she whispered, pausing. 'There are like…' she glanced around the table '…*fifteen* people here.'

Wasn't that the point of dinner? To socialise? He liked being around people, but she didn't seem comfortable. He took a closer look at her face. 'You okay?'

'I'll just fake it till I make it,' she muttered as she glanced again at everyone at the table before sitting down.

He wasn't even sure he was supposed to hear that little quip, but the honesty underlying it smote him. A small surge of protectiveness made him reach out to clasp her hand in his again as they sat side by side. Did she honestly doubt how stunning she was? Was she really intimidated by these others present?

Or was it that she'd wanted to dine alone with him tonight? His pulse struck an irregular beat. He couldn't remember when he'd last dined alone with a woman. Always he had extras with him—work colleagues and acquaintances, or another couple of women, friends of his latest lover. He liked being surrounded by busy, happy people. That was normal, right? And there was safety in numbers.

Too much time alone with a lover might lead to complications he didn't want.

All he really wanted from the women he dated was phys-

ical release and fulfilment—the delights of mutual pleasure.
If he took a woman home, he encouraged her to leave after
they'd had sex. Generally he'd drive her home, then would
drive alone for a while, enjoying the late night and the city,
the relaxed state of his body. Or if his lover was fast asleep
in his bed—as some of them pretended to be—he went into
his study and worked through till dawn. When a woman
woke up and realised he wasn't there, she soon got the message. Even when he dated a woman for a few weeks, he
wanted his own room at the end of each night. He needed
his intimate space to himself. Always. And—other than
amusement—he needed his emotions minimally engaged.

'Order something to eat—you'll feel better.' He opted
to tease Catriona into sparking back at him. Humour was
always good.

'I'm starting to think you must be an emotional eater.'

He laughed. 'No, I just recognise "hangry" when I see
it. You didn't stop for lunch—you must be starving.'

'And you know this because?'

'Paolo reported in to me.'

'Oh, so my every move is being documented and reported back to you?'

'Naturally. My fiancée's welfare is very much my concern.'

She glowered at the menu and he bit back his smile.

'Something wrong?' He waited, knowing she'd find
something. She was never going to make this easy for him.

'I'm vegetarian.' Her glance at him now was positively
sugary. 'So this whole French *foie gras* and raw steak thing
isn't working for me.'

Of course she was. 'Another whim of yours?'

She lowered the menu and turned to correct him. 'I've
been vegetarian since I was seven.'

'You just made that choice one day?'

'Pretty much.'

'Your parents agreed?'

'Of course not. So I went on hunger strike until they did.'

He grinned, imagining the stubbornness of a red-headed wilful child. 'How long did that take?'

'Just over a week.'

'That long?' He'd have given in to her much sooner. 'Why don't you wish to eat meat—for slimming or ethical reasons?'

She sent him a withering look. 'You really have to ask?'

'When you feel strongly about something, you go the whole way with it, don't you?'

'All or nothing.' She nodded blithely. 'Otherwise what's the point?'

'So when you're wrong, you're *really* wrong.'

'No,' she answered haughtily. 'I'm *rarely* wrong.'

'Oh? What about men?' He laughed, enjoying her cut-glass perfection. 'Third time lucky, do you think?'

'Once I'm shot of you?' she muttered so the others couldn't hear. 'I'm checking in to a nunnery.'

'Oh, no,' he chided. 'That would never do. You'll always need a release for that passion.'

'That's what my art is for,' she said airily.

He laughed, genuinely amused. Catriona had far too much fire for any kind of life of denial.

'What's so funny, you two?' one of the women across the table called to him.

'Alejandro delights in teasing me,' Catriona answered before he could.

He was going to delight in teasing her. Very much.

He listened as she assumed the role of society fiancée. Most of the guests were over from the States like him, a couple of younger ones for the first time, and Catriona efficiently schooled them in the 'off the beaten track' tourist ideas, getting in a plug for her brother's upcoming play too, he noticed with a wry grin. And, for someone who was 'faking it', she was doing a good job. When the food arrived she quietened, tucking in to the specially ordered vegetarian dish with gusto. All or nothing indeed.

'What are you thinking about?' he asked her gently when he saw the curve of a smile on her mouth.

Her eyebrows shot up. 'Seriously?'

'Yes.' He wanted to know everything that was going on in that head of hers.

'I was thinking how delicious that was.'

'So, despite the initial disappointment of the menu, we've managed to please you?'

'Mm hmmm.' She sat back with a satisfied smile and looked at him.

Her eyes sparkled in the light; her skin was so pale it was almost luminescent. She had such striking colouring and, whether she intended it or not, there was challenge in those emerald eyes. Challenge he could no longer resist.

He pushed his chair back and stood. 'Come with me; there's something you need to see.'

'We're leaving now?' She looked startled and glanced back at the other dinner guests.

'Only for a moment. This way.' He threw a polite smile at the others but firmly took her hand and led her out the back and down the gleaming black corridor. At the very end he paused and turned to face her.

'Why are we here?' She still looked bemused. And beautiful.

'To admire this painting.' He waved a distracted hand at a large modernist painting that was conveniently hung on the wall. 'As an artist, I thought you'd appreciate it.'

'I'm not really that much of an artist. And not the painting kind.' She frowned at the canvas.

'Okay, I brought you here because I wanted to be alone with you.' He wasn't afraid to be honest. He knew she wanted him too. And he wanted her to look at him again, not the stupid painting.

She faced him, that frown replaced by a laughing smile, but it still wasn't enough.

'I thought you liked dinner parties with billions of people,' she teased.

'Shh.' He'd hardly touched her all day and he couldn't resist now. He wanted to taste that smile, to press against the pretty pout of her full lips. He wanted to feel her softness and lithe strength, he wanted to claim her body with his own and see her buck and then break under the pleasure he could push her to—

Her eyes widened as she looked up at him. 'Alejandro—'

He caught her lips with his, groaning as he felt her part for him immediately. Caution and control faded. He tugged her closer, pressing her body against the hard ache of his, wrapping his arms around her waist so he could explore her shape. He couldn't get close enough. He tried to keep it gentle, but the kiss deepened. So did his frustration. He wanted to be alone with her. Warm. Naked. He wanted all the time in the world to explore her—to taste every inch and every secret part of her. But he had to make do with just her mouth. It was good. Too good. And it wasn't enough.

Kitty lost track of time and space and sanity. Never had she been kissed like this. Never had she felt as if she was so close to soaring—so high, so quick. There was only Alejandro, only this warmth, only this surging sense of delight. And need. She wanted to burrow closer, she wanted him to touch her more…there…everywhere. His kisses drugged and ignited desire. Never had she wanted a man like this. The way his tongue teased, the way he nipped the inside of her lip with his teeth, the soothing—then stirring—caress of his lips, the pleasure he promised with every stroke…

She writhed helplessly and recklessly against his firm hold, grinding her hips against his. Her wantonness shocked her. She didn't want this to stop. She didn't want this ever to stop. But—oh, God—that was why it had to. They couldn't. Not here. Not now.

She tore her lips from his, jerking her head back and reminding herself of where they were.

'Alejandro,' she pleaded breathlessly, pushing against his chest. 'There are people.'

They were making out in the restaurant corridor like teen lovers who couldn't go home to their parents' houses for privacy, and she felt out of control.

'We're engaged,' he lifted his head and pointed out with annoying reasonableness. 'Of course we're going to kiss. No one would ever believe I was engaged and not be touching my fiancée any time I could.'

She pushed back a strand of hair and sent him a baleful look, locking her knees to stop her legs from shaking. How could he remain so collected when he kissed like that? 'There's an occasional kiss, and then there's indecent behaviour. I only agreed to this so I *wouldn't* get arrested, remember?'

He looked amused. 'A few kisses aren't going to get you arrested. Or were you about to strip naked and have your way with me up against the wall?'

Oh, if he only knew. She jabbed her finger in his chest. 'Stop provoking me.'

'But it's the most fun I've had in years.' He pulled her close again and brushed another quick kiss on her lips. 'You respond so magnificently. Like lightning, you flare. You must be incandescent when you orgasm.'

A wave of heat almost turned her to cinders on the spot. 'Right now I'm incandescent with rage.' She wished the lighting in the corridor was dimmer so he couldn't see how violently he was making her blush. 'Stop talking like that.'

He bent his head and whispered in her ear, 'But it's turning you on.'

'Everyone is staring,' she hissed. Well, only the couple of people who'd ventured down the corridor, and they'd quickly gone again.

'I don't care.'

'Well, *I* do.' She pushed hard against his chest. If he kept kissing her like that she'd agree to anything he suggested and she refused to let him win so easily. 'It's past my bedtime.'

'You want to go home to bed?' He stepped back and looked wickedly at her.

'Alone,' she lied. 'Yes.'

'Then let's get you there.'

CHAPTER SIX

OFFICIALLY, PARKES HOUSE had eight bedrooms, all of them with private bathrooms. Half were on the second floor, the remainder on the third.

'Which room did you take?' Alejandro asked as they climbed the stairs. 'The one next to mine?'

'Of course not.' It had interested her to see that he'd claimed one of the smaller rooms as his, but maybe that was just because there was so much stuff shoved into all the others.

'So you know which is mine.' He grinned. 'Did you go in and take a good look at my things?'

'Naturally.' She battled her blush and tried to act as if she wasn't embarrassed. 'The more one knows about one's enemy, the better one is equipped to win the battle.'

'Enemy?' He laughed. 'Bit extreme, don't you think?' He took hold of her hand. 'Did you learn anything of use?'

She gently breathed out, trying to slow her pounding pulse. 'You're a show-off. As if you can read all those books at once.' The pile beside his bed had almost exclusively been non-fiction, on a wide and eclectic range of subjects.

'I like reading,' he said. 'You won't find the diamonds, by the way. I keep them with me at all times. They're too precious.' He looked at her curiously as they walked along the corridor of the third floor. 'So which room?'

Her heart still thudded too quickly. She had no idea how she was going to resist him. 'My own.'

His eyes glinted. 'And it's not one of these?' They'd passed all the doors now.

She shook her head.

'Show me.'

'Fine.' She led him to the stairwell again and went first.

'You were up in the attic? Servants' quarters?'

'Don't go thinking I was some kind of Cinderella,' she said gruffly. 'In some ways I was very spoilt.'

'Tell me something I don't know,' he drawled.

She glanced at him but he was smiling. At the top she went a few paces along the much narrower corridor, opened the door, flicked on the light switch and then stood back to let him go in first.

'Oh...' He muttered something under his breath.

'What?' She peeked around the doorway, stopping when she saw he'd halted only a few steps into the room.

He turned to face her. 'It's so light.'

She glanced at the white walls, white furnishings and the myriad small windows that gave the most glorious views to the skies. She couldn't help smiling because he was right—the light was what made this room. Even at night, it had a brilliant quality. She couldn't believe he'd not seen it before.

'Have you not been up here at all?' She was amazed as he shook his head. 'You bought this house and everything in it without even taking a proper look?'

'I liked the location, the convenience to work and the outlook.' He shrugged. 'Anything else I want I can add or rebuild later.'

Didn't he see what was special about the place—its history, its quirks, its sense of *home*?

'I liked the view up here. The light and the space.' She tried to explain it to him as she walked past him. The angles of the ceiling were random because of the roofline. When she'd turned thirteen she'd had the room enlarged to become both her bedroom and her first sculpture studio. Her father hadn't minded paying for the renovation and it had kept her occupied and away from the parade of women he was bringing home. She'd been unable to compete with those beauties who'd turned his attention from his children. She'd spent hours alone up here.

Alejandro was staring grimly at the narrow single bed in the corner with its plain white coverings. Then he turned those penetrating eyes on her. 'Did you sneak boys up here to share this bed?'

'Of course not. What kind of a question is that?' She stuck her hands on her hips and shook her head at him. 'You have such a one-track mind.'

He laughed at her reaction and her heart started its crazy trip-along pace again. 'Oh, come on, all those times using that secret hidden key of yours?' He folded his arms and leaned against the wall, looking utterly roguish.

'Absolutely not.'

Sneaking a lover in was totally the sort of thing *he'd* have done. No doubt he'd been sowing his wild oats since he was a youth.

'I was a good girl,' she added when he kept staring at her with those dangerous eyes.

'You amaze me,' he said dryly. 'Then why the need to sneak in and out if it wasn't to go wild?'

'I was exploring the art scene.' And pushing boundaries to get her father's attention. It hadn't worked.

'So you were the young muse for the Bohemian set?' He waggled his brows at her.

'Actually, my first boyfriend was three months *younger* than me. He was another art student when I was at *university*.'

'Was it sublime?'

Of course it wasn't. She turned her back on his low laughter.

'Poor Catriona. And then there was the dastardly fiancé.'

She hated that he guessed her lack of experience so easily. 'It's not that easy for everyone, you know,' she muttered grimly.

It was a disappointment. She would have liked to have been one of those free spirits who flitted from romance to romance and emerged unscathed, but it wasn't to be. She was nothing like Alejandro. And she didn't want to be with someone who she knew would let her down. Sure, she had his attention now—for whatever reason—but soon enough that attention would turn to someone else and she'd be left in the cold again.

His hands on her shoulders pulled, turning her to face him. 'I'd make it sublime.'

His smile was bewitching, but it was something in his eyes that really had her spellbound.

'You're full of promises,' she muttered gruffly, trying to settle her skipping pulse.

'Ah, so you want proof.'

She didn't know what she wanted any more. But she knew this moment had been building since they'd first set eyes on each other. It was normal for him but so outside her realm of experience she didn't know how to handle it.

'Do you always get what you want?' she asked, genuinely curious.

'When I've decided I want something, I stop at nothing until I have it,' he said, equally honest. Equally serious. 'So, yes, I do.'

'And right now you want me?'

He nodded.

'And you'll stop at nothing?'

He didn't answer. A smile, slow and amused, spread over his face. He tugged her that little bit closer and bent his head to kiss her. And she didn't say no. She didn't step back. She just let him. She stood there and let him pull her into his hot embrace.

And she liked it.

She moaned as he moved her that bit closer, his kiss claiming her. Soft kisses again, teasing ones, tender and tormenting. She pressed closer, seeking more. His hand swept down her back, resting on her hip. It was no longer enough. None of this was enough.

Her legs were shaking. She couldn't stand it any more. Literally couldn't stand.

But she didn't need to say anything. His arms had already tightened about her and somehow the bed was now at the back of her legs. With a smooth movement he eased her onto the narrow little mattress and then came down on top of her. She gasped, trembling at the sensation of finally having him there, so close to her.

He muttered something but she didn't catch it because he'd resumed stroking, trailing those torturously slow fingertips across her waist and up to cup her breast. Her body ached. She longed to burst free of her clothes, even her skin. She was *so* hot. He looked into her eyes for a wordless moment. Passion had darkened his eyes even more and she just drowned in them. His skin was slightly flushed. She didn't think she'd ever seen him look as gorgeous—or as dangerous. Every cell within her tightened in anticipation.

He smiled and she was lost. His hand framed her face, fingers tangling in her hair, and he kept her still so he could savour her lips, plundering her mouth with his tongue. Teasing, touching, until the yearning inside could no longer be contained. Then it wasn't as teasing, wasn't as gentle. Hunger sharpened.

He couldn't seem to get enough of kissing her. Which was good, because she couldn't get enough of kissing him. She arched, aching to get nearer, wanting him everywhere, in every way. Her legs splayed, allowing him the space to press closer, more intimately against her. She groaned as his hard length pressed against her, right there. So good. Uncontrollably she rocked, rubbing against him, trying to ease the need, skating closer and closer to an arousal that could have only one end. Her bra was too tight, her breasts were too full, her nipples too taut. Finally, finally, blessedly, he moved, kissing down the length of her neck until his hot mouth hit the high line of her dress.

She clenched on her muscles and cried out as need spiked within her as he pressed his open mouth against her jutting nipple, through the fabric and all. He stiffened above her then swiftly returned to kiss her full on the mouth. Not tender at all now, but ravenous. She couldn't contain another moan of desire, couldn't stop the ragged, short breaths of desire escaping her lips.

'I want to see you,' he muttered savagely.

His hands dropped to her thighs, to the hem of her dress. 'I want to see every inch of you.'

Kitty opened her eyes, his passion-roughened words shocking her back to reality. The light hurt. It was so light in here. She didn't want to be seen by him in this unforgiving brightness. She didn't want him to see all her imperfections. In that split second she couldn't help comparing herself to all the other women he'd known—all those beautiful women. She gripped his hand, stopping him from lifting her dress any higher. There were very, very few people who'd seen her naked. And it would never happen in this bright light. Not with him, not with anyone.

Her emotions spiralled out of control as she realised where she was and what she was doing and with whom and *what was she thinking?* This behaviour was so unlike her. Never had she wanted a man the way she wanted him. It shocked her. It almost scared her.

She froze.

He raised his head and looked down at her, his gaze both astute and tense, his smile rueful. 'You're not ready to let me in, Catriona?'

Dazed, she looked up into his face from where she lay half beneath him. For a fatalistic moment she thought she would *never* be ready to cope with him.

His smile deepened—a little strained, a little tender. 'I think you need to sleep on it.' He levered off the bed.

'You're…leaving?' Even though he was no longer pinning her, she couldn't move, she was stunned. And suddenly desolate.

'Perhaps I have more patience than you give me credit for.' He braced his arms either side of her, leaning over her again only to press a quick, light kiss on her lips. 'I will never do anything you don't absolutely want me to. Let's be very clear on that.'

He straightened and walked away from her before she could think what to say. Kitty sat up, watching him as he left the room. She was hot and cold and confused and part of her was relieved but the other part was nothing short of devastated. As soon as he'd closed the door behind him, she slumped back onto the bed—suddenly sorry that he'd been so restrained. She could have had an experience unlike any other if she'd not been so self-conscious. So insecure. So stupid.

If he'd kissed her for just a few minutes more she'd have been so het-up she'd have agreed to anything. But he wasn't going to let it happen that way. He was too sensitive to her moods. He wanted her commitment to their affair to be made beforehand—not in the heat of the moment. It turned out he was too damn chivalrous to make it easy for her.

She rolled onto her stomach and buried her face in her pillow in a swelter of confusion and desire and contradiction. It was only lust, right? She could get a grip on herself—it shouldn't be that difficult. But the thing was, she did want him and he knew it. He was just going to make her say it so there was no doubt.

Could she take the little he offered? Was it even that little? She'd never had that kind of an affair. Never had the kind of pleasure he'd already made her feel in just those few touches. Maybe she *could* handle it. And maybe, once it was done, it would be over. The desire would die because this driving need would have been filled. All she had to do was swallow her pride and say yes to him.

But she couldn't bring herself to do that either. She didn't want this to be that easy for him. She didn't want to be just another of his notches.

Basically? She was screwed.

She gave up on sleep and rose super early the next morning and grumpily trooped downstairs to the kitchen to find some fruit to freshen her up. But she encountered Alejandro on the second floor landing in shorts and a thin tee, looking hot and sweaty and, when he caught sight of her, grumpy. He'd clearly been out for a run or something. So that was how he did it.

'How I do what?' he asked.

She choked—had she uttered that thought aloud? She must have; he was gazing at her expectantly. But he still wasn't smiling.

Awkwardly, she tried to explain. 'Eat all that rich food but stay so...'

'What?' he prompted when she broke off.

'Fit,' she mumbled.

He didn't smile. If anything, his expression grew even grimmer. 'Is that what you wear to bed?' He gestured at her white pyjamas. 'You wear black during the day and white at night. That's very you.'

They stared at each other across the landing and for a moment neither moved.

'Please be ready to go out when I get home tonight,' he said gruffly. 'Unlike some, I work a long day and when I'm done, I'm hungry.'

Her spine stiffened. 'Certainly, darling. I won't make you wait a second longer than necessary.'

Her gaze clashed with his.

'God,' he muttered hoarsely, 'I hope not.'

* * *

Alejandro threw himself into work, determined to put Catriona out of his mind for the day and concentrate on everything else. But thoughts of her eroded his focus. He'd never met a woman like her—intriguing, contrary. Annoying. She made him laugh. And the feeling of her strong yet soft body arching to meet his? The sound of her breathy moans as her desire escalated?

He puffed out a long-held breath and turned away from his computer in disgust. He was getting nowhere. He fished in his pocket, then laid the diamond choker across the desk. He wanted to see her wearing it again. He wanted to see her wearing the diamonds and nothing else. But that was what had shut her down last night—when he'd said he wanted to see her, she'd stiffened in his arms. She had an insecurity there that he was going to have to sweep clear somehow.

He deliberately worked late because he wanted to prove to himself that he could stay away from her. That he was still in control of himself emotionally and physically. This was nothing, this was easy, this was still *safe*. But when he finally headed home, his pulse started pounding. It was all he could do not to bolt up the stairs and haul her into his arms.

He didn't bolt. He just walked. Still in control.

But his pulse sprinted.

He found her in one of the box-filled upstairs bedrooms. She was in black again—long-sleeved top, slimline trousers and thin black sneakers on her feet. Her hair hung loose down her back, as glorious as ever. His blood fizzed. Just seeing her was a pleasure, but her mouth was downturned as she bent over another enormous cardboard box. She had a clipboard beside her, ready to itemise everything she extracted.

He glanced about the room. He had little sentimentality, but maybe the loss of these things truly made her sad.

'What are these?' He nudged the box she'd been look-ing into.

'Oh.' She glanced up, startled, and coloured slightly. 'They're the Christmas and birthday presents I gave my father every year since I was about eight. My earliest sculp-tures. He obviously didn't feel the need to keep them.'

She shrugged.

Alejandro knew there were issues with her father. He'd found him to be somewhat unreliable in his business prac-tice—the amount left behind in the house had been totally downplayed, for one thing, and it seemed Catriona and her father were not close. But Alejandro knew some fathers were worse than others. His father was the worst of all.

Distracting himself, he lifted some of the pottery pieces out. Some had not stood the test of time. Or at least hadn't been kept in a safe place. There were chipped bits and a couple of broken vase tips at the bottom of the box. But a couple—especially one vase and a sculpture that looked like a lion—were very delicate and showed the develop-ment of skill. 'Some are—'

'Terrible, I know.' She interrupted him with a brittle laugh. 'I was just a kid. He didn't think I should study art; apparently I needed to get a real job. You know, the kind that earns money. Because that was what mattered most to Dad. The guy who'd married into an old wealthy family and managed to *lose* all the money...' She trailed off and glanced at Alejandro with a wistful smile. 'Your parents must be very proud of you.'

It felt as if a boulder had been lodged in his chest. For a second he gaped before collecting himself. She didn't know about his parents then. She didn't know...

He halted his thoughts. He didn't feel inclined to tell her. He never discussed it and ensured conversation never became personal enough for a woman to ask. Several busi-ness colleagues knew, but also knew never to mention it.

He turned away from the box. 'Are you ready for dinner?' he asked bluntly.

'Time sneaked away from me.' Kitty bit her lip, surprised to see icy reserve sweep over him. 'I only need five minutes if we're going out again?'

He'd totally stiffened up, no longer the suave conversationalist and tease.

'Of course.'

She sent him a cautious smile and left the room, quickly moving to change her clothes. Why had he frozen up when she'd referenced his family? It was unlike him to reveal so much; usually he teased to deflect a conversation. A million more questions followed—where did that slight exotic edge to his accent come from? Why was he so driven when he'd had so much success so young? He fascinated her and she wanted to know everything about him.

But at dinner she found that goal impossible to reach. The guests chatted animatedly about topical issues but no one pressed her for any detail about her relationship with Alejandro, no one asked how they'd met or when they'd become engaged. Which was polite. But no one asked him anything intrusive or illuminating either, which was disappointing. They sought his opinion on something to do with work, or debated politics and current affairs. It was all intelligent and interesting, but the only other thing she learned about him was that he was well read, had encyclopaedic general knowledge and would be an extremely useful addition on a pub quiz team.

And as the evening progressed she realised he didn't actually talk that much at all. He smiled and gave a thoughtful insight into something that was business-related or added an occasional witty comment, but, for the most part, his contributions were limited. He seemed happy just to be at the centre of the noise and chatter. Her curiosity deepened.

But she knew she wasn't the only curious one at the

table. The woman sitting opposite her had been avidly watching Alejandro, conversing with him loudly, unsubtle in trying to get his attention. Now she turned to Kitty—her curiosity unveiled as she raked her gaze over her, her eyes narrowing on Kitty's hand.

'Still no ring?' The woman's smile gleamed as she leaned across and spoke in an undertone. 'There's a smidge of hope for the rest of us then.'

The last thing Kitty wanted was to compete for Alejandro—not in any way.

'You're welcome to have him,' she replied directly, but with a smile. 'I keep trying to shake him off, but he's persistent.'

There was a moment of stunned silence around the table. Kitty swallowed; she hadn't realised she'd spoken *that* loudly.

'After Catriona's hurt over her previous engagement, she's decided an engagement ring is bad luck,' Alejandro said with urbane ease. 'I have agreed to surprise her on our wedding day when our vows are taken.' He placed his hand over hers and gave it a squeeze. 'She finds it difficult to trust, but I'm working on it.'

Kitty stared at him, unable to think of a thing to say to that. He met her eyes for a moment, and she saw the humour dancing in his, but there was something else too. Something she couldn't define and couldn't cope with. She turned and caught a stabbing glance at her from the other woman, but she was too floored by Alejandro to bother responding. Her body felt engulfed in flames. She was so embarrassed, but also somehow grateful. It was crazy. She was crazy. And so was he.

'You're a more outrageous liar than I am,' she whispered in his ear in the most provocative way she could manage once normal conversation had resumed, determined to take control of this mad roller coaster ride again. 'That was pretty good. But you know, I've changed my mind. I want a rock. Monstrous huge, please. The gaudiest thing you can drop a few hundred thousand on.'

She sat back and beamed at him.

He cupped her face and inexorably drew her close again so he could whisper in return, 'It's too late; the offer is rescinded. I like my story better about the bad luck engagement ring. It has an air of truth about it.'

He was so near she was lost in the depth of his black-brown eyes. Her heart raced. He was horrendously handsome. She scrambled to stay sane—to stay on top of what was just a game.

'You're heartless. Utterly heartless.'

He laughed delightedly; his warm breath stirred her hair. For a moment it was as if they were in their own bubble of amusement and heat.

'I have no need for a heart,' he muttered.

That hit like a cold wind. Could anyone really be that carefree? She pulled back, wary of the other diners watching them less than surreptitiously. With an effort she maintained her smile and reached for a glass of water.

'Lead me along as far as you dare, Catriona,' he added quietly so only she heard. 'I'll keep step. You won't scare me off.'

'I thought you were out to stop me from saying outrageous things.'

'I've decided I like them. The only person they really cause trouble for is you.'

And wasn't that the truth.

'I am chastened,' she admitted honestly. 'That's it—no more from me.'

He laughed, full bodied and sexy. 'Never. You're too impulsive for that vow to last long.'

The truth was she was trying as hard as she could to hold him off. Because this sparring—this foreplay—was fun. But once she'd given in to him—and to her own desire—it would be over. It was all in the thrill of the chase for him. He'd be off on the next hunt once he'd captured this prey. So, back at Parkes House, she didn't let him climb the stairs with her.

'No. No. No. No.' She scampered ahead of him and held up her hands like a metaphorical wall. 'You stay down there.'

He looked up at her, pausing with one foot on the first step. His mouth quirked. 'Not even a kiss goodnight?'

'No. Nothing. Not a thing.'

He leaned back against the railing and his smile broadened to positively smug. 'Finding it so hard to resist you can't even risk one kiss?' Amusement danced in his eyes. 'Not long now then.'

His arrogant laughter followed her. He was appalling.

And that was the thing, wasn't it? This wasn't ever going to be for long.

CHAPTER SEVEN

'I'M READY.' KITTY looked up as Alejandro walked in from a frustrating day.

His mouth dried. She was sitting on the sofa in the library with her ankles demurely crossed, clad in another slinky black dress that clung to her curves and suggested total sensuality while keeping her too damn covered up.

Was she ready for him?

He'd let her get away without so much as a kiss yesterday but now he'd had enough. This was the longest amount of time he'd ever invested in a seduction and seeing her sitting there so coolly perfect was the last straw. Hadn't she spent the day thinking of him? Wasn't she being eaten from the inside out by coiling desire the way he was?

'Alejandro?' Her eyes widened as she watched him stalk towards her.

He didn't reply as he pulled her up from the sofa and into his arms. This was what he needed. Her close in his arms, her mouth parting under his, her body softening.

He kissed her the way he'd been fantasising about all day. Long and deep and hungry. His arms tightened as he felt her lean into him. Desire raced as she kissed him back, her energy rising to meet his in a snap. Oh, yes. Ready. So ready.

He lifted his head to look into her eyes for the consent he so badly needed. But she pushed him back breathlessly.

'Stop it,' she panted. 'You're messing up my hair. It took hours to get it this smooth, you know.'

'And it looks lovely.' He reached for her again. He needed to do more than look—he needed to touch. Now. 'Come back here.'

'No—' she stepped further away '—I didn't do it for you.'

'No?' He smirked.

'Of course not!' She rolled her eyes. 'It's for all those wannabe lovers of yours. The troupe of women hanging on your every word. I have to show my cred to them.'

Alejandro paused, dropping his hand. That was ridiculous. She had nothing to prove. 'They think you're my fiancée.'

'Like that matters to them!' She faced him. 'Or to you.' She shook her head. 'If one took your fancy, you'd be gone in a flash.'

He frowned, his irritation building. The last thing he felt like doing was leaving her. And suddenly the last thing he felt like was sharing her with a bunch of other people around the dinner table either. He wanted all her attention on *him*. As his was on her.

'Can you even remember all their names?' she asked.

He stared at her, mystified.

'All your ex-lovers,' she explained grumpily.

It was his turn to roll his eyes. 'Can they remember mine? What does it matter?' They were irrelevant to this. 'What's wrong with living in the moment?'

'It's just so…meaningless.'

And? He really didn't see why she wanted complication, for things to be involved. 'Must you be so deep all the damn time? Must there be meaning in everything?'

'Not everything all of the time. But sometimes. Yes.'

'Work hard, play hard. That's the life I enjoy.' And he didn't see why his past should impact on his affair with her now. He didn't understand why she railed against what they could share in bed together. 'I already told you—I will never marry. I will never have children.'

She hesitated, her fire dropping a fraction. 'You don't like them?'

'It is not something that interests me.' He turned away from her pretty eyes.

'Oh, that's a shame. Who's going to inherit all your billions, then?'

He laughed, relieved to hear her tart tone. She was back to her best with him. 'I'm going to give it away to charity.'

'Nice.' She nodded. 'Just the one charity or are you going to share it around, the way you do your sex skills?'

Ouch. He rubbed his chest with the heel of his hand. 'You're not going to try to convince me to have children? Tell me I'd make a great father?'

'If you don't want them, you don't want them. Who am I to try to convince you otherwise?'

'You want children?' Oddly, his chest felt heavier now. The thought of Catriona cradling a small child made it hard to breathe.

'Possibly.' A wary expression flitted over her features. 'But I'd have to find a decent guy first. In my experience, they're thin on the ground.'

He chuckled, trying to recover his equilibrium. 'Poor princess. You've gone from—how do they say—from the frying pan to the fire.'

'You said it,' she agreed dramatically. 'I escaped the claws of a cad only to fall into the jaws of a shark.'

From one heartbreaking engagement to one fake one. The fake one was more fun, though.

'You'll survive,' he said soothingly. 'You might even have fun.'

Silently, she met his gaze. Her eyes sparkled. She was having fun now and they both knew it.

She drew in a breath and lifted her chin that fraction higher. 'So how many other people are going to be at dinner tonight? Will there be any other men for me to flirt with or will it just be women to fawn over you and stroke your ego?'

Yes, the game was on again. Tension coiled in his muscles at the thought of dinner; he didn't want any distractions now.

'It'll just be the two of us,' he muttered, making that decision then and there. They needed time alone together to get this sorted between them.

'Not the usual entourage?' She turned limpid eyes on him. 'Are you sure you can cope with the depth of conversation that might be required?'

'I think I can keep up with you.'

'So where are we going?' she asked softly.

He didn't know. He quickly texted his assistant to let him know that he and Catriona were not going to be joining the others for dinner then challenged the beautiful woman still standing too far away from him. 'You're the local; you lead the way.'

She skimmed a sharp gaze over his Armani suit and then looked down at her couture dress. 'I'm not familiar with all those super exclusive restaurants you seem to like.'

He shrugged. 'There'll be something nearby.'

He didn't want it to be too far from his bed. As far as he was concerned, tonight she was going to be his.

They ended up in a small Thai takeaway joint. She leaned against the Formica counter, laughing as she ordered a selection for them both.

'You like it spicy?' She sent him a coy look.

'I can't believe you even have to ask.'

'I don't like it too hot,' she said primly.

'I don't believe you.' He flicked her chin. 'I see through you.'

She turned so she faced the other way to see out of the window and watch the passers-by. 'Maybe I see through you too.'

Did she, now? He leaned closer. 'What do you think you see?'

'Someone who sells himself short.'

His eyebrows shot up. Uh, no, he didn't. He knew what he was good at.

'You have much more to offer than good-looks, money-making brains and superb sex skills.'

Both sassy and serious, she stole his breath.

'Oh?' He didn't want to ask. Didn't want it to matter. But suddenly her opinion had value. 'What else do I offer?'

'Humour.' She reached for the carrier bags from the waiter and then glanced at him. 'And you're kind.'

He stilled on his way out of the tiny restaurant. 'You've clearly mistaken me for someone else.'

'Oh, you can have your cruel moments.' She bit her lip ruefully and led him out onto the pavement. 'But you can't hide your underlying tendency towards kindness. You didn't drop me in it in front of all those people at your party. You're letting me sort my family's stuff even though a professional would be much faster, but you know it matters to me.'

He cleared his throat. 'I think you'll find that *kindness* isn't my motivation.'

Her eyes glinted but she shook her head. 'You're fundamentally okay,' she argued. 'I just don't think you realise it. You look after your staff, you go to great lengths to take care of your guests and you actually *do* give money to charity.' She turned and walked snappily along the path. 'Now, we could sit in the garden if you like. As long as you can handle eating with plastic cutlery?'

'I guess,' he muttered dryly, following a pace behind. But the number of times in his youth when he'd eaten with no cutlery… Hell, the number of meals he'd missed because there was no money even to buy bread. She might think she could manage on a bit of a budget now, but she had no idea of his reality. And she had no real idea of him.

Kind? He didn't feel in the least kind regarding her.

He sprawled back on the lawn, recovering from her direct assessment of him, his appetite lost. But he enjoyed watching her, listening to her chattering about her day, about the city, about anything, prompting her with a question when she fell silent. He needed her to distract him from the desire tightening his muscles.

The warm dusk slowly turned into a cool evening. The last of the sunlight made strands of her hair spark. Her vitality glowed. All he wanted to do was reach out and capture it—capture *her*. Yeah, not kind.

'It was good?' he asked as she helped herself to the last spoonful of his curry.

'Mm hmmm,' she mumbled as she finished the mouthful.

'So you do like it hot,' he muttered triumphantly.

She smiled at him and he was felled.

'Let's go home.' The words spilled out. But the second they left his mouth his innards chilled.

Since when did he think of Parkes House as his *home*? Let alone think of *her* as being part of that? And this desire to capture her and hold her close? He froze as his heart slammed his chest. He tried to block the fear trickling in. Catriona was just another woman he was seducing. That was all.

Just another lover who he could take. Or leave.

CHAPTER EIGHT

Kitty worked quickly and efficiently, categorising items before re-boxing them neatly, mortified her father had left such a mess for a total stranger to deal with. Much ought to be taken to the rubbish or recycling centre and the sooner the better because she was totally over the blow-hot, blow-cold enigma that was Alejandro Martinez.

He'd fallen silent on the short walk home last night and then vanished to his room without a word—no goodnight call, let alone goodnight kiss. He'd gone to work without speaking to her this morning as well. Which was *fine* and she was *not* disappointed and she should *not* have spent all day trying to work him out. Except he consumed her thoughts. Why did he sometimes seem so unhappy despite all his success? There were moments when she thought an expression of pure pain crossed his face—it had flashed out of the blue when they'd walked home last night. He'd utterly iced up. She didn't understand why—they hadn't been talking anything personal.

She sighed and taped down another box. The mystery of his life was no business of hers; she just needed to get a grip on her own reaction to him. She was not up for a roller coaster ride of his engineering.

The slam of the front door echoed all the way up to the room where she was working. She glanced at the clock. It was only four in the afternoon, way too early for him to have finished work already.

'How's it going?' he asked as he appeared in the library doorway the merest moment later, all tense angles in a navy suit, no tie and no smile.

'I hate my father for letting it get to this state,' she admitted honestly, trying not to stare at him, but failing.

Alejandro's edgy expression softened. 'Another day nearer to your precious necklace. You suffer so for your diamonds.'

'Why are you back so early?' She watched him hovering just inside the room. 'Shouldn't you be running your empire?'

'It's running successfully without me for a few hours.' He looked into the nearest box and poked through the contents. 'It's a test for the new employees.'

'Really?'

He looked back to her. 'No,' he said bluntly.

The atmosphere thickened. Her heart thudded too quickly for comfort. She was too acutely aware of that raw look in his eyes that she didn't understand. He looked as if he hadn't slept well.

Don't get curious. Don't think you're starting to care.

She tried to warn herself—her mother had fallen for a suave, charming swine and so had she in James. She didn't need to make that mistake again. She didn't need him coming home all intense and brooding and pulling her close only to then push away without a minute's notice. But an impulse was rising—she wanted to see his smile again. She wanted him to tease again.

Alejandro's gaze dropped and he sombrely studied the contents of the box nearest him.

'I was thinking you're right,' he said slowly.

Kitty's jaw dropped but before she could speak he flashed the quickest of grins.

'That I should understand more about this house,' he added, walking away from her, the smile gone again. 'And I might as well do that while you're here to explain it to me.'

She was wary of the intense energy emanating from

him. Of this seemingly random request. What did he *really* want?

'Where did you want to start?' she asked as he restlessly prowled round the room, picking up small items and replacing them haphazardly and seeming to avoid looking at her directly.

He fiddled with a small wooden figurine on the table. 'Show me your favourite things.'

She kept watching him steadily but he still didn't meet her gaze.

'I don't have favourite things as much as I have favourite places,' she said.

'Such as the library?'

She wrinkled her nose. 'I used to wait for my father here and it was always a disappointment. That's why Teddy left notes for me in the hidden compartment in the bookcase— to cheer me up.'

He'd left notes because most of the time Teddy was out, supposedly at sports coaching when in fact he was at the local drama club.

'So then it's your bedroom?' Alejandro guessed.

'That came later,' she corrected him. 'My favourite place of all is the secret room.'

He spun towards her, his eyebrows high. 'There's a secret room?'

She laughed, pleased at the flash of interest in his face. 'I know—it's pretty cool.'

'It wasn't on the plans.'

'If it was, it wouldn't be secret!' She rolled her eyes. 'Come on—it's downstairs. It's not huge; it's about the size of a lift compartment.'

'And it exists because…?'

'Because it was an extension of the butler's pantry and its entrance got sealed and hidden because one of my ancestors was a scoundrel and needed to hide from the long arm of the law.'

He stared slack-jawed at her. 'Seriously?'

He laughed as she nodded.

'That sounds like one of your family. Good God!' He walked to the door. 'Show me.'

She overtook him on the stairs, unable to stop her small smile at the thought of sharing the house's secret with him. She'd always loved this little room. 'So, through the kitchen and then out to here.'

'Where every kitchen appliance known to man is stored,' he said dryly.

'That's right,' she acknowledged ruefully. Her father had indulged their old chef back in the day before the money had dried up.

She walked into a corner of the pantry and pushed the old subtle knob that formed part of the decorated skirting board. There was a clunking noise and a part of the wall swung, revealing a narrow gap.

'Oh, my—'

'I know.' She interrupted him. 'Hardly anyone knows it's here.' She squeezed in the gap, her own excitement at being back in the small room rising. 'It's really cute.' She glanced into the far corner where, as a girl, she'd set up a cosy hiding place. Slowly she turned, suddenly remembering. 'But, whatever you do, don't—'

She broke off as he shut the door behind him.

'Don't what?' he asked.

The darkness was complete.

'Oh,' he said, quick to realise. 'We'll have to feel for the door handle?'

'Actually, there's a slight design flaw,' she mumbled in embarrassment. 'No lighting. No interior door handle.'

'Why am I not surprised?' he sighed. 'Are we going to suffocate to death?'

'No, there's a vent.'

'Thank heavens for small mercies. Do I need to break the door open?'

'No, don't damage it,' she said quickly. That old mechanism was too historic and she'd hate its secret to be exposed. 'Can't you call one of your assistants to come and direct them how to open it?'

'I don't have my phone with me.'

Oh. 'I don't either,' she realised. She'd left it on the table upstairs. 'We're stuck.'

Heat flooded her at the realisation. She was locked in, alone and in the dark, with one very sexually magnetic man who was the walking definition of unpredictable.

'There's really no way of opening it from this side?' he asked, a thin vein of irritation in his voice.

'No.' She'd tried hard enough as a girl.

He was silent for a moment and she heard him stepping around, getting the feel for the space. 'Paolo should be here in an hour or so to drive us to dinner. He'll come in through the kitchen entrance; will we hear him arrive?'

'Yes.'

'And will he be able to hear us if we yell?'

'Yes.' She'd yelled when she was a child a few times.

'Then…' He paused. 'I guess we wait.'

For an hour or so. She leaned against the back wall and slid down into her old familiar corner, blocking her mind from sending her images of what they could do to pass the time. She was *not* going to be that easy for Alejandro.

'You know this is dangerous,' he said a bit roughly. 'How did you get out of here when you were a kid?'

She cleared her throat. 'I taped a ribbon over the edge so the door couldn't quite lock into place, but it was almost shut so no one knew I was here.' Or at least that's what she'd pretended. The chef had always known and had always checked on her. Neither of her parents had.

'What did you do in here all by yourself?'

'Drew. Dreamed.' She'd sat with her torch and sketched fanciful creatures—fairies goblins, elves. She smiled self-consciously at the memory—which was stupid, given he couldn't see her. But it was that kind of place for her—secret and a little bit magic.

'You couldn't do that upstairs?'

'When Mother was at home, my father stayed out very late.' Her smile faded. She'd sat in the library and waited for him. 'And when she was away he brought a lot of "guests" home. I preferred to stay out of their way when they were here.'

'Female guests?' Alejandro asked expressionlessly.

'Naturally.'

There was a brief pause. She heard him moving nearer, then felt him sit down next to her.

'Your mother travelled for work?'

She bit back a sad laugh. 'No, she'd go on retreats to "find herself".' She paused. Her mother would routinely just check out of marriage and motherhood. 'After the attic was renovated, I stopped coming down here.' She'd hardly had to come downstairs at all. She could avoid her father's affairs and absence in her own room.

'And what happened to your mother?' That roughness in his voice gave the question an edge.

'Eventually she didn't come back from one of her retreats. Last I heard, she's in Australia. I guess she finally found herself. She gave Dad everything in the divorce—gave up all her material possessions and never came back.' She'd given up her children too.

But Kitty had had the *house* and the things she'd made to decorate it. And she'd had Teddy, when he could bear to be home.

Alejandro didn't say anything in reply to her admission. There wasn't really anything to say and she was glad he didn't bother with platitudes. But of course he wouldn't; he didn't seem to let anything touch him too closely. Or at least that was the appearance he was so determined to convey. But surely there was more than he showed. She saw those quicksilver flashes of emotion. Of depth. How did she push beyond his teasing, suave exterior?

'So your time spent drawing and sculpting led you to study art,' he said, interrupting her thoughts.

'Collection curation in the end.' She hadn't had the true talent to be an artist. 'While you studied...'

'Law, economics, commerce.'

'Oh.' She shivered at the thought of it.

'Very useful degrees.' He nudged her and she heard his short laugh. 'More so than art.'

'It isn't all about making money,' she fired up.

'So speaks someone who has never struggled to make the money to keep a roof over her head, or enough to eat. Would you eat cake when there's no bread left?' he teased.

'I'm not as ignorant or out of touch as all that,' she muttered. 'I just don't see why it all has to be about how much money you can make. I make enough for *me,* whereas you're out to make as much as humanly possible. Self-made guys like you celebrate the downfall of the likes of my father.'

'Not at all.' Alejandro laughed. 'I would never celebrate anyone's failure.'

No, but he was single-minded about success and ruthless in achieving it. He wouldn't give up at a setback; he'd fight back until he'd won in the way he wanted.

'He worked hard, you know,' she tried to explain. 'He just made mistakes. Plenty of them.' She sighed. 'He was trying to groom Teddy to take over the family business but Ted hated it and was hopeless. They fought a lot.'

'And you hung out in the attic.'

Kitty shifted restlessly; somehow she'd ended up talk-

ing more about herself and still learned nothing much more
about him.

'But you love your father, even though he let you down,'
Alejandro said.

'He has his weaknesses,' she replied. 'We all do.'

'I don't.'

She laughed, pleased to hear that amused confidence
in him again. 'Yes, you do. You're arrogant and stubborn.'

'What you call weakness, I call strength,' he countered,
unabashed as always. 'Stubbornness is determination and
it helps me succeed.'

'Bully for you,' she grumbled. 'There's no success that
comes with impulsiveness.'

'You think not?' He laughed softly. 'You successfully
bring fun. Laughter. The unpredictable.'

'Are you suggesting I'm unpredictable?' she asked
archly. 'Coming from you, that's high praise.'

'Are you suggesting that I've finally charmed you?' he
teased.

'Oh, no, I still see through you.' Except she couldn't see
him at all; she could only hear the warmth in his tone. 'I
know you only want one thing.'

Temptation whispered within her. She wanted it too.
And she was tired of fighting her attraction to him. Here
in the dark, no one would know. Here she could still learn
something about him. She could learn the physical. She
shivered again. She was too aware of his nearness, of the
possibilities.

'It really is pitch-black, isn't it?' she muttered, trying
to distract herself.

'Are you scared?' That thread of amusement sounded,
warming her.

Honestly, she was always scared when he was around.
Not of him but of her reaction to him. She felt him shift
beside her. His arm pressed against hers, so did his leg.

'I used to be afraid of the dark,' she confessed distractedly.

'But you got over it?'

'Teddy locked me in here once, not long after we first discovered it. I was terrified. But after a while I got used to it and I refused to let him know how much it bothered me. Then I found it didn't bother me anyway and I didn't have to pretend any more. This became one of my favourite places to hang out.'

'You faked it till you made it?' His chuckle was soft.

'I guess.'

'I like the dark,' he said gently.

'Oh?' She half expected some comment about his liking the dark because he was usually in bed then, but there was a serious note in his voice. 'Why?'

'It's safe—you can't be seen.'

His answer surprised her to silence. What—or who—did he want to hide from? Why didn't he want to be seen? Was he scarred in some way? Her mind raced with questions. She was about to ask but then she heard him—it was almost a whisper.

'You can't be found.'

'You liked to hide?' She never would have guessed that.

He drew in a quick breath. 'Mmm…'

He didn't elaborate. Of course he didn't.

Why had he needed to feel safe?

She reached out, unable to resist any longer—offering the reassurance of touch. His stubble was rough beneath her fingertips. Who was she kidding—this was what *she* wanted. Here, in the dark, no one would know. She couldn't see. He couldn't see. It could be secret, and maybe a little bit magic.

'Catriona?'

'Shh.' She just wanted to explore.

'Do you know what you are doing?'

She smiled in the darkness and leaned closer to press her lips to his jaw. His muscle jerked beneath her lips.

He turned his head towards her and she felt his breath on her face. 'Don't start something that can't be stopped. Not unless you are very, very sure.'

She would never be sure of anything much. Except that right now she liked exploring what she could of him. She liked it here in the dark where she too could hide and neither of them could see. But she could feel.

His hand cupped her chin, he gently traced her lip with the tip of his finger, and she couldn't resist a quick slide of her tongue. His finger paused and she heard his swiftly indrawn breath.

'This isn't a good idea,' he said roughly.

But, before she could reply, he kissed her gently.

'Yes,' she whispered when he drew back.

'Yes, this isn't a good idea or yes this—?'

'Just yes.' She pressed forward blindly, seeking his mouth again.

And it was a good idea. It was a very, very good idea.

Her kiss wasn't gentle. She sank into it, relishing the freedom. Here, in the dark, she relinquished her hold on her desire. It burst free—heating the small space. She wanted to explore him. She ached to touch every part of him, to feel the slide of his skin against her own. She wanted—

He groaned and reached out quickly. Unerringly finding her waist, he lifted her onto his knee, capturing her completely.

'I think you like to take risks, Catriona,' he muttered harshly.

'Alejandro…'

He answered her plea wordlessly, his hot mouth crashing down on hers while his hands explored, lifting under her tee. She moaned as he unclasped her bra and her tight breasts sprang free. He palmed them for a moment and she wriggled on his lap, feeling his hard erection digging into her. Oh, yes, this was what she wanted. This was everything she wanted.

She lifted her arms as he tugged the fabric up, ridding her of both the tee and the dangling bra in the one movement. Then he swept his palms over her naked back, pushing her forward so he could kiss her bared skin, working his way across her body until he sucked her painfully tight nipple into his mouth. She cried out as heat flamed low in her belly.

'I want to taste more,' he said gruffly. 'I want everything.'

He moved, lifting her and placing her on her back beside him. It took nothing for him to slip off her shoes and run his hands up her legs to unsnap the fastening of her jeans and then slide them and her panties down and off.

She was naked now. And hot.

'I want to see you,' he groaned.

But he couldn't and she was pleased because here in the darkness she was free. His hands were warm, his mouth hot as he licked his way up the inside of her thigh. Her legs splayed and he took control, pushing them wider to make room for him between them. He kissed her core, holding her in the most carnally explicit position she'd ever been in in her life. She couldn't control the sobs of pleasure as his tongue caressed her, teasing her most sensitive nub with swirls and licks until she shivered uncontrollably. She was so close.

'*Please*,' she begged him. 'I want you.'

He broke free to brace above her, his body pressing against hers in agonising temptation. 'You had to do this now? When we have nothing here? No bed? No protection?' He swore furiously and at length. 'You madden me.'

'We can just…' She drew in a shuddering breath and writhed under him. She was so close. 'I want to touch you.'

He paused and it gave her enough time to reach up, feeling for the buttons of his shirt. She undid them, sliding her hand beneath the cotton to feel the damp, silken heat of his skin. She tracked her hand through the light dusting of coarse hair and briefly wished she could see him. He shrugged off the shirt completely and she lifted higher, so her tongue could follow the path of her fingertips. His skin was warm and a little salty and she wanted to taste more too.

But he slid his hand between them. She moaned as he parted her, exploring. He swore again. She trembled as he stroked her, drawing her tension out, making it impossible to bear. Because it wasn't enough. His fingers, his tongue weren't enough. She wanted *all* of him.

'I can't take it any more,' she muttered brokenly. '*Please.*'

'Please what?'

In the darkness, in the warmth, in the delirium only he seemed to be able to stir, it was safe to speak. Safe to say exactly what she wanted from him.

'Take me,' she whispered in absolute hedonistic abandonment. 'Take me hard.'

'Oh, hell, Catriona!' he ground out, frantically moving against her. 'I can't resist feeling you—I'll ensure—'

She heard the slide of his zip and melted. 'Yes. Oh, yes.'

'I'm clean...I've never had sex without protection in all my life.'

She was so eager she didn't care. 'Just do it,' she begged. 'I want to feel you.' Inside. Here. Now.

'Just for a moment.' He flexed his powerful body, controlled and slow, but she felt his muscles shaking.

'Yes.' Just this once.

She thought she was going to die if she didn't experience it all with him.

He paused. Then thrust. Hard.

'*Alejandro.*'

One word shot from his mouth in reply—crude and very much to the point. But she was too far gone, her body rigid and locked on his. She gasped harshly, clutching him closer, her legs parting that bit wider, wanting him closer, closer still, even as he filled her so completely.

'I cannot stop,' he rasped hoarsely. 'I can't...'

'*Yes*,' she cried, trembling and twisting beneath and about him as her orgasm ravaged her body. So, *so* ecstatic.

Suddenly he moved—hard, rough. Pulling back, only to thrust hard again. His hands tightened, holding her in place so he could drive deeper into her, pumping faster and faster.

'Oh, yes,' she gasped, her breath knocked from her. She rocked, meeting every fierce thrust, pushing their pace faster still, her hands greedy on him. It was carnal and hot and wet, and he was big and bossy and she was going to orgasm all over again. '*Oh, yes.*'

She didn't want him to stop. Not ever. Undone at last, they pounded together, frenetic and free. She was hurtling towards another orgasm, her last barely over. Her mouth parted as cries of delight tore from her. It was so good. *So* good. But at that ultimate moment he suddenly pulled out of her. She arched high but it was too late. He was gone.

His seed spurted over her stomach in hot, pulsing bursts as he braced above her, his agonised groan ripped from deep within.

She moaned too, a sound of torn satisfaction, of frustration. She'd wanted to ride through that tornado of bliss with him this time, but he'd wrenched out of her embrace.

'It wasn't supposed to happen like this.' He groaned again and cursed softly. She felt the absence as he lifted right away from her.

She lay still, shocked by how rapidly their passion had escalated into something so out of control. So reckless. So breathtakingly sensational.

'Like how?' Gingerly, she eased up into a sitting position, licking her dried lips as she felt the literal distance between them growing.

'Over so quick. Too quick.'

And it was over. She didn't trust her voice to answer. Her emotions were all over the place and she didn't want to sound tearful. It had been the most sublime experience of her life but all that exquisite joy she'd felt had been snatched away. Suddenly she felt vulnerable. It had happened. They'd had sex. He'd got what he wanted from her. And now it was over.

'Damn it, what time is it?' he muttered roughly. 'We need to get out of here.'

Kitty didn't want to get out of here. She wanted to curl in a ball and stay hidden for ever. She didn't want to look him in the face again. He'd made her feel things no one else ever had. Never had she enjoyed sex like that before. But it meant so little to him—how could it mean so little?

She realised there was suddenly a small light illuminating his face—in that slight glow he looked serious and distant.

Her body chilled as she realised what he was doing. He was tapping the fancy watch on his wrist. He was sending a damn *message*? Eventually he glanced in her direction and now there was a small smile on his face, as if he was pleased with himself.

Oh, she'd just bet he was.

'Did you just use your smart watch to send an email to get us out of here?' She glared at him even as the light went out and she knew he couldn't get the benefit of the full death stare she had on him. 'Only *now*?'

'Only now, because I just remembered that I had it,' he replied calmly. 'Until now, I was somewhat distracted.'

'But you could have sent a message sooner. Before...' She trailed off then cleared her throat determinedly. 'You could have sent a message when we were first stuck in here. But you didn't.'

'Catriona.'

She didn't answer him. She was too busy whipping herself into a fury.

'Catriona.'

Eventually he sighed and she heard his low laugh but she was not finding anything funny right now. She felt around on the floor for her clothes, not bothering with her bra or undies. She tried wriggling awkwardly into her jeans but they were all twisted and she couldn't figure them out in the stupid dark and she hated knowing that he could hear her struggling and was probably laughing inside at her expense. In the end she shoved on her tee and hoped it was the right way round, and who gave a damn about her shoes anyway.

'Alejandro?' a voice called.

Of course Paolo would arrive in less than ten freaking minutes.

'In here!' Alejandro banged on the door. 'The mechanism is down to your right.'

Alejandro had stood but Kitty remained curled on the floor as far in the corner as she could fit.

Light streamed in.

'Thank you,' he said to Paolo, who'd unlocked the door but hadn't stepped in. 'Please leave us now. Immediately.'

Alejandro moved out of the room, leaving the narrow doorway open. He didn't look back at her, but Kitty could see him—still clad in his suit trousers and shoes. But his shirt was off. He was tall and muscular and just that bare back on show made her shiver. She was glad when he disappeared from view, leaving the entranceway empty. But she heard him talking in a low tone, and his brief, infuriating laugh.

Then nothing.

'He's gone,' Alejandro called eventually when she didn't appear, his amusement still evident in his voice. 'You're safe to come out.'

The *last* thing she was, was safe.

But she stood, clutching the rest of her clothes protectively in front of her as she strode out, determined to pack her bags and leave the house this instant. Damn the diamonds, she'd get the lawyer onto it, as she should have right in the beginning.

She stomped past where Alejandro stood in the hallway, heading straight for the stairs. She didn't even glance at him.

'Catriona.'

She ignored that dangerous edge in Alejandro's voice.

'*Catriona.*'

'I'm not talking to you.' She turned to face him, tried to ignore how devastatingly gorgeous he looked in just those low-slung, unbelted trousers and no damn shirt on. 'You took advantage of that situation. You manipulated it.'

'How did I do that, exactly?' he asked. 'I wasn't the one pleading. Stop acting like a teenager and creating drama where there is none. You wanted me. I wanted you. We still want each other. What does it matter when I sent the stupid message?'

Because she wouldn't have succumbed to him then and there. She could have held out. Because they hadn't needed to sit there in the darkness together and experience that sense of intimacy build. But it hadn't been real. Not to him.

'It doesn't make any difference, Catriona,' he said. 'Our having sex was as inevitable as the sun rising and you know it as well as I.' He ran his hand through his hair, leaving tufts upright and even more gorgeous. 'Don't try to tell me you regret it.'

Only now could she see those muscles and that delicious olive skin of his and appreciate him truly. He was like a god. And only now did she realise what he was holding in his hand.

'You got Paolo to bring you *condoms*?' she shrieked.

'It seemed like a practical solution.' He shrugged. 'I did not have any.'

She glared at him. He probably did that all the time—sent his assistants out for a coffee and cake and another two dozen condoms because he burned through them so quickly. He was a sex-driven devil. But, heaven help her, hadn't she just benefitted from all that wealth of experience?

'Have you *no* shame?' She turned and took to the stairs, furious with him. She heard his laugh behind her.

'You seem to have enough for the both of us.' He grabbed her arm, stopping her, and turned her to look at him. 'Truly, Catriona,' he said softly. 'There are far worse things to be shamed by.'

His words had that core ring of truth to them. But she didn't want to know the truth. She wanted… She didn't know what she wanted any more.

He waited three steps below her, his eyes just that little bit beneath hers. Beautiful, deep brown eyes. That half smile was so sexy. So assured. And so maddening.

Those hot moments in that small dark space had been the most erotic of her life. That was what she rebelled against. That a man she didn't want to like could bring her to her knees like that. So easily. So carelessly. How was she supposed to protect herself from him when he overwhelmed her so completely? How could she not get hurt in this?

'I don't want to want you like this,' she admitted with a raw edge to her voice. 'I'm leaving.'

His eyes narrowed. 'Do you really think you can walk away right now?'

'Why not?' She shrugged, dropping her gaze. 'We've finally had sex. It's over.'

'It is anything but over.'

'Once was enough.'

He laughed outright at that—but now there was little humour in the sound. 'Was it? Then why are you still fighting me? Why all this heated passion if it doesn't matter?'

'What matters is how you manipulated that to get what you wanted.'

'But it was what you wanted too. I'm not the villain here. I did what you asked me to.'

Heaven help her, she hadn't only asked. She'd begged. And she wanted to beg again.

He wasn't going to give her everything she wanted and needed. But did *that* really matter? She'd thought she'd found that with James and she couldn't have been more wrong. Maybe she did just need a release for once. Something easy and fun and meaningless. Something that wouldn't matter at all in the long run.

'I just hate letting you win,' she confessed.

And she wasn't that much of a prize anyway. Once he'd seen her—once he'd had her again...

'Don't you understand?' He climbed the two steps until he was right in front of her. 'We're both winning.'

'You really want to win this?' She swept off her tee, baring her entire body.

She'd never been as exposed to anyone. Never in the broad daylight like this.

His jaw dropped, his hungry gaze raked down her pale, freckled, angular body. 'Catriona.'

She didn't get the chance to reply or to run. She was in his arms and his kiss was utterly demanding. Utterly dominant.

And she surrendered totally. Her knees buckled and he lowered her exactly where she was, until she was prone on the staircase. He undid his trousers, kicking them off in a fury. That was when she completely forgot about how she looked. All her focus was on him—the expanse of golden skin and the play of powerful muscles just beneath the surface, the masculine whirls of hair on his chest that then arrowed down in a trail of delight to... She swallowed and her womb pulsed at the sight of him. He was physical perfection. She was hurled straight back into that maelstrom of passion and need and unquenched, unbridled lust.

'Please. Please. Please.' Not a plea, a command. She wanted to touch him. Taste. Feel. She was almost in tears with the need to have him.

He left her for a moment, muttering unintelligibly as he struggled to open the box of condoms and sheath himself.

But then he was back just a step below her butt, on his knees between her legs and grasping her hips firmly. He held her high, controlling her position so he could take her as completely, as dominantly as possible. And watch while he was at it—she was sprawled on the staircase before him, so exposed, and he devoured her with raw lust.

For a second he met her gaze; his eyes were dark and intense and so filled with desire. She panted breathlessly, spellbound. Never had she seen passion this raw. Never had she felt it in herself. The strength of it made her shake. Made her hungry. She was more aroused than she'd ever been in her life.

His gaze narrowed. He knew. He saw it in her, felt it in her. His face flushed. She saw his own control slip as his gaze burned down her bared body again—from her jutting breasts to her waist, to her slick, hungry sex.

'I just have to—' He held her firm and bucked his hips, impaling her to the core.

'*Yes.*'

'This time,' he groaned determinedly as he thrust deep inside her again. 'This time we can take our time.'

But there was no taking time for her. Not when he was grinding so hard against her and so deep inside her and all she could see was his powerful body pressing its passionate intent on hers. She was there already. Arched and taut as a bowstring.

'Alejandro!' The orgasm shattered her. She cried in unashamed ecstasy.

'Damn it, Kitty,' he growled as he held her hips more tightly and thrust harder, deeper, his eyes wide and wild as he stared down at her. 'You make me—'

He broke off as a guttural shout burst from him. His veins popped, his skin glistened as he strained, fighting the pleasure that had already consumed him. Because there was no taking time for him either. 'Kitty,' he choked.

She laughed with exultant delight as he thrust that one last time, striving for the ultimate satisfaction with her. She squeezed hard and tight, cresting again as he was ravaged. She rode the rigours rocking his body as his orgasm exploded, and she relished the lack of control he had in that moment.

Serenity and satisfaction flooded her cells as he slumped heavily over her. And then the cold trickle of reality came. She closed her eyes, needing to scrape together some sort of emotional defence. But she was shocked at the uncontrollable, furious chemistry they seemed to share. They'd just acted like wild animals, mating on the staircase in about twenty seconds flat.

Slowly he disengaged and rose to his knees, gazing down at where she still lay, sprawled down the stairs, naked and unable to move. His eyes glinted as he seemed to read her mind. 'You think we're done?' He shook his head as he bent and scooped her into his arms. 'We're very far from done.'

CHAPTER NINE

ALEJANDRO ROLLED ON to his back, appreciating the softness of the mattress beneath him as he pulled Kitty to rest on his shoulder. The bed was better than the hard floor but was too narrow for total comfort. He breathed out, satisfied. Finally he'd managed to have her the way he'd wanted to—taking his time, making her come again and then again before finally letting himself go.

He'd had to make it up to her because in all his life he'd never lost control as quickly as he had when he'd finally first entered her, locked in that little room. Her tight, writhing body had blown his mind, his orgasm impossible to delay. He groaned inwardly at the speed of it. It must have been the lack of condom—the first time in his life he'd taken such a risk. He knew it had been foolishness, but being with her had felt so good, his skin now goosebumped at the recollection. He still didn't know how he'd managed to pull out. It had nearly killed him at the time.

He couldn't take that risk again. He didn't think he'd have the strength to leave her like that a second time anyway.

But he'd had to have her again—especially when she'd started to build walls between them. That second time on the stairwell hadn't been much better, with his pleasure literally coming too soon. Even with a condom his control had not been brilliant. But *seeing* her body then, watching her response and the emotions flashing in her eyes? She was exquisite—her breasts high, her nipples dusky, her waist narrow and at that private heart of her there was a thatch of that fiery-coloured hair… And it turned out that the skin that had been silken and warm beneath his lips in the dark room was moon-pale and luminous, and gently dusted with rose-gold freckles—they covered her shoulders, arms, breasts, thighs…every part of her. He'd traced patterns of them with his tongue, desperate to taste every inch of her, *fascinated*.

She'd not liked being naked in the light. She'd not wanted to admit how much she'd wanted him again. Her anger had flared. But when it had burned off, pure desire remained. She'd become passion incarnate—as voracious and as victorious as he.

He'd carried her up to the shower, then had her again up here in her bed. Yet, even now, despite the residual ache in his muscles, he felt his hunger stirring.

She was stirring too—wriggling away from him. He turned to read her expression but she was studying the ceiling with grim determination.

'You can leave now,' she said quietly. 'It's a bit cramped in here.'

He froze. Was she ordering him from her bed? Seriously? Before he'd even had the chance to catch his breath and cool down? Not if he had anything to do with it. She was not calling time yet.

'It's not that small.' He inched down determinedly.

'I'm hot.'

His body stiffened in instinctive reaction to the dismissive challenge in her voice. 'Then we'll take off the coverings.' He kicked the blanket to the floor and pushed the sheet to her hips. 'You're sleeping naked anyway.'

And just like that he was ready again.

'I'm not planning on going anywhere,' he muttered, rolling to his side to lean over her. 'Except down on you.'

She was forced to look at him then. Her eyes were wide and dozens of emotions flickered through them. He kissed her before she could argue and worked his way down, down, down…

* * *

He woke early in the morning. He blinked at the light streaming in through the windows and saw the clear blue sky. He was cramped and achy all over. In the end he'd slept the night in her stupidly narrow bed. But he'd simply been unable to move—his muscles slammed by total exhaustion.

Now she was snuggled right into his side, her body soft and warm as it encroached on his. Her hair was like a mass of flames across his chest—soft and warming and with a faint fresh scent. He gently lifted a strand to see it glint in the light. His chest tightened and breathing suddenly seemed harder.

He wanted her to wake, yet he also wanted her to rest. He'd woken more than once in the darkness, unused to having someone with him right through the night. But she'd woken too and welcomed him when he'd turned to her, his appetite rapacious again.

Now she opened her eyes with that sense she seemed to have for when he woke. A pair of emeralds glittered at him, filled with accusation. 'You're still here.'

'Yes.' His throat felt raw and his voice sounded gravelly but, given how long and how harshly he'd groaned during the night, he wasn't surprised. 'I'm still here.'

He watched wariness enter her eyes. He tensed in anticipation. Regrets were not allowed. And this wasn't over yet.

She shifted as if to move away from him but he pressed his palm on her back, holding her in place against him. That tight feeling ventured further south—to familiar territory.

'Is that how you greet your fiancé good morning?' He smiled at her and shifted down her body. 'Maybe I should put you in a better mood, hmm?'

To his pleasure, she parted her legs, letting him in. Always he wanted her to let him this close. He adored doing this to her. Teasing her. Arousing her until she thrashed beneath him and begged for it. He didn't think he'd ever tire of hearing her excitement build. Of making her moan for him. Of making her hot and fierce. He smiled as he kissed her slick, sweet core. He didn't take her again, just licked her to orgasm because he imagined she was probably tender today. He'd not been gentle on the stairs. Or when they'd finally made it to the bed. Hell, even he was aching in parts he hadn't realised he could ache in. He blamed that on the cramped little bed.

'Oh… *Yes!*' The cry was wrenched from her as she clenched her hands on his shoulders, shuddering through another orgasm.

He stifled his groan as his need sharpened. He'd hold back this time. He kissed her gently through the aftershocks, feeling laxness grow within her and seeing sleepiness return to her green eyes. He gently stroked her hair until her eyelids fluttered shut. Then he moved. But at the doorway he turned, unable to resist taking in one long, last look before beginning his day. She was beautiful, enthusiastic and generous, and the most gorgeous challenge. He could hardly wait already.

It was mid-morning before Kitty woke again. She'd slept better than she had in months. She stretched languorously. *Oh, hell.* There were aches in places too private to be named. So many aches. And the worst?

In her heart.

Never could she regret what had happened yesterday. He had won. Totally. But it had to be done with. She'd finish sifting through all the family stuff and get out of here before she got too enmeshed in an affair that was only going to end painfully for her. Alejandro, for all his arrogance and immunity to emotional depth, was too easy to like.

She took her time in the shower, hoping the hot water would soothe her muscles and over-sensitised skin. But she was half aroused again already, just *thinking* of him.

It was the most rapacious case of lust ever. Who knew sex could be so addictive, so much fun and so intense? That it could be all those things at once was both mind-blowing and terrifying.

She fought for control over her own damn mind—making herself get dressed and head downstairs and get on with work. Once she was underway with the boxes, she was startled by a repeated knocking on the front door.

'I'm sorry to interrupt you, Miss Parkes-Wilson, but there's a delivery for the top floor.' Paolo didn't look her in the eye as he explained.

She tried to smile but she was mortified. The man had brought condoms when he'd busted them out of that room yesterday! So Kitty looked past him to where a beautifully tailored woman and a couple of brawny delivery men stood in front of a large truck double parked in the street.

'A delivery?' She blinked then stepped aside to let them in. 'Of course.'

Then she saw what it was—a massive, massive bed.

'For the top floor?' she questioned, her voice squeaking. This was going in *her* bedroom?

'Yes, the attic bedroom,' the woman said crisply. 'Mr Martinez requested I dress the bed for him and ensure it's perfect.'

Did he, now? Unable to answer, Kitty stood aside. It was his house now and she had no authority to argue. She went down to the kitchen and hid. A new, massive bed for her bedroom? The guy had serious nerve.

Almost an hour later she heard Paolo calling for her.

'All done?' She stepped out into the hallway, glad when he nodded.

'You don't wish to inspect it?' the woman asked.

'I'm sure it's lovely.' She led them to the front door and opened it. 'Thanks so much.'

She shut the door on them before her blush became visible to the astronauts on the International Space Station and, with a combination of avid curiosity and outrage, ran back up to her bedroom, freezing on the threshold when she saw it.

He'd replaced her ancient little bed with a monstrosity best suited to a whorehouse, with its four posts perfect for tying dominatrix straps to. Except that was her being over-dramatic. It wasn't tacky. It was beautiful. Freshly laundered white linen covered the whole thing so it looked like a soft cloud. The thing that annoyed her the most was that it was *gorgeous* and fitted her room perfectly. And she was turned on just at the sight of it.

She turned on her heel and marched out of the room, determined to get the sorting done even more quickly than she'd planned. The sooner she got away from Alejandro Martinez, the better for her emotional health.

'Darling, I'm back.'

Anticipation rippled through her body. Despite his sarcastic call, she heard the rough edge of desire underneath it.

'What took you so long?' she taunted, knowing full well he was home earlier than usual. Again.

He walked towards her, his gaze penetrating, that cocky smile curving his arrogant mouth. 'I take it the bed arrived? Let's go use it.' He grabbed her hand and led her to the stairs, carrying a plastic bag in the other. 'I walked into the store and chose what I wanted.'

Was this the new routine? *Now* this liaison was exposed as the blistering lust-fest that it was. No dinners out any more—or even in. It was just straight to bed to have sex the second he walked in the door. She ignored her own desire for exactly that—she couldn't let him have it this easily.

'It's too big,' she grumbled as they got to the top floor.

He sent her a sideways look that told her he wasn't

fooled. 'I figured we needed a little more space to be creative.'

She was not hot at the thought of that. She wasn't.

In her bedroom he set another box of condoms on the table. She stared at it, feeling the shifts deep within her treacherous body.

'I suppose the best thing is I'll have the space to be able to sleep without having to actually touch you,' she muttered.

'Yes, because you hated using me as your pillow last night.' He stood his ground as he began to unbutton his shirt. 'Why don't you come closer and try to tell me again how much you don't want me?'

She flung her head back, watching as with each flick of his wrist more of his beautiful skin was exposed. 'What's in the bag—sex toys?'

'Dinner.' He laughed and his muscles flexed in the most distracting fashion. 'I'll get the toys tomorrow now I know you want them.'

'Oh, so I actually get dinner?' she asked tartly. 'But it's takeaway. Disposable. Not the five-star restaurants any more.'

His smile was evil. 'I know what you want more.'

Her skin burned as she watched him strip. His muscles rippled; his body was hard and magnetic.

Two could play at that game.

'And I know what you want.' She lifted her top and whisked it off her head. She wore no bra—her nipples were too sensitive for lace today.

He retaliated by toeing off his shoes, then socks and finally kicking off his trousers and boxers in the one movement. Kitty's mouth dried as she drank in the response of his body; her hands shook as she peeled her jeans and panties off. Naked, trembling, she stared at him from across the room in a wordless but passionate duel.

'Come here,' he breathed his command.

Internally she battled—her pride, her need to deny him when he always got it *all*, versus her own desire for him.

No false declarations or meaningless promises.

This was what it was. The dam had burst and there was no containing it now until the lust had been drained. She needed it to be drained.

She stepped towards him until she was close enough for him to grasp her waist and slam her against him in that last step. She arched her neck, granting him full access even as she stared hard into his eyes and challenged him. 'Do you insist on such total surrender from all your women, the way you demand it from me?'

'No.' Despite gritting his teeth, Alejandro couldn't hold back his honest reply. 'There's just something about you that really ticks me off.'

Something that lit him up. Something he couldn't get enough of. Her, like this, naked and hot and welcoming him. Stripped back to the essentials, this was sexual hunger, unstoppable and fantastic. The sooner it was sated the better and it was killing him trying to hold back from thrusting hard and claiming her with no foreplay whatsoever.

He didn't understand *why* she needed to fight him, but he knew she couldn't help it. Something about him got to her. It was the same for him. He relished sparring with her, anticipated her arguments and ached for the moment she surrendered and welcomed him into her hot, wet body.

'So you want me to submit?' she asked.

And she did that now. Stepping back, she fell backwards onto the big bed, her arms and legs spread-eagled, positioning herself like an offering for him, except her eyes were alight with that challenge. She wasn't giving in to him without extracting something in return.

'Is this what you wanted?' she taunted.

He couldn't get the condom on fast enough. 'This is your fantasy and you know it.' He breathed hard, daring her to deny it but needing to hear something else. Something true. 'You like it when I pin you down and kiss every inch of you.'

He'd known from the second he'd seen her that it would be like this—their physical attraction was combustible. He caressed her until he heard her gasp. Slow. So Slow. Until, hot and wet, she sobbed for her release. Never had pleasuring a woman been so pleasurable for him.

'Yes,' she screamed. *'Oh, yes!'*

He rose in a fury, fired by her raw admission.

'You're obsessed,' she murmured as she spread her legs wider so he could take his place where she wanted him.

'Possibly.'

The words were a warning in his ear. Was this unnatural? Was this constant ache going too far? But he couldn't stop now. With a harsh groan, he buried himself deep inside her, growling at the exquisite torment of her tight silken body. He held fast for a moment, just to prove to himself that he could.

'Please,' she whispered beneath him, her arms holding him tight and close. 'Please.'

And there it was. He couldn't resist that request, couldn't deny her or himself. So, in turn, he too surrendered, driving hard, driving home.

Strong yet soft, she met him thrust for thrust. *'Alejandro.'*

He lay as limp and useless as a rag but despite his exhaustion he couldn't join her in sleep. She was the most sexually compatible lover he'd had. Not that he'd had as many as she seemed to think. It wasn't as if he spent every night with a new woman. Sex was merely a relaxation strategy to combat work hours and stress.

But this was different. This driving resurgence of desire only moments after completion? He felt inhumanly strong and the voracious hunger drove him on. It couldn't last, right? Usually a few days was enough with one woman before he eased off…but he wanted Kitty more than ever. He wanted so much more.

Any kind of obsession was unhealthy, but at least his obsession with work resulted in a productive, safe, outcome. To be obsessed by a woman? That wasn't safe.

And he was obsessed. He was addicted. Not just to sex with her, but to the way she stood up to him, the way she made him laugh, the way she made him feel alive. And he wondered about the wistful expression on her face as she packed up her family's history from this house, but at the same time he knew the connection she felt to this place was something he could never understand, no matter how hard he tried.

And he did demand her surrender. He was obsessed with that.

God, his brain was addled. Never before had he sat at his desk and discovered he'd lost five minutes in a dreamlike state, just thinking about a woman. He didn't want to think about anyone like that. He didn't want to lose control of himself in that way. He'd seen what happened when someone became obsessive. Became possessive.

Someone very much like him.

He couldn't let it happen now. Not with sweet, vulnerable Kitty. Not with anyone.

He had to protect her. He had to remember he had too much to do. Work had to take precedence. He breathed out, finally able to relax and sink towards slumber as he realised: work was the answer.

CHAPTER TEN

'I'M GOING TO New York for a week. You'll be all right here on your own?'

Kitty looked up from her checklist and hoped she'd hidden the way her heart had just thudded to the floor. 'Of course. It'll be a nice holiday from you,' she lied. He was home early again, but he wasn't staying. He was going away for *a week*.

'Me and my lecherous demands?' He caught her close and kissed her until she was soft and leaning against him. 'You're not going to miss me at all?' he teased.

'I'm going to catch up on my sleep.' She pushed out of his arms and brushed her hair back from her face.

It was mean of him to invite an admission like that when he'd never admit such a thing himself. She'd be out of sight and out of mind... She frowned.

'I'll call you and—'

'Don't,' she interrupted breathlessly.

A quizzical expression crossed his face. 'Don't call you?'

'Not if you're going to call me like you did Saskia that night. I'd rather you didn't call me at all. I'd rather not know.'

His eyes widened. 'What are you implying?'

'I just mean that when this is over I want you to tell me face-to-face, not a phone call. You think you can hold back from temptation for a week?' She held her head high, even though she hated how shrill she sounded. 'Because I don't think that's too much to ask of my fake fiancé.' She didn't want humiliation in that way.

'Catriona, I'll be working non-stop—'

'You'll have to eat sometime—'

'So I'll eat at my desk.'

She laughed a little bitterly. 'You won't go out to all those fancy restaurants?'

The ones with all those women who'd love nothing more than his attention and for him to take them home for a couple of hours' post-work 'relaxation'.

'I have a lot of work to do; that's all this trip is. For me to *work* hard. I'll play with you when I get back.'

And that was what this was. *Play*. A game that would be over soon enough. It was good to get the reminder.

She nodded and forced a smile, but it was small. 'Okay.'

She wanted to believe him, but past experience told her she was a fool to. Her father. Her real fiancé. And Alejandro himself wasn't one to maintain a relationship. He'd admitted that he didn't ever want to.

'I'll see you soon,' he said.

'You're leaving now?' She bit her lip as she realised how that sounded.

'Yes. I just called by on my way to the airport.'

For a moment she thought he was going to say something more, but he shook his head.

'Okay, then…' She struggled to think. 'Have a good trip.'

He sent her a sombre look, turned and left.

She stared at the empty space in the room that he'd left. That was it? Had he really gone so quickly—with just a few words?

Better get used to it. This was what would happen when they parted for good.

Swallowing back a horribly desolate feeling, she turned back to her checklist. She *wasn't* going to torture herself imagining him with a million women while he was away. She was going to get the work done so she could get away quickly and cleanly once he did return and keep herself from hurting more. And until then, when he was out of sight, *she'd* keep *him* out of her mind.

But she was lonelier than she'd ever been in her life. The house was too empty, that new bed too huge, the ache in her heart too unrelenting. She needed distraction—and plenty of it.

'What the hell is going on with you two?' Teddy's eyebrows were at his hairline as he poured her a coffee in the theatre's green room. 'You've really fallen for him?'

'It's impossible not to fall for him.' Kitty shrugged and forced a smile as she confessed the truth in the safety of a joke. 'Unfortunately. But he's away and I need something to do.'

Her brother eyed her for a moment, then pushed a mug of coffee towards her. 'We need help,' he said. 'We always need help. No one can source cheap props the way you do. Can't pay, though.'

Kitty laughed, grateful for the support. 'Well, duh.'

She enjoyed the theatre scene. Hunting for props was fun, creating them even more so. While Teddy's play was almost due to open, the play next in the schedule needed some items that she was happy to help conjure up. She hadn't done that in an age—not since before she'd had to get a 'real job' as gallery assistant.

True to her request, Alejandro didn't phone her. But that night he did send her a picture. It was of the empty soup container on his desk. His dinner. She sent him a selfie poking her tongue out at him.

The next night it was a pizza box. The night after that, a noodle box.

Less than halfway through his self-imposed respite week Alejandro wondered, for the millionth time, what Kitty was doing. Where she was. Who she was with.

Unease chilled his gut. Would she be out seeing friends? Would she have finished up at the house and left?

She hadn't wanted him to phone. She hadn't been able to meet his eyes when she'd asked him not to and he'd made her explain why. Now he felt embarrassed about that call he'd placed to Saskia in front of her. What an arrogant thing to do. He arranged for a bunch of flowers and a brief, apologetic notecard to be sent to Saskia. He hadn't meant to be cruel, but maybe he had been. Contrary to what he'd told Kitty at the time, he didn't know for sure if all Saskia had wanted was a quick fling. As usual he'd set out his expectations and just assumed she'd accepted them. But too often people hid their true feelings.

He counted down the days but time crawled. The nights were worse. His sleep was disturbed, but not by desire. Twice he woke with sweat filming his brow. That old helpless despair clogged his throat. He stared into the darkness and thought of her to make himself feel better. And worse. Because he couldn't stop thinking of her.

The fourth night away, he couldn't take it any more. He succumbed to the temptation and called Kitty's mobile. But she didn't pick up. The brief message on her answer service wasn't enough to satisfy his need to hear her voice. He tried the landline at Parkes House. She didn't answer that either.

He paced through his Manhattan apartment, his concentration in smithereens. He needed to know where she was. He needed to know *now*. Was she okay? Had she been in an accident? Was she with someone else?

A billion questions swarmed in his mind, stopping him from thinking properly. Slowly, a cold unease seeped into his belly and began to burn. This obsessing over her was becoming a festering wound. Who was he to demand to know the minutiae of her day? Since when was his head so filled with wonderings about a woman? He did not want to be this man. He'd *never* wanted to be this man—not obsessive, not possessive.

His phone rang and he pounced on it. But it wasn't Kitty; it was one of his junior consultants in the London office.

'I've had a question come up—'

'I'll come back early.' Alejandro fell on the excuse gladly.

'You don't need to—'

'I'll be on the first flight.'

It was night-time when he landed.

'Is Kitty at home?' Alejandro asked Paolo the second he saw him waiting for him at the airport.

Paolo looked evasive as he led the way to the car. 'She said she was happy using public transport.'

Grimly, Alejandro said nothing. Paolo was not a gaoler but he was a protector, and Alejandro should have made it clear that he needed to know she was physically safe and secure at all times.

After Paolo dropped him off, he unlocked the door, his anticipation building. But he knew as soon as he crossed the threshold that she wasn't home. He paced though the house, wondering where she was, who she was with, why she still wasn't answering her damn phone.

Finally, almost two stomach-churning hours later, he heard the key in the door.

She was in her usual black trousers, black top ensemble, not one of the designer dresses. Her hair was tied back and hidden under a black wool beanie of all things. She'd not been out to dinner? She was smiling—looking so happy— and she'd not seen him yet.

'Hey.' He couldn't choke out more of a greeting than that. The wave of emotion at seeing her again was too intense.

'Alejandro.' For a moment she looked shocked. But then her brilliant smile broadened. 'You're back early.'

That reaction soothed him, but not completely.

She put her large bag down and unwound the scarf from her neck. 'Did you miss me too much?' She looked sassy.

'I got the work done sooner than I'd expected.' He couldn't relax enough to walk towards her. 'Where've you been?'

She didn't take her gaze from him. 'At Teddy's play,' she said softly. 'It was opening night tonight.'

'You didn't answer your mobile when I called.'

'Because I turned it off. It's polite to do that when you're at a live theatre performance.' Her gaze intensified. 'Before you ask, I've spent the last few days helping out at the theatre with the props.'

'I wasn't going to ask.'

'No?' She chuckled.

He shifted on his feet, not able to bring himself to walk either to her or away from her. He hated the mess of emotion in his gut.

She came nearer.

'You're not a little jealous?' she teased lightly.

'I don't get jealous.' He couldn't even break a smile.

'No?' Her eyes danced. 'Maybe something you ate disagreed with you.'

'I'm not jealous,' he repeated. He hated this feeling. He wanted it to go away. He wanted her to come closer to him.

'You missed me,' he told her. It wasn't a question.

Her mouth tightened and her chin lifted. 'I missed the *sex*.'

Not a good enough answer. 'Not me?'

'And your grumpy mood? Hell, no.'

He reached out to curl his arm around her waist and haul her close so she was pressed against him. Hell, *yes*, that was where he needed her. Close.

'Every step of the way you try to deny this attraction,' he said roughly. 'You deny it even as you dance into my bed.'

'There are moments when I don't like you.' Her eyes

sparkled. 'But as I'm stuck in this situation I might as well use what little you can offer.'

His body tightened at the insult. 'What "little" can I offer?'

'Orgasms,' she answered airily.

'Is that all?'

She chose not to say anything more. Provoking him.

Alejandro gave her a gentle shake. 'Stop trying to annoy me. You won't like it if I retaliate.'

'You're the one being annoying.' She slipped off her beanie, released her hair from its elastic tie and shook it out. 'You're all talk.'

The anger he'd felt suddenly morphed into something else. The desire to control. To prove a point. Deliberately, slowly he lowered his head. Her response to his kiss was instantaneous and made the passion within him flare. But it didn't soothe the need coursing in his veins. He lifted her and carried her up the stairs, kissing her as he climbed. Passion, anger and relief combined, giving him a burst of strength. He couldn't get her naked quickly enough. But he didn't strip himself. Not entirely. He needed to retain some control for what he intended to do.

He forced himself to slow down, to caress—first with fingertips, then lips, then tongue. His blood quickened as he felt her skin warm, as he heard her breathing change. He knew her well now but it still wasn't enough. He couldn't stop touching her, greedy for the feel of her skin against his again. Need spiked. He wanted to kiss her everywhere, touch her everywhere, take her. *Now.*

Too fast again. He growled, pulling back.

She arched, reaching for him.

'Not yet, Kitty,' he said roughly. 'I don't feel like giving you that yet.'

But he was lying to her and to himself. He held her arms pinned above her head with one hand, and with his other he trailed his fingertips over her skin, feeling that silky smoothness and following the pattern of pretty freckles all the way down. She was so gorgeous, she tormented him. It would take nothing for her to come, and he knew it. But he wasn't giving it to her. Which meant he wasn't coming either.

Stalemate.

Kitty looked into his dark eyes, unable to stop herself arching up to him again. He was here, home, with her, but he was so controlled and so grim and so determined to have her total surrender. But she wanted his too. And she saw the flush in his cheeks, the sheen on his skin. She felt the barely leashed energy in his twitching muscles. The rapacious lust in his gaze only turned her on all the more, but no matter how she provoked him, he always had the last laugh. He always won. Suddenly she was angry—with herself for missing him so much, with him for always teasing and never telling the truth—with him for not acknowledging that this thing between them was…*more.*

Impulse burned. Before she thought better of it, she lashed out. 'Do you honestly believe I'm thinking about you?'

The look he gave her then was filthy, fiery fury. He rapidly thrust away from her in a rough motion. She raised up onto her elbows, watching as he stripped out of his pants and jerkily sheathed his straining erection. His lack of finesse proved just how angry she'd made him. She closed her eyes and slumped back in heated agony and anticipation. She'd wanted this. Wanted him to be unleashed. He grabbed her hips and pulled her down until her lower legs dangled over the edge of the bed. She felt him step between her parted knees.

'Open your eyes, Catriona,' he demanded. 'Open your eyes and look at me.'

He kissed the heart of her and she almost came on the

spot. She cried out when he left her just before she could crash over the edge.

'Open your eyes.'

This time she obeyed. Her heart thundered as excitement flooded her veins. He was standing over her, his muscles bunching, his body flushed. She ran her tongue along her dry lips.

'Say my name,' he said as he spread her thighs that little bit more with his broad hands and then bent to brace above her, one fist either side of her head.

'Alejandro,' she whispered, melting in the storm of arousal and need and anger.

'Louder,' he insisted. 'Don't stop saying it, or I'll stop. Don't stop looking at me.'

'Egotistical maniac.' She lifted her chin at the filthy look that flashed in his eyes.

'I just want honesty. Be honest,' he demanded.

He came down hard and thrust into her. One forceful movement.

'Then I expect the same from you!' she cried in his face as the exquisite sensation pushed her past her emotional limits. 'Be honest with me.' She clutched him close, utterly torn between happiness and frustration and the yearning for *more* from him. The need for everything. 'You were *jealous.*'

'I missed this,' he shouted back, his control breaking and he thrust hard and fierce. Uncontrollably, he pumped into her over and over, his passion pushing them both across the bed. 'Missed you,' he corrected brokenly. 'Missed you.' He groaned in tortured surrender. 'God, I missed you.'

'Yes!' she cried, her nails curling into his rigid muscles as she held him tightly.

She'd missed him too. So much. Now she wrapped around him, holding him closer than ever, feeling him there with her. So very *there*. Not just physically but in every way. She gazed into his eyes, swept away on the tide of emotion pouring out of him. Emotion that reflected her own—need, need, *need*.

The orgasm hit too quickly, too intensely. Everything shattered. It was easily the most beautiful experience of her life.

In the end she didn't think she'd ever be able to move again. He was slumped over her, his breathing still ragged, emotion continuing to radiate from him. She stroked his hair back from his forehead. His skin was burning, his face was still flushed from the insane effort he'd unleashed on her. She blinked back the tears that had welled in her eyes then swallowed so she could find her voice.

'I don't know why you make me so mad that I say whatever pops into my head to aggravate you,' she whispered, brushing her fingertips down the side of his face. 'I'm sorry I was such a witch.'

'I was not any better,' he admitted, his voice oddly subdued as he shifted to lie beside her. 'I'm sorry. I was… jealous.'

Peace settled within her as he admitted it and she smiled at him sleepily, her eyes closing.

But he didn't smile back.

Alejandro jolted awake a few hours later. Trying to stay quiet, he mentally counted to regulate his breathing. She was fast asleep, burrowed into his side, and he didn't want her to wake this time, not when his heart was racing, his skin was covered in a cold sweat and nausea roiled in his stomach.

He swallowed hard, his mind whirring as he tried to shut down the nightmare. He breathed slowly, hoping to calm himself. But he couldn't help examining the emotions she'd so easily identified. Emotions he'd never felt before. He'd not let himself feel them before.

He'd turned away from any teen crush, going with the girls who'd wanted something else from him. Something simple. The more he'd had of those, the more there'd been. It had become easy. Just sex. Just pleasure. Nothing deeper.

But now insidious fear crawled just under his skin. Memories scalded, choking him. The malevolence, the neediness, echoed in his head.

'You love him more than me.'

The demands. The obsession.

'You're not leaving. You're never leaving.'

He hadn't had these horror-soaked dreams in years. Hadn't thought about the past in so long. He was fine. Happy. Healthy. Living a great, successful life. But in the last few weeks it had changed. Now it didn't seem as great. Or as successful.

In those days while he'd been in New York, Kitty had been laughing, having fun. She hadn't been missing him at all. Which should be fine. Just as it should be fine for her to spend time with Teddy. How could he be jealous of her *brother*? It wasn't as if he was any kind of threat. Yet here he was, feeling jealous, fighting with her, wanting—what?

His feelings were out of control. *He* was out of control.

His worst nightmare had become reality.

CHAPTER ELEVEN

WHEN ALEJANDRO NEXT woke he discovered Kitty had already left the bed. He glanced at the time. It wasn't that he'd slept in; it was that she'd got up appallingly early.

Why?

He pushed back the sheet and tried to swallow down the burn of regret that she wasn't there for him to touch. It wasn't anywhere near as easy. Hell, he was suddenly so *needy*.

He forced himself to shower and dress before going downstairs in search of her. She wasn't in any of the bedrooms on the second floor, but he noticed how much she'd cleared and sorted. She was almost done. That was good. That had to be good.

He finally found her in the kitchen, working at the covered table with a soldering iron in hand, bent over an incredibly weird-looking object. 'What are you doing?'

She glanced up, guilt flashing on her face even as she smiled. 'I hope I didn't wake you.' She looked back at the mass of plastic, metal and wire she was working on. 'I know I should be finishing those last few boxes, but I promised Teddy I'd get this done in time for their rehearsal later.'

He stepped closer to the table. 'What is it?'

'A prototype gamma-ray shield for an intergalactic army.' A self-conscious giggle escaped as she set the soldering iron down. 'The next show at the theatre is a cowboy space opera.'

'Of course it is.' He leaned down to take a better look. 'You made it from scratch?'

She nodded and he was aware of the anxious look in her eyes.

He took a moment to study it. Yet to be painted, she'd constructed it using who knew what and had included details that most likely wouldn't be seen from the stage. It was a miniature work of art. 'It's amazing. Can I pick it up?' When she nodded he lifted it. 'It's so detailed. And exactly what a shield should be like.'

She flushed at his tiny compliment, which both pleased and annoyed him. Why hadn't her family complimented her more?

'But not too heavy?' she checked.

'No.' He carefully tested the weight. 'It's good.'

'Hopefully, if they like it they'll offer me more work. Paid, even.' An excited smile lit up her face. 'I can do it when I've finished here.'

When she left him? He stared, hating the feeling washing through him.

Her cheeks coloured slightly and she looked back to the shield as he carefully put it back down.

'You should come and see Teddy's play.' Her words were rushed. 'He's actually pretty good.'

'You're very loyal to him.' To the point of doing some breaking and entering even.

'Of course. He's my twin—I have to be his number one fan.' She rolled her eyes as she laughed. 'Don't you have any brothers or sisters?'

'No.'

He'd answered too tersely. Now he sensed her biting back follow-up questions. Of course she was curious; he would be too. He walked away so he couldn't see her expressive eyes. He might as well get it over with; she'd have to find out eventually. Obviously she hadn't done the stalker-style Internet search on him that he'd done on her. He shouldn't feel put out by that. He shouldn't feel half of what he was feeling. The nightmares had left a residue of discomfort which left him tired and irritable. Telling her would be good. It would be the beginning of the end.

'My mother is dead,' he said bluntly. 'My father killed her in a jealous rage because she dared try to leave him. The police shot him.'

His blood rushed to his head, making the room spin, and he put his hand out to the wall. He'd not had to say it aloud for a while. He'd forgotten how much it impacted. He tried to count in his head. That numbness that he'd employed for so long came in handy now.

'What?' Her voice was a shocked whisper. 'Alejandro…'

'Everyone knows,' he said brusquely. 'There's no point trying to hide it. It happened. I was a child. I have accepted it and moved on.' He licked his very dry lips. 'I was sent to the States to live. I was very lucky.'

He had been very lucky. After the first two shots, his father had pointed the gun at him. He'd been seconds away from death when the police had killed his father. His mother had been lying just in front of him; she'd stepped forward when she'd seen what his father had in his hand. Nothing could take that image away from him. Nothing could lessen the impact. Nothing could change it.

And he could never be the man his father had been.

'Where were you?' she asked.

'That's why they shot him. He was pointing the gun at me.'

Alejandro turned to look at Kitty in time to see two fat tears rolling down her cheeks. Her simple, heart-rent reaction touched him more than words ever could.

'I'm okay,' he muttered quickly, his breath shortening. 'Better than okay. I was fostered. I focused on school. It was my way out. I got good scholarships. I studied really, really hard.'

Somehow he was standing right in front of her and his arms were around her. She leaned in.

'You're not supposed to comfort me—it's supposed to be the other way round.' Kitty wrapped her arms around him, holding him as tight as she could, wishing she could absorb even some of the pain that was intrinsically bound within him.

He'd told her that truth so baldly, so mechanically.

She wanted to ask so much more. Wanted to know when, how old he'd been, who'd helped him... But it all seemed so inane, those details unnecessary, because they couldn't change the pure horror of what he'd endured. It couldn't make it better. Nothing could make this any better. What about the poor child who'd witnessed that brutality? Who'd lost his mother at the hands of his father?

No wonder he lived his life determined to skate along the superficiality of good times and simple fun. He didn't want complicated. He didn't want emotional.

He didn't want to be hurt again.

'So that's why you don't want marriage or children,' she said when she lifted her face.

'Why would I?' he answered bluntly.

Why, indeed.

'Don't try to change me,' he said softly, his voice a little rough.

'I wouldn't presume to think I could,' she whispered.

'Don't pity me.'

'Don't try to dictate how I'm supposed to feel.' How could she not feel sorry for him, knowing this?

'You only need to feel pleasure.'

His hedonism made total sense now. *He* only wanted pleasure. Only light and easy fun. But life was never like that. Not in the end.

He'd built an impenetrable shell around himself. Always

out, always with people, always having fun. Always that superficial delight. No real emotional intimacy.

'I only want fun,' he warned her one last time.

She gazed at him, then slowly nodded. 'Then let's have fun.'

Alejandro jolted awake. Again he froze so he didn't disturb her, but his heart raced as he blocked the lingering image in his mind. He tried to focus on work instead. But that didn't help much either. Alejandro stifled a groan of despair. He had to go back to New York tomorrow but he was dreading it. He already knew time and distance from her weren't going to help him regain his perspective. He'd thought that if he indulged in her for a couple of days, he'd have had enough. Instead he just wanted more. He liked the way she teased him. He liked listening to her talking about the house, the theatre, the restaurants. He liked her. Maybe telling her about his past had been a mistake—it had broken a barrier within him and she seemed to be able to slip closer than before.

Now he was worried.

He didn't want to feel the gaping loss he'd felt the last time he'd left her—not that massive 'something's missing' sensation. He didn't want that worry, nor the nagging jealousy of nothing. If she was with him, he wouldn't feel that.

Too tired to resist the temptation, he turned and gently roused her. It only took a moment. 'Come with me.'

A twinkle lit her slumberous eyes. 'I did already.'

'No. To New York. Come with me.'

She froze mid-stretch, suddenly looking unsure. He hated that wariness in her, as if she couldn't trust or believe what he was saying.

'I don't want to have another night without you,' he said, her vulnerability forcing him into honesty. Then he smiled. 'Come wear your ridiculous dresses over there. I dare you.'

* * *

He made himself work for a while on the plane—just to prove he could. But the rest of the time he sat comfortably as Kitty curled next to him, engrossed in the movie she'd selected. The limo ride to his apartment took too long and it was dark when he finally led her into his building. It wasn't until he'd flicked the lights on and turned to see her reaction that he realised her pallor.

'Are you okay?' He stepped forward and grabbed her shoulders. She looked as if she was about to fall down at any second.

'I'm just really tired.' She grinned apologetically. 'Like really, really tired. I think the flight got to me more than I thought it would.'

'Then straight to bed.' He led her to the guest bedroom and put her bag just inside the door. 'Come on.'

'I want to explore first.' But she stepped into the room. 'Wow, fancy.'

He glanced around at the sleek interior, with its private bathroom with his-and-hers basins. This wasn't his room; this was the room he used when *entertaining*.

He frowned as he followed her back into the living area. 'You like it?'

'It's very tasteful. Very different to Parkes House.'

'Less full of stuff, you mean.'

'Yeah.' She winked at him and made a beeline for the bookshelf.

But it wasn't the books she was checking out. It was the photo.

'My mother,' he explained, even though he knew it was obvious.

'She looks like you.' She smiled at him shyly. 'Except for your eyes.'

An acrid feeling burned in his throat. 'I have my father's eyes.'

She glanced at the shelf but of course there was no photo there of his father. No other photos at all. For the first time he thought about how boring his apartment must look. The only personal things in it were his books.

'I think you're right,' she said quietly. 'I really need to get some sleep.'

He looked at her; she'd paled again. And suddenly he didn't want her in that bedroom. He didn't want the memory of other women in there with them. He wanted it to be theirs alone.

'Come with me.' He led her up the spiral staircase to his secret space and opened the door to let her past him. 'This is where I usually sleep.'

Her eyes widened as she looked at the small room, her mind processing. 'When you're alone.'

'Yes.' It was small and very simply decorated, safe and quiet, up high on the mezzanine floor. 'You'll sleep better in here.' He cleared his throat. 'It's darker—the curtains are...' He was making excuses. He just didn't want her in that other room.

'Okay,' she said. 'Thanks. I'm sorry I'm so tired.'

So was he, but not because he was desperate to slake his lust. He wanted her to be okay. 'Don't worry, just sleep.'

He climbed in beside her and drew her close so her head rested on his chest. Slowly he relaxed as he felt her sink into sleep in his arms. Warm weariness stole into his bones, and that feeling of anxiety eased until he slept too.

'Alejandro?'

His eyes snapped open; his heart was thundering. Kitty was leaning over him, her eyes wide and worried. He realised the reading light beside her was on and—

'Are you okay?' He sat up and checked his watch. It was only just after two in the morning. 'What's wrong?'

'N-nothing.' She eased back, turning away from studying him so intently. 'I'm fine. I just...'

He waited, rubbing his hand through his hair. His forehead felt damp—had he been dreaming again? He froze.

'I just—I don't know about you, but I'm *starving*.' Kitty suddenly slid out of the bed and sent him a dazzling smile. 'I'm going to go fix something.'

Food? Fantastic. 'I'm not eating noodles,' he muttered.

'Who said I was cooking anything for you?' she said tartly, her spirit snapping. 'Honestly, your arrogance...'

He laughed and rolled out of the bed, inordinately happy that she was back to her best. 'I'll cook. But I can't believe I have to cook vegetarian.'

'You've never used any of this, have you?' She looked around the sterile kitchen while he headed to the pantry, praying he had something edible in there.

He stepped out, brandishing a couple of cans and a bag of rice. The freezer revealed more possibilities.

'Are you sure it'll even work?' she teased as he flicked a switch on the oven. 'I bet you've never turned it on even once before.'

He grinned at her. 'You know I'm very good at turning things on.'

She rolled her eyes.

'Not noodles,' he said pointedly as he placed a steaming dish of rice and vegetables in front of her fifteen minutes later.

'Oh, so good,' she mumbled after the first forkful. Then she glared at him. 'Is there anything you aren't good at?'

'So many things,' he said lightly. 'I won't bore you with the list.'

Only a few hours later, when he got up to go to work, he tried not to disturb her, but she sat up anyway. She still had shadows beneath her eyes. He frowned. He'd been selfish, all these nights of interrupted sleep had taken a toll on her.

He'd been little better than an animal. But she'd wanted it too. She'd pushed him. She'd welcomed him. Even so, she clearly needed a break.

'Lie back down and sleep in,' he told her.

'And miss the chance to explore New York?' she pretty much shrieked. 'Never.'

'Please.' He wanted that pallor to return to a more normal shade. 'Just have a couple more hours' rest then meet me for lunch. I'll send a car.'

'I can find my own way.'

That determined independence annoyed him. It was so unnecessary. But he knew there was no point arguing.

In the end she stood him up for lunch. She sent a text saying she'd meet him back at the apartment before dinner. Apparently she'd got distracted at the shops.

Disappointed, he worked through, but he was glad she must be feeling better. They'd go out tonight, just the two of them. He contacted a friend to find out the city's best vegetarian restaurant and then phoned to secure a table, bribing his way in.

When he finally got home she was ready.

'Where are we going?' she asked before he'd even said hello.

For a moment he didn't answer; he was too busy staring. Now he understood why she'd got distracted. She was in a designer dress, but it wasn't black. It was a beautiful bottle-green and cut to perfectly emphasise her slim waist. The low-scooped neckline showed her delectable freckles. The first time she'd ever worn anything that revealed them. The first time she was in colour. She looked stunning.

He saw the wary hesitancy in her eyes and the way she was holding herself very erect, and knew he was going to need to tread carefully. If he said the wrong thing she'd flare up at him. And for once he didn't want to do that.

Maybe there wasn't a right thing to say. Only a right thing to do. He walked to her and cupped her face in his hands.

'Look at me,' he commanded softly when she avoided his eyes.

Slowly, reluctantly, she met his gaze.

'I can't kiss you or we'll never get out of here tonight,' he muttered hoarsely. 'You've gone to too much trouble to stay home.' For once it hadn't been for anyone else. It had been for him. It touched him more than he could bear. 'You are beautiful.'

She pushed back from him, not meeting his eyes as she blushed. 'You'll sleep with anything.'

'You really know how to insult a man.' He grabbed her hand so she couldn't walk far. 'But you insult yourself the most.'

He had no way to prove how attractive he found her. No way other than sleeping with her—again and again and again.

'I'm not a beast who roots whenever, however, with whatever I can,' he said bluntly. 'I can sleep with none but the world's most beautiful women. A list of models a mile long. Yet I choose to screw you. And only you. Over and over. Why do you think that is?'

'You're going through a phase.'

He laughed and released her hand, giving up on convincing her. 'You wish to burn yourself with insecurity about your appearance, that's your choice.'

Her head whipped as she turned to stare at him, her jaw slack. Suddenly she laughed.

'What?' He queried the change in her demeanour. All of a sudden she was *glowing*.

'You're right.' She giggled again and actually wiped a tear from her eye. 'You're absolutely right. I've been stupid.'

He cupped her face again. 'Not stupid.' He knew she'd

not got the security she needed from her father or her ex-fiancé. 'Sweet.'

She tilted her chin, her eyes glinted, her lips still curved. 'Not that sweet...' she murmured wickedly.

'No,' he muttered hoarsely. 'We need to leave. We're going to the most lauded vegetarian restaurant in the city. You've no idea the hoops I had to jump through to get us a table at such late notice.'

Delight shimmered and she leaned even closer. 'You're going vegetarian for me?'

'Just for tonight,' he drawled. 'So for once you get to choose anything from the menu—you're not limited to one or two same-old, same-old dishes. So let's go.'

But she didn't move; she just smiled up at him and his chest was too tight again and he couldn't seem to move. His heart couldn't pound hard enough. She was sparkling now—her eyes glittering like jewels.

'Kitty—' He pulled the diamond choker from his pocket.

Her soft lips parted as she gazed at them, then back up at him. 'You have it with you?'

'All the time.' He didn't know why. He felt close to her when he had it in his breast pocket. It was stupid, but there it was. 'Please wear it.'

It would look stunning on her.

She shook her head, her smile resolute. 'I can't. It's not mine to wear.'

'You wish it was?' He'd buy them for her if he could.

'It's just not meant to be that way.' She turned away from him.

She deserved more than that. She ought to have her heart's desire. She had such a generous heart.

'You took such a risk for them.' He smiled as he remembered her stealing in to the library that night, all sleek determination and fire.

'Isn't there someone for whom you'd do anything?' she asked lightly. 'No matter the cost or the risk?'

He maintained his smile, but an emptiness gaped in his stomach. She loved in a way he couldn't. The cost of loving like that was too great.

CHAPTER TWELVE

'KITTY?'

It couldn't possibly be morning. It just couldn't. Kitty groaned as she opened her eyes.

Alejandro was already up, dressed in jeans and looking gorgeous as he held a mug towards her. How had she slept through his getting up? She always woke when he did—and not just in the morning, but in the middle of the night when he had those dreams that made his whole body flinch and her heart ache because she didn't know how to help him. The dreams that seemed to be occurring more and more frequently and were more and more frightening for him.

'Coffee?'

'Oh, no, thanks.' She tried to turn her grimace into a smile and rolled over so he couldn't see how bad her attempt was. But the smell was making her gag. She screwed her eyes tight shut and wished she was back in that warm, deep sleep. Yesterday, as the day had worn on she'd felt better, but once again she'd woken feeling so very tired. And queasy as—

Her eyes flashed open and she stared at the white wall of his cosy private bedroom. *Queasy?*

Her mouth filled with bitter spit and she forced herself to swallow it back without moving. Her feminine intuition had kicked in way too late. When was her cycle due? She frowned. She was usually pretty regular and she should have had her period at the end of that first week that Alejandro had been in New York. But she hadn't had it and she'd been so distracted she'd not stopped to think about it at all. Until now.

'I thought I'd take the day off,' Alejandro said huskily

as he sat on the edge of the bed. 'Thought I'd come with you on your sightseeing trip today.'

Her heart would have leapt if it wasn't too busy beating at a billion thuds per second.

'Oh.' *No.*

Not today. Not this. Oh, please, not this.

She shrank into the mattress as her mind scurried. She needed time to figure herself out. Time to reassure herself that she was panicking over nothing and only having an irregular few weeks or something. Her pulse hammered in her ears as she tried to think of an excuse to put him off. 'I'm still feeling tired—I think I need to sleep some more. Maybe later today?'

But he'd offered to take time from work and spend it with her—and she had to turn him down...? She bit her lip, holding the heartbreak and fear inside.

'Are you okay?' He leaned over her and looked at her intently. 'Do you need to see a doctor?'

'No,' she lied and avoided his eyes. 'I'm just tired.' She forced a coy smile. 'I guess I'm not used to the all-night bedroom antics the way you are.'

She felt him withdraw at that flippant comment, but she hardened her heart. She had to have a couple of hours to herself this morning because she was too anxious to maintain a facade of carelessness until later.

'Text me later then.' Alejandro stood. 'I'll see where I'm at.'

'Okay.' She forced herself to snuggle back down in the bed.

He paused on his way out of the room, then turned and walked back to where she was, now almost totally hidden in a tight huddle under the sheets. 'Rest well.'

He pressed his lips to hers. At first she was too scared to be able to relax into the kiss but then that warmth flooded her, overwhelming her as it always did. As *he* always did.

But the moment she heard the door close she sprang out of bed, ignoring the return of the bitter taste in her mouth.

She quickly dressed and then took the elevator down to the ground floor. She smiled confidently at the doorman as he held the door for her to leave the building. She wasn't going to make the mistake of asking him for help finding a pharmacy—that information would be bound to filter back to Alejandro at some point.

She strode along the busy pavement, trying to look as if she knew where she was going. Down two blocks she finally stopped and asked a café worker for assistance.

Five minutes later she handed over the cash for the home pregnancy test. Her fingers were freezing and she almost dropped the change. The chances were so very low, right?

But their first time in that secret room… Surely there'd be only the slightest risk from that? He'd pulled out before he'd orgasmed. How unlucky could they be if a baby had been conceived in that so-brief moment?

Back in his apartment the result flashed almost immediately.

Pregnant.

Kitty stared fixedly at the result, her brain working overtime. She repeated the test. And got the same result.

All kinds of emotions swooped in so quickly she felt faint. She sat down on the floor of the gleaming bathroom. This could *not* be happening.

But it was. Slowly, a feeling of utter certainty and conviction stole over her, giving her an unexpected sense of calm.

She ran her hand over her still-flat belly. There was a tiny life in there. Alejandro's child. Her heart almost burst beneath a wave of unconditional, absolute love. Her muscles flexed in a surge of protectiveness. And suddenly she didn't feel unlucky at all.

But then she thought of Alejandro and how he would

react to this. Her ballooning heart ruptured and she gasped as she realised the hurt they both faced.

This was the very last thing he wanted and it was the very last thing she wanted to do to him.

He didn't want this. He didn't really want her—not for good. Her eyes filled as she realised the happiness she'd felt in the last few days had just been a facade.

She quickly stood. She had no time for tears. She had to leave. She had to think about how she was going to handle everything before telling him. She had to have a sure plan in place before she could even *face* him.

Galvanised into action, she methodically packed her clothing and left the building again with another confident wave at the doorman. She rounded the corner of the block before hailing a cab and heading to the airport. She used the last of the available credit on her card to buy a ticket for the next flight back to London.

She switched her phone off and left it off—from the time she left his apartment, through all the hours during the flight and the time she travelled across London. When she switched it on to phone Teddy, it rang immediately.

Alejandro.

Her heart spasmed. But she didn't answer it yet. She couldn't. Not until she'd figured out a plan that would work. He didn't want marriage, he didn't want children and she knew he wasn't going to change that stance—not for her. But she had that tiny fear that he would try to 'do the right thing'—that he would be as chivalrous and generous as she knew him to be.

So she had to show him that she could handle all of this on her own. That it would make no difference to his life. That he could remain free.

The fact was, he would have lost interest in *her* soon enough anyway. She'd been that temporary aberration, a different kind of fling for him. But her heart sputtered in a last little fight at that thought—she'd started to believe it might be something a little more special than that.

But that wishful thought could never be tested now because she would *never* use this pregnancy to lay *any* kind of claim on him. She had to shut him out for now, until she'd proven her total independence.

'Kitty?' Teddy sounded puffed as he answered her call on only the second ring.

'Yeah—'

'Alejandro has been calling me round the clock wanting to know if I knew where you were and if you're okay. Are you okay?'

She closed her eyes. 'I need your help. Please. Where are you right now?'

Teddy spoke rapidly, his concern audible, but she couldn't tell him anything yet either—only that she needed a safe haven, and quickly. She didn't stop at Parkes House— she went straight to Teddy. And, from him, to a train.

It was another ninety minutes after seeing Teddy before she summoned the strength and courage necessary to phone Alejandro himself. By now she'd been operating on automatic flight mode for so long, it wasn't difficult to sound detached. And that was good. She just had to keep blocking the pain for a few moments longer.

'Where the hell are you?' Alejandro demanded as soon as he heard her voice. 'Kitty, what's happened?'

'Nothing. I just realised I'd made a mistake and wanted to return to London.'

'A mistake?' he queried harshly.

'It's over, Alejandro.' She couldn't get her voice above a whisper.

'What kind of mistake?'

'Coming to New York with you. Us having an affair.'

There was a pause.

'Is there someone else?' he asked, a different tone in his voice. Fear.

Kitty shut her eyes tightly and grasped hold of the excuse he'd just handed her. 'Yes.'

'I don't believe you,' he said bluntly. 'Something's happened. Tell me what's happened.'

She swallowed and repeated her stance, determined to stick to her game plan for forcing him away from her. 'It's very simple. I've met someone else. I wanted to tell you before you found out some other way. It was fun while it lasted.'

Alejandro stopped pacing across the floor of his empty apartment and listened harder, trying to ascertain something—anything—in the resulting silence.

'Kitty?' He couldn't believe she'd just said that.

Now he replayed the cruel words in his head and realised that they echoed those he'd said to Saskia those few short weeks ago. Saskia and every other woman before her. The irony wasn't lost on him. And now his anger began to build.

Had she done all of this deliberately? Was she out to teach him that 'lesson' she'd long ago said he deserved?

'You're back in London?' Now he'd heard from her and could tell that—physically at least—she was safe, he was sure of it. 'I'm on the next flight.'

He walked out of his apartment and locked it as he spoke. He'd been packed and ready for the last twelve hours while he'd been desperately trying to track her down.

'Don't!' she suddenly snapped, her voice rising in pitch and volume. 'You won't find me, Alejandro. Accept it's over and move on.'

She ended the call.

For a moment sheer rage blinded him. He'd find her and find out the goddamn truth or—

What? What would he do?

His blood iced but bile boiled up his throat. Shame burned at how angry he'd felt less than a second ago. And, now, how hurt he felt.

But as he replayed her last desperate words in his mind, he heard the pain evident in her tone. Something was wrong. Very wrong. And when Kitty was hurt or upset she ran away. She'd run to Cornwall when her fiancé had cheated on her. She'd gone to her secret room as a child when her father had let her down.

It was what she always did.

When he called her phone back again she didn't answer. Not the first time. Or the fifteenth.

CHAPTER THIRTEEN

TEDDY PARKES-WILSON STRAIGHTENED up and shook his head. 'I'm never going to tell you where she is,' he said before Alejandro had a chance to speak. 'Say what you like. Do what you like. You'll never get it out of me.'

'Relax. I'm not about to beat it out of you.' Alejandro stared into the younger man's eyes. 'I wouldn't ask you to betray her trust. I wouldn't expect you to and I wouldn't respect you if you did.'

He shoved his hands into his pockets, hiding the way his fingers had curled into fists in frustration. But he meant what he'd said; he wasn't about to bully anyone. That was the whole point. 'I know you're loyal to her,' he said to Teddy, unable to hide his bitter censure. 'Even though you take advantage of her.'

Teddy looked annoyed, but accepting. 'That's why I won't tell you. I owe her and I know it.'

Alejandro had known Teddy wouldn't give his twin up. But he wasn't giving up either. 'I will find her.'

'Even though she doesn't want you to? You'll still hunt her down?'

'Yes.' Alejandro forced himself not to flinch, hating the way Teddy seemed to think he was some kind of monster—what had Kitty said to him? 'Because she and I need to resolve this face-to-face.'

He needed to see her one last time. If only to understand. If only to reassure her that she didn't need to run away from *him*. He didn't understand why she'd run and the least she could give him was that explanation. He refused to be someone who was feared. That was his worst nightmare.

'I think this belongs to you.' He pulled the diamond choker from his pocket and held it out.

Teddy's face flooded with colour in that sudden way his sister's did. 'It does, but I don't deserve it.' He took the necklace. 'I'll give it to her.'

Alejandro walked out of the small rehearsal studio none the wiser as to where Kitty actually was. Not Cornwall this time—that would be too obvious. Not Corsica to be with her father. He guessed she'd probably used some of Teddy's resources. But he had resources too. And he'd use every last one of them to track her down.

He hated the darkness of his thoughts, yet he couldn't stop them consuming his mind and time. He couldn't bear the thought of her with another man and refused to believe she actually was. Yet doubts wormed. Jealousy festered. He had to know the truth behind why she'd ended it.

He had to know she was okay.

But it was almost a full month since she'd left New York before his phone buzzed with a profitable call from the private investigator he'd engaged weeks earlier. A month in which Alejandro had worked around the clock. A month in which he'd been unable to sleep, in which he'd not gone out to dinner because he couldn't face the feeling of isolation in crowded places, in which he'd paced the empty rooms of her former family home and wished she was there with him.

A month of hell.

'There's a crofter's cottage on the Highland estate of one of the brother's theatre friends that's sometimes rented out as a holiday home,' the investigator said briskly but with obvious excitement in his tone. 'It's been booked out for the next few months.'

'And she's there?'

'I believe it's her but I'm sending you a picture now for confirmation.'

Alejandro rang off and stared at his phone impatiently,

waiting for the photo to land. When it did he drew in a sharp breath and was glad he was sitting down. His muscles emptied of energy. His heart stopped.

The shot was taken from a distance but with a long lens to get a close-up on her face, which meant it was slightly blurry. But he instantly recognised her. She was wearing a woollen coat—black, of course—and her hair was loose. Her skin was as pale as ever, her freckles as pretty. But there were no sparks in those emerald eyes.

He phoned the investigator back. 'Give me the address.'

'I've texted it to you already.'

Alejandro closed his eyes. 'Is she staying there alone?'

'Yes.'

He cut the call, groaning in bitter relief. He'd go there this instant. He broke into a run, storming out of his office in the early morning, abandoning the meetings scheduled and not giving a damn.

He worked out it was fastest to fly to Glasgow and drive from there. But it still took too long—hours of adrenalin, of a mounting headache that threatened his vision, of a tightening in his chest that made it hard to breathe. Hours of trying to work out what to say to her first.

But when he finally parked up outside the small cottage in the early evening he could see at once that it was empty. The curtains weren't drawn, there were no lights on, no other vehicle on the driveway. He clenched the steering wheel of the plush rental car and bit back his bellow of frustration. Had she somehow heard he was on his way? That was impossible. He'd told no one where he was going.

He got out of the car anyway to peer into the windows of the cottage and see if any of her stuff was visible. In the first window he couldn't see much. There was an open-plan lounge and kitchen with a number of impressive paintings on the wall, a plump armchair placed near the window to catch the sun and the low table next to it had a used teacup and a book on it, but there were no identifiable clothes draped anywhere…

He realised the barking in the distance was growing louder. He stepped back from the window to walk along the small veranda and rounded the corner so he could see behind the cottage.

An Irish red setter bounded towards him ahead of a slim figure walking behind it. She wore a beanie but her fiery hair flowed out from underneath it. And she wore black, of course. Not the cute little tailored trousers; this was an exercise combination—leggings and a sleek merino top that clung to her…*curves.*

She'd been out for a walk. There was colour in her cheeks. That colour drained the second she saw him.

Alejandro's eyes narrowed as he stared hard back at her.

For a heartbeat her pace faltered. Her hand lifted in a barrier across her belly. A small giveaway gesture of protectiveness. That book on the table inside flashed in Alejandro's mind. The title that he'd seen but not really registered.

Pregnancy & Beyond: A Guide to Baby's First Year.

And the expression in Kitty's eyes now?

Guilt.

'How did you find me?' Her voice shook as she neared enough for him to hear her.

He couldn't answer. He couldn't stop staring at the changes in her body—tiny changes, yes, but even in the slimming black attire they were obvious to him. Her breasts were fuller, as was her slender belly. She was pregnant. He was certain of it. And he knew to his bones that it was his.

This was why she'd left him.

He only needed to look into her eyes for a second to know what she was going to do and he'd not expect anything less from her.

She would have the child. She would love the child.

For a second he was blinded and his gut burned. Molten rage scoured his ribs. He had not felt so hurt since—

He shut his eyes. Blocking the memory and the wave of emotion that threatened to overwhelm him.

This was not what he wanted. This was *never* what he'd wanted.

'That bastard's blood—' he choked. Unable to move. Unable to utter another word.

He'd never wanted this. Never, ever. He'd wanted the whole sorry mess to die when he did. He'd forced himself to forget it for almost all of his life. It was over. Only now it wasn't.

'Alejandro—'

He threw out his hand to stop her from stepping nearer to him. He was too angry.

'I need time,' he snapped. 'You've had...*weeks* to get used to this. Give me...give me...'

Kitty stopped in her tracks as shame burned. He *knew*. He'd found her and he knew and he was so very angry.

She didn't blame him. She should have told him so much sooner. But the days had slipped by and she'd been focused on finding a quiet place to settle for a while. On keeping well. On *hiding*. She'd been such a coward. But she couldn't be now. She swallowed and made herself speak.

'I'll be in the cottage,' she said quietly. 'Whenever you want to talk.'

She wouldn't blame him if he got back into his car and drove away. He'd hate her for this and maybe he was right to. And wasn't that what she'd wanted? Hadn't she done this deliberately to force this kind of response from him?

Yes, she was that much of a coward.

But she left the door to the small cottage open and stood with her back to the door because she couldn't cope with watching him, waiting to see what he would choose to do. The dog let her know when Alejandro stepped inside. She turned as he barked and saw him run up to Alejandro, his tail wagging crazily as he nuzzled Alejandro's hand, asking for a pat.

Alejandro complied, but he didn't look down at the animal. He was too busy staring at her and so obviously keeping himself in check. Emotion burned in his eyes. The trouble was she didn't know what emotion it was.

'Are you keeping well?' he finally asked.

'I'm fine, Alejandro. I'm okay.' She walked over to him and closed the door.

He didn't take a seat, though; he just stood there—too large for this room. Too big for her heart.

She saw his pallor and the torment in his eyes and her willpower broke. She couldn't help reaching out to cup his jaw. But he flinched and pulled back before she made contact. She curled her fingers into a fist, hurt by his rejection even when she knew she deserved his anger.

She turned away. 'I'll put the kettle on,' she said lamely.

'Don't,' he said shortly. 'This won't take long.'

She hadn't got even halfway across the room. Now she turned back to face him.

'So there is no one else?' he said quietly.

She lifted her chin. 'There's the baby.'

The emotion in his eyes flared as she referred to it. Confirmed it.

'I know you don't want children,' she said quickly. 'That's why I left. I don't expect anything from you. I never will.'

He turned on his heel, strode to the window and stared out of it at the darkening sky. 'You didn't give me a chance. You ran away without talking to me. You have made your decision without me,' he muttered in a low voice. 'I suppose there is nothing more to be said.'

Yes, that was what she'd wanted, right? For him to say nothing. For him not to fight. Not to try to 'step up' and be the husband and father to her child that secretly she so very badly desired. But having him behave as she'd thought she wanted him to hurt.

'You might not want this child, but I do,' she said defensively.

He turned his head and glared at her. 'You want it for the wrong reasons.'

What wrong reasons? 'To trap you into paying money to me?' she guessed wildly. Her hurt morphed into sudden, vicious anger. 'I said I don't want anything from you.'

Which was a lie, but what she truly wanted she could never have.

'You want this baby because you want someone to love you,' he snapped.

Shocked, she just stared open-mouthed at him, feeling as if she'd been ditched—hanging fifty feet up a cliff with no foothold. 'I wasn't the one who didn't bother with the condom. I wasn't the one who—'

'All your life you've wanted someone to adore you and now you think you've got it,' he interrupted coldly.

'I didn't *plan* this—' she fought back.

'But what are you going to do when it gets hard? Are you going to run away and abandon it when times are tough?'

'Of course not.' She flung her head, stung by his attack. 'And you know what? There's nothing wrong with wanting to be loved.' She burned inside—so wounded, so bereft. 'Or with wanting *to* love someone. At least I'm not afraid to put myself out there and *try*.'

His nostrils flared as he whirled to face her, his stance widening as he braced.

But she stepped forward, too hurt to stop.

'You don't let anyone into your life. Not properly. You basically buy their company with your success and your... skills.' She saw him flinch but she carried on anyway. 'It's not the sex that bothers me. It's the *superficiality*. You keep everything shallow so you can't be hurt.'

He paled in front of her and she felt a twinge of remorse. 'I cannot imagine the horror you experienced as a child… But you're stopping yourself feeling anything except shallow pleasure. You use sex as a temporary muscle relaxant. You're worth more than that.'

And so was she.

'You don't understand,' he said gruffly.

'Then help me understand. Talk to me.'

'The way you talked to me?' He stared at her pointedly.

She slumped into a seat. 'I'm sorry, okay? I'm sorry I didn't tell you.' She glanced up at him. 'I'm sorry if I hurt you.'

'It's not about stopping me from getting hurt,' he muttered. 'When I came back from New York that first time I was away from you, I was jealous of your *brother*.' He closed his eyes for a moment and then looked at her bleakly. 'I can't become that obsessed, Catriona. I can't become that monster.'

She straightened, surprised at his bitter words. 'You'd never be a monster.'

He threw her a pitying look and shook his head at her naivety. 'It's started already,' he argued. 'I took you to New York because I couldn't bear the thought of wondering what you were doing. Who you were with. What I was missing out on. Am I going to become so controlling that I can't leave you alone? That's not normal.'

In that moment hope sparked within her. Had he felt that deeply about her? Did he want more than just a temporary fling with her?

He looked tortured. 'I never wanted to spread the poison that's in my veins.'

Now she realised the hell he was putting himself through. She put her hand across her belly. 'This is a totally innocent baby. Just as you were a totally innocent child. You're not him, Alejandro—you'll *never* be him.'

'I have his eyes.'

'You have your own eyes. You're your own person.' She'd had no idea that this was what he feared. Was this what caused his nightmares?

But he shook his head. 'I can't take the risk. I can't get...' he glanced down at her body and then back up to her face '...I can't get involved.'

It hurt to hear him say it so bluntly.

'Are we not worth the attempt?'

He didn't even want to *try*. She understood that he was hurt, but it hurt her too. So much. Why couldn't someone ever love her the way she loved them? What was it that was wrong with her? Why did she have to miss out again?

'You deserve better than this, Kitty. Better than me.'

That wasn't true—she deserved better *from* him.

'Everybody struggles with their emotions sometimes.' She attempted a smile as she tried to reason with him. And to be as honest as she could. 'I've been so jealous of all those women of yours. I've been so insecure.' She still was. 'But I keep on *trying*. You're worth it to me. This is worth it.'

'So worth it, you ran away without giving me any kind of explanation.' His cheeks looked hollow; he was even paler than before.

'I was scared.'

'Of me,' he said heavily.

'Not because I thought you'd hurt me physically. It was just that I wanted more than you wanted to give me.' She drew in her lip and bit down on it hard. But there was no reason to hold back now. 'I want you to love me. Because I love you.'

He shook his head. 'That can't happen.'

'Because you don't want to get hurt again?'

'Because I cannot do to my child what my father did to me,' he corrected her furiously. 'He ripped me apart, Kitty. He destroyed everything I had.'

'Not everything. You're still here. You've rebuilt so much. People get help for all kinds of issues...' She stood up and walked towards him. 'Why let him steal your future? Your happiness?' She reached him, her heart thundering. 'By shutting yourself away you're letting him win.' She gazed into his beautiful troubled eyes. 'He didn't want anyone else to have your mother. No one else to have you. You're letting him win by locking your heart away. You should show him the middle finger and fight to have a full and happy life. You could get some help; I could help—'

'I can't be the man you need me to be,' he snapped. 'I can't be him. I just can't.'

The finality in his tone devastated her. 'Because you don't love me.'

Not enough to want to try. That was what hurt so much. Not her. Not even the tiny baby she carried. Always, she wasn't enough.

'It's because I *do* love you that I can't,' he roared.

'What?' She stared at him fixedly. 'What did you say?'

He looked back at her; that emotion in his deep eyes was nothing but heartbreak. 'Don't,' he whispered. 'Don't, Kitty.'

Don't make him say it again? Don't make it harder? Don't step closer?

Her eyes filled with tears as her heart broke for both of them. Why couldn't he try for her? She framed his face in her hands, feeling the roughness of his evening stubble. His skin was so warm and he was so beautiful to her. Her heart filled to bursting—with disappointment, with desire, with aching love. She reached onto her tiptoes and kissed him.

He was as still as a statue as she kissed him. But he wasn't cold like marble—he was hot and straining as he held back. She didn't want him to hold back any more—not in any of his emotions.

She kissed him more deeply—winding her arms around his neck. She didn't care about anything else in this instant. There was no point in trying to argue any more. In trying to think. In this one moment of life there was only the need to touch and to feel him again. To have him with her.

To love him.

His hands came to her waist and she pressed closer to him, needing to feel his strength against her now more than ever. And she wanted to reassure him somehow. She wanted him to know how she felt. She wanted him to believe that this could work. This strong, gentle man was so scarred that he couldn't see himself as he really was.

He kissed her back now and suddenly turned her so her back was pressed to the wall—his natural inclination to dominate resurging. She welcomed it—helped him, shimmying down her pants as she leaned back against the wall and then fought with the zip of his trousers. She needed him in this way at least. She'd missed this so much—the searing, unstoppable attraction. The need to take and be taken. She sealed his mouth in that hot, deep kiss, silencing any opposition of his or the spilling of more of her secrets. The kiss told him everything anyway.

She wanted him. She needed him. She loved him.

For once it wasn't the culmination of a challenge, or the finale to a playful flirt. This was nothing but pure emotion. A final kiss, a final connection. All the pain of goodbye. All the love that was being lost.

'Please.' She arched in readiness as he angled her hips in that delightfully sure way. He was hard and she was wet and he pushed to his hilt in one powerful thrust. She cried out at the physical pleasure—at the emotional pain. She felt such completion and yet her heart was being torn apart.

'I'm so sorry.' His voice broke as he paused, looking

into her eyes with such torment in his. 'I never wanted to hurt you.'

'It doesn't matter,' she muttered as he gave her the one thing he could.

It was worth it. It would always be worth it.

She rocked her hips, riding him, their coupling hot and wet and as easy as always. But tears coursed down her cheeks as she met him thrust for thrust. He brushed them away but they kept tumbling.

'Kitty,' he pleaded as he pressed deeply into her again and again. His brow was wet, his frown pained. 'I'm sorry.'

Fearlessly, unashamedly she looked into his eyes—she would not hide her feelings from him now. She wrapped her arms more tightly around him and kissed him again and again and again. She loved him. She loved doing this with him. She would never regret any of it. And she never wanted it to end.

But all of the emotions were too big for her to hold— they had to burst free from her. She cried out as the sensations became too exquisite for her body to bear.

He buried his face in her neck. He shuddered violently and his pained, pleasure-soaked groan rang in her ears. She squeezed hard—holding him as deep and as close and for as long as she possibly could. Because it was her last moment with him.

But in the end the intense spasms of pleasure wreaked havoc on her muscles—rendering her limp and weak and leaving her with nothing but words.

He was still. Silent. And, in some ways, stronger than her.

In another heartbeat it would end.

'I love you, Alejandro,' she whispered. 'And I would have loved you no matter what.'

He didn't reply—no word, no look, no action. For one last breath she had him with her. But then she felt his muscles ripple. He flexed and then disengaged—from her body, from her embrace. It took only a moment for him to straighten his clothing and step back from her. His head was bowed so he avoided her eyes. But she wasn't afraid to look at him. There was nothing to be afraid of now. The worst had happened. *Was* happening.

She watched as, without a word, he walked out of her life.

CHAPTER FOURTEEN

KITTY RECEIVED A parcel from Alejandro's lawyer less than a week later. Delivered by courier, the documents explained that a large settlement of money for the child was to be held in trust, together with a monthly allowance that was enough to house, feed and clothe ten children, not just one tiny baby. And he'd gifted her Parkes House and all its contents. No strings. No reversion to the child once he or she was of age. It was hers and hers alone.

There was a note in the letter, penned by the lawyer, informing her that Alejandro was returning to New York and that he planned to stay in a hotel on the occasions he needed to return to London for his work.

She knew he'd avoid it as much as he could. He'd almost never be there.

Her heart solidified. He might be trying to mean well, but she didn't want any of what he was offering her. Not money or physical security.

Time stagnated. The days dragged, but the nights were the worst—she paced, unable to sleep. She missed him. Ached for him. Loved him. And was so angry with him.

A few days later she heard the sound of a car pulling up outside the cottage. Her heart raced for the first time. She opened the door. *Alejandro?*

'Hey, sis! You went quiet—' Teddy broke off from his cheery greeting as he got out of the car and stared at her. His expression morphed to total concern. 'Kit—'

'Don't,' she begged him. 'I know I look... Don't say anything.'

'Jeez, you better get back inside and sit down.' He followed her into the cottage and sat on the sofa opposite her armchair. 'Talk to me.'

'I'm okay, Teddy.'

'Oh, sure you are.' Her twin rolled his eyes. 'You've seen him then?'

She nodded. 'It's finished.'

Teddy frowned then reached into his pocket. 'Alejandro gave it to me.' He handed her Margot's diamond choker. 'But let's face it. It ought to have been yours in the first place.'

Kitty curled her fist around the gleaming coils of platinum and diamonds so she couldn't see it. 'Would you be devastated if I sold it?'

'Why do you want to do that?' Teddy looked shocked.

'Because I need to be independent from him. I can get some capital from this, then sort myself out.' If she was having this baby on her own, she didn't want anyone else to have to pay for it.

'Are you sure the two of you can't work it out?' Teddy leaned forward. 'He looked a wreck. So do you.'

Kitty closed her eyes. 'It's more complicated than… It's just better this way.'

'But you're both miserable. I don't see how that's better than trying to sort it.'

'He doesn't want to try, Teddy,' she said brokenly and the tears finally tumbled. 'That's the point. He doesn't want to *try*.'

Half an hour later, Kitty's tears were dried and she was curled up in the chair watching her brother as he made her a couple of pieces of toast that she didn't feel like eating but knew she had to.

Alejandro wasn't coming back; she accepted that now. No more waiting for a car to arrive. It was over between them. He'd made his decision and she had to move on too.

Maybe Alejandro had been right. Maybe she did run away when times got tough—but not any more.

And maybe part of her wanted this child because she wanted someone to love her. Was that so terrible? But she was the parent here and she was damn determined to ensure that her child felt utterly, *unconditionally* loved. No matter what. Her baby would never feel like he or she wasn't good enough, would never come second to another all the time. Kitty would do everything she could to make her child emotionally whole and secure and happy. The hurts of past generations would not be passed on by her.

And it was beyond time that she pulled herself together and got on with it.

'Can I get a lift back to London with you?' she asked Teddy as he handed her the plate of hot buttered toast.

'Of course.'

New York. The city in which to forget everything. The city where he could get anything, everything and anyone.

Except the one he wanted.

Alejandro stood up from his desk and shrugged on his jacket, ready to go to one of his favourite restaurants. Now was the time to get on with his life. He'd been in a kind of stasis during that month when he'd been unable to find her—he hadn't been able to go back to 'normal' until he'd cleared the air with her. But now he'd done that. More than that, he'd made provision for her and the baby.

His conscience was clear. He'd done all he could.

He'd enjoy his life again. He just needed to get on with it again.

'We haven't seen you here in a while, Alejandro.' The maître d' smiled at him. 'Your guests are already at your usual table.'

'Thank you.'

He'd return to his easy, shallow social whirl.

But it wasn't easy. They welcomed him with bright smiles and barely veiled curiosity that he ignored. He listened to the dinner party chatter. It now seemed inane. Where was the passion? Where was the love for something—anything—other than a party? He glanced around the table, unable to raise a smile. The women were intelligent and beautiful, the men equally talented and all were competitive and driven.

'Are you ready to order, sir?' The waiter interrupted his thoughts.

Alejandro put the menu card down. 'Actually, I've changed my mind. I'm sorry everyone—' he cast a smile around the table '—I won't be dining with you tonight after all.'

He decided to bury himself in work instead. That at least he was passionate about. That at least was productive.

He worked such long hours he lost track of when it was day and when it was night. That was the good thing about having offices in different countries—one was always open. There were always emails to send and markets to watch. Nightmares to avoid. Loneliness to deny.

Who are you going to leave your billions to?

He thought about a tiny baby with hair the colour of a bonfire. Once he'd let that thought whisper in, the rest tumbled behind it in a flood. The memories he'd been blocking for days. The way she'd challenged him. The way she'd laughed with him. The way she'd looked at him. The way she'd held him.

I love you, Alejandro.

She'd felt so good. But then she'd looked so sad. And she was right—he was such a coward. She deserved so much better than him.

So become the man she needs you to be.

He fought against that little voice—the nagging thread of hope. Of possibility. The dream. He was doing the right thing already. She'd get over it. She was better off without him and the risk he bore.

It was almost midnight several days later when the email landed. He stiffened when he saw Teddy Parkes-Wilson's name as the sender. Had something happened? Was she well? Surely Teddy would phone if it was something bad?

He clicked to open it, suddenly fearful of what her brother was emailing about. He'd pulled the investigator off her. Her life was hers; he was not spying on her. He was not becoming that creep.

But there was no message in Teddy's email—only a link to another website. Great, he was being spammed by her brother. He clicked the link anyway.

It took him to an online auction site—specifically to a series of listings from one vendor. His eyes narrowed as he recognised the first few items. All those designer black dresses. Those shoes. Kitty had placed everything she'd bought with his money up for auction. There was a high-lighted comment in the blurb on each stating that all the proceeds would be donated to a leading charity for the sur-vivors of domestic violence.

His throat burned. Shame hollowed him out. But he couldn't stop scrolling down. There were so many memo-ries attached to those dresses. Even the ones she'd not had the chance to wear.

He paused when he came to the emerald dress that she'd worn that last night they'd had together in Manhattan. But it was the entry just beneath that which broke his heart.

The antique diamond choker. This time the proceeds were not listed as going to charity. Alejandro knew ex-actly why.

Teddy had given it to her and she was using it to gain a foothold on her future. He knew the money in the account he'd set up for her had been untouched. She'd save it for the child but not use a cent for herself. Her integrity and pride wouldn't let her. Now she was doing what she thought she had to do, to make her way independently. She was willing to sacrifice something she loved, for the benefit of someone else. She always put others first, even when it wasn't necessary.

Well, not this time. He wasn't letting her.

CHAPTER FIFTEEN

'WHAT DO YOU MEAN, the auction site is down?' Kitty glared at the wall as she tried to understand what the man on the helpline was telling her. 'None of my items are up there any more.'

'I know; we're looking into it. We can phone you back once we've located the issue.'

She didn't want them to phone her back; she just wanted it fixed. But she hung up with a sigh and turned back to her new creation on the dining table. She needed to keep focused, keep working, keep moving forward.

Someone banged on the front door just as she was about to begin sketching a 'laser nozzle' for the interstellar transporter. She wiped her hands and went to the door.

'Alejandro.' She stepped back almost instantly, suddenly self-conscious in her splattered tee and ancient leggings. He might have helped her address her body confidence issues, but she'd still rather not be in her painting rags.

'May I come in?' he asked.

He looked better than the last time she'd seen him—not as pale or angular. His eyes were brighter and vitality radiated from him. That was good, right? He was obviously doing well.

But it ripped her heart all over again.

'Of course.' She brushed her hair behind her ear. 'It's still your house.'

He didn't respond to that as he walked in ahead of her. Nervously, she ran her hands down the sides of her legs and followed him.

'You're making more props?' He turned into the kitchen and noted the clay sticking to her tee with a small grin.

'Yes.' She summoned a smile to match his. 'They liked the shield and commissioned more.'

'I'm not surprised.'

She nodded and then looked at him, her heart thudding. 'How can I help?'

He drew his hand from his pocket. She gasped as she saw what he held—Margot's diamonds.

'Where did you get that?' she asked.

'You're not to sell it, Kitty—it means too much to you.'

'How did you get it?' She'd left it in the safe at the auction house.

'I bought it.' A wry grin crossed his face. 'It and several rather stylish dresses.'

'You *didn't*. From my auction?'

He nodded.

'You bought everything?' That was crazy.

'I know it's stupid, but I couldn't bear to think of anyone else wearing them.'

'But you paid for them all *twice*.'

'I don't care.'

'Oh, Alejandro.' Tears pricked her eyes. He melted her, every time. 'Why did you do that?'

Alejandro turned and walked away from her. There was too much he had to say and he lost track of everything when he looked at her. 'I need to tell you about my father.'

He heard her sharp inhalation.

'You don't have to do that.'

'I do. Please.' He took a seat at the furthest end of the table from her so he wasn't tempted to touch her. He had to get this off his chest. He had to get her to understand. 'I don't like to talk about it much, but there's a lot I remember. There'd been other incidents before that day. He was possessive. Jealous. He hit her. And me.' He dragged in another shuddering breath. Saying this aloud to her was harder than he'd thought it would be. But he'd worked on it with his new counsellor, and he was determined he'd get himself sorted. For himself and for Kitty. 'He'd get jealous of me. He'd say she spent more time with me than with him. That she loved me more than him. Like it was a competition.'

Kitty didn't say anything; she just came forward and sat in the chair next to his.

His father had been wrong. His father had been evil. But he had his blood in his veins.

'When she took me and left him for good, he flipped out.' Alejandro avoided looking at Kitty's face as he said it. 'He tracked us down and came after her. She stepped in front of me. She died protecting me.' It hurt so much but he could never forget. And until now he'd never really understood what had driven her. 'That's what mothers do, isn't it? They fight for their young. They'll do anything for their children. Fathers should too.' He lifted his head and looked at her. 'And fathers should love their daughters every bit as much as they love their sons.'

Her sweet face crumpled. 'Alejandro—'

'I think my father confused love with possession. He held on to her and refused to let her go because he saw her as *his*.' He fought back the emotion clogging his throat. 'And I promised myself I was never going to be like that with any woman. I wasn't going to marry. I wasn't going to have kids. It was all so clear and so easy for so long. And then you stole into my new home and I turned into a demanding creep.'

'No—'

'I locked you in the library,' he growled. 'For heaven's sake, Kitty, I was awful to you that night.'

But she shook her head. 'You weren't that bad. I was the one who'd broken in. I was the one in the wrong.'

'But I took advantage of that. I saw you and I wanted you so I used every chance that came my way to keep you with me.' He'd taken total advantage of everything to do with her. 'All you wanted was what should always have been yours. The necklace.'

'But I also wanted you,' she said softly with a small shrug. 'I took one look at you and…you fascinated me. Maddened me. But I wanted you the second I saw you. You were more honest about that than me.' She licked her lips. 'And then I got to know you. You didn't bully me into staying there with you. You didn't threaten me with violence. Not once.'

'But you had to stay only because I had something you wanted.'

'What I really wanted was you.' She smiled sadly at him. 'And if I had really wanted to leave, you wouldn't have stopped me. We both know that.'

Did they? Would he have let her walk out? Not with the diamonds, but without. Yes, he would have.

Her smile deepened as she watched him. 'You would have figured out the ownership of the necklace and returned it. You're not dishonest. You're just. And that night with the necklace was the catalyst for the attraction between us. My staying here was convenient for us both. It's just that I couldn't admit it at the time. I never wanted to admit how attracted I was to you because it overwhelmed me. But I stayed and then really got to know you. That's when I was really in trouble.'

Alejandro couldn't dare believe that she truly cared for him. He didn't deserve it when he'd been so arrogant and so damn dismissive. 'I don't want to make you unhappy. I don't want you to feel trapped. I need to be able to let you go. I have to let you go.' He ruffled his hair distractedly, unable to get the words right. 'Because I'm afraid of myself.' He looked up at her. 'But now I'm more afraid of life without you. I'm so sorry I walked away from you that day in Scotland, Kitty. I'm so sorry.'

Kitty was struggling to believe that he was here. That he'd bought all those dresses all over again. That he was gifting her the diamonds.

Most of all that he'd opened up to her about his father and about his fears.

And she was too afraid to really question why. She couldn't bear to have her heart broken twice over.

'There's something I need to tell you,' she said quickly. 'I had my first pregnancy scan yesterday.'

He paled and she saw the fear flare in his eyes.

'It's okay,' she added quickly. 'Everything is okay.' She swallowed. 'Better than okay in some ways.' She breathed out, struggling to stay in control. 'I'm having twins.'

'Twins,' he echoed softly, his eyebrows lifting.

'Two babies. Twins. Yes.' She still couldn't believe it herself. 'That's why I'm showing so much more at this stage.'

'I thought that was just because you're not very...' He trailed off. 'Twins...' He looked dumbfounded.

'Yes. It's in the family.' She half smiled.

But his expression was shuttered.

She kicked herself for the reminder about genetics and the passing on of particular traits. 'Not that we inherit...'

'No, it's okay.' He huffed out a breath. 'It's just that I don't want you to think I'm here because of the baby... Babies.' He rubbed his hand through his hair. 'The pregnancy isn't relevant—it's you I want.'

Her pulse pounded loudly in her ears and she was glad because she was terrified of hearing what he was going to say next.

'Kitty—'

'You know that marriages with multiples are more likely to fail?' she interrupted in a rush. 'Financial pressures. Lack of sleep. Extra stress.'

He smiled at her—a slow, tender, vulnerable smile.

'We won't have financial pressures and we can get help—nannies, cooks, cleaners, whatever it takes. We're in a better position than most. The thing is, I don't know how to be a father,' he said huskily. 'I didn't have a good example.'

She shifted on her seat, moving nearer so she could hear every one of his almost whispered words.

'And I've never had a relationship last much longer than a month.' He leaned closer to her too. 'But I want it all with you, Kitty. I want you. I love you.'

'I don't really know how to be a mother yet, either,' she offered shyly. 'A bit of instinct maybe, some help from the experts, and we'll be okay.'

'More than okay. I know I need help processing everything.' He looked intense. 'I know you know about the nightmares. I hadn't had them in so long, but then with you I guess everything opened up…' He trailed off and cleared his throat. 'I thought I had it all together, but I didn't. I wince at the way I treated those women. I was cavalier. I thought I was doing no harm. But I was.'

She reached out and framed his face with her hands. He needed to stop beating himself up. He needed to believe in himself the way she did. 'You're okay, Alejandro. You're a good guy. And I love you.'

'You've changed my life,' he said simply. 'I love you so much. I want to be the man you need. I'm going to be.'

There was the determination she loved in him.

'You already are,' she promised him. 'You *are*.'

A half smile lit in his eyes and he reached into his pocket. 'I got this for you.'

There was a rushing in her ears as he opened the small box and she saw the diamond ring.

'The jeweller worked round the clock to match the style to the choker, but if you don't like it we can get another.'

'I don't want another.'

'You don't have to wear it.'

She laughed through her tears. 'Stop it. I love it. You didn't have to do that—just coming here was enough. All I wanted was *you*.'

'Oh?' He reached into his pocket again, some of his cocky arrogance returning. 'But I got these too. For, I don't know...next week?'

She stared at the heavy matching wedding bands in his palm.

'Too soon?' There was an edge of anxiety in him now.

'No,' she whispered. 'Oh, Alejandro.' She launched into his arms. 'I need to feel you again,' she confessed. 'So much.'

His laugh was brief but exultant and he stood and quickly turned, flinging the rings to the floor so both his hands were free—to hold her close. Caress her. Claim her.

The kisses were fiery and frantic and the fabric separating their bodies tore. But then, just when he was so nearly hers, he stilled.

'I've missed you.' He trembled as he held back. 'I don't want to hurt you—'

'You won't. It's okay. I want you so much.'

He was gentle anyway, holding her protectively in his arms as they reconnected again in this most intimate, most emotional of ways.

'I love you,' he told her.

Again. Then again. Until her tears flowed and he kissed them away and made her sigh in unbearable pleasure. She'd never imagined it was possible to be *this* happy.

'Two babies,' he breathed hoarsely as he rolled onto his back and lifted her so her head rested on his chest. 'Heaven help me if they have red hair.'

'And freckles.' She mock-shivered. 'The poor kids.'

'They'll be lucky to have them,' he said, idly tracing hers now with a lazy fingertip. 'They're beautiful on you.'

She pushed up and rolled so she was astride him. She

shook her head, letting her hair tumble to tickle him, and delighted in the way he looked at her. Finally, she believed in them both. 'You're crazy.'

He smiled into her eyes, relaxed and free, able to enjoy the tease. 'About you. Absolutely.' He kissed her tenderly. 'Always.'

* * * * *

If you enjoyed
CLAIMING HIS CONVENIENT FIANCÉE,
why not explore these other
Natalie Anderson stories?

THE FORGOTTEN GALLO BRIDE
THE MISTRESS THAT TAMED DE SANTIS
THE SECRET THAT SHOCKED DE SANTIS

Available now!